TYRANT MEMORY

ALSO BY HORACIO CASTELLANOS MOYA

AVAILABLE FROM NEW DIRECTIONS

The She-Devil in the Mirror

Senselessness

Horacio Castellanos Moya

TYRANT MEMORY

TRANSLATED FROM THE SPANISH
BY KATHERINE SILVER

A NEW DIRECTIONS PAPERBOOK ORIGINAL

Published by arrangement with Horacio Castellanos Moya
and his agent and publisher, Tusquets Editores, Barcelona.

Originally published in Spain as *Tirana Memoria* by Tusquets Editores.

Publisher's Note: The epigraph from Canetti's *The Agony of Flies* (Farrar, Straus & Giroux) was translated by H. F. Broch de Rothermann.

Manufactured in the United States of America
New Directions Books are printed on acid-free paper.
First published as a New Directions Paperbook (NDP1204) in 2011
Published simultaneously in Canada by Penguin Books Canada Ltd.

Library of Congress Cataloging-in-Publication Data
Castellanos Moya, Horacio, 1957–
[Tirana memoria. English]
Tyrant memory / Horacio Castellanos Moya ;
translated from the Spanish by Katherine Silver. p. cm.
Originally published in Spain as: Tirana memoria.
ISBN 978-0-8112-1917-4 (pbk. : alk. paper)
1. Revolutionaries—El Salvador—Fiction.
2. El Salvador—History—Revolution, 1944—Fiction.
3. El Salvador—History—1944–1979—Fiction.
4. El Salvador—Politics and government—20th century—Fiction.
5. Hernández Martínez, Maximiliano—Fiction.
I. Silver, Katherine. II. Title.
PQ7539.2.C34T5713 2011
863'.64—dc22
2011002587

3 5 7 9 10 8 6 4 2

New Directions Books are published for James Laughlin
by New Directions Publishing Corporation
80 Eighth Avenue, New York 10011

CONTENTS

TO J.C.R.,
TO WHOM I ONCE GAVE A PIPE

Would it be better if nothing remained of our lives, nothing at all? If death meant our instant obliteration in the minds of all who have had images of us? Would this be more considerate of those who follow? For it may well be that what remains of us constitutes a claim on them, a burden they are forced to carry. Perhaps human beings are not free because they contain too much of the dead and because this surplus refuses ever to be abolished.

— Elias Canetti, from *The Agony of Flies*

Part 1
Haydée and the Fugitives (1944)

Haydée's Diary

Friday, March 24

It's been a week since Pericles was arrested. I expected him to be released today, as has always occurred on previous occasions, when they let him come home after a week. But now the situation is different. Colonel Monterrosa told me as much, at noon today in his office, with a look of regret on his face because he respects Pericles: "I'm sorry, Doña Haydée, but the general's orders are final: Don Pericles will remain under arrest until further notice." I began to suspect that the general is angry or afraid about something else when, on that first day, I found out they hadn't locked him up in the room next to Colonel Monterrosa's office—he's the chief of police—but instead had taken him to one of the cells in the basement; the colonel told me he was very sorry, but the decision to deal more firmly with Pericles had come straight from the top. During his previous imprisonments, my husband could receive visits from friends authorized by the colonel, and we always ate lunch and dinner together in that room, where I'd bring the food María Elena and I had prepared. Now, Pericles is isolated, and they allow him to come up to that other room only once a day, at lunchtime, to meet me. But I suppose I shouldn't complain: Don Jorge's situation and that of other political prisoners is much worse.

After speaking with Colonel Monterrosa, I returned home and called my father-in-law to ask if he knows why Pericles isn't being released. My father-in-law told me the general has his reasons, and the best thing for me to do is bide my time. I did not insist. My father-in-law is a man of few words, loyal to his general, and Pericles's articles criticizing the government upset him greatly; every time I've ever asked him why they arrested my husband, he answers simply that acts of disobedience cannot go unpunished.

Then I called my parents' house to tell them the bad news. My mother asked me how Pericles is taking it. I told her he seemed to have been expecting it, his only remark being, "It appears the man is very frightened." My husband never calls him "the general" or "Mr. President," or "the Nazi warlock," like my father and his friends do; he simply calls him "the man." My mother asked me if Betito and I were going to come over for dinner. I said yes; the youngest is always the favorite grandchild.

Our neighbors came over for a visit this evening. The Alvarados expressed their regrets that Pericles had not been released, though they are very careful when it comes to discussing politics. Raúl is a doctor, but astronomy is his true passion; he has a telescope and whenever a special phenomenon is about to take place, which he always knows about, like a meteor shower, he invites Pericles to stay up with him to watch it. Rosita, his wife, brought me some women's magazines she got from the Neighborhood Circle, a club sponsored by the American Embassy, of which they are members—I'd like to join but Pericles does not think very highly of it.

Saturday, March 25

I find relief from my solitude writing in this diary. It's the first time since we were married that I have been separated from Pericles for more than a week. When I was a teenager I used to keep a diary, a dozen or so are stored away in my memory trunk; I used to spend days in my room reading one novel after another, lost in my own fantasy world. Then came marriage, children, responsibilities.

This morning, before my father left for his finca, we had a long conversation. I asked him if he could think of any way to pressure the general to release Pericles. He told me that in a few days the coffee-growers' association would meet with the American ambassador, and he would present Pericles's case as one more violation of freedom of the press, he said it wasn't enough for the dictator to detain Pericles's boss, Don Jorge, and to keep the Press Club closed since January, but now he has gone after the columnists. But he warned me that the Nazi warlock has gone off the deep end and doesn't listen to anybody, "not even your father-in-law," he told me. My father respects my father-in-law, even though sometimes he calls him "the cantankerous colonel," and he doesn't approve of his total obedience to the general.

At noon, I brought my husband books and tobacco. We ate in silence. I then talked to him about family matters; he told me he is weary of the lack of natural light, and the damp. I don't like his pallor or that cough of his, which is becoming chronic. He repeated that "the man" feels besieged, trusts no one, otherwise he wouldn't have consigned him to this basement cell, and wouldn't keep him locked up.

Clemen dropped by this afternoon. He's outraged that his father is still behind bars. I told him his grandfather has recommended patience, for there is nothing to be done at the moment. My eldest son is hot-blooded, imprudent; he was cursing the general, calling him "that little shitfaced dictator," saying that nobody wants him anymore, he should step down and leave the country. I suggested he show some restraint with his words. He promised he would come for lunch tomorrow, Sunday, with his wife and children.

Later in the afternoon, Carmela came by, and we had a cup of coffee on the terrace; she is still my best friend, has been ever since high school. She brought a delicious lemon pie. She was very sorry to hear that Pericles had not been released, and she warned me that there are new rumors of a coup d'état.

A short while ago, just as I was sitting down to write, my sister Cecilia called. I told her about Pericles, but we soon started talking about the cross she bears, much weightier than mine: her husband, Armando, has become an inveterate alcoholic, and every time he gets drunk he turns aggressive, violent; he has never hit her, because he's afraid of my father, but he always gets into serious trouble and ends up at that house of ill repute. They live in Santa Ana, the city where we were born and raised, where I married Pericles; it's also where my grandfather's old mansion is, which my father has turned into a coffee-processing plant.

Sunday, March 26

Patricia called from Costa Rica quite early this morning. I told her that her father was still in jail. There was a long silence. She is the most sensible of my three children, the one most like Pericles, the one who's closest to him. She asked me how her father's spirits were. I told him that his spirits aren't a problem but his cough is. She told me her husband also has a bad cold. Patricia and Mauricio were married last December first in San José; such a lovely wedding. She asked me to call her the moment Pericles is released. My poor daughter: this is the first time she has been far away when her father is in jail.

Then I went to eight o'clock Mass, as I do every Sunday. I prayed for my husband to be released soon, even though he doesn't believe in religion or want anything to do with priests—he has always respected my beliefs, as I respect his. On my way out of church, I stopped to chat with Carmela and some other friends. They invited me to accompany them to the Club, but I had several chores to do at home, particularly because María Elena has gone home to her village. One weekend a month she visits her family, at the foot of the volcano, near my father's finca.

I spent the rest of the morning making chicken with rice and a beet salad. Betito had gone to swim at the Club, and he returned a little before noon to accompany me to the Black Palace—that's what we call police headquarters. They don't let Betito come into the room where I meet with Pericles; he must remain in the waiting room. Those are the general's orders: I am the only person authorized to see my husband and only for half an hour a day. Pericles was in a very good mood: I assumed he must have had some good news, but he didn't say anything. I have been warned to never talk about politics during my visits, because the walls have ears.

Clemen, Mila, and my three grandchildren arrived punctually at one o'clock. The children are rambunctious and poorly behaved. Marianito is five years old, but he is already a little demon; the twins, Alfredito and Ilse, just turned three, and they seem headed in the same direction. Pericles quickly loses patience with them; he doesn't like how destructive, willful, and ill-mannered they are. He says that Clemen and Mila do not make the best couple. "What else could come from a union between a frivolous man and a shifty woman?" he complained angrily once when the children got into his library and tore apart several books; I told him not to talk like that. This afternoon, they started running around the house asking for their grandpapa the moment they arrived. When he is calm, Marianito is a tender, sweet child, the spitting image of Clemen at that age.

After lunch, while Mila was out on the patio watching the children play with Néron, our old dog, I asked my son what would happen to his father if he were in prison during a coup d'état. Clemen said, without hesitating, that it would be for the best, that a coup was, in fact, the speediest means for Pericles to regain his freedom. Then I asked him what would happen to his grandfather, Colonel Aragón, who has always been so loyal to the general. He answered that this would depend on the position his grandfather takes during the coup. I don't share Clemen's confidence that the best way to secure Pericles's release is a coup d'état. I'm fearful; I'd rather be with my husband if something like that happens. I don't understand very much about politics, but my son is rather rash. And the general has been ruling this country with an iron fist for twelve years.

I went to the Club this afternoon. I learned that Betito had been drinking beer with some friends from school, secretly—he's only fifteen years old. When I got home, I scolded him, I told him he should have more respect for me and not take advantage of his father's absence to do foolish things, for Pericles is very strict and would punish him on the spot; years ago he had the same kinds of problems with Clemens.

After dinner, I spoke for a long time on the phone with Mama Licha. The poor thing suffers from arthritis, which makes it difficult for her to walk. She told me that every single day she asks my father-in-law when they will release Pericles, and every single time the Colonel answers her with an irritated harrumph. My mother-in-law adores my husband, her firstborn. She asked me how Patricia is, and she complained that neither Clemente nor Betito had come to visit her in the last two weeks. Cojutepeque is about twenty-five miles away; the colonel's the governor there.

Later, my mother called to tell me they had just returned from the finca, where they had lunch with several couples, friends of theirs, including Mr. Malcom, the British commercial attaché, and his wife. I assume the men, as usual, spent their time in heated discussions about the war in Europe, then mocking the general and his wife; my father says the English simply can't understand how that Nazi warlock has been able to hold onto power, nor why the Americans make no concerted effort to remove him. My mother asked if there was any news about Pericles.

Raúl and Rosita came by for a while this evening. We listened to the radio, drank hot chocolate, and ate delicious vanilla biscuits. Raúl has his clinic, but he also teaches at the university, where, according to him, the atmosphere is quite heated and new protests are being planned against the general. Both are very worried about Chente, their eldest son and a medical student, who seems to be involved in planning the protests and refuses to accompany them to the beach for the Easter holidays.

Monday, March 27

It's strange how sometimes when I write in this diary I feel nostalgic for my adolescence. Then I remember I turned forty-three last October, I have three children and three grandchildren, and I started writing this diary as a substitute for my conversations with my husband. I needed this time alone, Pericles's long absence, to get me to open this beautiful notebook and begin to let my fountain pen glide across its bone-colored pages. I bought it nine years ago in Brussels, when we'd already moved into the house on Boulevard du Régent; in the mornings, after Pericles had left for the embassy and Clemen and Pati for school, I would roam around the city for a few hours with Betito, who at five years old was too young to go to nursery school in a foreign language. I bought this notebook at a shop near Saint Catherine's Square. I saw it in the window, I loved the design on its hard cover, and I immediately decided to buy it to write down my impressions as a stranger in that city, a fantasy I'd been harboring ever since we crossed the Atlantic by steamship. But I never wrote in it, not till now.

This morning, María Elena returned from her village later than usual; usually she's here by eight, but today it was almost eleven before she arrived. She explained that Belka, her daughter, has a terrible flu, and they had to take her to the hospital early in the morning; Belka is six years old, spirited and charming, and lives with María Elena's parents and siblings, and we only get to see her when we visit the finca; María Elena's family has always worked for my family. I asked her to finish cooking the meatballs and rice that were already on the stove while I packed the rest of the food in the basket I take to Pericles every day: a thermos of coffee, hard-boiled eggs, milk, and sweet rolls for breakfast; and ham and cheese sandwiches for dinner. What matters most is that he not have to eat that filthy food they serve at the palace.

My husband was very upset today: he found out that the general didn't have him arrested because of the article he wrote criticizing him for violating the Constitution so he could get re-elected president, but rather because somebody had told him that Pericles had agreed to join the group headed by Don Agustín Alfaro, the leader of the coffee growers and bankers who are now opposing the general, most of whom are Father's friends. I told him that was nonsense, the general knows very well that none of them agree with Pericles's ideas, which they consider communist. But gossip is gossip. And this wouldn't be the first time it's happened: a few years ago, when the War in the Pacific began, the general kept Pericles in jail for a week for no apparent reason, though subsequently we learned that someone had told him that my husband was spreading rumors about the general concocting a plan to re-supply Japanese submarines on Mizata Beach and another plan to land Japanese troops in California, and supposedly those stories had turned the government of the United States against "the man." But these accusations against my husband are groundless, the whole world knows of the general's sympathies for the Germans and the Japanese and of his plans to assist them.

When I returned home, I called my mother-in-law to tell her what Pericles had told me, hoping she would pass it on to the colonel, who has privileged access to the general. Mama Licha said she would do so without delay, she said it's unheard of that her son should be kept in jail because of a silly piece of gossip, and it's high time he be released. My father-in-law belongs to the military old guard, those who supported the general's coup d'état twelve years ago and have remained loyal to him ever since; both my husband and my mother-in-law call him "colonel," never his given name, even I stopped calling him Don Mariano, or Father, years ago, and now I also call him only colonel.

This afternoon I went to the Estradas' haberdashery. I am going to knit a sweater for Belka; the poor dear surely suffers from the cold, that's why she comes down with the flu so often. The eldest Estrada, Carolina, was in school with me. She showed me a skein of beautiful crimson-red yarn; then she asked after Pericles, she said it's unacceptable for respectable people to be treated so poorly and that nobody agrees with that evil man's latest whims. Then I stopped by Mariíta Loucel's shop, located in the same building, the Letona, next to the Estradas' shop. To my surprise I ran into my nephew, Jimmy, the son of Angelita, Pericles's first cousin. Mariíta and Jimmy were whispering secretively in French. When they saw me enter, they stopped, as if I had caught them in flagrante, but then they immediately greeted me, asked after Pericles, and told me a few bits of news and gossip as if everything were perfectly normal. I was still suspicious, however, may God forgive me for thinking badly of anybody; Mariíta is, after all, a year older than I am, and Jimmy is the same age as Clemen. What I mean to say is that Mariíta is known for the positions she's taken against the general, and Jimmy is captain of a cavalry regiment.

As I was leaving the Letona Building, I ran into César Perotti, the maestro. He asked after Pati, expressed his regrets that her wedding had been in San José and not here, where he would have been delighted to take part, sing his best songs. The maestro used to be Pati's piano and singing teacher; he gave her lessons twice a week for five years and always praised my daughter's discipline and musical talents. At times it's difficult for me to understand that mixture of Spanish and Italian he speaks so haltingly. This time he abstained from moving his hands about so extravagantly, and right there, sotto voce, he told me not to torment myself over Pericles for soon things would change; he said that in all the good homes where he gives classes, people are speaking out against the general, and a situation like this cannot possibly last long. In Plaza Morazán I took the taxi that belongs to Don Sergio, Pericles's driver, a man of few words, something quite unusual for someone in his profession.

Betito and I ate dinner at my parents' house. I told them what Pericles had told me. Father said the Nazi warlock is a scoundrel, that he's now pretending to adopt socialist ideas so he can remain in power and fears my husband will expose the farce; then he again started railing against the increased coffee export tax, a subject that drives him completely mad and makes me fear he will have a fit while he's eating; he also mentioned rumors circulating about the growing discontent among younger army officers because of their low salaries. Then we started talking about the new house my parents are building in the Flor Blanca district. My father would like to bring stonework directly from Italy, the land of his father, but that won't be possible because of the war, and he will have to make do with what he can find at Ferracuti's warehouse. I love the new house, but I am sorry it is out in the suburbs—it's so much more difficult to get there by foot.

At night, Betito came to my room to give me a notice from school requesting Pericles's presence to discuss some problems related to my son's conduct. Wasn't he ashamed, I asked him, causing such problems while his father was under arrest? He told me it wasn't his fault, the principal has it in for him. Pericles is extremely strict about discipline, and it infuriates him that neither of our sons has inherited this virtue; only Pati resembles him in that way.

Tuesday, March 28

I listened to Clemen's shows on the radio as I do every morning. He reads the news on Radio YSP, but he also has artistic, thespian inclinations, and performs in two radio dramas. Pericles was the chief news editor of the station, and he got Clemen his job. Thank God, my son seems to finally be settling down. He didn't want to study at the university, despite his father's pressure, nor at the military academy, where his grandfather the colonel wanted to send him; he tried working with my father managing the estate and in the coffee-exporting company, but Clemen has never known how to handle money, and my father ended up firing him under rather unpleasant circumstances. Now, gratefully, he's been at the radio station for two years.

My mother called after breakfast to remind me about the wedding shower this afternoon for Luz María, Carlota de Figueroa's daughter, to tell me I mustn't forget; and she came by in the late morning so we could go together to buy the presents. I took the opportunity to go to La Dalia department store to buy the Cuban cigars Pericles likes; Don Pedro, the owner, is so kind, he made me a gift of a special cigar to take to my husband.

I got to the Black Palace a little before my visiting hour so I could meet with Colonel Monterrosa. Don Rudecindo, as many call him, is from humble origins, like the general, and has a very bad reputation, but he has always been very kind to me. I told him the time had long come for my husband's release, he has committed no crime other than expressing his opinion in a newspaper article. Don Rudecindo told me his hands are tied, and he advised me to go and speak directly to the general; he also told me it was perhaps better for my husband to remain locked up because there are rumors that the communists are conspiring against the government, and this way Pericles would not be implicated. Evil tongues say the general will never forgive my husband for betraying him, for having become a communist agent. But everyone knows the general accuses anybody who opposes his government of being a communist. I did not tell Pericles what Don Rudecindo recommended: I know all too well that my husband would consider asking "the man" for any favor whatsoever to be the worst possible betrayal. As I was leaving, I gave a few coins to Sergeant Machuca, who is the one who buys newspapers for Pericles early every morning.

Luz María's shower was at the Casino. My sister came from Santa Ana wearing a new celadon green dress, very elegant; Cecilia is Carlota's best friend and wouldn't miss her daughter's shower for anything in the world. There was an exquisite raspberry tart; some of us stayed afterwards to play canasta. My friends expressed their regrets about Pericles's situation; they shared the latest jokes about Doña Concha, the general's wife, a quite ordinary, uneducated woman who has somewhat oddball ideas and is the laughingstock of society. There was also a discussion about whether Dr. Arturo Romero is the most intelligent and handsome politician at the moment; Don Arturo is a gynecologist, urbane and refined, trained in Paris, and is shaping up to be the leader of the opposition. Carlota said she found the doctor engaged in a pleasant chat with Mariíta Loucel in her shop this morning, they were speaking French and the conversation ended abruptly when she entered; this made me think of Jimmy and Mariíta, though I didn't mention it. My sister seemed worried all afternoon; she came from Santa Ana with Armando, who went straight to Lutecia Bar to drink himself into a stupor.

At night I called my mother-in-law to ask her if she'd had any news from the colonel. She told me that he explained to her that the general is quite angry, furious, in fact, because he is certain that many of his ex-collaborators are conspiring against him and being paid to do so by a group of rich people and the Americans, so it might not be helpful to bring up the issue of Pericles right now and might even make matters worse. Mama Licha said she hopes this storm passes quickly and the general enters his mystical period and orders my husband's release. Sometimes I can't tell if my mother-in-law is being serious or speaking in jest. The general is a theosophist, he holds séances, he believes in invisible witch doctors, and he demands that his close circle of friends call him "maestro." At first, people respected his eccentricities, but ever since he began to give lectures every Sunday in the auditorium of the university, and broadcasting them over the radio, we realized that "the man" isn't in his right mind. For months now, those broadcasts have been the butt of all the after-lunch jokes at the Club and the Casino on Sunday afternoons.

My sister is spending the night at my parents' house; Armando hasn't shown up nor will he until he is completely inebriated. My father is furious; he will send her back to Santa Ana tomorrow with his chauffeur. I always remind Cecilia to offer thanks to God that her children have not inherited their father's vice: Nicolás Armando is father's most trusted employee at the coffee company, he married well and is a responsible man; Yolanda and Fernandito are also very decent young people.

Wednesday, March 29

Pericles's friends called this morning, one after the other, as if they'd planned it, all asking the same questions, all receiving the same answers. The first was Serafín, who is running *Diario Latino* while Don Jorge remains in jail; then Mingo called, the poor man told me he was laid up with a migraine all day Sunday and Monday; and finally, Chelón, Carmela's husband. All three repeated their regrets at not being able to visit Pericles because of the general's orders that he be kept in isolation.

Serafín says he feels a bit guilty because he should also be in jail, he's the one responsible for the newspaper, though Pericles is the one who wrote the article. I responded just as my husband had to Don Rudecindo, when he arrived at the palace under arrest: the authorities should have locked up Don Hermógenes, the censor, for not having done his job more diligently. "Your old man is incorrigible," Serafín said, laughing, because it sometimes seems as if poor Don Hermógenes is Pericles's employee, he is so intimidated by him. And Serafín knows as well as I do that neither he nor the censor really has anything to do with this, this is an issue between the general and my husband. Before hanging up, he said we should remain alert, many rumors are circulating in the city, and many people's nerves are on edge.

It worries Mingo that Pericles is locked up in a cell in the basement. Years ago, Mingo was held for a few days in the room next to the police chief; at that time, he was the owner of the newspaper *Patria*, where my husband began working after he resigned as ambassador and we returned from Brussels. Mingo is a highly sensitive poet, his health is precarious, and he still trembles when he remembers his arrest; but the general showed him a lot of consideration, because Mingo also was practicing theosophy at the time, though he has now returned to the church. I told him not to worry about Pericles's spirits, he is tough and resilient, it's not for nothing that he graduated from the military academy as a second lieutenant; then I asked after Irmita, his wife, who suffers from chronic lung disease, some kind of asthma she got while living with Mingo in Geneva.

I told Chelón that if he was calling, it was because he had nothing better to do, surely he was lazing about, waiting for inspiration for his next painting. He knows better than anybody what is going on, thanks to Carmela, for she and I speak every day. Then I told him that my mother-in-law is hoping the general will enter his mystical period so he'll free Pericles, and since he, Chelón, is also a mystic who believes in invisible forces, he should conjure them up and instruct them to enter the general and dispel all his anger at my husband. Chelón is a dear man, and an artist, but he knows nothing whatsoever about politics.

There is no news to report from my visit with my husband. I brought him the books he asked for. He gave me a letter for Serafín, who sent someone to pick it up at my house as soon as I told him about it. I told Pericles that my father is still pressuring Judge Molina, the president of the Supreme Court—a spineless coward who's completely subservient to the general—to define his legal status, for it is illegal to hold someone under arrest for an unlimited amount of time for an alleged violation of the anti-defamation laws. Because Mr. Pineda, my husband's and the newspaper's lawyer, has come up against a brick wall in the courts. "Excuse the expression, Doña Haydée, but the law doesn't mean a damn thing to that warlock," he said, discouraged, the last time we talked. I asked him to keep applying pressure, to not give up, but inside I know that Pericles will never be set free until "the man" cools off.

Clemen dropped by this afternoon, tipsy, talking up a storm, as he always does when he has too much alcohol in his blood and is on the verge of doing something foolish. He assured me something is brewing, the general is going to have to leave, his days in power are numbered because the Americans are sick and tired of him. For a moment I suspected Clemen had some specific information about a plot or even that he might be involved in one, because his tongue starts wagging when he drinks, and he might just end up in jail like his father; then he told me he had come from a journalists' luncheon held at the American Embassy. I made him a strong cup of coffee, but he started nodding off anyway and fell asleep in the armchair. My poor son, so like his Uncle Lalo. I let him sleep even though his absence from work might cause him problems; anything's better than seeing him drunk.

I had planned to go to the bank then to visit Carmela after the worst heat of the day had passed, in the afternoon, but I chose to stay home until Clemen woke up; I feel uncomfortable leaving him alone with María Elena. He woke up an hour and a half later, complained that I hadn't woken him up earlier, and rushed off to the radio station. I begged him not to stop on the way to quench his thirst with a beer. The reasons we have the children we have has always been a mystery to me: who could have predicted, when Clemen was a baby, that he would have so few of my traits, or those of Pericles or his grandparents, and instead would inherit all the good and the bad of his Uncle Lalo, my father's youngest brother, charming and scatterbrained, always on the lookout for revels and women? I have accepted God's will and have made my peace with it; Pericles has had a more difficult time doing so. My father claims that since Uncle Lalo was killed just a few weeks before Clemen was born, his spirit entered him.

Thursday, March 30

Pati called to tell me that she is pregnant; the doctor confirmed it this morning. She is happy, though she says that Pericles's situation casts a pall over the joyous news; I warned her against confounding her feelings: one thing is her sadness over her father's imprisonment and quite another the happiness that he himself will have when he hears the good news. And so it was: Pericles was delighted when I told him. What I didn't tell him is that I have hopes he will be freed tomorrow, Friday, two weeks from when he was arrested, because then comes Palm Sunday and the Holy Week, and it is reasonable to expect the general to soften up and order his release before going on vacation; and I didn't mention this to my husband because he has a particular dislike for creating false hopes, for what he calls weak minds who believe in "pipe dreams," whereas he believes only in the facts.

My parents were also very gladdened by the news of Pati's pregnancy. I stopped by their place after my visit to the Black Palace. My father shares the hope that Pericles might be released tomorrow; he said that if this happens, we'll have a big party on Sunday at the finca and invite the whole family, to celebrate both events: my daughter's pregnancy and my husband's freedom. The next day, on Monday, my parents will leave for Guatemala, where they like to go for the Holy Week; when I was a teenager, I loved going with them to see the carpets of flowers in the streets, the massive processions, especially the one for the Holy Burial.

When I got back home, I told María Elena we must make the house spotless for Pericles's return, there shouldn't be a speck of dust in his study or on his bookshelves; we discussed the best dishes to make for lunch, for I expect they'll release him in the morning, as has been the case on other occasions. We will make a watercress and bacon salad and the spinach lasagna with cheese that Pericles likes so much; for dessert we'll have *dulce de leche*. We'll finally bring out the new flowered tablecloth my sister gave me.

I think it's a splendid sign that the rosebush in the garden has bloomed precisely today; no more being alone. Tomorrow morning early I'll go to the beauty salon for a cut, shampoo, and styling. I want my husband to find me beautiful and elegant, he deserves nothing less, without a trace of the anguish and loneliness that I can now see on my own face.

I wonder if tomorrow, when Pericles is again by my side, I'll have the need and the steadfastness to keep writing in this lovely notebook, and I tell myself that surely I won't, I must consider this diary a friend who came to visit me from far away, who keeps me company and comforts me during these moments of solitude, and once her duty is done, she'll leave, though with some wistfulness, the same wistfulness I'll feel when I return this notebook to my memory trunk.

Friday of Sorrows, March 31

Oh, the horror of it! The general has ordered Pericles transferred to the Central Prison. There's no judicial writ, no legal process, that evil man is simply taking revenge on my husband, who knows for what reason. I found out late this morning after I returned from the beauty salon when I called the Black Palace, hoping to hear of Pericles's imminent release. There was a tone in Colonel Monterrosa's secretary's voice—evasive, and he refused to give me any information—that made me wary, then afraid that my husband was going to remain behind bars; my wariness turned to suspicion when Don Rudecindo refused to take my call. "Colonel Monterrosa isn't here," his secretary told me, and by the way he enunciated each word I knew the colonel was there but didn't want to talk to me. So I hung up and dialed the palace again, but this time I called the receptionist and asked to speak to Sergeant Machuca, for I was certain he would tell me if something had happened, not only because of his respect for Pericles but also because he owes my father-in-law more than one favor. And so it was. The minute he took the phone, he began speaking in an undertone so nobody would overhear him tell me that if I wanted to see my husband I shouldn't wait till noon, I must hurry to the palace at that very moment, because he heard that Pericles was going to be transferred. I asked him where they were taking him, and why. But Sergeant Machuca said he had to hang up, and told me not to tarry. I didn't waste a second. I asked María Elena to call my parents and my in-laws immediately to let them know that Pericles was being transferred to another prison, and that I was on my way to the Black Palace to find out what was going on. Fortunately, my mother had lent me Don Leo, their chauffeur, to help with the morning chores; I asked him to drive me there as quickly as possible. He asked me if there had been an accident; as we drove across the city at full speed, I told him about Pericles's imminent transfer, how on other occasions these transfers had been a way of masking the general's secret intention to do away with his political rivals. We soon reached the palace. I ran upstairs to Don Rudecindo's office; the secretary tried to stop me, but I had already pushed open the door. The colonel was talking on the phone, and his face changed when he saw me. I stood right in front of him and demanded to know where my husband was. Don Rudecindo covered the mouthpiece with his hand, asked me to have a seat and wait a moment, then motioned to his secretary to leave the office. After hanging up, he looked me in the eyes and said, "This morning, the president called me personally and ordered me to transfer Don Pericles to the Central Prison." I was in a rage, possessed. I told him, between clenched teeth, that this was a travesty, that carrying out an unjust order was an act of cowardice, and I would cling to my husband and force them to take me with him. Then Don Rudecindo, glancing up at the clock on the wall, as if he hadn't even heard my insults, said that perhaps at that very moment Pericles was entering the Central Prison. I became quite distressed because I had assumed that my husband was still in the cell in the basement, but it turned out that shortly after Sergeant

Machuca had hung up, Pericles was taken to the vehicle that transported him to his new location. I stood up and, as if spitting out my words, muttered: "What is he going to do to my husband, that . . . !" I was going to say "so-and-so warlock," but I controlled myself, even mentioning him was degrading, so I stared with profound disdain at the general's portrait hanging on the wall behind Don Rudecindo. He told me that nobody was going to do anything to my husband, the president's intention was to gather in one place all those arrested on charges of acting against the political order while the prosecutor's office completed the legal procedures and filed formal charges, and I would be able to visit him as prescribed by the law. I turned my back on him and left.

Don Leo had parked and was waiting for me in front of the palace; I asked him to drive me to the Central Prison. Then I thought I should have tried to find Sergeant Machuca to get more information. I couldn't remember at that moment who the director of that prison was; I would have to go home to make a few phone calls and try to pull some strings. But the most important thing at that moment was to make sure that Pericles was there, that this didn't turn out to be some kind of ploy to secretly take him elsewhere. The guards refused to let me enter until I mentioned my father-in-law's name and rank. It seemed as if the prison director was already expecting me, surely he'd been warned by Don Rudecindo. His name is Eugenio Palma; he's a colonel, ugly as sin, and his manners were quite uncouth. I demanded to see my husband that very instant. He told me those were not visiting hours. I was adamant, I insisted this was not for a visit but rather to verify that Pericles was there. He called an assistant and gave him instructions; he explained to me that he would carry out my request as a special and personal courtesy, but he also warned me that he still didn't know what the visiting policy for my husband would be, he was awaiting orders, then out of the corner of his eye he looked at the portrait of the general hanging behind his desk. Not even five minutes later Pericles walked into the office, escorted by the assistant. I rushed up to him happily and kissed him on the cheek; I would have embraced him, as one might embrace someone who has been brought back from the dead, but my husband is quite averse to public exhibitions of emotion. The colonel introduced himself with a military bow, he assured Pericles he would be treated with respect and in accordance with the law, and he repeated that the visiting policy had still not been determined, but in the meantime I could leave his food and clothes with Sergeant Flores, the assistant. A moment later the colonel gave the order for Pericles to be taken away. I gave him another kiss on the cheek to say goodbye; Pericles whispered in my ear that Don Jorge had not been transferred, that he was still in the palace basement. Before leaving, I told the colonel I would call him later to find out the daily visiting hour; he informed me that inmates at that prison have the right to one visit a week on the weekends. I argued that Pericles is not a criminal, but rather a prisoner of conscience, who has not even been formally charged. He promised to inform me as soon as he received his orders.

I got into the car and asked Leo to take me to my parents' house. He asked, quite concerned, about Pericles's situation; Don Leo is a highly trusted family employee, the son of a mechanic my grandfather brought here from his town in Italy. I told him my husband was well, but that I still didn't know when I was going to be able to visit him; as I spoke, and watched the people and houses going past the car window, I felt suddenly overwhelmed by an urge to cry, to unburden myself, but I held back. As soon as I entered the house, my father gave me a hug, asked me if I had visited Pericles, how he was, and told me he had just spoken with Mr. Malcom, the British commercial attaché, and he told about the latest vile act the Nazi warlock had committed against my husband; he also spoke with General Chaquetilla Calderón, ex-minister of the interior, to ask him why they had transferred Pericles to a prison for thieves and criminals; General Calderón said he knew nothing about the case, but as soon as he had any information he would let him know. My father has a special regard for General Calderón because he was the military leader in charge of putting down the communist uprising in January of '32 in the region near the volcano and the family finca; but this man, Chaquetilla, despises my husband, precisely because during the uprising, when Pericles was "the man's" personal secretary, he expressed his reservations about the excessive cruelty he, Chaquetilla, was using against the indigenous population. I immediately called my father-in-law, who naturally was already aware of the development, and the only thing he said was that I mustn't worry, perhaps remaining locked up for Holy Week would force my husband to reflect on the advisability of showing some respect for order and authority; I would have liked to answer him with a strong riposte, but I sensed the helplessness and sorrow behind his words; then he asked me about Clemente, if I had any news of my son, which took me by surprise and made me fear that he had been drinking too much again and that news had reached Cojutepeque. But at that moment I didn't have time to concern myself about Clemen. I called Mr. Pineda, the lawyer, and informed him what was going on; he told me there would soon be a court hearing. Lastly, I managed to get in touch with Ramón Ávila, minister of foreign affairs and justice, who is quite fond of my husband; I asked him to please intercede on his behalf with the general, I told him I was making this request without Pericles's knowledge because I am very concerned over the direction events have taken; he expressed regret about the situation and told me I could rest assured, he would do everything in his power. I do trust Mr. Ávila, he behaved honorably even when Pericles decided to resign as ambassador to Brussels, whereas that Chaquetilla, I'm certain, is behind the conspiracy against my husband.

I returned home so María Elena and I could prepare the basket of food and clean clothes for Pericles. We arrived at the Central Prison just before noon and asked for Sergeant Flores. They would not let me past the foyer; only after I persisted did the sergeant come out to see me. He took the basket and told me I could visit Pericles tomorrow between three and four o'clock in the afternoon. I asked him if this would be my daily visiting hour; he answered that he had information only about Saturday, only what he just told me, and nothing more. I stood there with María Elena in front of the gate of the Central Prison, stunned, then with deep sadness, because I realized that I might not be able to eat lunch with Pericles again until he is released.

When I got home, I went to my bedroom, closed the door, and cried. Once I'd unburdened myself, I tried to call Clemen at the radio station, but he wasn't there. Then Betito arrived, I told him about his father's transfer, and we ate in silence; my poor boy is so angry and finds no way to express it. I think perhaps I shouldn't tell Pati, it might adversely affect her pregnancy. My sister Cecilia called me quite dismayed, she asked if I wanted her to come from Santa Ana to keep me company. I thanked her but told her there was no need, she mustn't worry. This time I called Clemen at home. Mila answered, she sounded drunk, was completely beside herself, and began cursing my son and warning me that he had gotten himself into who knows what kind of a fix, he was out partying with the Castaneda brothers, who knows in which whore house, he almost never comes home. My daughter-in-law is an ordinary woman; I once heard rumors that she had committed adultery. My son is no better. I pray for both of them, and for their children.

As I look back over this day in the silence of the night, feeling calmer now only because I am utterly exhausted, I reproach myself for clinging to that foolish hope yesterday that Pericles would be freed, and now it seems as if I was carrying that hope for a long time, as if an eternity rather than a mere twenty-four hours had passed. My greatest comfort was a visit from Carmela and Chelón: we dined together, Chelón spoke about the new book of poems he plans to publish, he proposed jokingly that I should let him dig around in Pericles's papers, taking advantage of his absence to find the verses he writes in secret, which he so categorically denies doing. And then, when Carmela mentioned that yesterday morning she had seen Clemente leaving the Letona Building, Chelón tried to mimic the way Mariíta Loucel recites her poems. We almost died laughing, because the truth is it seemed he was mimicking Clemen, that clown, mimicking Mariíta. They were particularly amusing, as if they had deliberately set out to entertain me, offer me a pleasant respite, talk about other things; I am so grateful to them.

A few moments ago, just as I was finishing up writing about my day in this diary, I received a strange telephone call; it was General Alfonso Marroquín, leader of the First Infantry Regiment. He asked to speak to Pericles, as if he didn't know that he was still under arrest and had been transferred to the Central Prison. I brought him up to date. He said nothing; he apologized for disturbing me so late at night, then hung up. General Marroquín is a close friend of "the man"; Pericles considers him a cruel and contemptible general.

Saturday, April 1

There'll be no more privileges, that's what Pericles told me this afternoon while we were talking in the room where the other prisoners also receive family visits. I felt disoriented, I didn't know whom to turn to, how to ask for a minimum of privacy, unnerved by the fact that my husband and I were being treated like common criminals, disoriented the moment I had to stand in line, show my documents, be searched, and wait like everybody else, when my mentioning Sergeant Flores served no purpose whatsoever, for they informed me that he didn't work today, nor had he left any instructions; on the other hand, I was quite impressed by the solidarity among the families of the prisoners, the camaraderie among people of differing social classes who all seem to be victims of the same great injustice. Pericles told me that he was doing fine there, that he shares a cell with two students, by the family names of Merlos and Cabezas, who have also been arrested for political reasons and who show my husband great respect and consideration, as I myself could ascertain when they approached us with their respective families to introduce themselves. As I commented to my parents later, Pericles seemed genuinely animated, even optimistic, as if contact with different kinds of people was his oxygen. He told me the routine is almost like in the military, it feels good to exercise in the early morning in the prison patio, his conversations with the young students have been stimulating, and the most outrageous rumors are circulating about the imminent fall of "the man." Then I told him as discreetly as possible about the strange late-night phone call I had received from General Marroquín; he sat thinking for a few moments but didn't say anything. I'm concerned about the hygiene of the facilities, because in the Black Palace he had access to the officers' washrooms, whereas in the Central Prison he must use the same toilets as all the other prisoners. As I was leaving I asked the guards if I could visit him tomorrow at the same time, but they told me the prisoners who are allowed a family visit on Saturday are not allowed one on Sunday, and vice versa. I asked to speak to the man in charge, but, just as I suspected, to no avail. I came home quickly to get the personal telephone number of Colonel Palma, the director of the Central Prison, to request authorization to visit tomorrow and to request some kind of clarification of the situation before the Holy Week holidays; his wife answered, she told me the colonel was not in and promised to give him my message. I didn't hear from him all day. My father tried to get in touch with that general, Chaquetilla Calderón, to see if he could personally intercede to get permission for me to visit daily, but it seemed Chaquetilla hadn't been seen since noon at the Military Casino after he had already ingested half a bottle of whiskey. Fortunately, I brought Pericles food for two days.

Clemen showed up before dinner, tipsy again, and unusually agitated. I asked him what he had been up to in the last few days; I complained that I'd been trying to get in touch with him at the station and at home and hadn't been able to. He acted very mysterious: he admitted he was deeply involved in something of utmost importance, but he couldn't yet reveal any information. I didn't insist because it makes me furious to see how easily he lies, another characteristic he inherited from his Uncle Lalo. We spoke about his father's situation; he told me he knew about the transfer, he regretted not having been able to accompany me either yesterday or today to the Central Prison, but we must remain vigilant, he said, for soon that swine of a general would get what was coming to him. I told Clemen that if I manage to get permission to visit his father tomorrow, it would be good if he came with me, at the Central Prison there aren't the same restrictions as at the Black Palace, others can also visit the prisoner. He told me I shouldn't get my hopes up, there are rumors that this Sunday is going to be a dangerous day, and it would be best if I stayed home. There was a certain excitement, a fervor in his eyes that worried me. I preferred to ask him about the children. Then he ranted and raved against Mila: he can't stand her anymore, she accuses him of being a drunk when she's the one who never puts the bottle down, she spends all her time playing poker with her friends and does nothing to educate the children or improve their home, he is sick and tired of her reproaches and that's why he goes home only late at night to sleep. After he was done letting off steam, María Elena came into the living room and asked if he would like a cup of coffee. My poor son left me with a rather nasty taste in my mouth.

Betito left this morning for the beach in Zunzal with his school friends; most of them will stay there the whole week, but Betito will return on Monday so he can accompany me to the Central Prison to visit his father. My father has to go to the finca, as he does every Sunday; my mother will stay home so we can attend Mass then have lunch together; she says she wants to cancel her trip to Guatemala rather than leave me alone during Holy Week with Pericles in jail. I've told her several times that there is no need for her to cancel her vacation.

At eight at night, María Elena and I sat in the living room listening to the America Radio Drama; the program was quite interesting, and we enjoyed it immensely. I've been trying to read, but I am oddly uneasy, as if the uncertainty about Pericles's release were pinching my nerve endings, as if I were entering a new stage of life I am not prepared for and which I would prefer not to have to confront. I must pray more fervently.

Palm Sunday, April 2

Coup d'état! Clemen is involved up to his eyeballs: he was the one who announced the beginning of the uprising against the general on the radio this afternoon, and he is one of the announcers who continues to report the events, calling on the people to support the coup. I couldn't go to the Central Prison to see Pericles because the military is patrolling the streets. The air force has bombed the area surrounding the Black Palace; now I thank God my husband was transferred. Father is at the finca and Betito is at the beach; there's been no way to contact them because all communications within the country and the routes into and out of the city have been cut off. Clemen announced that the rebels have taken over the National Telephone and Telegraph Company. María Elena and I have come to my parents' house, and we will spend the night here. Fortunately, I brought my diary with me; I am now writing in what was my bedroom when I was a teenager, by the light of a candle, because the entire city is in blackout. It is eight o'clock at night. Hope is spreading, but more so, confusion.

The day began with bad omens: I wasn't able to get in touch with Colonel Palma to have him authorize a visit to Pericles; on the phone, his wife said the colonel had left that morning, and she had given him the message but he had left no reply. "You know how these men are, Doña Haydée," she said, as if to apologize. Then I received a call from Pati in Costa Rica: she was alarmed to learn that her father was still in jail and that we have no idea when he will be released; I had a guilty conscience because I had to lie when she asked me if anything had changed. Mother and I went to eight o'clock Mass; in his homily, the priest again criticized those who distance themselves from the Catholic Church and promote exotic religious doctrines that are far removed from the true faith, all this an allusion to the general's occultist beliefs. Friends stopped to talk as we were leaving church; nobody had the vaguest notion that the coup d'état would begin this afternoon: there have been so many rumors flying around for so long. I went to the Central Prison later in the morning, with new provisions for Pericles and the hope of seeing Sergeant Flores or convincing the officer in charge to let me enter and at least give the basket directly to my husband. It was the visiting hour for common criminals; they didn't let me in, a guard with a roguish face told me that he would give Pericles the provisions, and I returned home with a horrible feeling of impotence, and despair.

To cheer me up, Mother convinced me to eat with her at the Casino; she even made me drink a rather strong aperitif. We ate a delicious paella, and for dessert, an exquisite guava tart. After coffee we decided to leave, despite the insistence of some friends that we stay to play canasta; now I can only thank God for watching over us. Mother dropped me at the house, where I found María Elena getting ready to go out: she was on her way to a three-o'clock show at the Teatro Colón. I laid down on the sofa to take a nap. Half an hour later, María Elena woke me up, frightened, to tell me that she had turned on the radio and heard there had been a coup d'état. I'd been in such a deep sleep, and I was so lethargic, at first I found it difficult to react. She explained how she couldn't get downtown because there were troops everywhere, how she soon started to hear the rat-a-tat-tat of machine guns and saw war planes flying over the city and dropping bombs. Then I heard Clemen's voice on the radio: he announced exuberantly that the dictator was dead, the air force and the infantry have joined the rebels and the only resistance left are the police and the National Guard; then, other professionals and radio announcers took turns at the microphone, most of them friends of Pericles, and the most important words were spoken by Dr. Romero. When I finally understood the magnitude of the events, I thought of my husband and what might be happening at the Central Prison. I tried to call Clemen to get more information, but I couldn't get through; nor could I communicate with Mother or my in-laws. I told María Elena I would go to the Central Prison to see what was happening there, perhaps they had already released Pericles; she warned me it was most likely extremely dangerous to be on the streets at that moment, but she said she'd accompany me. I told her she should stay home in case anybody called; she insisted on coming with me. The Central Prison is located about seven blocks from the house. People were walking quickly down the street, everybody very tense. In the distance I saw airplanes flying toward downtown. Many people were standing on the sidewalks in front of the open doors of their houses, waiting, their radios blasting, celebrating the general's death. Two blocks from the Central Prison, a group of soldiers stopped us in our tracks and ordered us to go back the way we had come. I protested. But there was no way to convince them. Also, just at that moment, two airplanes flew very low overhead and loud explosions could be heard coming from near the Black Palace. Then I got frightened. I told María Elena that it would be better for us to walk toward my parents' house. There were no streetcars. I ran into several acquaintances in the street; there was tremendous excitement. It was God's will that Mingo drove by at that moment. I told him we knew nothing about Pericles's situation in the Central Prison. He explained that nobody knows anything about anything, the situation is very confusing; people knew only what Clemen and the other rebels were reporting on the radio: that the First Infantry Regiment was battling the police in the area around the palace, the general was dead, and the air force was supporting the coup. He told me he would drive me quickly to my parents' house, and I should call him if I needed anything at all. Mother was beside herself: Don Leo had gone to get me and found nobody at home, she had not been able to get in touch with Father, and Clemen's voice on the radio made her fear the worst. Slowly, she began to calm down. Soon a few phone calls got through, from friends who live in other parts of the city, and we spoke with the neighbors. We found out that the airplanes had missed their target, the bombs didn't fall on the Black Palace but rather on the block of the Casino, and there were fires and many dead in the streets. Mother explained that we have only God to thank that the three of us are alive, because the Teatro Colón, where María Elena had been headed, is on the same block, and it is still in flames now, late at night. Later, one of the Castaneda brothers, Clemen's friends, announced on the radio that the general is not dead, he's barricaded in the Black Palace. "That warlock is going to win!" my mother cried out in horror. I hushed her, told her not to repeat those words for they would bring bad luck. I was stupefied when I realized what could happen to Clemen and Pericles if the coup failed: the general's rage, his need for revenge. God help us!

Before it got dark, Don Leo drove us to my house to pick up some clothes so we could spend the night here, and to lock up all the doors and windows, in case any robbers thought to take advantage of the chaos; I put my diary and my rosary in my overnight bag; I left a note on the table in case Betito or Pericles showed up. María Elena helped her Aunt Juani prepare dinner; Juani has been working for Mother for twenty-five years, and the poor thing suffers terribly from varicose veins. After dinner I spent some time in the kitchen where the servants eat: María Elena was talking about how, when the coup began, she was going for the third time to see the movie *Flor Silvestre,* with Dolores del Río and Pedro Armendáriz, in which a poor young peasant girl marries the son of a rich landowner, but now she'll never be able to see it again because the movie surely burned up in the Teatro Colón. It was so touching to hear her. I returned to the living room; Mother suggested we pray a rosary. But just then the phone rang: it was Clemen. I asked him if he was alright, if he knew anything about his father; I told him about my futile efforts to get to the Central Prison. He told me right now all efforts were focused on the assault on the Black Palace, where the general has taken refuge, first the beast must be finished off in his lair then there would be time to go to the Central Prison; he said he was spending the night guarding the station, and if he heard anything about his father he would call me immediately. I asked him what was going on there. He told me not to worry, they would level the Black Palace at the latest tomorrow, he said everything would have been easier if that idiot Lieutenant Mancía had captured the general on the highway to the port, which was the plan, but he had slipped out of their hands, in disguise and in a private automobile, the sneaky devil. Clemen spoke excitedly, his voice hoarser than usual; I assumed he'd been drinking whiskey and smoking for many hours. I wanted to ask him about my father-in-law, but we got cut off.

After praying the rosary, well-nigh unable to give it my full attention because of all the emotions churning inside me, I went to my bedroom. Now that it is night, the planes have stopped dropping bombs, the heavy artillery fire has also stopped, though from time to time and with certain regularity, there are flurries. Dr. Romero, who has been proclaimed the civilian leader of the coup, announced on the radio that the forces opposing the general will cease their attacks during the night to avoid innocent casualties; he made an appeal to the population to join the democratic movement; he confirmed that

General Marroquín and Colonel Tito Calvo are leading the military rebellion; they are half brothers, and dislike my husband. Then the transmission ended.

I'm going to lie down for a while, just to rest, I'm so distressed I don't think I'll be able to sleep; I want to believe everything will turn out well, that the general will be defeated, and Pericles will be freed any moment, but at the same time I fear the worst—I have terrible premonitions.

(Midnight)

Father arrived a little before ten. I had already fallen asleep; the noise in the living room woke me up. He arrived with friends. Soon I got out of bed and was listening to their reports about the latest events. Father heard about the coup while he was still at the finca; he was taking a siesta when Don Toño, the foreman, woke him up to tell him what he was hearing on the radio. He went immediately to the coffee-processing plant and the other warehouses to make sure everything was in order and to warn the security guards to remain very vigilant, there has been a coup d'état, and criminal elements would take advantage of the anarchy. Then he went to Santa Ana, to my sister Cecilia's house, where he met with his coffee-growing colleagues to find out who was leading the movement and figure out how to lend them support; the local military detachment has joined the uprising, according to Father. Then he decided to return to San Salvador. Some of the men warned him it would be better to remain where they were for the night, it was already getting dark and the roads would be dangerous. But Father is stubborn, and once he makes a decision nobody can get him to change his mind. He said he'd had no problems leaving Santa Ana, but when he got to San Juan Opico he encountered the first checkpoint, then another as they approached Santa Tecla, and lastly entering the capital; at each checkpoint it took him a long time to convince the soldiers to let him pass. It's obvious Father had been aware of the possibility of a coup but knew nothing about the details or the exact date; he's vexed they didn't inform him. He was quite enthusiastic about Clemen's participation in the seizure of the radio station. "Finally, he's decided to do something worthwhile," he said. Mother does not share his opinion, she thinks it imprudent to expose oneself so openly; she said that if the coup fails, there will be weeping and gnashing of teeth. Father asked me if Captain Ríos Aragón, who'd been mentioned as the commander of the troops that had taken over Ilopango Airport, is Jimmy, Clemen's cousin; I said, yes, he is, he's the eldest son of Angelita, Pericles's first cousin.

Juan White, Güicho Sol, and my Uncle Charlie were quite frantic, pacing around the room, whiskey glasses always in hand, complaining about how useless the military is, wondering how they could possibly have let the general slip out of their hands, and the pilots were even worse, instead of bombing the Black Palace, they dropped the bombs two blocks away, destroying the Teatro Colón and all the shops in the vicinity. Mother piped up and asked if the Casino had also been destroyed; they told her it hadn't been; fortunately, it was untouched. Güicho said it seems the leaders of the coup don't really want to carry out the assault but instead only scare the general, as if they could possibly win like that, only the faint of heart would be foolish enough to suspend the assault at night, when they should be delivering the coup de grâce to the Black Palace and finishing that Nazi warlock off once and for all. Güicho said he doesn't trust General Marroquín, the commander of the First Infantry Regiment, which is leading the charge on the palace. Then I thought about why General Marroquín might have called Pericles on Friday night: why would he have wanted to contact him when it's common knowledge my husband is in jail? Father wondered to what extent the American Embassy supports the coup. Güicho said he had spent some time that afternoon with the ambassador, and there would be no support or any statement of support until the outcome became known. Juan is livid because he hoped the American troops would come to the support of the rebels. After drinking another couple of shots of whiskey, Juan and Güicho left. Only then did Father ask me if I had been able to speak to my father-in-law; I told him I hadn't, the telephone lines to Cojutepeque are out, but undoubtedly the colonel is beside himself because of Clemen's participation in the coup. I expressed my anxiety about Pericles's situation. He told me that we should immediately mobilize all our contacts to get him released, taking advantage of the opportunity, now that the general is under siege and on the verge of being overthrown. But he couldn't get in touch with either Chaquetilla Calderón or Judge Molina, president of the Supreme Court, or Don Agustín Alfaro, the director of the coffee-growers' association, who they say is inside the garrison of the First Regiment with the rebels. He told me he can't understand why Clemen hasn't persuaded any officers to go with a contingent of troops to the Central Prison to liberate his father and the rest of the political prisoners.

I've returned to my bedroom to rest for a while. Father is still out in the living room with his friends, drinking whiskey by candlelight, discussing the latest rumors, going over the names of the officers involved in the coup. I keep thinking about how worried Pati must be, how she'll hear about all this so suddenly and not be able to get in touch with any of us; Betito is at the beach with his friends, perhaps without the slightest idea what is going on. And I think about Pericles, how uncertain things must be at the Central Prison, where, after all, God has seen fit to keep him safe, because if he had been at the Black Palace he would be at the mercy of the general's fury. I will pray for this Holy Monday to be a good day, when at long last the spell that warlock has cast over our country and over all our lives will be broken.

Holy Monday, April 3

Today feels like the longest day of my life. I'm amazed I still have the strength to sit here and write, to consign to paper some of the events that are burning inside me as nothing ever has before. The coup failed. My fears became reality: the general took control again, the rebel officers surrendered, Clemen is in hiding, Pericles is still in prison in a very precarious situation, isolated, without any possibility of receiving anything from the outside world. I am home, unable to sleep, tormented by my fears; Betito is sleeping at his friend

Henry's house. Fortunately, the electricity and the telephone have been working normally since noon. Pati has called twice, the poor thing is in so much anguish, she even offered to get on a plane to come help me; I'm afraid all this stress will affect her pregnancy. I've also spoken to my mother-in-law, who told me with great sadness that if Clemen gets caught he is a dead man. Two plainclothes policemen have been watching the house since dusk; María Elena saw them when she came back from buying tortillas. In the streets, chaos and panic reign supreme.

Where, dear God, is my poor Clemen now? I have told myself not to think about him, that I must take him out of my mind or the anxiety will destroy me; I keep repeating to myself that there is nothing I can do for him, only God and fate can save him now. The last time we spoke was at one in the afternoon; I managed to get in touch with him at the radio station. He told me they had not lost hope that the infantry and artillery regiments could launch a decisive assault against the Black Palace, though he admitted that a defeatist attitude was beginning to take hold, many with him there at the station had begun to talk about the embassies where they would seek asylum if the coup failed. I asked him what he would do if that happened. He told me he still didn't know, he was weighing his options, but I shouldn't worry. He sounded exhausted, almost like a zombie; I assumed he had barely slept and that the excitement and the alcohol had taken their toll. By this time Father and his friends had already given the coup up for lost, he said the rebel officers had been remarkably idiotic: negotiating on the telephone with the Nazi warlock, trying to force him to surrender, when precisely the opposite was really going on—the general was the one tightening the screws on them. By then I had already found out that my father-in-law had publicly announced his full and unconditional support for the general and had angrily condemned Clemen's actions.

So, the entire city is on tenterhooks, there's no end to the rumors and hearsay: Colonel Tito Calvo was driving a tank through the streets bragging about how they were going to demolish police headquarters with cannon fire; the pilots had dropped bombs on purpose on the block of the Casino and the Teatro Colón because they didn't really want to finish off the general, just give him a scare; the ambush of the general failed because the general had infiltrated the ranks of the rebel officers; many vagrants have been killed by gunfire in the vicinity of Parque Libertad; the Nazi warlock has made a pact with the devil, he conducted a black mass in the basement of the palace and will now execute all those who plotted against him; troops from Cojutepeque and San Vicente are marching to the capital from the east and have the support of the people along the way, and they have already taken back the garrison at the Ilopango Airport.

One horrible rumor is that the general lashed out yesterday against poor Don Jorge. They say that once he felt safe in the palace, the first thing he did was order Don Jorge to be tortured; he was then taken out of his cell and executed in the street, where his body was left as a warning to the rebels. It appears they shot Don Jorge and left him for dead, but he somehow managed to survive. Horrific. I've called his house to talk to Teresita, his wife, but the line is dead. I pray to God, please, make this be only a rumor.

I tried to get to the Central Prison early this morning, but the same checkpoint that stopped me yesterday was there again today. This afternoon, when it was already evident the rebels had lost, I attempted again, and finally I managed to get through. But it did me no good. Soldiers were surrounding the prison, still afraid of an assault by the rebel forces. I was carrying the basket of food for Pericles; I approached the casemate to ask them to call Sergeant Flores. In vain. Several groups of prisoners' families were standing around outside; the guards had told them that everything was fine inside the prison, no visits were allowed until further notice, and they should leave, take themselves out of harm's way. I recognized the mother of Merlos, one of Pericles's cellmates; her eyes were red from crying, she was drying them with a handkerchief. I feared the worst. I was alarmed and asked her what had happened. She said she was afraid the general would now decide to execute the political prisoners, take his anger out on them. It was the same fear eating away at my insides. I told her what I tell myself: this cannot happen, her son and my husband are innocent, they have been locked up, they have had nothing to do with the plot, played no part in the coup, and had no responsibility for it. Then, when I stopped talking, an image of Clemen struck me full force. She saw it in my face, for she immediately said to me, "Let us pray to God that your son escapes." I was on the verge of collapsing, crying my heart out right there in the middle of the street, in front of the guards who were watching us and the rest of the families; I felt a huge lump in my throat and two tears fell out of my eyes and down my cheeks. But I managed to control myself. I hastily said goodbye to Doña Chayito, that's Merlos's mother's name, turned around, and made my way back home. After so many years with Pericles I have learned to hold back my tears. But what I didn't let out in the street, I did at home, in my bedroom behind closed doors, until I felt that I didn't have a single tear left inside me and that my husband was watching me, frowning severely.

A few minutes after three this afternoon, Father called the house to tell me the rebels had just surrendered. "That warlock broke the backs of those spineless sissies," he said bitterly; he told me a white flag was flying over the barracks of the First Infantry Regiment. "The elation lasted less than twenty-four hours," he said. I didn't know where he was calling from, but I could hear his friends shouting in the background, they were surely drinking and bewailing the turn of events. He told me we now had to find a hiding place for Clemen, help him escape. He asked me if I had spoken to him in the last few hours. I recounted to him the conversation we'd had at one in the afternoon. Then he suggested that Betito stay with them, Mother was hoping he'd spend the night there, the worst thing would be if the warlock's henchmen decided to take it out on him that his brother had participated in the coup; I told him Betito is at his friend Henry's house, and he will stay there where he is safe. Father insisted I remain at home, in case Clemen called again. It wasn't Clemen who called, though, but rather his wife, Mila; it was the third and last time I spoke to her today; she was completely out of her wits, ranting on and on, a whole litany of complaints, insulting Clemen for his total lack of responsibility. She said that neither she nor the children should have to pay the price for that exhibitionist getting mixed up in such stupidity just to impress his secretary at the station, whom she said is his lover. I "turned off the lights," as Pericles calls it, when one's mind simply departs from where it doesn't want to be and doesn't hear what it doesn't want to hear, until I heard Mila say that if the general condemns my son to death, he deserves it. "You are talking nonsense, Milita, and you are going to regret it," I said, and immediately asked her if she had spoken to Clemen in the last few hours. She answered that that "you-know-what" hadn't called since noon, but that she had taken that opportunity to rub his face in how stupid she thinks he is, just look at what he's done, even getting his own grandfather, Colonel Aragón, in trouble; she said she told him she's going to ask for a divorce once everything settles down. I didn't say a word: it never rains but it pours.

Fortunately, I then spoke with Mama Licha. My mother-in-law is solid as a rock: there's not even a tremor in her voice in the face of all these catastrophes. She affirmed that the colonel supports the general on principle, because for him authority and order are the most important things; but he is also a human being, a father and a grandfather, and as such he suffers in silence; she wanted to let me know that the colonel will do everything in his power to help Clemen escape, but that if he is arrested, nothing will save him from the general's fury. Then she asked after Pericles; I told her it was impossible to visit him at the Central Prison. She encouraged me to be strong, to not lose faith. She knows of what she speaks: when she was a young girl of twelve, she watched her father's execution in the main square in Cojutepeque.

I hurriedly transmitted Mama Licha's message to Father, hoping he would find a way to pass it on to Clemen. Father told me that under the circumstances he didn't trust the colonel, but we would talk about it later, in a few minutes the general's radio message would begin, he'd call me as soon as the warlock's tirade was over. I had turned off the set because my nerves were already frayed; I asked María Elena to turn it on right away. I sat in Pericles's chair, something I rarely do, and suddenly I found myself mimicking him when he's paying close attention to something; María Elena remained standing in the kitchen doorway, rubbing her hands together with a terrified look on her face. And while I was listening to "the man," instead of concentrating on the content of what he was saying, I started counting in my head the number of times he said the word "treason," and by the way he pronounced that word I sensed the rage of omnipotence defied, the exultation of a man who is about to exact revenge. When, in conclusion, he announced the immediate imposition of a state of siege and martial law, I stood up and went to the kitchen to get something to drink. María Elena moved aside for me and as I passed by her she muttered in despair: "Poor Don Clemen."

Father came over for a while before dinner: he told me that nothing is yet known of Clemen's whereabouts, that most of the rebels have been racing desperately from embassy to embassy looking for asylum, that many have already been captured, and that the population is terrified because the Nazi warlock will reconvene the war council to sentence all those who betrayed him to execution by firing squad; however, several friends are willing to give a helping hand in whatever way they can; he warned me that anything related to Clemen would be better discussed in person, not over the phone. I told Father that we should never stop reminding friends and acquaintances who are close to the general that Pericles has had absolutely nothing to do with the coup, he has been in isolation for more than fifteen days, and moreover at the palace, where everybody remained loyal to the general; I already told my mother-in-law and my brothers-in-law the same thing, that this could never be repeated too often, given these dire circumstances.

Later I got a call from Angelita, Pericles's first cousin. She was in despair and sobbing because she has heard nothing from Jimmy, the government forces have already taken control of the airport, and they have not mentioned her son among the rebel officers captured. I told her I was in the same situation with Clemen, I have heard nothing about his whereabouts since noon, before he left the station. We must pray to God, she said, for the general to forgive them; I agreed, but I also warned her that most importantly they must escape, and I told her what my mother-in-law had said about the firing squad that awaits anyone who is captured. It is vaguely comforting to know that someone else shares my anguish, though it brings no peace. Where is Clemen right now? What will become of my son and my husband? I feel as if my soul were being stripped bare, and I'm completely exposed, raw. I've had a cup of lime-blossom tea to settle my nerves, and so I can sleep a bit. I'm grateful to have this outlet where I can write down my sorrows.

Holy Tuesday, April 4

A day from Hell. Despair, anguish, rumors, helplessness. And terror everywhere. Still absolutely nothing about Clemen: friends call to tell me they heard somebody saw him somewhere; others tell me they've heard he's been seen somewhere else. The telephone hasn't stopped ringing: everyone asks after him, gives advice, tries to offer me words of consolation. On the radio they keep repeating the names of the officers who have been captured, and they call on those who have fled to turn themselves in, to have faith in the general's mercy. *Diario Latino* and the other opposition newspapers have been shut down. Father and his friends are planning something, but it's all top secret, and they don't include me at all. Poor Mila called me early this morning to say that if Clemen gets in touch with me, I should convince him to turn himself in, there's no point in running away, she will also try to convince him; then she called back, hysterical, because a detachment of policemen had come to the house looking for my son, they wreaked havoc, terrified my little ones, and the cowards killed Samba, that beautiful dog, Nerón's daughter, who never did anything bad to them or anybody else. I wouldn't be surprised if they burst in here any moment now. Those rumors about Don Jorge turned out to be true: the poor man is hovering between life and death and has undergone very complicated surgery. I went to the Polyclinic to keep Teresita and her family company; I left, deeply moved. By the afternoon, I thought I was going to collapse, I felt like I was having a nervous breakdown: I got into bed and slept deeply for three hours. I woke up feeling like a zombie. Right now I wish I were in a bubble, in another world, far away from all this and alone with Pericles, so he could caress me, and we could talk as we always talk; but then comes a wave of anxiety, and I feel like I'm drowning, and I must do something, though I don't know what; I somehow believe my son and my husband will suffer terrible consequences unless I can muster all my strength. But the streets have been taken over by the general's troops, nobody can get near the barracks, the government buildings, or the Central Prison; the authorities are telling people to stay at home. Thus my agitation flounders in a sea of impotence. I will finish knitting Belka's sweater.

Fugitives (I)

1

"Hold still . . . ," Jimmy says, startled, bringing his index finger to his lips to demand silence. He lies stretched out and lanky on a mat on the wooden floor; he's barefoot and shirtless, wearing olive-green trousers and a belt with a silver buckle.

The knocks on the front door are gentle but insistent.

"Who could that be?" Clemen asks, wordlessly, gesturing with his mouth; he's sitting on his mat, his arms wrapped around his knees, also barefoot and shirtless.

Jimmy presses his ear against a crack in the wooden floor.

"Just a moment! Coming!" shouts one of the girls from the back of the house.

Under them, they hear the slapping of flip-flops passing through the house on the way to the front door.

"Who's there?" the girl asks.

They hear a woman's voice but can't make out the words.

"Seems like a neighbor," Jimmy whispers.

They hear a loud bang.

Clemen is startled.

"Fuck! What was that?" he cries out, in a whisper, his face twisted in terror.

"The girl dropped the door latch," Jimmy mumbles, without turning to look at him, his ear still pressed against the crack in the floor of the loft.

"I thought it was the Guard," Clemen exhales, with relief.

They hear animated voices, laughter, goodbyes, then the latch drops again as the door closes. The slapping of the flip-flops passes under them, on the way to the back of the house.

"They brought a gift for the priest," Jimmy says and lies back down, face up on the mat.

"How do you know?"

"I heard."

"I don't believe you," Clemen says; he also lies down on his back on his mat, his hands clasped behind his neck.

"I gotta get out of here as soon as possible," Jimmy says, talking to himself, pensive. "This is a hell hole."

"Where are you going?"

"Better you don't know. Might bring bad luck . . ."

"I'm not budging from here, not unless that priest throws me out. They'll catch us in a second out there."

"Don't have any illusions you're safe here."

"More than in the streets, we are."

Then, suddenly, Clemen sneezes, making so much noise that even he sits up and looks scared.

"Sorry," he says, "I couldn't hold it."

Jimmy turns to look at him disapprovingly.

"If someone happened to be walking by, the game would've been up," he warns.

"I said I'm sorry. It's all the dust in here," he mumbles, and looks around at all the junk in the corners, the cobwebs, the layer of dust covering the floor.

They sit in silence, alert, but they hear no sounds from outside.

"I don't think anyone could hear it in the street," Clemen says.

"Just a minute ago, we couldn't hear what the women were saying at the front door, so outside they can't hear what we're saying, either."

"I guarantee you, even the girls in the back of the house had a fright," Jimmy says irritably.

"What time is it?" Clemen asks. "The priest should be back already."

Jimmy pulls a pocket watch out of his trouser pocket, places it under the light from the skylight, and says, "It's only five-twenty. He said he'd be back at six."

"I've been shut up here for four hours, two more than you ... I gotta take a piss."

"Think about something else, because you can't here."

"It's my nerves," Clemen says. "I need a smoke, I need to stand up, walk around," he adds, looking at the slanted ceiling a few feet above their heads. "This attic is like being in a dungeon."

"Just be thankful we've got somewhere to hide, you ingrate. You don't see me complaining, and I'm taller than you. Go ahead and tell me again how they dressed you up as a housemaid ...," Jimmy asks, cracking a smile.

"I told you, it was Gardiner's idea, the vice-counsel."

"How the hell did you think to hide there?"

"I'm good friends with Tracy. Luckily, she was home. I spent the night in their guest room and this morning, after they dressed me up, they took me out in their car ..."

"Were you wearing make-up?"

"You bet, and a wig, and I got plucked, just as pretty as can be. Look," Clemen says, passing a finger over an eyebrow. "And I was wearing underwear and a slip, and a bra stuffed with wads of wet paper under the uniform. If the police had made me get out of the car, the only way they would have found me out is if they'd touched me between the legs ..."

"And since your balls are probably about so small," says Jimmy pressing his fingertips together, amused, "there's no way they could have caught you."

"You can make fun of me as much as you want, but it worked."

"I wish I could've seen you: the ugliest housemaid in history..."

"Go ahead, keep making fun of me, see if I care. I wouldn't have been here otherwise, that son-of-a-bitch general of yours would've been smashing my balls like he did to that dimwit Tito Calvo."

"Poor guy...," Jimmy says, serious now, frowning.

"They're a gang of fucking sissies..."

Jimmy looks at him disapprovingly.

"Only a bunch of ass-fuckers could have let that warlock slip through their fingers on the highway," Clemen upbraids him bitterly. "Why didn't the tanks blast the police headquarters when the bastard was there?" His voice has risen, impassioned. "Eh? Why did the airplanes drop their bombs on the streets around the barracks and not on the only target that mattered?"

Jimmy sits up and orders him firmly, "Lower your voice, they're going to hear us."

"Go order people around in the barracks, you turd," Clemen answers.

They hear loud knocks on the front door.

Clemen sits up; all color has drained out of his face, and he swallows in terror.

Jimmy stumbles over to the corner where his jacket, gun, and infantry boots are lying; he picks up the gun and presses his ear against the crack in the wooden floor.

The knocking continues, insistently.

Nobody from the back of the house answers.

"Where did they go, those girls?" Jimmy wonders.

Clemen is terrified.

Now they hear somebody's steps running from the back of the house, the noise of the latch, an exchange of greetings, laughter, the latch again, the steps return.

"What's going on?" Clemen asks, anxiously.

"Maybe this is all normal. It's a priest's house: people are always visiting, bringing gifts," Jimmy says as he puts the gun back in the corner and lies down on the mat.

"I'm worried those Indian girls will rat on us."

"Supposedly they don't even know we're here."

"Could they be that stupid ..."

"That's what the priest told me, they have no idea this loft even exists," Jimmy says. "They didn't see me. He brought me straight to the prayer room and showed me where I had to climb onto the wardrobe and push in the false tile on the ceiling."

"You scared me to death ..."

"You yellow belly."

"They saw me. I even ate lunch here ..."

"In your housemaid costume?"

"Uh-huh ... When they cleared the table, the priest told them he had to confess me, and they should stay in the back of the house. I think they'd never seen a servant in uniform. Then we went into the prayer room, I took off the uniform and wig, stuffed them in a bag, he gave me these trousers, which are too long and baggy, and I climbed on top of the wardrobe."

"You're really fucked, you don't even have clothes to leave with."

"I already told you, I've got nowhere to go, unless the priest takes me to another hiding place. And you, you think you'll be able to walk down the street with that officer's uniform on without anybody recognizing you?"

"That's how I got here," Jimmy says. "Anyway, the priest's clothes will fit me, we're almost the same height, but you look like the village idiot."

"I don't understand how my grandfather could have sent you here, knowing I was already here ...," Clemen wonders as he slowly tries to stand up, still bent over looking for the highest spot in the loft so he won't bang his head on the ceiling.

"It stinks of whiskey here," Jimmy complains, sniffing around him.

"Where?" Clemen asks, suddenly excited, looking eagerly at the pile of junk. "I can't smell anything with all this dust and mildew."

Jimmy stares at him, then leans over and sniffs.

"Oh, it's you. You're sweating whiskey."

Clemen looks at him in disbelief; then he sniffs his own arm.

"You're right," he says with a smile, surprised. "Too bad I can't drink it," he adds, licking his arm.

"Some nerve you've got. Big rebels you civilians are," Jimmy says indignantly. "While we were out there in the thick of battle, risking our lives, you guys were partying it up, guzzling the booze. And you still have the nerve to complain that things turned out the way they did ..."

"Don't give me that shit, Jimmy. You guys were much worse than us. When that Colonel Tito Calvo of yours got to the American Embassy, he was so drunk he was falling over himself as he got out of the tank ..."

"You weren't there."

"But the consul told me, and he was. Falling down drunk and shitting himself he was so afraid, begging them to give him asylum. There you have your great military leader," Clemen says disdainfully. "Don't start on me with your sermons right now."

"It wasn't like that in the air force ..."

"The coup failed because that spineless sissy was afraid to order the tanks to attack police headquarters. If they had, there'd be a whole different ball game right now."

Clemen lies back down on his mat.

"Things aren't that simple," Jimmy mumbles, moodily.

"Damn right, you gotta have balls."

"I thought the same thing when I was in communication with the First Infantry Regiment, and I pressed General Marroquín to begin the armored attack on police headquarters, then he told me there were important political prisoners in the basement, friends of ours, people from good families, who might get killed, so he didn't give the order."

"Bullshit. They should have attacked right away, without giving them a chance to react."

"Who knows. If your father had been there in the basement, you'd be singing a different tune," Jimmy says; he picks up his folded shirt and places it under his head to use as a pillow, then settles in as if to go to sleep.

"That Marroquín is Tito Calvo's half brother, and he's buddies with that motherfucker, your general. I don't know how they could have ever considered putting that pair of clowns in charge of the coup."

"That wasn't the idea," Jimmy explains, then turns on his mat, his back to Clemen. "The idea was that Colonel Aguilar would command the coup, but things turned out differently. Let me sleep for a while, wake me up when the priest arrives . . ."

"I don't think you'll be able to sleep."

"If you shut up I will."

Clemen lies on his back, gazing blankly up at the tiny skylight; it's a dirty pane of glass, about four square inches, surrounded by roof tiles, through which an increasingly faint light filters into the room.

"Good thing we have this skylight," he says.

Jimmy breathes heavily and rhythmically with his eyes closed, as if he were sleeping.

"I hope the priest lets us sleep down below. It'll be horrible here," Clemen insists.

Some bells ring nearby.

"Is it five thirty or a quarter to six?" he asks. "I wasn't paying attention. Jimmy . . ."

"Leave me alone . . . ," Jimmy says, without moving or opening his eyes. "You're a real pain in the ass . . ."

"Don't be so pigheaded, you're not going to be able to sleep. Anyway, the priest will be back any minute now."

"He told me he'd try to get here by six," Jimmy explains. "You slept off your hangover all nice and cozy at the American consul's house, so you're pleasantly rested. But I spent the night out in the open, don't forget . . ."

"What? Weren't you at the Novoa's house by the lake?"

Jimmy sits up, rubs his eyes, and looks at Clemen with irritation.

"The worst part is that you're a deaf pain in the ass . . . I never said I slept at the Novoa's; I told you that Lieutenant Peña and I managed to break through the blockade of enemy troops and escape from the Ilopango Airbase in the late afternoon, then we walked for three hours through the coffee fields to the lake, then hid out near the

Novoa's vacation home until very late at night, always on guard to make sure that nobody took us by surprise, that nobody would even know we were there. Only then did I go to the caretaker's, whom I've known for years, and asked him not to make any noise or tell anybody we were there, and to help us cross the lake. We left in a canoe at three in the morning. Now you understand why I haven't slept?"

"Nice guy, that caretaker. Hope he doesn't rat on you . . ."

"It won't matter now."

"What if they find the canoe?"

"What stupid things you think of . . . Is that why you woke me up?"

"I have a feeling I know that Cayetano Peña . . ."

"He's brave, that lieutenant, determined, without him I wouldn't have been able to get through the blockade . . . I got out of the canoe in Candelaria and walked for two hours toward Cojutepeque; he kept going all the way to the other side of the lake, where he has a friend, near San Miguel Tepezontes."

"I hope he made it . . . ," Clemen says and gets up again, bent over, his neck pressing against the perpendicular ceiling. "And I hope that goddamn priest gets here, my bladder's about to explode."

"That 'goddamn priest' is the person who's saving our necks. Maybe you could learn to show a little more respect."

"Don't start giving me one of your sermons," Clemen says, pressing his hand against his genitals. "I've known Father Dionisio for as long as I can remember."

Jimmy has lain back down on his mat; he takes the folded shirt out from under his head and puts it over his face, covering his eyes.

"What I don't understand is what the hell you, a cavalry captain, were doing at Ilopango Airbase, instead of leading your troops against the barracks where your general was taking cover. That's why things turned out the way they did, everything was badly organized, you people did everything ass backwards."

Jimmy doesn't move.

"Be thankful I'm exhausted," Jimmy mumbles. "If not I'd smack you for being such an ass. The air force doesn't have its own troops, and we went to protect the airbase, it's as simple as that."

Clemen has sat down, his knees bent; his legs are moving around restlessly.

"Maybe there's a can somewhere I can piss in," he says, looking around.

"What a pig. You'll stink the place up. Don't you realize there's no circulation in here."

"This is no joke. I can't hold it any longer," Clemen says as he crawls over to the corner where the junk is.

"Keep your voice down, they're going to hear us," Jimmy urges.

Clemen rummages anxiously around through the broken furniture, the rusty pieces of iron, the moldy clothes.

"Don't make so much noise."

"Fuck you, stop giving me orders. All you military bastards know how to do is give orders."

"Stop making so much noise, you dimwit. You're putting us in danger," Jimmy insists, still lying down, not moving, his folded shirt covering his eyes.

"Look what I found!" Clemen exclaims with excitement, lifting up an empty paint can.

"What is it?" Jimmy asks without budging.

"A can I can piss in . . . ," Clemen says as he returns to his mat.

"That's disgusting, you're not going to . . ."

Suddenly, a pile of junk falls to the ground with a loud crash.

Jimmy jumps up; his head hits the ceiling.

"Moron!" he spits out between clenched teeth, furious, and starts to come at him threateningly.

"It was an accident . . . ," Clemen says apologetically with a whine, lifting his hands to protect himself.

At that very instant, in the midst of that tense silence, they very clearly hear someone's footsteps running from the back of the house.

"We've been discovered," Jimmy mumbles, still furious, sitting down on his mat. "Let's see how you explain your stupidity to the priest."

Clemen brings his fists to his temples and rubs them, pressing hard, his face twisted in pain and his eyes closed, as if his head were about to explode.

"I don't even have to pee anymore," he says as he pushes the can away and lies down on the mat.

"What are we going to do?" Jimmy wonders out loud, now looking worried.

"What?"

"What if the girl got frightened and has decided to go out and tell someone?"

"I don't think they'd go out without the priest's permission."

"I'm not so sure. They might even think it's the Devil," says Jimmy as he puts on his white undershirt.

"You think?"

"Put yourself in their place: a whole ton of weird noises coming from the roof over the prayer room, over the altar."

Jimmy buttons up his olive-green shirt and starts to put on his boots.

"You're right," Clemen says, smiling, now confident again. "They must be scared shitless . . . But what are you going to do?"

"I'm going to go down and tell them we're doing some work for the priest, repairs, and that they shouldn't be afraid."

"What if there's someone with them who's not to be trusted?"

Jimmy stops to think for a few seconds. Then he takes his watch out of his pocket.

"It's five to six," he says.

"If you want, let's both go down, then I can take a leak. But Father Dionisio means what he says, and he made it very clear I wasn't to go down until he got back."

"He told me the same thing," Jimmy says, indecisively.

"We don't want him to get angry and throw us out."

"I don't think he ever would."

"Because you don't know him. Let's wait five more minutes, and if he doesn't come, we'll go down."

Jimmy lies down so he can press his ear against the crack in the wooden floor.

"We'll wait," he says, "but if I hear one of the girls about to leave, I'm going to go down and stop her."

He moves over to the loose floorboard that covers the entrance to the loft.

"Let's keep quiet, then," says Clemen in a circumspect tone of voice.

"That's what I say: keep your mouth shut."

The light abruptly turns gray, as if the setting sun had been obscured by a cloud or some foliage; a flock of parrots make a racket as they fly over the house.

"Soon we won't be able to see anything," Clemen says.

Jimmy reaches for the edges of the board he'll have to lift in an emergency; he turns and gives Clemen a scornful look, but Clemen doesn't notice.

"We were left in the dark like this at the radio station," Clemen continues, "from one minute to the next they cut our electricity and, that was that, the party was over ..."

"Shh ...," Jimmy demands silence.

"I don't see how they could have forgotten to send troops to take over and defend the power station."

Jimmy looks at him in disbelief, then anger.

"You participated in planning the coup," Clemen continues. "There wasn't anybody with enough sense to think of taking over and defending the power station?"

"Are you going to shut up once and for all?" Jimmy mutters.

"Don't worry, if the girls haven't gone out yet they're not going to, the priest forbids them from going out without permission. They'll wait and tell him about the noise."

Clemen sits down and grabs his genitals again.

"That was a major fuckup, but it wasn't ours, it was yours, the civilians," Jimmy says. "None of you thought you'd need electricity to keep the station running ..."

"I can't hold it anymore," says Clemen, reaching for the empty can. "I'm going to take a leak."

"You're a pig."

"I don't have time for niceties."

On his knees and with his back to Jimmy, Clemen has unzipped his pants and is peeing into the can; as the stream starts to flow, he lets out two short farts.

"Sorry . . . ," he says, looking relieved.

Jimmy shakes his head back and forth in disbelief. Then he puckers up his face in a look of disgust and covers his nose with his palm.

They hear distinctly the front door opening.

Jimmy grabs the edges of the board, ready to lift it; Clemen hurries to pull his pants up.

"I'm here, girls, and so is Doña Chon!" Father Dionisio exclaims in his hoarse voice and his Castilian accent. "Come get the tamales!"

They hear the flip-flops slapping against the floor, a greeting, the priest giving his blessing to Doña Chon, and the door closing.

"Father, Doña Ana brought you some cheese a while ago."

Clemen and Jimmy remain still and alert, the latter without removing his hand from his nose.

"Which Doña Ana, my child? There are several."

"From the pharmacy, Father."

"How nice, because we are going to have two guests for dinner. But how many times have I told you not to open the door to anybody when I'm not here."

"I'm sorry, Father . . ."

"I don't want it to happen again. Tomorrow I'm going to hear your confession, because the Devil always has his way with you girls."

Mockingly, Clemen makes an obscene gesture with his right middle finger into a hole made with his left thumb and index finger.

"Father . . ."

"Yes?"

The voices sound as if they are right beneath them.

"There are some animals up above . . ."

"Where, my child?"

"There, in the roof, Father, in the prayer room . . . We heard some loud banging."

"Some rats must have gotten in. We'll put out some poison. Don't you worry, my child. Go back to your sister and help her fix dinner. And stay in the back, in the kitchen, until I call you. Don't disturb me."

"As you wish, Father."

The flip-flops walk away. The door to the prayer room has been closed. A moment later they hear a light tapping under the floor of the attic.

"Come down," the priest says.

Jimmy picks up the board, climbs down through the hole, resting his feet on the wardrobe, then jumping onto the floor; Clemen follows behind him, being very careful; first he places the can on the wardrobe, then jumps down.

"What's that?" the priest asks, curious.

"I was pissing my pants, Father. Forgive me. I couldn't hold it any longer. Luckily I found this can."

Jimmy makes a face of disapproval.

"You have no self-control, Clemen. Take it to the bathroom . . . Make sure the girls don't see you from the kitchen."

Father Dionisio is a tall, hefty, ruddy old man with a gray beard, bulbous nose, and knitted brow.

"Come to my room and I'll give you some clothes," he says.

Clemen goes to the bathroom while the other two enter Father Dionisio's room. The priest opens a wardrobe, takes out a shirt, a pair of trousers, and a pair of shoes, and says to Jimmy:

"We're about the same height. They'll be a bit roomy on you, but nothing noticeable. Try on the shoes, those boots of yours stink like the Devil, they'll scare people away."

Clemen enters with the empty can.

"You are the same size as the colonel. I brought you two changes of clothes and a pair of shoes," the priest says, pointing to a brown paper bag on the floor.

Jimmy has already quickly changed his clothes, as if he were getting ready to leave right away; Clemen asks the priest if he brought any cigarettes.

"Look inside the shoes," the priest says.

Jimmy anxiously asks him what he's heard about the situation.

"I'll tell you soon. It's terrible."

Clemen has finished getting dressed; he picks some matches up from the priest's nightstand and lights a cigarette.

"Father, please forgive me," says Clemen, "but is there any chance for a beer, a shot of something, anything?"

Jimmy turns around and looks at him in astonishment.

"Let's go to the prayer room. Then I'll get something for you."

After closing the door and gesturing to them to have a seat on one of the benches, the priest speaks quietly and in a grave voice: the coup has been completely defeated, most of the rebel officers are in the hands of the dictator, there's no news of the civilians who took part, the National Guard is patrolling the roads and conducting searches on the least suspicion; everybody is terrified.

"But we're safe here, aren't we, Father?" Clemen asks.

"You are not safe anywhere, my son."

"I've got to get out of the country," Jimmy says. "If the general gets his hands on me, I'm a dead man."

"We are too far away from the border," the priest says.

Then he tells them that the head of the National Guard in Cojutepeque is an old enemy of the colonel, and even though the colonel is the governor of the province, he wouldn't be surprised if the chief were keeping an eye on the colonel, knowing that Clemen participated in the coup and might try to seek protection from his grandfather.

"We must find somewhere else to hide you, farther away from the city."

"But here on the outskirts, nobody would suspect anything," says Clemen, swallowing hard and taking a few final deep drags off the cigarette.

"The head of the Guards is shrewd, and a lout," the priest says and points to the plate under the candlestick where he can stub out his cigarette. "I wouldn't be surprised if he suspected me because of my friendship with your family, and took advantage of my absence during Mass to come and search the house."

"I have plans to leave as soon as possible," Jimmy says.

The priest turns to him in surprise.

"Very good, son. You'll tell me all about it while we eat dinner, anxiety stimulates my appetite," the priest says as he gets ready to open the door, then adds, "This will be your last meal down here. From now on you must remain above, I'll leave your food on the wardrobe, and you can come down at dawn and at night, once the house is all locked up, to take care of your business."

"What about the girls?"

"Don't worry about them. They are my goddaughters. They talk only to people I give them permission to talk to, and they never go out without me. I will forbid them from coming into the prayer room. And they won't know you are here. Anyway, they spend most of their time in the back of the house, in the kitchen, the washroom, and their quarters.

The priest goes out onto the patio and claps several times, his signal that dinner should be served; Jimmy and Clemen pass into the dining room and sit down across from each other at the rectangular table.

"The refreshments, Father?" Clemen asks.

"All in due time, son," the priest says.

He opens a cabinet and takes out a bottle of rum; Clemen's face lights up. The priest pours out three glasses and sits down at the head of the table.

Two girls, just barely adolescent, short and thin and with indigenous features, enter the dining room carrying plates of food. They say "good evening" but keep their eyes down, not daring to look any of the men in the face. They place beans, rice, fried plantains, cheese, cream, and tortillas on the table.

"What if someone knocks on the door while we're eating?" Jimmy asks, worried, once the girls have left.

"Everybody in the congregation knows not to disturb me during dinner."

"What about the National Guard?" Jimmy insists. "Is there a back exit through the patio?"

The priest, who at that moment was helping himself to some plantains, suddenly looks at him with fear; Clemen gulps down his whole glass of rum.

"You would climb into the loft immediately and without making a sound," the priest says after recovering his composure. "But I don't think they'll come tonight; they're only now getting organized. Eat quickly, then go up."

Nervous, but without saying another word, they eat their fill.

"What's the plan you mentioned, my son?"

"To go east as soon as possible, Father. My idea is to reach the Gulf of Fonseca. I have a couple of friends at the American base there."

"The roads are all blocked," the priest explains. "National Guard soldiers are patrolling in pairs and the regional forces are everywhere, demanding documents from anybody they don't know, and they check the names against the list of coup participants that was wired to all the command bases in the country this morning. Your names are on that list, that's what the colonel told me."

"May I pour myself another one, Father?" Clemen asks; from the look on his face it's clear he is undergoing a panic attack.

"Last one . . . Otherwise you'll have to relieve yourself in the middle of the night."

"We have to find a way for me to leave," Jimmy says.

"For you to leave together," the priest says, still with his mouth full.

Jimmy and Clemen look at each other in surprise.

"I don't want to leave, Father," Clemen says.

"And I don't want him coming with me," Jimmy adds.

"You won't be able to be up there for long without being discovered, son," the priest warns Clemen, as if he hadn't heard what Jimmy said. "This house receives many visitors. Then we'd all be in trouble, even your grandfather. We must find a way for you to leave together."

Jimmy takes a sip of rum.

"With all due respect, Father, I think the military should go one way and civilians another. It would be best if Clemen found a new hiding place and I continued on my way. It won't be easy to reach the gulf, I might encounter dangerous situations, and my cousin here simply isn't prepared..."

One of the girls enters with more tortillas. They stop talking. She asks the priest if she should bring three cups of coffee. He nods, without looking at her, and keeps chewing.

She leaves quickly, her sandals making the same slapping sound as she walks away.

"Maybe you know a guide you trust, Father, someone who could take back roads to the train tracks in the middle of the night?" Jimmy asks in a low voice, sidling up to the priest, as if he fears the girl has stayed behind the door listening.

The priest wipes the plate with a piece of tortilla, sopping up the remains of the beans and the cream; he scrunches up his face, as if mentally searching through the roster of his congregants to find the man Jimmy needs, then he places the piece of tortilla in his mouth and shakes his head.

"Wouldn't do you any good," he says, once he finishes swallowing. "There's a pair of soldiers on every train, and they inspect every car."

Clemen nods in agreement with what the priest has said, throws Jimmy an I-told-you-so look, then takes a tiny sip of rum, hoping this way it will last all night.

"What's up with you?" Jimmy says irritably. "The rum already went to your head, didn't it?"

"No, I just think you've got to be nuts to want to go out in the middle of the night and get caught by a patrol."

"If I want your opinion, I'll ask for it, you hear?"

"Well, just in case you wanted it..."

"Boys," the priest interrupts them, having heard quite enough. "Right now it would be best for you to finish eating, take care of your business, and climb back up to the loft. There's nothing like a good night's sleep for the Lord to enlighten us with new ideas."

At that moment the girl comes in, her head still down, carrying three steaming cups of coffee; Clemen watches her carefully, and as she leaves, he checks her out from behind.

2

"Jimmy, are you awake? ... What was that?" Clemen whispers.

The other keeps snoring.

"Jimmy ..."

Clemen gropes around in the darkness until he touches Jimmy's shoulder; he gives him a few pokes.

"Jimmy ..."

Jimmy opens his eyes like a frightened animal; it takes him three seconds to realize where he is and with whom.

"What's going on?" he whispers.

The darkness is almost total: the filthy skylight lets in barely a trace of the night's glow.

"Did you hear that noise outside?"

"No."

"Sounded like soldiers marching."

They are lying next to each other on the mats, a few feet apart.

"I don't hear anything."

"They went by while you were snoring, that's why I woke you," Clemen whispers.

"Have you been up for a while?"

"I had a nightmare."

"You sure you heard troops marching by or was it part of your nightmare?"

"The nightmare woke me up a while ago, and the marching happened just a minute ago."

"Strange ..." Jimmy whispers.

"Yeah, it is. I'm not imagining it."

Downstairs they can hear Father Dionisio's rhythmic snores; above, the wind is whistling through the trees.

"What time is it about?"

"I don't think I'll be able to see in this darkness," Jimmy whispers, and he takes his pocket watch out of this trousers.

"I've got matches."

"Are you crazy? The reflection will show through the skylight."

"You think?"

"We shouldn't risk it."

Jimmy sits up and holds the watch face up to the skylight.

"I could light a match close to the floor and shield it with my hands so nobody can see it outside," Clemen whispers.

"It's midnight. Twelve fifteen."

"I thought it was later ... We came up here really early."

Jimmy has lain down again; he yawns and turns over to go back to sleep.

"The priest is right," Clemen whispers. "Anybody would lose their mind stuck too long up here in this attic."

"You'd better get used to it. It's not going to be easy to find somewhere else."

Clemen sighs.

"This is fucked," he complains. "How could everything have gone so wrong?"

"Complaining won't do you any good. Let's just thank God they haven't caught us."

"You aren't married and you don't have kids, so what do you care? Poor Mila must be having a really hard time ..."

"I don't think they'll do anything to her," Jimmy tries to comfort him. "They're not going to involve either her or the kids."

"And my poor old man, a prisoner ... Who knows what they'll do to him ..."

"He was in jail, so he couldn't have known anything about the coup. The general wants us, the rebel officers. He'll never forgive us for betraying him."

"That damned motherfucking warlock has made a pact with the Devil," Clemen says angrily, raising his voice.

"Shh ... quiet down, you're going to wake up the priest."

Clemen tosses and turns on the mat, restless.

Jimmy feels around on the floor to make sure his gun is by his side. Then he whispers, talking to himself, as if trying to convince himself of something:

"If they catch me, I'm a dead man."

"Are you really going to go off on your own?"

"I'm going to rest tonight, recover a little. I'll ask the priest for detailed information about ways to get to the train tracks. And tomorrow at this time I'll start off..."

"You're nuts... What if you meet up with a patrol?"

"That's why I have this gun and why I'm a military man. I still have two clips."

"They're going to kill you..."

"That's the risk I'll have to take," Jimmy whispers. "When you get involved in the affairs of men, you've got to have balls... I told you Lieutenant Peña and I were surrounded, and we shot our way out. I'm not going to let them capture me."

"You should stay here a few days until the situation clears up," Clemen whispers, cautiously.

"The situation is already very clear. I'd rather take my chances on the move than holed up here like a rat."

They hear noises in the street; heavy footsteps approach the house.

"Listen. They're coming back."

Jimmy has now sat up, wide awake, clutching his gun on his lap.

They remain silent while the marchers pass by; then they hear the voice of the commanding officer repeating as they march away: "One, two, one, two..."

"It's a patrol," Jimmy whispers.

"National Guard..."

"No, local forces," Jimmy explains. "Didn't you notice that some were marching out of rhythm?"

"Fuck, I'm scared shitless."

"Shh..."

They've gotten used to the darkness: Clemen can make out Jimmy's hand pointing down, toward the room where the priest was snoring a moment before and that is now totally silent.

"Why are they out marching at this time of night?"

"Emergency patrols. There's a curfew."

"Don't you think they're trying to tell us they know we're here?" Clemen groans.

"Calm down and lower your voice," Jimmy orders in a whisper.

"If they knew we were here they would have already come in and gotten us."

Jimmy keeps listening intently, but the priest has started snoring again.

"Let's keep quiet for a while until the priest falls back to sleep."

"He must be scared to death, like we are ..."

"Shh ..."

Jimmy has lain down again; he places his gun next to the cushion he's using as a pillow. They each have sheets and a glass of water. And they swept the floor.

"I'm not going to be able to fall asleep," Clemen whispers.

"At least let me sleep."

"I need whiskey."

"Drink water."

"It'll just make me have to pee. And in this darkness, I might miss the can and it'll end up all over the floor."

The priest coughs, clears his throat, then turns over in bed.

"I told you: shut your trap," Jimmy whispers, irritated. "Let us sleep."

Clemen sits down. He feels around for his glass of water; he takes a sip. He stares at the dirty skylight.

"I wish we could see the sky," he whispers. "Looking at the stars would distract me."

Jimmy has turned his back to him.

Clemen stretches, then lies down, clasping his hands behind his neck.

Jimmy's breathing becomes heavier, more rhythmic; he seems to have already fallen asleep.

"The minute I found out that the ambush had failed, and the warlock had managed to get to police headquarters, I had a premonition everything would fall apart ...," Clemen mumbles, bitterly, talking to himself. "But it wasn't my fault."

Suddenly, an owl hoots very close by, as if it were on the roof of the house. Clemen listens carefully: he hears a buzzing from afar.

Jimmy moves around on the mat.

"What wasn't your fault?" he asks, curious.

Clemen sits up anxiously.

"I need a smoke," he whispers.

"You know the priest asked us not to smoke up here."

"But I'm really anxious . . . Did you hear that buzzing?"

"Sounds like an engine . . ."

"Sounds like it's coming closer."

They both concentrate on the distant buzzing.

"It comes closer, then moves farther away," Jimmy whispers. "But anyway, what were you talking about?"

"That it wasn't my fault the son of a bitch went to police headquarters."

"Who said it was?"

"That bastard Juan José, because I announced over the radio that only the police and the National Guard weren't supporting the coup, and that's why the bastard went straight to the Black Palace . . ."

"I heard you say that," Jimmy whispers.

"But everybody was saying it. And that bastard Juan José was the first to go on air when we took over the station, and he claimed that the general had been killed in the ambush on the highway to the port . . ."

"You civilians always run off at the mouth."

"And you military men don't do jack shit. First you duped us with your deadly ambush that never was, then you supposedly had the Black Palace under siege, and then you let him slip right through your fingers like water . . ."

"Shhh . . . keep your voice down."

"That Juan José . . . accusing me . . . even Dr. Romero announced on the radio that the general was dead, and the National Guard and the police weren't supporting us. We were all left in the lurch by you people."

The priest clears his throat again.

"It's a truck and now it really is coming closer," Jimmy whispers.

Clemen cups his hand behind his ear.

"You're right," he whispers, then swallows hard. "It's the National Guard..."

"Or the army..."

"It stopped... It's about two hundred yards away."

"Troop transport," Jimmy murmurs, wide awake now. He sits up, pushes off his sheet, and picks up the gun.

"You think it's coming here?"

"I hope not," Jimmy whispers.

"Why did it stop?"

Jimmy remains alert; he barely shrugs his shoulders.

"They keep revving it, as if they're waiting for someone," Clemen whispers; he is squirming, anxious. "Could they be doing a house-to-house search?"

"We must be prepared..." Jimmy says.

"How? What do you plan to do?"

"If they come in the house, we'll retreat into that corner," Jimmy whispers, pointing to a spot in the back of the attic.

"Don't go shooting off your gun or they'll kill both of us," Clemen whispers, right then scurrying toward that corner.

As he moves, nervous, his knee hits the glass of water.

"Shit... the water spilled."

"Was it full?"

"No..." Clemen whispers, curled up in the corner.

"I hope it doesn't seep through the wood."

"I don't think it will... Here they come. Listen."

The roar of the engine approaches the house.

"Keep driving, keep driving..." Clemen mumbles as if he were praying.

"Shhh..."

The truck has stopped in front of the house. Orders ring out, there are loud footsteps. Knocks on the door.

"Open up. National Guard."

"It's not here," Jimmy whispers. "It's the house across the street."

Clemen is paralyzed, his face full of terror.

They hear the priest's bed creaking; they see a ray of light through a crack in the floor. Then they hear the priest's slow footsteps to the front door.

"What's he doing? Why is he opening the door when they haven't knocked here?" Clemen groans.

"Shhh..."

The priest has opened the door.

"Why all the racket, Sergeant Marvin? Did something happen?"

"Good evening, Father." The sergeant's voice sounds heavy, as if his words were sticking together. "Sorry for the disturbance, we're just alerting the residents because we've received information that several communist traitors are hiding out in this zone..."

"At this time of night?"

"Yes, Father. We just got word. Some officers who were at the Ilopango Airport during the rebellion. They say they came in this direction."

"Come over here, Sergeant."

"Yes, Father."

From up above, they hear the footsteps enter the living room. Clemen squeezes into the corner; Jimmy doesn't budge.

"You have been drinking on duty, Sergeant," the priest says curtly, with reproach.

"No, Father Dionisio, just one little drink, I swear, just to make the long night easier."

"One drink... Don't swear in vain, Sergeant, and don't go around frightening people in the middle of the night, this is Holy Week and it will be your fault if they get too scared to come out for the processions..."

"No, Father. I'm just warning the residents in my zone. I'm just following orders... And the girls?"

Jimmy and Clemen look at each other.

"They are sleeping, son. At this time of night only lost souls stay awake."

The footsteps move back toward the front door.

"May God be with you, Sergeant. And rest assured... if I hear of any strangers in the vicinity, you will be the first to know . . ."

"Not all of them are strangers, Father," he says, lowering his voice, as if he were telling him a secret. "My lieutenant suspects that one of the colonel's grandsons, the one who insulted the general on the radio, came here to hide out . . ."

Clemen tries to make himself even smaller and opens his eyes big and round like two saucers; Jimmy gestures with his hand for him to calm down.

"If that happened, the colonel himself would turn him in," the priest says, with a slightly indignant, disapproving tone. "The colonel is more loyal to the general than all the rest of you put together. And don't you forget that."

Now out on the sidewalk, the priest issues a warning:

"Be careful with that truck, don't go destroying the carpet of petals the congregation has made such an effort to spread around the streets."

They hear the sergeant shout out orders, some running steps, the truck door slamming, then the engine revving up. The truck pulls away; the priest stays at the door.

"Good night, Father Dionisio . . . ," a voice sounds, from afar, not the sergeant's.

"It's the neighbor across the street," Jimmy whispers.

"Good night, son. Go back to bed . . ."

When the priest closes the door, Clemen lets out a loud fart.

"Sorry," he mumbles.

Jimmy looks at him with disgust and brings his hand to his nose.

The priest has crossed his room; his bed creaks, the ray of light shining through the crack in the floor disappears; after clearing his throat, he sighs:

"Thank the Lord!"

In the darkness, Jimmy's eyes shine with the desire to strike Clemen down.

"You're disgusting," he whispers, without removing his hand from his nose.

Clemen moves very carefully back to his mat; then he whispers:

"Fuck, what a nightmare... You think they'll come back?"

"I hope not."

"How could that lieutenant have found out I came here?"

"The sergeant said his lieutenant suspected, he didn't say he'd found anything out," Jimmy whispers as he straightens out his mat. "And the priest warned us about this lieutenant, that he has it in for your grandfather, though he can't do anything because of his rank."

"So, why did they come precisely to this house?"

"They were scoping out the area. You heard him."

"Too many coincidences..."

"Maybe the sergeant made such a big to-do because he likes one of the priest's girls," Jimmy wonders out loud.

Clemen keeps staring at him with astonishment, as if suddenly he too understood.

"It's true. He asked about them..." he whispers, and then, in a mischievous tone and bringing his hands to his genitals, he adds, "The one who served us dinner is just about ripe for the plucking... You think the priest has had her?"

"Shhh... He's going to hear you. The things you think of..."

"She would feel so good...," he sighs, without letting go of his crotch.

They grow quiet. The night is cooler. A cricket begins to sing inside the attic, near the piles of junk.

"I'm not tired anymore," Jimmy mutters.

The priest is snoring again.

"She's going to turn us in...," Clemen whispers, suddenly quite agitated.

"Who?"

"The little Indian girl who served us our dinner, the one who's ready to be plucked..."

"She doesn't even know we're here."

"I bet the sergeant will come to court her when the priest isn't here, and she'll tell him that two strangers had dinner here."

"I'll warn the priest, but he said they were completely under his control."

"Nobody controls women, least of all when the priest is out of the house at the processions all week."

"You're right."

"If that sergeant starts sniffing around the house," Clemen whispers, anxious, "it won't take him long to find us."

"We've got to leave here as soon as possible."

"But, where?" Clemen moans.

"The colonel and the priest will find you someplace more remote, further up in the mountains. And I should continue with my own plans ..."

"What plans? You don't have any plans ... Go out there and let them find you? Get on a train so the National Guard can nab you? Stop pretending to be some kind of hero ..."

Jimmy turns to look at him, at first in disbelief, then with disdain.

"I'm not going to bother explaining it to you. Of course, I have a plan. What I need is fake ID or a disguise so I can ride the train without being recognized, just like you got out of the capital dressed as a housemaid."

"Even if you dress up as a whore, they'll find you."

Jimmy sits up; he picks up his glass and takes a sip of water.

Suddenly Clemen stares at him with astonishment.

"I have an idea," he mutters.

Jimmy lies down with his back to him, annoyed, as if he weren't listening.

"I have a great idea ...," Clemen repeats, sitting up, increasingly excited.

Jimmy remains quiet.

"Did you hear me? I have a great idea for how you can ride the train without anybody recognizing you and I can get to a different hiding place, no problem ..."

"Wow ...," he mumbles peevishly.

The priest coughs; his bed creaks.

Haydée's Diary

Ash Wednesday, April 5

Clemen has not been captured, and I pray to God he manages to escape altogether. As to his whereabouts, all we know is that he left the radio station on Monday, moments after he spoke to me, a few hours before the rebel officers surrendered; since then, nothing. My whole being trembles just imagining that they might capture him. The rumors are gruesome. They say officers are being savagely tortured to get them to reveal the names of everybody who collaborated with them, the general himself is in the Black Palace overseeing the interrogations, they've already begun to prepare for the war council, and soon they will begin ordering executions. There's a desperate stampede. They also say the Peruvian embassy is full of people requesting asylum; apparently things didn't go well for those who sought refuge in the Mexican embassy, they didn't know that Ambassador Méndez Plancarte is a fervent admirer of the general—he has boasted of it more than once right in front of Pericles—and he would never open the doors to any rebel officer. They also say Colonel Tito Calvo arrived at the American Embassy in a tank, certain that the United States would give him political asylum, but when he descended from the tank to enter the compound, the Marines blocked his way; the colonel had a shouting match with them, rained curses down on them, then returned to the tank to go to another embassy, and that's when the general's troops fell upon him and took him away.

I went to the Central Prison twice today, demanding that they let me see my husband, but I had no luck. Colonel Palma refused to see me, and Sergeant Flores didn't even come out so I could give him the provisions I'd brought for Pericles. Outside the Central Prison, I met up with the mothers of Merlos and Cabezas; we shared our concerns and fears. Thank God my mother-in-law called me before dinnertime to tell me we must pray for Clemen but that nothing will happen to Pericles, the general will not retaliate against those who did not participate in the coup, the colonel is certain of that—the president himself knows that General Marroquín and Colonel Tito Calvo have always had grudges against my husband. I felt greatly relieved. I called Doña Chayito, Merlos's mother, right away to tell her what my mother-in-law had just told me; she promised to tell Doña Julita, Cabezas's mother, tonight. We agreed to meet tomorrow at nine o'clock in front of the Central Prison.

Pati called to tell me that she and Mauricio are trying to pull strings to get Clemen asylum at the Costa Rican embassy. I explained to her that the problem now is that all the embassies are surrounded by the general's police, and nobody can go in or out without them knowing; I was going to tell her not to worry, we are dealing with the problem from here, then I remembered Father's warning. Pati suggested we send Betito out of the country, have him spend some time in Costa Rica. I told her that Betito is a teenager, he is not involved in politics, so nothing will happen to him, even though the truth is that at this moment nobody in this country is not involved, even the children are talking about it.

A few minutes before eight I went to the servant's room to look for María Elena, to tell her that the radio broadcasts were back to normal and invite her to listen to a new Cuban comedy show with me—we need a bit of distraction in the midst of so much misfortune. I found her on her knees, her face buried in the bed, as if she were praying, but she was actually crying inconsolably. I asked her what had happened. She said it was nothing and she was sorry, she'd soon be fine, and she got up and wiped her face off with a towel. I was very touched by the sorrow in her eyes. I told her not to worry, Clemen would weather this misfortune, God is watching over us. Sometimes you must pretend to be strong, full of faith and hope, even if inside doubts and fears are tearing you apart.

Holy Thursday, April 6

No news of Clemen. Everybody reminds me that no news is good news. But we mothers want some proof that our fugitive child is well, a word from someone who knows he is safe; without that, anguish festers in my heart.

My mother-in-law dropped by unannounced this morning, accompanied by my sister-in-law Bertita, Pericles's younger sister. They explained that they had left Cojutepeque on the first train, at five in the morning. Mama Licha urged me to quickly prepare everything I wanted to take to my husband; they had come from the station in a hired car that was waiting in front. We soon left for the Central Prison. We had no problem getting in; Sergeant Flores was expecting us. They brought Pericles into the room where we were waiting; I couldn't control myself, I ran up to embrace him and whispered in his ear that Clemens had managed to escape, and that Don Jorge was still alive; his eyes looked heavy, his clothes were a bit soiled, but he seemed to be in good spirits. "And you, what are you doing here with your rheumatism?" Pericles asked his mother, affectionately and with apparent surprise. All she said was that she'd had an urgent need to see him, to be certain he was doing well, and thanks to God the opportunity had arisen to pay him a twenty-minute visit, but she didn't mention the colonel's good offices. During the entire visit Pericles talked as if he was certain that somebody was taking detailed notes of our conversation: he asked after the family, Pati and Betito, Mila and the children, my parents and my sister, but not a word about the colonel or Clemen; he told of the hours of uncertainty he'd spent inside the Central Prison during the coup, prisoners and guards listening to every word broadcast over the radio, and wagers even being placed on who would win, the rebels or "the man"; he mentioned how tense the officers in charge were, how they kept expecting an assault at any moment; under his breath he cheered the outbursts of enthusiasm of a group of guards who dislike the general; he declared scornfully that anybody in his right mind wouldn't even dream that a couple of cowards like Marroquín and Calvo would be able to defeat "the man"; he expressed sorrow at the fates of some of his acquaintances, and he made reference to several arrests I didn't know about. I realized that more information is available inside the Central Prison than outside, and my husband, though he spoke in generalities, was surely right in the center of it all. I would have liked to finally ask him if he had foreknowledge of the coup, of Clemen's participation, but he would never have forgiven such imprudence. We drank coffee and ate sweet rolls; Pericles ate a few bites of the provisions we brought him. The minutes flew by. Colonel Palma, the director of the Central Prison, came personally into the room to inform us that our time was up: he greeted my mother-in-law with a deep bow, then turned to me and Bertita; he exclaimed in a stentorian voice that Pericles had no cause to complain about how he was being treated, and he announced that now that the vicious traitors had been defeated, things would slowly return to normal, adding that next Sunday, Easter Sunday, as proof of the general's magnanimity, I would be allowed to visit again; then he said it would be his honor to accompany us out. Mama Licha stood up and gave Pericles her blessing. When we embraced before parting, he whispered in my ear that I should tell Merlos's and Cabezas's families that they are both well, and he kissed me on my ear lobe, which he knows I love. As I watched them lead him out, I held back my tears and felt my heart clenching, as if I had found him after having lost him for a long time, and now they were taking him away from me again. At the large front doors, and with the same false obsequiousness, Colonel Palma sent a respectful greeting to my father-in-law and also to my "dear parents," as if he knew them personally.

I looked around for Doña Chayito and Doña Julita, the students' mothers, but it was early, and they still hadn't arrived. My mother-in-law asked me to accompany her to Clemen's house, she wanted to see her great-grandchildren and say hello to Mila; we all got in the same car, which was waiting for us. As we were driving, I suddenly felt lighthearted, as if a great sadness had lifted; my mother-in-law made a few comments about the procession, about how pretty the carpets of flowers were in the streets of Cojutepeque. A contingent of secret police was posted at the intersection in front of my son's house; a couple of them approached to sniff around when we got out of the car. Ana, Clemen and Mila's housemaid, opened the door for us; she said the señora had just gone out and the children were playing on the patio. Mama Licha asked her if Mila would return soon; Ana, who is María Elena's cousin, said she didn't know, though I had a feeling there was something she was keeping to herself. Marianito came running up to us, such a lovely child, my favorite, and shouted with joy; Alfredito and Ilse ran up behind him: they're still upset about Samba's death; they led us to the patio, showed us the exact spot where the police had killed her. We stayed only a short while. Then my mother-in-law and Bertita dropped me off at my house; they were going to pay a couple of other visits, then return to Cojutepeque on the noon train so they would arrive in time for the procession of Jesus carrying the cross. María Elena greeted me with a message from Doña Chayito, who had been waiting for me in front of the Central Prison. I called to tell her what had happened.

Father was not surprised that we were granted permission to visit Pericles so unexpectedly, thanks to my in-laws. He says that right now the Nazi warlock doesn't trust any of the younger officers, so he is relying heavily on the older officers like Colonel Aragón, who have always been loyal to him; he also reminded me that the general claims that the wealthy are now his enemy, not those with socialist ideas, and he includes my husband among the latter. Father left at noon for Santa Ana with Betito, who will stay with Cecilia and Armando for a few days; mother insisted on staying with me to keep me company, in case there is an emergency. Father complained that yesterday he had to obtain a pass from the Black Palace; the authorities now require one for all cars leaving the city.

Mingo dropped by this afternoon for a cup of coffee. I told him about our visit with Pericles; he told me that Colonel Aragón's support had been vitally important to the general during the coup, and surely my father-in-law wants to guarantee that there be no reprisals against Pericles, knowing, as he does, that there is little he can do for Clemen. He confirmed that Serafín has sought refuge at the house of the Guatemalan consul, he is very frightened, the poor thing, afraid the general's troops will burst in and arrest him; it's anybody's guess when the newspaper will appear again. He then began to recount one story that is spreading like wildfire: the general managed to save his own life and defeat the coup because of the efforts of Father Mario, a Guatemalan priest who I think is a good man but Pericles believes to be scheming, ambitious, and unscrupulous. They say that Father Mario was the first to call the general at his house at the beach to inform him of the uprising and warn him of the ambush planned by Lieutenant Mancía, even advising him to return to the city in a different car so he could slip by unnoticed. And that is not the end of it. Mingo asserts that Father Mario himself drove to where the ambush had been laid and convinced Lieutenant Mancía to let the general pass, and that is how he was able to waltz right into the Black Palace. Unbelievable. According to what Mingo said, Father Mario also took it upon himself to convince General Marroquín and Colonel Calvo, not only to call off the tank assault against the palace but also to negotiate with the general through his own mediator, as well as to surrender with the guarantee that the general would spare their lives. How I miss Pericles whenever I hear political gossip such as this: he knows so well how to discern the truth from the fantasy.

Carmela and I went to the procession in the afternoon. Both our husbands are nonbelievers, both have ideas neither of us understand even if we do respect them; this strengthens our friendship. Mother had a headache and preferred to stay home. We caught up with the procession in the Candelaria district. The ritual was the same as every other year, but there was a different atmosphere, there was fear in people's eyes. I met the mothers and wives of men who had participated in the coup; we exchanged embraces and shed tears. I felt a claw digging into my throat, and I found it difficult to repeat to everybody who asked that I was grateful to our Lord that Clemen had not been captured. People who recognized us offered their support, patted us on the shoulder. Angelita, Jimmy's mother, was with mothers of other young officers who are already under arrest. Some had turned themselves in, trusting the promise the general had made to show mercy, but it has now been announced on the radio that they will be court marshaled. Fortunately, Jimmy has not been caught, either. Nobody has been allowed to see those locked up in the basement of the Black Palace, and the rumors about torture are getting worse and worse. There is enormous uncertainty.

Where is my son at this very moment? I look at his photo on my dresser and tears come to my eyes ... I asked María Elena to stay with me on these days of the Holy Week; father will go to the finca and give Belka her sweater and some other gifts. I think there are many of us, women alone, burdened by the sorry fates of our men. Mila and the children are staying at her father's house; the poor thing was traumatized by the search. Nerón has howled several times tonight; at first it frightened me, I thought somebody was trying to break in, then I told myself that animal has a sixth sense and knows about Samba's death; then, when I heard the howls of other dogs in the neighborhood, I remembered it was a full moon.

(Dawn)

I just dreamed that Clemen was hiding at Father's finca, in a shed in the middle of the coffee fields; in my dream, Don Tilo, María Elena's father, led the soldiers there, and they burst in on my son. I woke up in a cold sweat at the very moment he was fleeing under a hail of bullets. I haven't been able to shut my eyes again.

Good Friday, April 7

Still no news. The opposition newspapers are still shut down; not even the two that support the general appeared today. The radio stations are broadcasting only Holy Week programming, as if nothing extraordinary were happening, and when there is a brief news report, it consists of a litany of praises for the general and accusations and threats against his adversaries.

This morning I went to the Polyclinic: Don Jorge remains in critical condition. Several journalists were visiting; they all asked after Clemen and Pericles, all showed great concern. Mingo and Irmita also came. Everyone's right in asserting that nobody is safe any longer, for if the general dared to perpetuate such brutality against Don Jorge and has gotten away with it with total impunity, the same could happen to anybody. Don Jorge is not only the owner of the newspaper, he also belongs to one of the country's best families. It's true, he is rather rebellious, and sometimes irascible, and he does frequently insult the general and make fun of him, but nobody deserves to be tortured and shot down in the street like a rabid dog. I thank God Pericles has always shown restraint, in his columns he has criticized the political measures taken by "the man," but he has never attacked him personally; he knows him well, he was his private secretary for two years, he knows how spiteful and implacable he can be, hence he has always been circumspect when recounting his experiences during that period. As I was saying goodbye to poor Teresita, a delegation from the American Embassy was coming to visit. Mingo and Irmita offered to take me to my mother's house. According to Mingo, the general will not execute either General Marroquín or Colonel Tito Calvo: the first because they are old friends, and in the last analysis, he surrendered to him; the second because he was not captured in front of the embassy, as I was told and many were led to believe, rather he managed to enter the foyer where Ambassador Thurston was meeting with others from the diplomatic corps, none of whom offered to give him asylum, at which point Mr. Thurston convinced him to turn himself in after speaking on the phone with the general to request he show mercy. "If the ambassador turned him over to the general, he can't shoot him," Mingo said; I hope this is true, and may he also pardon Clemen and all the others who have been accused. When we arrived at Mother's house, I invited them in to stay and have lunch with us, try the delicious cod and the jocotes in honey, but they had a family engagement.

Mingo also confirmed that Mariíta Loucel has disappeared; they say she is neither at her house nor at her finca. Now I understand she must have known about the coup, that's why Jimmy, Dr. Romero, and even Clemen went to see her; that's why they were speaking French, so the general's spies wouldn't understand. I never would have thought she could be so audacious. I hope she managed to leave the country. Nor is anything known of Dr. Romero's whereabouts; perhaps they fled together. Pericles says that Mariíta would have been a great poet if she hadn't devoted herself to so many things at once, for she wants to excel as a businesswoman, a defender of women's rights, a landowner, and a politician. The poem of hers I like best is called "You Are Mad, I Suspect," I even know it by heart. I love it when Pericles recites it to me in his deep voice:

Write no more poems, you say? You are mad, I suspect
as if such a thing were nothing to request.
I can never please you, try as I will.
As if you'd asked death to no longer kill.
As if you'd wished the babe in my womb
to remain forever as if in a tomb.
My verse is the offspring of a homicidal pain.

It's a beautiful poem, though of course I prefer the ones Pericles has written for me. A little while ago, surrounded by the silence of this somber night, I reread them and felt so wistful ... The ones he wrote when he was courting me bring back so many memories, but I am more moved by those he wrote during the first year of our marriage. There are many of them, I've realized, now that I have gone over each one, written with green ink on marble-colored sheets folded carefully and duly sealed. It's so vivid to me, how each time he gave me one he would repeat that it was a gift for me alone, nobody else should read it, and they should never be published, each poem is something exclusive, personal, between him and me. This idea is so deeply ingrained in me, I would not even dare to transcribe one into this diary; it would be a betrayal of him.

I spent all afternoon and part of the night with Mother. We joined the Holy Burial procession for a spell, then returned home. The Club, the Casino, and the Círculo Militar remain closed by order of the general; neither parties nor family gatherings are allowed without prior authorization; a bit more and they'll forbid the processions. The secret police have been given carte blanche; they are everywhere, listening, spying, even at today's procession, where they were easily recognizable and it was all people could do not to jeer at them, they were so indiscreet; the ones keeping watch on the house are still there, prowling around. "The man" must be very frightened; we are more so.

María Elena came to tell me that this has been the saddest Good Friday of her life; I feel the same way. She went to the procession as well, with her cousin Ana, who has to sleep alone at Clemen's house every night, with the doors locked, trembling with fear, terrified that the police will burst in and rape her. Poor dear. I told María Elena to suggest that she come sleep with her here, but she says that Mila won't allow the house to be left alone. And I don't have the strength to take the chance of my daughter-in-law being rude to me.

Holy Saturday, April 8

I had a terrible shock this afternoon before leaving for the procession of the Virgin: the colonel showed up at the house without warning. My father-in-law comes to San Salvador under only extraordinary circumstances usually related to his work; at seventy years old, he says traveling aggravates him, puts his nerves on edge. He came to attend a meeting of regional leaders called by the general. He was here for about fifteen minutes, sitting in Pericles's rocking chair on the porch facing the patio. I was on my guard, watchful, knowing the colonel doesn't pay courtesy visits; he came solely for the purpose of telling me something. He accepted the glass of tamarind juice I offered him; Nerón came to lie down at his feet. He asked after Pericles; I told him that he is well, that tomorrow I will be able to see him again. He bewailed Clemen's "stupidity," that's what he called it, and said I should pray to God they don't capture my son; I told him we should all pray for that. He said he would like to be able to do that, but God no longer listens to his prayers. Nerón got up and went out to the patio, suddenly, as if he smelled danger in the air. Then, with no further ado, he came right out with it: the war council will meet, and Clemen will most likely be sentenced to death. I felt as if I had been stabbed in the chest; I was in shock. Then I reacted: I told him my son is a civilian, and war councils are for trying military officers. Not if the charge is treason, he muttered, clearing his throat. I told him what I had heard about the offers of amnesty, the guarantees of mercy. "You, more than anybody, Haydée, know how the general reacts in these situations," he said categorically. Then I remembered the final days of January 1932, when Pericles would return exhausted from the Presidential Palace, very late at night, and recount his conversations with "the man" regarding the fates of Martí and the other leaders of the communist revolt who would soon be executed. "It's them or us," I murmured, my voice shaking, because those were the words the general had used when Pericles asked him if he was going to reconsider the sentence. My father-in-law took a sip of his tamarind drink. I asked him, horrified, if he would participate in the council, if that's why he had come to the city. He told me he wouldn't, it wasn't his duty for he did not belong to that particular organizational structure of the army, nor did the general need to have him undergo a loyalty test of that kind. I asked him if he could do anything to prevent that sentence; he barely even bothered to shake his head. He stood up with some difficulty and said he had to go. As we walked through the living room, I asked him when the council was going to convene; he said he did not know exactly, but soon, very soon, once the holy days were over. I watched him walk to his car, he looked older, with the stiffness of somebody long accustomed to hiding his sorrow. I managed to reach the sofa, where I collapsed, I was a wreck, the tears welling up, forming a lump in my throat. María Elena came to comfort me, she must have guessed what I had just heard.

Father returned to the city late in the afternoon: he said a group of soldiers had come to the finca on Wednesday looking for Clemen;

they interrogated the workers, entered the manor house, searched the entire property, then spent the night in a nearby hamlet, where María Elena's family lives; the next morning they came back and scoured the entire property with a fine-tooth comb, asking about caves or possible hideouts. They found nothing, but they threatened the peons. Father told me that several acquaintances who participated in the coup have crossed the border into Guatemala, also some of his fellow coffee growers are on the lam, afraid of the Nazi warlock's rage. I asked him if Clemen has managed to cross the border; he said we would have heard if he had. That's when I told him about the colonel's visit and what he told me. He left the house immediately to go see his friends, to tell them of the tribulations that await us.

At the procession I spent some time talking to Angelita, Jimmy's mother. She was with Linda and Silvia, her two daughters, both of whom married quite well and are staying with her during this difficult period; she was widowed ten years ago when Dr. Ríos died, and her other son, Salvador, is a seminary student in Rome. I didn't want to bring up the war council, as it serves no purpose other than to make someone else worried about what is inevitable anyway. But she already knew. For a short stretch we carried a heavy statue of the Virgin, and we said several rosaries during the procession so that our sons would avoid capture. Angelita harbors the hope that the American military will defend Jimmy if he falls into the general's hands: Jimmy did a course at the Infantry and Cavalry School in Kansas, then he was stationed for another semester at a base in Laredo; the poor boy returned to El Salvador to rejoin the army only nine months ago. I expressed my doubts about the Americans sticking their necks out for an individual. But Angelita whispered in my ear that she is certain that if Jimmy got involved in the coup, it was with the approval of the American military, she knows for a fact that her son met frequently with Mr. Massey, the embassy's military attaché, with whom he enjoys a close friendship. That's when I noticed a spy circling around closer and closer, not taking his eyes off us; I warned Angelita. We resumed our prayers.

Betito will spend the weekend with my sister's family at their house on Lake Coatepeque. I must think carefully about what to say to Pati tomorrow, as I don't wish to make her more alarmed than she already is; I hope that after my visit with Pericles my spirits will improve, my mind will clear up. Because today I will go to bed as a lost soul, desolate, with a black cloud hovering over my home, my loved ones.

(9:30 p.m.)

Father came over a while ago, unexpectedly, to tell me the incredible news about Clemen's escape. He says that Monday afternoon, after my son left the station, he took refuge at the home of Mr. Gardiner, the American vice-consul. He managed to sneak in through the service door, thanks to his acquaintance with the servant and his friendship with the vice-consul's wife; my son's radio drama is very popular, his charm wins people over, though Father said, who knows what Clemen has going with that servant girl. Mr. Gardiner was at a meeting at the embassy and wasn't aware of Clemen's presence in the house until he returned that night. He then warned him that he could not offer him political asylum, but at that point he could not very well throw him out on the street, either, where the general's police would have immediately arrested him. Clemen spent the night at their house. On Tuesday morning, wearing one of Mrs. Gardiner's wigs and dressed as a housemaid, they took him in a diplomatic car to another hideout. That's all I know; Father didn't want to tell me how he found this out, and he warned me not to utter a word of it to anybody, not even to Mr. and Mrs. Gardiner.

Easter Sunday, April 9

It's eleven at night. Many of us are awake, our hearts in our mouths. The war council was convened tonight, between eight and nine o'clock, in the Black Palace. The general has not respected the holy day; his apostasy is great, and greater still will be his thirst for revenge. It was meant to be held in the greatest of secrecy, but word spread like wildfire. Everybody knows everything in this city. They say that

Tonito Rodríguez and Memito Trigueros are acting as defense attorneys; General Luis Andréu is presiding. The whole city is petrified, sunk in a deathly silence. The ten o'clock curfew and martial law are still in effect. My parents wanted me to stay with them, but I preferred to stay at home. I have said several Rosaries with María Elena. There's nothing more I can do. And answer the telephone, for we, the families of the accused, can at least offer each other comfort.

I couldn't get in to see Pericles. By dawn the streets were swarming with National Guard troops and police. The official newspapers and radio stations claimed the government had received information that the communists were planning an insurrection to commemorate the one-week anniversary of the coup; they called on people to remain at home, reminded everyone that today was not a day of processions, and requested that everyone inform the police about any gatherings whatsoever. It's madness. And there was no way María Elena and I could get to the Central Prison; we couldn't get past the police barricades. I was in despair. At one particular moment I remembered what my father-in-law had told me, about the imminence of the war council, but in a situation like this, nothing is certain. My greatest fear is that they will send Pericles back to the palace by mistake, because they say some of the coup participants were at the Central Prison for a while; but I quickly remind myself that there can be no confusion about my husband, by now the general must know every single detail of the conspiracy. I remember what happened to Don Jorge and I tremble.

I know nothing about Clemen's whereabouts. Father insists that if they haven't captured him by now, he must have managed to escape. I pray this is so. And I try to tell myself that this horrible experience will at least serve to get my son to settle down once and for all, nobody can stare death in the face and then continue along the same path as if nothing had happened.

My trepidation is too great; I find it impossible to continue writing.

(Midnight)

I'm still awake. My nerves fell like red-hot coals. I know I won't know anything until daybreak, but I cannot sleep. I am certain Pericles is also awake, knowing that the war council is in session, because in the prison they get news directly from the palace that we sometimes never hear. How I would love to hear your voice, my love, explaining what must be going on at the trial, calming my torments . . .

Monday, April 10

They've sentenced Clemente to death! And they executed General Marroquín, Colonel Tito Calvo, and eight more officers! The radio repeats the news over and over again. This is a heavy blow. We are all filled with dismay. The executions were carried out at eight this morning: Marroquín and Calvo were put in front of the firing squad on the patio of the palace, and the others were executed in the cemetery. I thank the Lord my son has not been captured! At this very moment I would be mourning him! Accursed warlock. . . As soon as they started reading the list of the condemned over the radio, I knew my son would be on it. And there he was. It's impossible to describe my anguish at that moment. We were in the living room, María Elena and I, listening to the radio. She began to sob, quietly; I simply threw myself back in the armchair and begged Our Lady with all my heart to please help Clemen flee the country . . . Nobody believed that monster would murder his own people so mercilessly. Not only did he kill Marroquín and Tito, but also their younger brother, Captain Marcelino Calvo. Three sons of the same mother! That poor old woman! That poor family! And here I thought I was the most unfortunate woman because my son is a fugitive and my husband is in jail . . . They also sentenced Jimmy to death, as well as Dr. Romero, Don Agustín Alfaro, and many others who have so far managed to escape, including Dr. Mario Calvo, Marcelino and Tito's brother. That brute will exact his blood revenge.

They had only just finished broadcasting the news on the radio when friends and acquaintances began to offer their support. The Alvarados arrived immediately; the phone didn't stop ringing. The same thing happened at my parents' house and at my in-laws'. Everybody tells me I should trust in God, Clemen will manage to save himself; some advise me to get Betito out of the country. Father assures me the general will not lash out at a minor who has not done anything; I want to believe him, but at moments I am assailed by doubts. Mother insists we should immediately send Betito to Guatemala City, to my Aunt Lola, who has been living there for many years; she says the border is so close to Santa Ana, and my brother-in-law Armando could drive him. Pati also is begging me to get her brother out immediately, either to Guatemala or San José. Only my mother-in-law reassures me, telling me that nothing will happen to Betito, if I am worried I should send him to their house in Cojutepeque, the colonel will guarantee his grandson's innocence. I spoke with Betito this afternoon: he said he doesn't want to leave the country, he doesn't want to leave me alone under these circumstances, tomorrow he is coming home, my sister and Armando will bring him from Santa Ana.

It seems Mila has completely taken leave of her senses; Ana told María Elena she has been drinking like a fish for several days. I called to ask her to bring my grandchildren here, but I couldn't reach her; Ana told me they are staying at her parents' most of the time. But the worst part isn't that Mila finds solace in drink during such a catastrophe; much more serious is what María Elena told me with shame and sorrow, because she is afraid I will think she is a gossip, but it was with the best of intentions, to spare me from a bigger shock later: she said that Ana told her that the señora talks on the telephone to a colonel by the name of Castillo and frequently goes out with him, and that she speaks disparagingly of Clemen in front of him, and on one occasion she told him on the phone that she believed her husband, "the coward," was hiding at Father's finca. I want to find excuses for my daughter-in-law, I want to tell myself she simply isn't prepared to deal with a situation as extreme as the one we are now facing, but what María Elena has told me tonight defies any justification. Mila is a scoundrel, a traitor. My hand is shaking as I write this. Pericles said as much a long time ago, when Clemen first started seeing her, he said the girl was "shifty" and not to be trusted; Pati also never took to her. I've always been the one to remind them not to be so judgmental, to accept people as they are. I'll make an effort not to think about her until Clemen is safe and sound, I don't want to be devoured by bitterness.

Mother says that Clemen's jocular, disrespectful, wild character has been his downfall; he never should have ridiculed the general on the radio, much less insulted him—mocking his personal defects, repeating jokes about him that are told on the street, even making fun of Doña Concha. That's why many other professionals and radio announcers who spoke on the radio in support of the uprising have not been sentenced to death, only Clemen—he even joyfully broadcast the news of the general's supposed demise. According to Father, it is the curse of Uncle Lalo.

In this city, we are breathing anger, mourning, and fear. Father managed to speak to Memito Trigueros, a member of the condemned men's legal defense team, who told him it was a summary trial: each lawyer had only ten minutes to argue his case, sentences were dictated at two in the morning, and by five the general had rejected requests for an appeal. Memito confirmed that the war council has not been adjourned, that they will meet again tonight to pass judgment on the rest of the coup participants, for the list is long and includes many who are in custody and others who are still at large.

I have been moving heaven and earth to find out if Pericles is still at the Central Prison. I managed to speak on the phone with Colonel Palma, the director: he assured me my husband was there, and perfectly fine, but that visiting privileges have been suspended until further notice, he said I must understand that these are extraordinary times. It's odd, but instead of arrogance, which is what I expected, I had the impression that Palma was frightened. I mentioned this to Mingo, who dropped by the house for a cup of coffee after lunch. He explained that there is much unease, fear, and mistrust among the officers in the army for, as it turns out, more of them than anyone could imagine were aware of or involved in the coup. As if this were not enough, Mingo told me, everybody also knows full well that Ambassador Thurston turned Tito Calvo over to the general after receiving a promise of clemency, that many of the officers who took part had recently returned from special courses in the United States, like Jimmy, and it would be not be surprising if the majority of the top brass saw these executions as the desperate thrashings of a drowning man, assuming the Americans have already turned their back on him completely. That's what I like sometimes about talking to Mingo, it's as if Pericles himself were explaining to me what was going on.

Mingo also told me that among those executed was one Lieutenant Mancía, a commander of the detachment that was supposed to ambush the general on his way back from the beach, and apparently the general owed his life to him because Mancía let him get to the Black Palace, thanks to Father Mario's efforts. Poor lieutenant! The general doesn't forgive the least hint of betrayal nor does he like to owe anything to a subordinate, that's what Pericles has always said. That came up this afternoon while Carmela and Chelón and I were eating *cemita* cakes and drinking coffee on the porch facing the garden and discussing the events of the morning; the sun was starting to go down, the heat was letting up a bit, and we were making fun of Nerón snoring. Chelón brought up the time the general invited him to the Presidential Palace, around 1936, a few weeks after he executed Lieutenant Baños, which upset us all so much at the time because the poor young man had done nothing but mouth off in a drunken outburst, yet the general had wanted to establish a precedent of zero tolerance for criticism from within the ranks of the army. "He likes to speak about the beyond, the invisible world, but he has a very strange relationship to death, he denies it has any meaning, and he has made a hodgepodge, to suit his needs, of many Eastern doctrines, especially those dealing with reincarnation, that's why he says it is worse to kill an ant than a man because the man will reincarnate and the ant will not," Chelón said. Then he added: "He was cajoling me, asking me about the heavenly bodies, about the development of the chakras, about traveling through time to remember previous incarnations, for he'd heard that I was knowledgeable about these things; but I was cautious, I pretended to be a curious neophyte, I didn't want him to take an aversion to me if he discovered that I knew more about some subjects then he did. In any case, he didn't like me and never invited me again." "Fortunately," Carmela said. Then I recalled, without mentioning a word of it to my friends, what Pericles told me the morning of the first of February, 1932, as he was about to get into bed after being up all night: at dawn, when he arrived at the Presidential Palace from the cemetery to give his eyewitness account that Martí and the other communist leaders had been executed, he found "the man" in his office, his eyes red and moist, as if he were suffering a bad conscience, trying to expiate his guilt for his crime, aware that he had stepped over a line and that there was no going back. Those tearful eyes, that expression of weakness in the face of the first executions of his political career, is a secret Pericles has always kept, one he told only me in the privacy of our bedroom. I now wonder if that silence might be what's kept him alive.

Fugitives (II)

1

"I almost fell and broke my ass!" Clemen exclaims, still trying to catch his breath after their mad dash and collapsing into the seat next to Jimmy in the first row of a half-empty train car, behind all the other passengers.

"Brother, shame on you for speaking that way!" Jimmy admonishes him, then looks at him disapprovingly. He is sitting next to the window. "What *is* the matter with you?"

Clemen turns and look around, afraid somebody may have heard.

"Forgive me, Father. I repent . . . ," he says, still panting, but with a mischievous twinkle in his eyes after verifying that no other passenger could possibly have heard him over the loud clattering of the train. "I meant to say I almost fell on the stairs . . ."

"Your appearance is reprehensible, Brother," Jimmy says, as he checks to make sure his own cassock has not come unbuttoned.

They ran onto the train just as it was pulling out of the station to avoid the National Guard and prevent anybody from recognizing them at the ticket window.

"What do you expect?" Clemen grumbles, whispering in Jimmy's ear. "After almost a week shut up in that attic, be grateful we didn't get cramps." Then he suggests: "We should look for a compartment."

They are sitting and facing the direction the train is moving. Jimmy again looks at the other passengers scattered around the car, then at the mountains through the window, and says:

"We'll wait for the conductor, he'll find us one."

Clemen is wearing gray trousers and a white shirt; he's carrying a backpack. Jimmy is draped in a black cassock; a large crucifix is hanging around his neck and he has a Bible in his hands.

"Good morning, Father," says a woman entering the car holding a little girl by the hand; she immediately crosses herself.

"Good morning, daughter."

Clemen adopts a docile expression and smiles like an idiot. Jimmy looks at him and whispers in his ear:

"You don't have to make yourself look like a mongoloid. Not all sacristans are mongoloids."

"Let me play my part the way I think I should," Clemen responds, irritated, into Jimmy's ear. "I've got more experience in these things than you."

"Sure doesn't seem like it . . ."

Clemen takes advantage of Jimmy looking out the window to poke the crown of his head with his middle finger, right in the middle of his new tonsure.

Jimmy is about to react angrily, but at that very moment several passengers enter the car and greet him with reverence.

"Good day, my children," Jimmy responds, blessing them with the sign of the cross. "May God be with you."

Clemen turns to them with his foolish grin.

"What an imbecile you are," Jimmy says angrily in his ear. "How dare you do something like that? If someone had seen you, we'd be in serious trouble."

"Nobody saw me," Clemen whispers.

"I can't believe it. You don't take anything seriously. You're playing games with our lives."

"The tonsure suits you," Clemen says, teasingly. "Nobody would recognize you."

Jimmy passes his hand over it, then solemnly declares, "Father Dionisio knows what he's doing."

"Maybe he was a barber before he became a priest..."

"He made you look like an orphan in the poorhouse," Jimmy mutters between clenched teeth without turning around to look at him, and without losing the severe expression on his face. "You look better now than you did before..."

Clemen passes both his hands over his shaved head.

The train car has filled up; the engine whistles furiously.

"Move over to this seat," Jimmy orders him under his breath. "It's better if we sit facing each other.

"I don't like facing backwards, I get sick," Clemen answers. "I'm just fine here."

"Brother, I am ordering you to change your seat," Jimmy says sternly.

A young, good-looking woman is standing next to them; she has put down the two suitcases she was carrying. The train sways; she grabs onto a handle, about to lose her balance. Clemen jumps up to help her.

"Good morning, Father. May I sit here?"

Clemen quickly moves the suitcases onto the seat facing Jimmy and gestures for her to sit in the one next to it.

"You are very kind, thank you," she says.

Her skin is light, as are her eyes, she is slender, and she is wearing a cream-colored close-fitting dress, her hair pulled back with a red scarf.

Clemen looks at her, surprised and eager, then immediately gives her his foolish smile. She smiles at him as she sits down—a gorgeous smile: full fleshy lips and perfect teeth.

Jimmy looks at her for a second out of the corner of his eye; he remains in a state of deep concentration, as if he were praying, his Bible on his lap and held firmly in both hands.

"Did you just get on?" Clemen asks with feigned sheepishness.

"No," she answers. "I boarded in San Salvador, but I changed cars because there are a lot of children in the other one, and one was vomiting, the poor dear . . . , " she explains, making a face of disgust. "Forgive me for mentioning it, Father," she adds, turning to look at Jimmy.

He barely glances up at her with his placid gaze, then subtly nods in her direction, as if granting her forgiveness.

Clemen is making an even more idiotic face, but he is so enchanted he doesn't take his eyes off her.

"Are you quite alright, Brother?" Jimmy asks, turning to look at Clemen with a stern expression; he then turns to the woman. "He gets a bit dizzy. He's not used to traveling by train."

"I'm fine, Father," Clemen says and flashes his idiot smile. Then he asks her, "How far are you going?"

"I'm getting off soon, in San Vicente. And you two?"

"Usulután . . ."

Clemen has placed his knapsack on the ground between his legs; he bends over to open it and rummage around inside, as if he were looking for something; he takes the opportunity to sneak a peek at her knees.

"I went to spend the Holy Week with my aunt and uncle, but everything was so nerve-racking because of the coup . . . ," she complains.

"Were you in any danger, my daughter?" Jimmy asks.

"It was horrible, Father. My uncle's house is in the El Calvario district, near the Second Infantry Regiment. I thought we were all going to die with all the shooting . . . ," she says with a groan as she crosses herself.

"Calm yourself, my child, let us thank the Lord that it is all over now . . ."

Clemen is still bent over, rummaging around in his knapsack, furtively glancing at the woman's knees. Jimmy turns to him and asks sternly:

"Have you lost something, Brother?"

"An orange, Father."

"Perhaps you left it at the church."

"I was sure I brought it with me," he says, sitting up.

"I have an orange," she says, opening her handbag.

"No, please, my child," Jimmy stops her. "It won't be good for him to eat on the train; it will upset his stomach."

Clemen glares at him, then quickly resumes his meek expression.

The conductor appears next to him with his blue uniform, his cap, and his thin, well-groomed moustache.

"Good morning, Father," he says, greeting him with a little bow.

The woman takes her ticket out of her bag and hands it to him; the conductor punches it and returns it with a smile that wants to be polite but oozes lust.

"We'll pay you now for ours," Jimmy tells him. "We got to the station too late to buy them there. We were accompanying some of our congregants and almost missed our train. I hope that's not a problem."

"Not at all, Father. Where are you going?"

"We boarded at San Rafael Cedros, and we're getting off at Usulután."

Clemen takes some banknotes out of his trouser pocket and hands them to the conductor, the idiotic smile still on his face.

"Do you think you could possibly arrange a compartment for us . . . ?" Jimmy asks solicitously.

The conductor looks at the woman.

"For the sacristan and myself," Jimmy explains. "This has been a quite exhausting Holy Week, and I would prefer the faithful not to see me nodding off . . ."

"There are none available at the moment, Father. I'll see if I can get you one in San Vicente."

He hands the tickets and the change to Clemen.

"The Lord would be most grateful, my son."

The conductor starts to walk away, giving the woman one last look before he leaves.

"Are you from San Vicente?" Clemen asks the woman.

"Yes," she answers. "I was born there and still live there."

"A lovely town," Clemen says, obsequiously.

"Thank you."

"Do you live with your parents?"

"Yes."

"Do you work?"

"I'm a primary school teacher, I teach in the afternoons."

Jimmy, irritated, clears his throat; he has closed his eyes, as if trying to concentrate on his prayers.

"How interesting," Clemen exclaims. "You must love children . . ."

"Very much," she says, smiling.

"What's your name?"

"Ana María," she answers. "Ana María Fuentes. And you?"

"Tino, they call me Tino," Clemen answers, flashing a full smile. "How lucky for you that you'll soon be at your destination. Your boyfriend will probably be there waiting for you, won't he?"

Her face turns bright red.

"Brother, you know very well the Lord does not approve of gossip," Jimmy warns him in a strict voice, looking at Clemen out of the corner of his eye. "Please restrain yourself. Focus on your prayers."

She lowers her eyes, ashamed. She opens her bag, takes out a newspaper, unfolds in, and begins to read, holding it up between her and the two men.

Jimmy and Clemen's jaws drop, they are in shock, their eyes glued to the front page: REBELS EXECUTED, the headline reads in huge bold letters. They swallow hard and exchange looks, their faces as white as sheets.

"How terrible," she says. "Those poor men . . ."

Jimmy clears his throat, feigning ignorance, as if he hadn't read anything.

Clemen's idiotic expression has twisted into one of fear; now he looks like a total moron, or madman.

"Who did they execute?" he mutters, his mouth parched, trying to muster his courage.

"The leaders of the coup," she says, lowering the paper.

She's about to hand it to Clemen, but first she turns to Jimmy and asks him shyly, "Would you like to read it, Father?"

"Let's see, my child. Let's see what was going on while we were celebrating Easter Sunday."

"No, Father," she corrects him. "The executions occurred this morning. The newspaper had just arrived hot off the press when I was about to board the train."

Jimmy reads carefully, trying to control any hint of eagerness; Clemen anxiously tries to read over his shoulder.

"Mr. Tino, that is quite rude," Jimmy scolds him, folding up the paper and returning it to the woman. "It's not polite to read over another person's shoulder."

Clemen practically grabs the newspaper out of her hands.

"Can I see?" he says.

Jimmy shoots him a disapproving glare, then turns to her with a gesture of resignation.

"They never really learn . . ."

Clemen, pale and shaking, has glued his eyes on the list of the condemned; Jimmy turns to look out the window and pretends to be nodding off.

The car is swaying, but Clemen seems too much in shock to be aware of anything.

"I would be happy to leave you the newspaper, Mr. Tino, but my parents will want to read the news," she says, in a quiet voice so as not to disturb Jimmy.

"They-shot-ten-of-them . . ." Clemen says, enunciating each word carefully, as if he could barely read.

"Brother! Put that down, it will only upset you!" Jimmy orders him categorically. "Take your Bible out of your knapsack and practice calming yourself . . ."

But Clemen continues in a stupefied state and begins to mumble the names of those who were executed.

"Ge-ner-al-Al-fon-so-Ma-rro-quín, Colo-nel-Ti-to-To-más-Calvo, Ma-jor-Fau-sti-no-So-sa . . ."

Jimmy is about to grab the newspaper out of his hand, but he catches himself; the woman has lowered her eyes, clearly embarrassed by the situation.

"Let us pray for the souls of those poor sinners," Jimmy says, now fully composed; he joins his hands at his chest, then takes his rosary out of the pocket of his cassock and, with the Bible on his lap, he intones, "*Domini homini, domini nostro*. For the word of our Lord is our guide and our salvation ..."

"Amen," says the woman contritely.

Clemen turns to look at Jimmy, as if he didn't understand, then quickly shakes his head and repeats, "Amen."

He hands her the newspaper, opens his knapsack, and takes out a Bible.

"Our Father who art in Heaven ..." Jimmy begins.

" ... hallowed be thy name, thy kingdom come, thy will be done, on Earth as it is in Heaven ...," the woman and Clemen repeat in unison.

At that very moment, a pair of National Guard soldiers enter the car; they stop next to them to get their balance, and watch the scene with surprise. They greet them with a reverential nod of the head, careful not to interrupt their prayers. They are wearing boots with gaiters, green uniforms, helmets, and are both carrying rifles.

" ... and lead us not into temptation, but deliver us from evil ..."

The soldiers walk over to the passengers in the next row and ask to see their documents.

"Hail Mary, full of grace ...," Jimmy continues in deep concentration after shooting a scathing glance at the soldiers.

The passengers in that row, obviously frightened, have quickly pulled out their documents; the soldiers have a list they check the names against. Clemen, extremely pale and still with the idiotic expression on his face, doesn't lift his eyes from his Bible.

"Our Lord is with thee. Blessed art thou among women, and blessed is the fruit of thy womb, Jesus ..."

The soldiers continue on to the next rows; they order one passenger to stand up and step into the aisle; one of the soldiers immediately pats him down.

"Our Father who art in heaven ..." Jimmy repeats.

The man has turned white; because of the swaying of the car he can barely keep his balance while he holds his arms out and the soldier searches him.

"... hallowed be thy name, thy kingdom come, thy will be done..."

The soldier ties his thumbs together behind him and shoves him forward.

"But I haven't done anything," the man cries out, terrified, on the verge of tears, and barely able to walk.

The guard gives him another shove.

"Father, help me," he begs as he almost falls on top of the woman.

"Careful, Doña Ana María," Clemen exclaims, rising to protect her.

"May you go with God," Jimmy says to the man with kindness, his right hand tracing the sign of the cross in the air. "And confess your sins..."

The man almost falls on his face with the next shove.

"Saint Michael the Archangel...," Jimmy prays.

"Protect us," Ana María and Clemen respond in unison.

The soldiers follow the man out of the car.

"Saint Raphael the Archangel...," Jimmy prays

"Accompany us always, O Lord, protect us from all dangers of body and soul," they respond.

"Amen," all three say. They cross themselves.

The whistle blows.

"What might that poor man have done?" she wonders, still upset.

Jimmy lifts his eyebrows and turns his gaze out the window.

"He's probably a pickpocket who managed to escape, because they immediately recognized him," Clemen says in his normal voice, forgetting his role for a moment.

"Brother, do not judge others, our Lord is the only judge," Jimmy warns him sharply, without even turning to look at him.

Clemen quickly makes himself look like an idiot again.

The woman watches him with curiosity; he looks back at her and grins foolishly.

"We are approaching your city, Doña Ana María," Jimmy says. "I can already see the first houses."

She turns to look out the window.

"You're right, Father," she says.

Clemen has opened his Bible; he's mumbling as if he were reading, but he has placed the book on his lap in such a way that he can see the woman's knees without her realizing it.

"Excuse me, Father," she says timidly, "what is your name?"

"Justo, my child," Jimmy answers, and looks at her with benevolent eyes; she lowers hers.

"I'm so lucky to have met you, Father Justo," she says. "After the fright I had in the capital because of the coup, I don't know how I would have felt if you hadn't been here when they took that man away."

"We must have faith and trust absolutely in our Lord Jesus Christ," Jimmy says solemnly.

She nods and crosses herself. Then she picks up one of the suitcases from the seat next to her and tries to move it into the aisle, but Clemen quickly stands up and takes it from her.

"I'll help you," he says solicitously.

He picks up both suitcases and carries them into the aisle.

"You dropped your Bible," she says, and bends over to pick it up; she places it on Clemen's seat.

The train is slowing down.

"I'll go with you to the platform," Clemen says, still grinning like an idiot.

Jimmy watches him carefully, then turns to her and says, "Please, my child, make sure this young man gets back on the train. He is very absent-minded, and I wouldn't want to lose him."

"Don't worry, Father," she responds, smiling and getting ready to stand up, "I won't budge from the platform until Don Tino has boarded the train again. Right, Don Tino?"

He nods, moving his head quickly up and down.

"Thank you, and may God be with you, my child," Jimmy says.

Clemen walks toward the stairs in front of her. Jimmy throws him another wary look. Then he nods to the other passengers who are walking toward the exit, an aloof and formal goodbye.

2

"Holy shit, we've been sentenced to death!" Clemen repeats, still in shock and forgetting that he is playing the part of a sacristan, now that they are riding alone in a compartment where the conductor brought them.

"What did you expect?" says Jimmy, very worried. "I warned you, that bastard won't forgive anybody. Even Don Agustín is on the list."

They speak under their breath, guardedly; Clemen has placed his knapsack and his Bible on the seats facing them to discourage other passengers from joining them.

"If they capture us, they'll execute us immediately," Clemen mumbled, swallowing hard.

Two women are walking down the aisle; they look into the compartment: they see the priest and the sacristan, then the knapsack and the Bible on the other seats.

"Forgive us, Father," one of them says, then they continue on their way.

"I shouldn't have left my gun at Father Dionisio's house," Jimmy says with regret.

"It wouldn't do us any good . . ."

"Sure it would. I'm not going to let them take me prisoner."

The train is picking up speed.

"Hopefully those soldiers won't show up again," Clemen says.

"Remember the story we're going to tell them if they ask for our documents, don't let your nerves get the better of you . . . No, better if you let me do the talking, as we agreed."

"You really screwed Major Sosa: it's completely your fault he was executed," Clemen says, distraught.

Jimmy looks out the window at the dry hills and the bottom of the Jiboa Valley. Then he says drily:

"It wasn't my fault. He was a moron for letting himself get caught. I told him he was done for, even though he didn't support us, I told him we used his name in the communiqué calling for the uprising. But he didn't believe me."

The train starts descending along the side of the valley.

"Really, you warned him?"

"Uh-huh," Jimmy says and shifts in his seat. "What hurts most is that they executed Second Lieutenant Max Calvo ..."

"He was under your command at the airport?"

They can see the Jiboa River through the window, and further on, the wide Lempa.

Jimmy nods vaguely, lost in his thoughts.

"Goddamn warlock: he killed all three brothers," Clemen says.

"Alfonso and Tito paid for their cowardice," Jimmy mutters, "but Max could have saved himself if he'd come with us ..."

A man, obviously drunk, appears at the door to their compartment; he sways back and forth, it looks like the movement of the train is going to throw him flat on his back.

"Good day, Father. May I sit with you for a while?" he asks, his voice slurred.

Clemen looks at Jimmy.

"You mustn't disturb us, we are about to begin our prayers."

"Just a little while, Father. All this swaying has made me dizzy ..."

"Your dizziness smells a lot like alcohol ...," Jimmy replies, and he gestures to Clemen to pick up his Bible.

The drunk falls into the seat facing Clemen; he's a short, squalid-looking man wearing filthy clothes, as if he'd been sleeping on the streets, with no socks and scuffed shoes.

"Forgive me, Father," he mumbles, after letting out a loud belch. He looks at Clemen, his eyes unsteady, and says, "What an ugly sacristan you've found yourself ..."

Jimmy smiles; Clemen is again grinning like an imbecile.

"Don't be misled by appearances, my child, for beauty resides in the soul."

Clemen turns to Jimmy, looking even more docile.

"This guy looks like a retard," the drunk man says, disdainfully, without taking his eyes off Clemen; then he turns to Jimmy.

"Forgive me, Father."

"My knapsack ...," Clemen says, getting up to grab it and taking the opportunity to stamp on the drunk's foot.

He lets out a groan. "What's the matter with this retard!" he exclaims, and gives him a shove.

Without warning, Clemen punches him hard in the stomach. The drunk keels over, his mouth gaping open.

"Brother!" Jimmy shouts.

"He's going to throw up!" Clemen says, retreating into the aisle.

At that very moment, the two soldiers appear behind Clemen, who doesn't notice them.

"Officers, please!" Jimmy cries out, and points to the drunk with a look of disgust.

Clemen turns to look at the soldiers; the blood drains from his face, as if he were in shock. They request permission to enter and remove the drunk, who is clutching his stomach and trying to catch his breath with his mouth hanging open.

"You got away from us, Hoot ...," says the taller, darker soldier with wiry hair.

"Forgive us, Father, but this bum always sneaks on in San Vicente and proceeds to harass decent people," says the other one, chubby with fair skin and a gold tooth.

The soldiers pick him up and take him out. Clemen moves aside; again his face has assumed a meek expression.

"That retard hit me ...," the drunk mutters, still breathing with difficulty.

"We're going to hit you harder," the darker-skinned soldier says, shoving him down the corridor.

Clemen returns to his seat: he takes a deep breath, picks up the Bible, and opens it at random. He sits there reading, and perspiring. Jimmy looks at him out of the corner of his eye.

"What's the matter with you?" he asks in an undertone.

"That piece of shit pushed me over the edge ... I'm too tense."

"Take it easy. Our lives are at stake. We were lucky those soldiers didn't see you. If they'd come a few seconds earlier ..."

"I hope they don't believe anything he says ...," Clemen says, looking scared.

The whistle blows three times. The train slows as it descends into the valley.

Clemen swats at a fly buzzing in front of his face.

"Hoot ... what a name ...," Jimmy says. "He didn't look like an owl, did he?"

"Nope."

"Are you still angry?" Jimmy asks, mockingly.

"God damn piece of shit ... He even brought flies in here."

Jimmy looks off into the distance; then, with a touch of apprehension, he says:

"I hope one of the Whites is at the hacienda."

"Yeah ... but it's okay even if they're not. If we make it there, we'll be safe. We'll get on a plane ..."

"Whatever you say, Mr. Lindbergh. You'll fly it, then?"

"There's always a pilot and a plane at the hacienda. I know that for a fact. Either Pepe Dárdano or Moris Pérez can fly us out."

"Let's pray," Jimmy says.

Clemen turns to him in surprise, then says sarcastically:

"You've even tricked yourself into believing you're a priest ..."

The clattering increases as the train brakes through the descent.

"It feels weird—no mustache after so many years," Jimmy mumbles, rubbing his upper lip.

Suddenly, one of the soldiers appears in the doorway; it's the chubby one with the gold tooth. Clemen is caught off guard, but quickly makes himself look like an idiot again.

"Forgive me, Father, but I'd like to speak with you for a moment," the soldier says, removing his helmet to show his respect.

"Would you like to confess, my son?"

The car sways around the curve.

"Not exactly, Father. I just want to ask you a question ..."

"Come in, my son," Jimmy says, and invites him to sit down on the seat in front of him. "But leave your weapon out there, you can't be armed when you speak to God."

The soldier tries to lean his rifle between the seat and the wall of the compartment, but the movement of the train makes this impossible. So he sits down and lays the rifle across his legs and the seat next to him, along with the helmet.

Jimmy points to the weapon and says:

"Not like that, my son. I repeat: you cannot be armed if you wish to speak with a representative of our Lord."

The soldier looks confused, it seems he had a difficult time deciding to approach the priest, and now he doesn't know what to do with his rifle.

"Don Tino," Jimmy orders, "take this good man's gun and hold onto it out there in the corridor. And keep still, I don't want you to hurt yourself with it."

The soldier seems relieved. Clemen goes out to the corridor, sits on the floor with his knees up, and holds the barrel of the rifle, resting the butt on the floor.

"Pray speak, son," Jimmy says.

"Nobody's listening?" asks the soldier, turning to look at Clemen, then leaning over in the seat to get closer to Jimmy.

"No, my son, not with this racket," Jimmy answers, also leaning toward the soldier. "Don't worry . . ."

The soldier scratches his head nervously, his eyes glued on the floor.

"What is your name, my son?"

"Eulalio . . ."

Then he stops; he takes a deep breath, as if trying to muster his courage.

"Why don't you confess, my son? It's easier . . ."

"I can't, Father," he says, then turns and looks where Clemen is sitting.

"Why can't you? Of course, you can. I am here. And the Lord always listens to the faithful."

"It's just that it's not something that's happening to me," he says, stammering, "but to my brother."

Jimmy looks at him with a stern expression; he doesn't speak.

"That's why I can't confess . . . ," he says.

"You're not hiding behind your brother, are you, son? That would be a very serious sin."

"No, Father," he answers, his eyes still staring at the ground.

"Look at me, son . . ."

The soldier lifts his head; he looks Jimmy in the eyes for a few seconds, then turns to look out the window, uncomfortable.

At that moment Clemen jumps up, frightened. They both turn to look: the other soldier rushes into the compartment.

"Hoot's gotten away," the dark-skinned guard exclaims in alarm.

"I have to go, Father," Eulalio says, getting up.

"Come back afterward, son, so we can finish . . . ," Jimmy tells him. "Where are you going?"

"Usulután, but first we're stopping off at La Carrera Hacienda . . ."

"I'll be back if I have time," he says, his helmet already on, as he grabs the rifle Clemen holds out to him.

Jimmy takes a medal with a picture of the Virgin out of the pocket of his cassock; he holds it out to Eulalio and says:

"Pray to the Virgin, she will guide you . . ."

"Thank you, Father," he says and rushes out after his partner, down the corridor.

Clemen remains standing until he makes sure the soldiers have left; then he comes and sits down in his seat.

"What did that jerk want?" he asks anxiously.

"The secrecy of confession is sacred, Brother," Jimmy says.

"Don't fuck with me. Tell me," he insists, raising his voice, "I was shitting myself out there . . ."

Jimmy energetically motions to him to keep his voice down; Clemen turns to look at the door of the compartment: nobody's there.

"To confess," Jimmy says. "But he didn't have the courage . . . or the time."

"I can't believe it," Clemen says.

"Soldiers also confess."

"It's not that."

"So, what is it?"

"Forget it. How much longer?"

The train has descended into the valley. The engine whistles, then takes off full steam ahead.

Jimmy takes out his pocket watch.

"We'll reach San Marcos Lempa in about half an hour," he says. "It's another half hour from there to the hacienda."

The warm wind of the valley swirls through the compartment.

3

"Very impressive!" Mono Harris exclaims with admiration. "I actually didn't recognize you."

They are in a large luxuriously furnished living room, sitting in armchairs around a table where there's a bottle of whiskey, a pitcher of water, and an ice bucket; through a large picture window can be seen other buildings—sheds, processing plants, sleeping quarters—and a parking lot, and cotton fields that stretch to the horizon. This is the manor house of the hacienda.

"Well-planned, wouldn't you say?" Clemen brags, gulping down the whiskey left in his glass.

"Very well-planned," says Mono Harris. "Nobody would have recognized you."

"Ah . . . this tastes so good," Clemen says, licking his lips, and lunging at the table to pour himself more.

"Where were you all this time?" Mono Harris asks, still in astonishment. He has pale skin, graying sideburns, a bulbous nose, and green eyes; he's wearing blue mechanic's overalls.

"Near Cojutepeque," Clemen says, "locked up in an attic."

"I can't believe it!"

"Yup," Clemen exclaims, settling back comfortably in his big chair, his glass on his lap. "Six days stuck there."

"Why didn't you come sooner?"

A tractor rumbles into the parking lot.

"It was better to wait till Holy Week was over," Jimmy explains, "so it would seem more natural that we were traveling. And we were hoping to get false papers, but there was no way . . ."

"Anyway, we had to give this one a tonsure and train him to become a priest," Clemen explains mockingly. "What's fucked up is that he can't stop playing the part, and he keeps saying Mass . . ."

"I'm a much better actor than you are, you can't deny it. . . ," says Jimmy, rubbing his upper lip where he used to have a mustache.

"You're excellent," Mono Harris interjects. "Until you told me who you were, I didn't recognize you."

"Whereas this one, the man himself," Jimmy says, gesturing with his thumb at Clemen, "the only thing he could do to make himself look like a sacristan was to act like a mongoloid, which is a cinch for him ..."

Mono Harris chuckles.

"Eat shit ...," Clemen says, without losing his sense of humor.

"Tell him about the drunk ...," Jimmy says, laughing.

"This asshole came looking for a fight, and I punched him in the gut ... Scared the shit out of him because he thought he was dealing with some dumb sacristan. So don't go on about how you're a better actor than me."

"You don't even come up to here on me, look," Jimmy says and makes a cutting movement with his hand at the level of his knees. Then he turns to Mono Harris and says boastfully, "One of the soldiers on the train wanted to confess to me."

"You're kidding! That's incredible! ... A toast!"

They toast and drink.

"What did he confess?"

"Nothing, in the end he held back, but here at the station he very politely helped me off the train," Jimmy says, smiling.

"I don't believe it !" Mono Harris exclaims.

"Yup," Clemen interjects. "'Thank you so much for everything, Father ...,'" he adds, imitating the chubby soldier, and letting out a laugh.

"The soldiers knew you were coming here?" Mono Harris asks, suddenly wary.

"Yeah, it was unavoidable," Jimmy says. "But there's no problem; they didn't suspect us at all. And the idea is to get out immediately, as soon as we finish our drinks, if that's possible."

"Which pilot is on duty?" Clemen asks.

"Pepe Dárdano will be here in a few hours ..."

"Perfect!" Clemen exclaims.

"I'm going to take off this cassock, I'm boiling hot," Jimmy says.

"Wait a minute, you plan to leave here by plane?" Mono Harris asks.

They both nod.

The expression on Mono Harris's face has changed.

"Where to?" he asks, frowning.

"The American military base in Punta Cosigüina, in the gulf," Jimmy answers.

There's an awkward silence. Mono Harris empties his glass.

"There's no problem," Jimmy explains. "The general doesn't have any planes. The pilots flew all of them into exile; my troops covered the last takeoff. So nobody can follow us ... And the officers at the American base are my friends, and they'll be waiting for us."

"The problem isn't the arrival," Mono Harris mutters, "it's the departure."

"Why?" Jimmy asks.

"There's a National Guard post here at the hacienda, and everybody who flies out has to report to them, with their IDs. That's the order."

Clemen and Jimmy look at each other, taken aback.

"It can't be ...," Clemen stammers, his mouth suddenly parched.

The three sit in silence.

"There's got to be another way," Jimmy mumbles.

Mono Harris leans over the table to pour himself another glass of whiskey; he looks increasingly concerned.

"Anyway," he says, "no pilot is going to want to take you. Whoever does it won't be able to come back. If he's caught, he's a dead man."

"I'll talk to Pepe and convince him!" Clemen shouts excitedly, as if he'd suddenly found the solution.

Mono Harris turns to look at him, now very serious, and sits up in his chair.

"I think," he says, and takes a sip of whiskey before continuing, "the most prudent thing would be for nobody to know you've come here. Things are very ugly."

"We found out about the executions on the train," Jimmy says.

"They say the warlock is going to continue the executions, and you two are on the list of those sentenced to death."

Clemen, pale, swallows hard; he drinks down the rest of his second whiskey.

"That's why it would be best for us to leave right away," Jimmy says. "Colonel Stuart is stationed at the base in Cosigüina; he was one of my instructors in Fort Riley. He knew about the coup, he gave us his support, and he told me that if I needed to retreat, I should go there."

The atmosphere has turned leaden.

"I told you: there's no way you can leave here by air."

"There's no other runway nearby?" Jimmy insists.

Mono Harris looks out the picture window: workers are loading bales of cotton onto a truck. He rubs his face with his hands, as if he had just woken up.

"The problem isn't the runway," he says. "If we make that flight, we risk the pilot, the airplane, we get the whole hacienda in trouble, and the ones who have to pick up the pieces are us, the owners, Juan and I, and we've already got enough problems with the warlock. He's got us in his sights. It's only because we are American citizens that he hasn't fucked with us."

"So?" Clemen asks, in anguish, squirming in his chair.

"So, we have to find another way out of this," Mono Harris says, pensively. "I'm not going to throw you to the lions ... Let me make a phone call."

He stand up, shakes his head, and walks over to the telephone, on a table in the back of the room.

"Don't mention our names, the lines are being tapped," Jimmy warns.

"Of course not ... Don't worry."

Clemen has poured himself another glass of whiskey and is compulsively taking little sips.

"You're going to get drunk ...," Jimmy scolds him.

"Don't fuck with me, you shit head, I don't care if you are a bishop. What are we going to do now?"

At that moment Mono Harris says hello to Don Mincho on the phone, tells him in English that there are some cattle buyers who are very interested in seeing the herd on the island, says he trusts them completely and that they are interested in staying at the house for a few days, is that possible?

Jimmy and Clemen turn to look, their eyes narrowing.

"Perfect," Mono Harris exclaims before hanging up.

He returns to the table; he empties his glass.

"What happened?" Jimmy asks, rubbing his hands together.

"Drink up and let's go."

"Where?" Clemen asks nervously.

"You, Jimmy, put on your cassock," Mono Harris says, without paying any attention to Clemen's question; he's moving quickly, nervously. "You have to leave here exactly as you came: a priest and a sacristan."

"I don't understand," Jimmy says. "What's your plan?"

"I'm going to take you to Mincho's island before those soldiers get back here looking for you. You'll stay there a few days while we figure out a way to get you out of the country."

"Can we take the whiskey?" Clemen asks, picking up the half-full bottle.

Mono Harris agrees with a nod.

Clemen puts the bottle in this knapsack.

"I'm going to pack you some clothes in another knapsack," Mono Harris says, and he quickly disappears down the hallway leading to the bedrooms in the rear.

"What do you think?" Clemen asks.

Jimmy has put his cassock back on.

"If we can't leave by air, we'll have to find a way by land or by sea," he says as he walks over to the window; at the back of the parking lot he sees a soldier standing in the shade of an almond tree, talking to the tractor driver.

Mono Harris returns with a knapsack.

"Leave that bottle," he tells Clemen. "I put a full one here in the knapsack."

"We can take both . . ."

"No, you'd leave me with nothing. And I'm not going to town before tomorrow."

Clemen takes out the bottle and places it on the table.

"If the soldiers come here asking for you, I'm going to have to say something," Mono Harris says. "Did you tell them why you were coming here?"

"No," Jimmy answers. "But if they'd asked me, I was planning to tell them I was sent here to check out the possibility of building a chapel."

"Perfect," Mono Harris says as he approaches the hat rack.

"I'm Father Justo and the mongoloid is called Don Tino," Jimmy says, pointing at Clemen.

Mono Harris takes a gun out of the cupboard and slips it under his belt.

"You got another one for me?" Jimmy asks.

Mono Harris points to the knapsack.

"We'll drive to the bay and from there we'll take the boat to the island," he says, as he walks to the door and takes some keys out of his pocket. "Along the way you'll get rid of that cassock and turn into cattle buyers."

They emerge into the boiling breath of the afternoon.

Haydée's Diary

Tuesday, April 11

This morning in the cemetery they executed a young man named Víctor Manuel Marín. I didn't know him, nor had I ever heard his name. They say he was one of the organizers of the coup, his brother is Lieutenant Alfonso Marín, one of the officers of the Second Artillery Regiment who held out against the counter-coup until the very end. Doña Chayito and Doña Julita, the mothers of Merlos and Cabezas, paid me a visit today; they brought me some delicious guava candy. Doña Chayito told me she knows the Marín family because Víctor Manuel worked at the Tax Collector's Office, where her husband was the head accountant; she said the young man's parents are devastated, especially because they discovered that he had been brutally tortured; they pulled out his nails, his teeth, and one eye, and they broke his arms and legs and had to prop him up on sawhorses so he could face the firing squad. According to Doña Chayito, Father León Montoya, who gave him extreme unction and visited his parents this morning to console them, confirmed that he suffered as much as Jesus on the cross. I shudder to think of it.

Doña Chayito also told me they have met with the mothers of other political prisoners, including those sentenced to death, and they came to invite me to join them at one of their next meetings. But we couldn't continue the conversation because Raúl and Rosita, my neighbors, dropped by. It turns out Raúl is a professor in the same department where Doña Chayito's son, Paquito Merlos, as they call him, is studying, and he is two years ahead of Chente. As Pericles always says, the world is as small as a handkerchief. As she was leaving, Doña Chayito told me she'd call me tomorrow to see if I would like to join them.

Wednesday April 12

I have just discovered the worst of all infamies: Colonel Castillo, whom Mila is involved with and to whom she speaks so disparagingly of Clemen, was the special military prosecutor at the war council. Since yesterday I've been devoured by curiosity, and I didn't stop till I revealed the treachery. The first thing I did this morning was ask María Elena to wheedle the colonel's full name out of her cousin Ana; she remembered that when Mila is drunk she calls him Aníbal. The rest was easy, as I remembered having read in the official government newspaper that someone named Colonel Castillo had taken part in the trial. My insides are twisted in knots. I was so enraged I couldn't control myself: I tried to call her at home and at her parents; it was fortunate I didn't find her because I would have flown off the handle. Then I went to Mother to tell her what was happening; she was aghast. She asked me if I was absolutely certain; I told her it was highly unlikely for there to be two colonels by the name of Aníbal Castillo. She told me we should keep it to ourselves for now, we had to think very carefully about how we were going to handle the situation; she told me she would tell Father tonight, after they were already in bed, to avoid an intemperate reaction. When I told Carmela, she said perhaps the best thing that could come from such a bad situation would be for that woman to leave Clemen's life for good, no matter how unforgiveable the treachery. But what about my grandchildren? No matter how hard I try, I have not been able to stop thinking about them: at moments I feel I'm spewing venom. I keep reminding myself that there is justice and that that Harpy's time will come; then I feel remorse for harboring so much hatred. María Elena made me a mug of lime blossom tea.

I have been making every possible effort to get them to let me visit Pericles, but all to no avail. It seems "the man" trusts no one and is finding conspiracies hatching even under his own desk. Not a single bureaucrat, moreover, wants to stick his neck out; they are all terrified of coming under suspicion. Father tried to speak to that Chaquetilla Calderón fellow, but his efforts yielded no results. My mother-in-law says I must be patient, for now, Pericles is safe at the Central Prison. This afternoon, I happened to run into Dr. Ávila, the minister of foreign affairs, in front of the Polyclinic: he was there to visit his mother, who recently suffered a cerebral hemorrhage, and I was there to visit Don Jorge. He looked haggard, seemed evasive, as if he were ashamed, and his tie was crooked. I mentioned my troubles and asked him to please intercede on my behalf so I could visit my husband; he begged me to understand that for the time being nothing could be done. Fortunately Don Jorge is beginning to react positively to the treatments and now has a better chance of pulling through.

Betito has returned from Santa Ana. High school and university classes don't resume till next Monday, by edict of the government, for fear of student protests, which anyway seem poised to erupt the moment they open the university, according to Chente, Raúl and Rosita's son, who came by this afternoon to talk to Betito and tell him about the protests being planned; he says students continue to organize despite the curfew and martial law, and those at the medical school, supporters of Dr. Romero, are the most active. Chente is a short young man, very serious and diligent, and he's full of curiosity; sometimes he comes to talk to Pericles. When we moved into this house, the poor thing fell in love with Pati, but she's two years older and was already engaged to Mauricio. I suspect Betito is more deeply involved than I had thought. He asked me if I have any idea where Clemen might be hiding; I told him I neither know nor want to know, the fewer people who know the safer his brother is. "If I were Clemen, I'd already be in Guatemala," he said proudly, then mentioned that he knows secret ways to cross the border in the area around Güija Lake, near his friend Henry's estate. He told me his cousins in Santa Ana were excited about the coup, many people there think we need to make another big push to finally get rid of the Nazi warlock, that for the next coup the Americans will come and drag him out by his hair. I perceived in his words the enthusiasm of adolescence. I have pleaded with him to act with prudence.

Doña Chayito called tonight to tell me that tomorrow she is hosting a wedding shower for Leonor, Doña Julita's daughter, and that I am cordially invited, at three in the afternoon, but since it was organized at the last minute due to recent tragic events, I mustn't worry about bringing a gift, and she gave me her address in the San Jacinto district, near the market. I was quite surprised, at first I didn't understand, because I had not thought about them all day, but I was then quite impressed by her audacity. I told her I would definitely attend and would bring a delicious chocolate cake.

I have never taken part in politics on my own initiative but have always gone along with Pericles, supported his decisions, trusting fully that he knew what he was doing and why he was doing it, always certain that my duty was to remain by his side. So it was when he decided to become the general's private secretary after the coup d'état that brought him to power, or, two years later, when he accepted the embassy posting in Brussels, or when he decided to break with the government and return home, or when we had to go into exile in Mexico. I will attend the meeting at Doña Chayito's place in the same spirit; as soon as I am able to speak with Pericles, I will tell him all about it and follow his dictates. I admire women like Mariíta Loucel, who fight in the front lines for their political ideals, but she is French and had a different education. My place is by my husband's side.

Thursday, April 13

I asked Don Leo to take me to Doña Chayito's house and pick me up an hour and a half later; first we stopped at the Bonets' patisserie to buy the chocolate cake. Today has been stifling hot. I wondered what I should wear; I didn't want to call attention to myself. Fortunately, my life with Pericles has taught me how to adapt to different social milieus. As we drove up the hill toward the San Jacinto church, I had a strange sensation, a kind of dissociation, as if it wasn't really me who was in that car. I arrived ten minutes late because I stayed chatting with Montse Bonet at the patisserie. Doña Chayito welcomed me with deference, even a bit of relief, or so it seemed to me, as if she had begun to wonder if I was really going to come. I apologized for my lateness and handed her the cake; she led me to an interior patio where Doña Julita, her daughter Leonor, and two other ladies she introduced me to were sitting around a table full of coffee and pastries. They were Doña Consuelo, the wife of Dr. Colindres, and a young and beautiful, though beleaguered, young woman dressed in strict mourning, named Mercedes, the wife of Captain Carlos Gavidia. It was cooler on the patio, thanks to the shade of two trees, a leafy mango and an avocado. I noticed a couple of gifts on the table; for a moment I wondered if this really was a wedding shower and if the political part hadn't been simply the fruit of my fertile imagination. But soon Doña Chayito explained that Dr. Colindres was arrested after the coup because he belonged to Acción Democrática, the party led by Dr. Romero, and although at first he was held at the Black Palace, it is now believed he has been moved to the Central Prison; she then told me that Captain Gavidia was arrested a few days ago as he was attempting to cross the border into Honduras, near Chalatenango; Merceditas doesn't know for certain where her husband is being held, though she believes he is still in the basement of the palace; and the captain's younger brother, Lieutenant Antonio Gavidia, was executed by firing squad on Monday at the cemetery. I crossed myself, greatly dismayed, and gave my condolences to Merceditas, who immediately began to cry, quietly, with so much sorrow I felt my heart breaking. A third brother, Pepe, a civilian, was arrested by the police the very night the coup failed, she muttered, and they've heard nothing about him, either. Doña Chayito poured me a cup of coffee, and as I cut the cake, I told them about Pericles and Clemen; I had the impression this was not the first time the four of them had met. Then a servant came to say that someone was at the front door, someone she didn't know. We all grew quiet and turned to look at Doña Chayito, who immediately stood up and went to the front door. I was nervous; my companions seemed even more so. All we could hear was a melodic bolero playing on the radio in the living room. I asked Leonor if she was really engaged and about to be married; she said she wasn't, but if the police arrived or someone asked why we were meeting, she would say that she was engaged to Paquito Merlos, Doña Chayito's son. Our hostess returned looking rather worried: she said it was a man claiming to be a soap salesman, and he was quite insistent that she let him in to show her his wares, but he looked to her like a police informer. I was quite surprised by Doña Chayito's sangfroid. She went to the living room to turn up the volume on the radio. She then explained that the purpose of the meeting was to organize a committee of mothers and wives of political prisoners in order to pressure for the immediate release of our family members and prevent those found guilty of having participated in the coup from being executed. Doña Chayito is a very outspoken woman: she said several mothers and wives had met previously, but now we must put more effort into organizing ourselves; she indicated that Doña Consuelo will be in charge of maintaining contact with Acción Democrática and certain professional organizations, Merceditas with the families of the officers who have been sentenced to death, and Doña Julita and she with the university students and the employee unions; she asked me if I would agree to pursue contacts with the diplomatic corps. I told her I would gladly try. Doña Chayito then asserted that we must get to work drafting a communiqué demanding a general amnesty as well as the immediate release of all political prisoners. She went into the house to bring paper and a pencil. Doña Consuelo didn't stop eating the chocolate cake and praising the Bonets' patisserie; Doña Julita sat very quietly, somewhat absentminded, as she always is when I see her, as if she were Doña Chayito's shadow, though I did manage to exchange a few words with her, during which I found out her husband is an engineer and works in the Ministry of Public Works, her son is also studying engineering, and the Cabezas and Merlos families are neighbors. Doña Chayito began drafting the communiqué on a piece of graph paper in a notebook; she had in hand a manifesto the university students had written, demanding the release of their fellow students and the end of the general's dictatorship, and she copied it almost entirely, then added a paragraph asking for amnesty for those who'd received death sentences and wrote at the bottom the name of the Committee of the Families of Political Prisoners. She asked us if we agreed, we all said yes, except Doña Consuelo, who warned that the slogan "Long live the families of political prisoners!" imitating the university students, seemed inappropriate, and might make us sound like communists. Doña Chayito crossed out that sentence and said she would type up several copies, tomorrow morning she would send each one of us a copy, and we should make more copies to distribute to the sectors we were individually responsible for. Everyone agreed it was vitally important for me to get it to the American Embassy as quickly as possible. We drank tamarind juice, finished eating the pastries, and finalized the details; I learned that Doña Chayito and Doña Consuelo are both teachers at the Central Girls School. Doña Julita mentioned that she'd heard a rumor that they are going to allow visits to the Central Prison on Saturday. I didn't feel the time flying by. Again someone was at the door: we were all frightened, but it was Don Leo coming to pick me up. I asked if anybody wanted a lift home; Merceditas, the poor thing, who had been rather withdrawn during the whole meeting, said she would be grateful. Before we said goodbye, Doña Chayito insisted on giving us bags of avocados, she said that tree produced fruit all year round.

Riding in the car, crossing the city on our way to the San José district, where she lives, Merceditas told me she was twenty-three years old, the mother of two children, and she doesn't know what she'll do if they execute her husband. Her mother-in-law has taken to her bed and hasn't eaten a bite of food since Monday, Antonio's execution has destroyed her. Merceditas says she still has hope her husband will be pardoned because of pressure from the Americans, for he received the highest possible marks in the training course he attended in the United States, where several military leaders had taken a real liking to him; she explained that the Gavidia brothers had been persuaded to participate in the coup by Captain Manuel Sánchez Dueñas, whom they executed along with Antonio. I realized Merceditas knows a lot about the coup, details only people in the military could know; I also discovered she is a young lady of very strong character (for a moment she reminded me of Pati), determined to do everything in her power to stop them from executing her husband and her brother-in-law, and if she seemed so withdrawn during the meeting it was because her grief is so devastating. Merceditas told me that this Captain Sánchez Dueñas, whom I'd never heard of, was the real organizer of the military coup: he was the top student in his graduating class and had been demoted for insubordination two years ago, and then there had been an order for his arrest, which forced him into exile; but he had returned clandestinely last Christmas to organize the conspiracy. My surprise was great when Merceditas said that this Sánchez Dueñas had been hiding out at an estate north of the city, where he'd been joined by other captains from his class, including, of course, her husband, Captain Gavidia, and that the estate is known as "La Layco," and is owned by Mariíta Loucel . . . I didn't have a chance to respond because at that moment we arrived at Merceditas's house, but after saying goodbye to her, and while Don Leo was driving me home I kept thinking, with astonishment, that maybe Mariíta was the one who had organized the coup, and not the late Captain Sánchez Dueñas. Don Leo brought me back to the here and now when he said that a car with plainclothes policemen, according to him, had been following us at a prudent distance the whole way from Doña Chayito's to Merceditas's house.

Friday April 14

Doña Chayito dropped by at ten this morning; she was carrying a copy of the communiqué hidden under her slip. She reminded me that I needed to make as many copies as possible to distribute among my acquaintances, it was the only way to spread the word about us, and the printing presses are all controlled by the general's spies. I told her I had tried to speak with Colonel Palma to find out if they were allowing visits on Saturdays, but he still wasn't taking my calls; we agreed to meet tomorrow in front of the Central Prison. Doña Chayito stayed only a very short time. I suggested she be very careful, my house as well as hers was under surveillance. I immediately got down to work: I sat down in front of Pericles's typewriter and churned out a dozen copies. At noon I went to my parents' house. I asked Don Leo to come pick me up and take me there; I was carrying four copies folded up in an envelope, stuffed into my stockings on the inside of my right thigh. I told Father what I'd been up to; I listed who the copies are for: one for the business attaché at the British embassy, one for the board of directors of the coffee-growers association, another for him to take to Santa Ana, and another for him to keep; I asked him to make as many more copies as he could to distribute among his friends and acquaintances, especially in the diplomatic corps. He asked me if we'd already sent one to the American Embassy. I told him not yet, but I would find a way to personally give one to Mr. Gardiner, the vice-counsel, considering his friendship with Clemen. Father said he was impressed by my initiative; he said that the decision to sentence Don Agustín Alfaro, Dr. Guillermo Pérez, the director of Banco Hipotecario, and so many other respectable people to death has convinced everyone that we must overcome our fear and find some way to get rid of that criminal warlock. He then promised to send a copy to the American Embassy through his own contacts. He warned me to act with the utmost discretion.

By the afternoon, I'd made a decision: I wouldn't go to the embassy but rather to Mr. Gardiner's house, where Clemen spent the night after the coup, the last place he was seen; that way I wouldn't compromise Pericles, who doesn't like the gringos at all (and they don't think highly of him, either). I called Doña Tracy, Mr. Gardiner's wife; she knows me from certain social events and also thanks to my family, though we have never been particular friends. I asked her if she might have a moment to spare for me this afternoon, I wished to converse with her in person. Surely she thought this had to do with news about Clemen, for she responded very politely: she said she was at my disposal. I left right away for her house. I had the impression that the servant who opened the door for me, a brunette girl with delicate features, had been eagerly waiting for me: she led me into a living room, where Doña Tracy was talking on the telephone, and offered me a glass of myrtle juice. The vice-counsel's wife is an outgoing young woman, platinum blonde, who once dreamed of being an actress and likes to socialize with young Salvadoran artists. After our greeting, she asked me if I spoke English, for she prefers to converse in that language; I told her I am quite out of practice, even though I studied it as a teenager. Then I told her the purpose of my visit; she told me she would gladly give a copy of the communiqué to Mr. Gardiner, and she would personally make more copies to distribute among her women friends in the diplomatic corps because it is unacceptable for that "evil man" to remain in power, ruining the country and assassinating its best men. I was surprised by her vehemence. Then, without further ado, she asked me if I had any news about Clemen. I was prepared to broach the subject only if she brought it up, because one never knows what secrets or complications there are in such a situation. I told her the truth: that I know nothing about my son's situation, and I pray he has managed to leave the country and find a safe haven. Then she asked me, with a mischievous look on her face, if I had heard that Clemen had hidden in that house after the coup failed; I answered that I had heard something to that effect, but that I understood one mustn't inquire, one must be discreet about such delicate matters. She recounted the long night they'd spent, she and Mr. Gardiner, conversing with Clemen about the ins and outs of the coup; she went into great detail about how they snuck him out disguised as a domestic servant; she made affectionate reference to his wonderful sense of humor and his thespian talents. At that point the servant girl, whom she called Indalecia, entered; she served us more myrtle juice. It was because of Indalecia's friendship with Clemen, Doña Tracy said once she'd left the room, that he'd had no trouble getting into the Gardiners' house. On the way home I felt lighthearted, happy, content, not only because I had carried out my duty effectively but also because those affectionate words regarding my son soothed my spirit, so wounded by Mila's infamy.

I invited Carmela and Chelón and Mingo and Irmita to dinner. I told them to come early, at six, so we would have more time, because the curfew begins at ten. María Elena and I made the ripe plantain empanadas filled with refried beans that Chelón is so partial to; also *chipilín* tamales and *pupusas* stuffed with cheese flavored with *loroco* flowers. I suppose I longed for some conviviality in the midst of so much misfortune, needed to feel my husband through his closest friends, even if he couldn't be present. Pericles has always said that Mingo is an excellent poet pretending to be a journalist, and Chelón a great painter pretending to be a poet. We dined to the tune of political gossip, nobody talks about anything else in this city; we also laughed at Serafín's expense, the poor man still hiding out at the Guatemalan embassy. Carmela brought some delicious cashew-apple butter for dessert. After dinner, Mingo told a story that made all our jaws drop: Major Faustino Sosa, the air force squadron commander who was executed by a firing squad on Monday on the patio of the Black Palace along with General Marroquín and Colonel Calvo, was, in fact, innocent, had absolutely nothing to do with the coup; the rebel officers who took over the airport under the command of Jimmy, Angelita's son, had even locked Sosa up in a barracks because he refused to support them and was critical of their disloyalty to the general. So why did they execute him? we asked. Nobody knows whose idea it was to include his name among the rebel leaders that were listed on the circular they sent to the regional commanders to demand their support, Mingo explained, and the poor man remained locked up, never suspecting that he was implicated in a rebellion he opposed yet would nevertheless cost him his life. Once the coup had already failed, Mingo continued, and the cavalry troops Jimmy commanded were being forced to retreat from the airport by the contingents loyal to the general, Major Sosa was freed, but nobody knows if he was warned that they had used his name in the communiqué; in any case, the innocent man went happily to meet the government troops, not knowing that they would immediately place him under arrest. Carmela said she simply couldn't understand: if Sosa hadn't participated, and if everybody knew he hadn't participated and that the rebels had used his name without his consent, why was he executed? Mingo shrugged his shoulders: he said it seems the general wanted to make him pay for the betrayal of the pilots who had flown into exile, taking all the planes with them, and leaving the general without an air force.

Not a single meal with Mingo and Chelón can end without them getting embroiled in a discussion about the occult, while we wives, who are Catholic, barely pay attention and carry on with our own concerns, especially because they make sour faces if we offer our opinions on the subject. Pericles greatly enjoys playing the role of devil's advocate and provoking them. Mingo knows a lot about theosophy and is now an implacable critic of it, whereas Chelón declares himself an agnostic, affirming that all theories regarding the spirit are pointless, and the only thing that matters is one's own personal experience. Last night, fortunately, they didn't get into thorny subjects, discussing instead the general's malevolence: how can a man who pledges to respect all things spiritual be such a cruel and perverse murderer? I maintained what I always do: there must be some hell where this man will pay for all the evil he has done us.

Before they left, while I was serving cognac to the men and cherry liquor to the women, I told them about my adventures with the Committee of the Families of Political Prisoners and showed them the communiqué. They looked at me in astonishment, almost admiration, I would say. I suggested they take a copy, especially Mingo, who is in contact with foreign journalists, whose presence in the country we should take advantage of because the newspapers that oppose the general are still closed. He told me it was very dangerous for him to walk around with compromising papers at that hour of the night, and said he'd come by tomorrow to pick it up; Chelón folded a copy and gave me a wink as he stuffed it in his shirt pocket. Both made me promise to let them know when visits to the Central Prison were allowed, so they could go talk to "the old man," as they like to call Pericles.

Betito called to report that he was at the home of his friend and classmate, Flaco Pérez, and would spend the night there to avoid being in the streets after curfew; I asked him to come home early tomorrow to accompany me to the Central Prison to visit his father. María Elena warned me that "little Betito"—as she sometimes calls him in spite of how much this bothers him—and his friends are organizing protests in the high schools, she said she was telling me not to gossip but because she thinks it better for me to know; she also again brought up the subject of my visit to the Gardiners' house, which I had told her about while we were making dinner, and it had greatly amused her to hear how they had dressed Clemen up as a housemaid, but now she wanted to know more details about Indalecia's uniform and what she looked like.

Before coming to bed to jot down these words, I looked at myself in the mirror for a long time: I think new wrinkles have appeared around my eyes, I look pale and disheveled. How much have I changed in these nine days I haven't seen Pericles? And how might he be after such a long confinement? I hope with all my heart we can see each other tomorrow.

Saturday April 15

I couldn't visit Pericles. No visits are allowed. We were a motley crowd in front of the prison at eight o'clock this morning: families of both political prisoners and common criminals. Many from the lower classes. I didn't realize that visits to common criminals have also been suspended since the coup. Fortunately, Betito was with me; crowds frighten me. People were indignant, the atmosphere was tense, they were taunting the guards, demanding they open the doors once and for all. I had difficulty finding Doña Chayito and Doña Julita; they were both there with their husbands. We stood talking next to a cart selling oranges and mangos. The insults being hurled at the guards became sharper and sharper. Doña Consuelo arrived with her children, a look of disgust on her face; she complained about the rabble. I feared that at any moment there would be an altercation. Then two squads of National Guard troops arrived to protect the entryway: silence fell over the crowd like a thick cloud of fear. But a minute later the taunting and cries of protest resumed.

I heard one woman, her voice hoarse and defiant, shout: "The warlock wants to execute our sons." It was like detonating a bomb. It incited the crowd, they began to chant louder and louder and more and more defiantly: "Freedom! Freedom! Freedom!" At first I was afraid, but when I turned to look at Betito and the women, I saw they were also shouting and shaking their fists. I joined in. And as I shouted with increasing fervor, I felt a mixture of anger and joy, as if finally I could express the bitterness that had been eating away at me ever since Pericles was arrested. Then the guards pointed their rifles at us: in a moment of panic I looked around for Betito and saw that he was still chanting, and just like the others, not backing down. Fortunately, at that moment, a military officer and several functionaries of the prison came out the gate: they ordered the families of the common criminals to get into one line with their documents in hand, visits would begin in fifteen minutes. There was a great uproar, shouts of joy, pushing and jostling for a place in line. That's when Doña Chayito shouted to the officer, asking where the families of the political prisoners should form their line. The officer responded rudely that no visits would be allowed to the political prisoners today, perhaps tomorrow. "Scoundrels!" the shout burst from my lips, and even now, I don't understand how. The families of the common criminals jeered at the officer, whistled and called out insults, and they shouted from where they were standing in line, "Murderers! . . ." Some offered to relay messages and carry in what we had brought, they said they would give them to their own family members who would pass them on to ours. Pericles had told me that the political prisoners were in a special section and had no contact with the common criminals. In any case, there was no harm in trying, so I gave my bag of provisions to a stout woman wearing an apron, obviously a vendor in the market, who said I had no reason to worry, her husband was an honorable man and would give the bag to "Don Pericles," as if she already knew him, and she said that she and her friends prayed every day that the warlock's henchmen wouldn't capture Clemen or any of the other "heroes." I was astonished, but just at that moment the line started moving, and pandemonium broke out. We withdrew to the sidewalk across the street; there were about fifty of us, the families of political prisoners. Doña Chayito said we must do something, but the officer returned to order us to disperse, we could no longer remain there. I had a sudden attack of weakness, a lightning-fast switch from outrage to despondency; I clung to Betito, who was still mumbling angry insults. Before we had all dispersed, Doña Chayito and Doña Consuelo passed out copies of the communiqué; we agreed to meet tomorrow at the same place at the same time. Doña Chayito walked with me a short ways: I told her I had gotten the communiqué to the embassy; she told me there would be a meeting that afternoon at four o'clock at Doña Consuelo's house, and she gave me a piece of paper with the address.

We returned home. I didn't feel well, as if my blood pressure had suddenly dropped. I made a cup of black tea with a lot of honey. María Elena isn't here: she left early this morning for her village to see her family, and she will return on Monday; I sent a little dress with her for Belka, I hope it fits, at that age children grow so quickly. I spoke with Mother, my mother-in-law, and Carmela, to tell them what had happened. Betito said he was going out with his friends; I lay down for a while. I dreamed about Clemen, he was running desperately in the rain, and then I was woken by a loud knocking on the door. It was Mila, with the children; she told me she needed to leave them with me for a few hours, she had an urgent appointment, Ana had gone to her village, and her parents weren't in town. I was still woozy from my nap. I told her there was no problem, but she should come get them before three because I also had an appointment, and María Elena had left with Ana; she assured me she would come at two-thirty on the dot, and she left in a hurry. Her appearance was so unexpected—only when I closed the door did my blood start to boil. The children ran to the patio to play with Nerón. I locked Pericles's study, placed all the fragile ornaments on a high shelf in the living room, and checked to see how much food María Elena had made. A moment later Marianito came into the kitchen saying he was thirsty.

After preparing them some melon drinks, I sat in the rocking chair on the porch and watched them play. I realized it's not healthy to keep what I feel and think about Mila inside. At that moment I was absolutely certain that she had left the children with me so she could wallow in sin with that colonel who wants to murder my son, her husband. I don't like having such poisonous thoughts, but this one time I couldn't get rid of them. Fortunately, Betito arrived half an hour later; he came with Chente, who asked me for copies of the communiqué to take to his companions at the university; he told me that they are organizing a strike and other activities to protest the atrocities committed by the general, and as soon as they open the university next Monday things are going to heat up considerably. I gave him my remaining copies of the communiqué, keeping only one for myself. Chente explained that the students have been holding secret meetings the whole time the university has been closed, and they agreed that their top priority was to launch a campaign demanding freedom for all political prisoners, and he would speak to his fellow students to ask a group of them to accompany us early tomorrow morning to the Central Prison to demand visiting rights. I told him I would present his offer to the ladies in the committee this afternoon, who also had contacts with students, and I didn't want to make decisions that weren't mine to make, and we should talk again at night. But I still find it surprising that such grandiose words and such determination can come forth from someone as thin and scrawny as Chente.

Mila came to pick up the children a bit before three. She didn't stay for more than a minute: she acted erratically, with all the anxiety of someone burdened by a great sin that's eating away at her; she shouted at the children to hurry up and say goodbye to their grandmother, then she thanked me and said she was sorry for being in such a rush. I wonder if that woman knows I know, or if it's her own sense of guilt that makes her so flustered.

The Colindres' house is only a few blocks away from ours. I got there a few minutes before four. Doña Consuelo told me I was the first to arrive, she led me into a living room set up with trays of sandwiches, a thermos of coffee, and pitchers of water and fruit drink; I noticed a beautiful oriental carpet she had over the back of a sofa. Minutes later Merceditas arrived; she was still dressed in strict mourning but her aspect was improved: she told us that the officers and civilians who had been imprisoned in the basement of the Black Palace, including her husband and brother-in-law, had been moved to the Central Prison, which is a hopeful sign. Doña Chayito came alone, with regrets from Doña Julita, who was suffering from a severe migraine; she immediately suggested to Doña Consuelo that we move to another room or to the patio, because the windows in that room look right out onto the street, and the police informers would easily be able to hear what we were saying. Doña Consuelo called the servant to clean off the table on the patio and help us move the sandwiches and drinks. Fortunately, the sun had gone down. Doña Chayito said it was urgent we discuss two issues: the election of the committee board and the request for a meeting with the diplomatic corps to explain our situation and ask for assistance. She explained that, due to martial law and the state of siege, it was impossible for all the families to assemble at once, hence she and Doña Julita had been holding meetings with small groups, such as this one, and they proposed that the two of them be designated as the coordinators so they could speak on our behalf. The three of us agreed, though Doña Consuelo warned that she had no interest in getting involved in political intrigue, she only wanted to work for the release of our family members. And also to demand amnesty for those condemned to death, Doña Chayito added, at which point she turned to look at Merceditas. Of course, Doña Consuelo said. Then we discussed the second point: Doña Chayito said we had to form a delegation that would go to the American Embassy early Monday morning to ask to see the ambassador so we can give him the communiqué, then request that he, as the senior member and representative of the diplomatic corps, make a personal request that the warlock halt all executions and free all political prisoners; she believes the ambassador will receive us immediately, and said we should call a press conference. I asked her how many people, in her opinion, should be in the delegation. She said at least six, among whom could be Merceditas,

Doña Consuelo, the mother of Lieutenant Marín and poor Víctor Manuel, the wife of Dr. Valiente, she, and I. We all agreed. Then I told them what I had talked to Chente about earlier, including his suggestion that a group of university students come to the Central Prison tomorrow to show their support for us. Doña Consuelo said she had a bad feeling about it, the university students might create trouble, and we would lose our chance to be allowed to visit our family members. Doña Chayito explained that she also received offers of support from a group of students, perhaps it would be best to first meet with the diplomatic corps, and if the warlock didn't respond and held fast to his policy of prohibiting visits, then we could ask the students for support. At that moment two tears starting running down Merceditas's face. I understood, painfully, that she had not seen her husband since they'd captured him, nor had they given her a chance to say goodbye to her brother-in-law, Lieutenant Gavidia, before he was executed by the firing squad. Only the enormous lump of rage in my throat prevented me from falling apart as well. Doña Chayito and Merceditas left together; I walked home.

Chente came over after dark. I told him what we had discussed; he said that anyway he and a couple of his friends could accompany me tomorrow if I would like them to, and they'd promise not to do anything untoward. I told him it was better to wait till Monday. I was alone in the house, because Betito was at Henry's. There was a moment when I thought I saw something else in Chente's eyes, a certain passion, some kind of longing, I don't know, but the fact was I furrowed my brow and he, blushing, looked away. Even now I'm not sure if it was all in my imagination. Pericles's absence begins to wreak havoc in me.

Sunday April 16

Pati called very early today. I told her I had no good news to report: I know nothing about her brother nor have I been able to see her father. I went to eight o'clock Mass. I confessed to Father Evelio: I admitted to feeling a lot of hatred toward a person who has betrayed a beloved member of my family. The priest asked me if I am sure about the betrayal or if I am allowing myself to be swayed by hearsay. I explained that it is very difficult for me to prove the betrayal but I had a serious and trustworthy source of information. He insisted on asking me if it was a betrayal or an infidelity. I told him it was a mortal betrayal, and I asked him to advise me how to behave toward this person. The priest told me we cannot judge others, our Lord is the only judge, and I should forgive and cleanse my heart; then he instructed me on what prayers to recite in penitence. I would have liked to give him more details, but as Pericles says, one must never tell priests names because priests are also men, and men can never keep secrets.

We went directly from the church to the Central Prison. Mother and some friends excused themselves, but others accompanied us. We were about thirty strong, including of course the members of the committee whom Doña Chayito had summoned to church. Betito hates to get up early on Sundays, but he came with me to Mass and then to demand that they allow us to visit his father; Chente and several other young people who had attended Mass also came with us. We walked the three blocks to the Central Prison. We stood in front of the gates. Doña Chayito suggested that she and I demand a meeting with the officer in charge. To my surprise, Sergeant Flores, the assistant to Colonel Palma, the director, who seems to have gone into hiding and takes nobody's phone calls, appeared at the gate before we spoke to the guards. The sergeant said that he regretted to have to inform us that he had still not received orders to authorize visits, if it were up to him he would let us in, but we must understand how delicate the situation is, surely Monday morning, when everything returns to normal, orders will be issued; he swore on his mother that all the political prisoners were doing fine and nobody at the Central Prison is being either tortured or placed before a firing squad. Doña Chayito raised her voice, saying that if we weren't allowed to visit our loved ones we would stay there the entire day with our protest signs, outside the gates of the Central Prison. I didn't know anything about the signs nor did I think it sensible to remain there the whole day if it wouldn't further our goal of getting them to let us visit, but Doña Chayito had already spoken. The sergeant warned us that this would have only negative repercussions for us, all political demonstrations were prohibited because of the state of siege, National Guard troops would disperse us, and we might even be arrested. "Better for us to leave, ladies, and wait to see what happens tomorrow," I heard Doña Consuelo say behind me. The majority agreed with her.

Betito and I walked to my parents' house. We had a family lunch: Cecilia, Armando, and the children came from Santa Ana; several uncles and aunts were also there. The clubs, along with the newspapers, remain closed by order of the general. Mother and Cecilia made paella. I told them what had happened at the Central Prison; everybody is indignant, they insist this situation cannot continue, something simply has to happen soon to make that Nazi warlock go away. "We all want him to leave, but not one of you is doing anything to get rid of him," Father said reproachfully. "Hail, Lenin," responded my Uncle Charlie jokingly. The men in this family are impossible: they joke about everything. Without any real information, we live off hearsay: they say they captured so-and-so, they say there will soon be new executions, they say the gringos are preparing something big against the general. I told them we are planning to go to the American Embassy to get the diplomatic corps to support our demand for immediate amnesty. "Mr. Thurston is waiting for you," my Uncle Charlie said somewhat ironically. He is, in fact, good friends with the ambassador. I told him to stop joking, I was speaking seriously. "I am also speaking seriously," he said, with another smile. I don't know what to think; most likely he's having fun at my expense.

Later this afternoon I asked Don Leo to drive me to Mingo and Irmita's house. I told Mingo about our plans and asked for his help notifying the foreign correspondents. He told me very few had remained in the country, but I can rest assured, he can guarantee that at least two from the American press will show up. We drank coffee and chatted a while. Irmita seemed worse; in my opinion she's suffering from something more serious than just chronic bronchitis.

Angelita came to visit me: the poor thing is just like me, she has no information about Jimmy, and her only comfort is knowing he hasn't been captured. She had hoped her son had left in one of the airplanes the pilots escaped in when they saw the white flag flying over the First Infantry Regiment barracks and were sure the coup had failed; but no, she just found out that the last pilot to take off was the son of Don Chente Barraza, a young air force student who had participated in the bombing of the Black Palace, and he had offered Jimmy a seat in his plane. But Jimmy decided his duty was to stay and organize the retreat of the cavalry troops he commanded, which were being surrounded at the airport by troops loyal to the general. That's what the Barraza family told Angelita. They also told her that their son Chente flew to the North American base in Punta Cosigüina, on the Nicaraguan side of the Gulf of Fonseca, where the few pilots who hadn't flown to Guatemala had gone, and now, fortunately, they are all safe and sound in the Panama Canal Zone. Angelita was in the middle of telling me this story when the Alvarados stopped by for a visit. They didn't know each other, but soon they all felt quite comfortable; all this anguish and uncertainty brings people together. Raúl predicted that things are going to get more difficult starting tomorrow, the university will be a cauldron of activism, and tragic events will undoubtedly occur; Rosita bewailed Chente's involvement in the protests, she fears the worst should he be captured, and she confirmed that the students plan to call a strike. Raúl said he has met with his medical colleagues, all of whom are wondering what has become of Dr. Romero, two weeks have passed since the coup, and there's been no word, except that he was sentenced to death. This is the same situation we are in with Clemen, Jimmy, and so many others, who are surviving on the lam, who knows where or under what conditions.

I must get ready for tomorrow: we will all wear black to the embassy. At this hour of the night, when I lie down in bed, I feel like I'm floating in the sea, face up, without moving, my eyes closed under the setting sun, being tossed about in the waves, while Pericles watches over me from the beach.

Monday April 17

A feverish day, as if the city had woken up in an altered mood. We arrived at the American Embassy at precisely eight in the morning. Indeed, just as Uncle Charlie had predicted, Mr. Thurston made us wait only ten minutes, then welcomed us warmly and was eager to be of assistance; he offered his condolences to Merceditas and the Maríns' mother. Doña Chayito was our spokesman: she gave him the communiqué, explained the situation of the prisoners, and formally requested that his government and the diplomatic corps intervene and pressure the general to declare an amnesty for all political prisoners. The ambassador said the first priority was to prevent more executions; he would call an urgent meeting of the diplomatic corps so they could present the general with a unified position; and although they cannot request amnesty because that is not within the purview of foreign governments, they can request that the government show "mercy." I don't know why, but at that moment I could clearly hear Pericles saying that the general had always been a loyal husband and as far as women goes he knows a Concha but no Mercy. The meeting was brief: a photograph was taken of all of us with Doña Chayito handing the ambassador the communiqué; as we left through the front door we were approached by journalists, not only three or four foreign correspondents but also some from our own newspapers and radio stations shut down by the general, journalists Mingo had surely informed of the event. Once in the street, and much to our surprise, a group of students, including Chente, were cheering for us and chanting antigovernment slogans. We turned our steps to the Central Prison to again demand the right to visit our family members. Colonel Palma refused to see us; again he sent Sergeant Flores, who assured us that visits would be allowed by next weekend. "We want to see them now!" Doña Consuelo shouted angrily; we all seconded her demand. Doña Chayito gave a copy of the communiqué to the sergeant and said, "Take this to the colonel. And tell him we just came from the American Embassy. The ambassador told us that sooner or later you will pay for your villainy!" Doña Chayito's boldness impressed me, though afterwards I wondered what Mr. Thurston would think if he found out what she had said. Suddenly, the young people started shouting at the sergeant, "Nazis! Nazis! Nazis! . . ." The expression on the sergeant's face changed: his eyes filled with hostility, he ordered us to disperse and threatened to call the National Guard that very moment to come and arrest us. We realized he wasn't bluffing; we left quickly.

María Elena was at home when we arrived; she had just gotten back from the village. She asked me where I was coming from that I was so agitated. I brought her up-to-date on the most recent events, including how frightened I was by Sergeant Flores's threat. María Elena told me that in her village and in the entire region around the volcano, people are fed up with the general, nobody can forgive him for having executed General Marroquín and Colonel Calvo in cold blood; in addition, squadrons of National Guard troops keep scouring the fincas and threatening the peasants, they suspect that several people who participated in the coup are hiding in the area. She told me the dress fit Belka perfectly, and her whole family sends me their gratitude and best wishes; she brought bags of fruit and the curdled cheese I love so much. María Elena said that when she walked out of the bus terminal, she had the sensation that this was the first day San Salvador had returned to some semblance of normalcy since the coup, but after what I told her, she no longer felt that way.

I received a phone call from my mother-in-law. She told me that Colonel Palma called to express his regret that he couldn't allow visits to Pericles, but orders are orders, and they come from the very top. I told her he is a coward for contacting her instead of returning my phone calls. I've been aware that my in-laws have known him for a long time, that there was a certain intimacy between them, I even suspected there were favors owed. Mama Licha warned me that the situation continued to be very delicate, it seems that rather than dissuade the officers from expressing their dissatisfaction, the executions have had the opposite effect. I was surprised that my mother-in-law would talk about such things on the telephone, she is always so cautious and circumspect. Something quite serious must be happening.

This afternoon rumors started circulating that Dr. Romero has been captured. I didn't believe them. I received phone calls from many people; everybody in the street was talking about it. I heard wildly different versions: that he was shot while being arrested, that they applied the law of flight—which allows them to shoot fleeing prisoners—that they are torturing him at the Black Palace. But it wasn't long before there was a news bulletin on the radio. First it was announced only that he had been captured, and more details would be given soon. Then there was a government press release stating with great fanfare that the "communist leader" Arturo Romero had been captured by a peasant patrol in the eastern part of the country, very close to the Honduran border; it said the doctor attacked his captors in an attempt to escape, and he was wounded in the ensuing struggle and taken to a hospital in the city of San Miguel. I froze: that scoundrel will execute Don Arturo, I said to myself. It was as if we were all thinking the same thing, because immediately a kind of silent wave of outrage rippled through the city. By then it was late in the afternoon. Betito and I went to the Alvarados' house; we were lucky to see Chente, who just happened to have stopped by to pick up some clothes and sandwiches because he was going to spend the night at the university. He told us a student delegation from the medical school was going to take the train to San Miguel as soon as possible to safeguard Don Arturo, for the National Guard troops who captured him had assaulted him brutally with machetes, he has a very deep wound on his face, and the doctors at the San Miguel hospital are doing everything possible to save his life; he also told us that preparations for the university strike are moving along, and that's what he's going to spend the night planning. Then he left quickly. All poor Rosita could do was ask God to watch over him and sit there biting her fingernails.

We returned home. Betito went to Henry's; I asked him to be very careful. Doña Chayito called to tell me she had just spoken to the ambassador, who said the doctor's arrest was bringing things to a head, the entire diplomatic corps approved the request for immediate clemency for all coup participants who are under arrest and requested a meeting with the general for the afternoon, and as soon as she had heard anything she would call me; she said we should meet at eight in the morning in front of the Central Prison. I assured her I would be there. I had just hung up when Raúl and Rosita came over to invite me to dine with them, then Mingo also arrived, asking me to tell him every detail of our meeting with the ambassador. In the end we stayed in: Rosita went to get the fried plantains and beans she had made, and María Elena served some meatballs left over from lunch. I was surprised by Raúl's sudden change; he is very upset by Don Arturo's capture, he said the entire medical society would do everything possible to prevent his execution, his friends are in contact with colleagues in San Miguel, and once they get him out of immediate danger they will stretch out his treatment as long as possible to prevent them from taking him to the prison hospital. He also said that on this first day of classes the political ferment among the university students has been intense, in classes nobody talks about anything besides the executions and how the general should be thrown out, and everybody's nerves are on edge.

Betito didn't return until a few minutes before ten; I was already getting worried. I scolded him: it is irresponsible to run the risk of being caught on the streets after curfew. He told me that he and his high school friends are getting better organized so they can join the university protests that will take place in the next few days. I warned him not to neglect his studies, whatever the circumstances, and not to misbehave at school: he is still a minor who must do as he is told, and he knows how strict his father is.

I'm exhausted, but my spirits are good. I hope I'll soon fall asleep. I don't want to stay awake thinking about Don Arturo's fate, because then I will grow worried about Clemen and Pericles. The one who is staying up all night is Chente, along with his classmates; he looks so inoffensive with his glasses and scrawny body, but that boy has turned out to be quite tenacious.

Tuesday April 18

A detachment of National Guard troops had taken up position on the street in front of the Central Prison with orders not to allow us to approach. The atmosphere was charged: I was afraid and decided to return home to wait for the other ladies. Doña Chayito called a bit later: she said she'd verified that the guards would surround the prison indefinitely to prevent us from approaching; she also confirmed that the representatives of the diplomatic corps were received last night by the general and they presented him with their request for clemency, though they received nothing but an assurance that everything would proceed according to the law. And again I could hear Pericles saying, "That's the only clemency the man knows: the National Guard." We will meet tomorrow at Doña Consuelo's house.

I spent the rest of the morning grocery shopping, feeling a bit guilty when I thought of the unpleasant things Pericles must have to eat. María Elena accompanied me from store to store; everyone is mumbling hateful insults against the general under their breath, though fear abounds. In Plaza Morazán we took Don Sergio's taxi; he says he misses my husband, his favorite client.

Then I went to the beauty salon—I was in a sorry state, I have been taking such poor care of myself, as if punishing myself for Pericles having to remain in jail. Silvia, the one who brushes my hair, told me she had just waited on Doña Tina de Ávila, the wife of Don Ramón, minister of foreign affairs, who swears that her husband and several other ministers would like to resign, but they don't see how or when, and they don't agree that there should be more executions and would rather the sentences be commuted, especially Dr. Romero's, but they are afraid to raise their voices because then the general would accuse them of treason and retaliate. I am certain this is the case.

I felt like a new woman when I left the beauty salon. Then I went to my parents' house. I noticed several young people on the streets wearing black ties. I brought Mother up-to-date on my recent activities; she advised me to be very careful, not depend on the fact that I am a respectable lady, she said, because the worst kind of animal is a cornered animal. I mentioned what Doña Tina had told Silvia at the beauty salon; Mother already knew—she's friends with Doña Tina and also with Doña Telma de Escobar, the wife of the treasury minister. She says the situation would be comic if it weren't so tragic: before each meeting with the general, most of the ministers agree to explain to him the virtues of adopting a more moderate policy and taking into consideration the advice of friendly foreign governments, but once they are face-to-face with him in his office, they all tremble, not one dares express the slightest dissension, least of all regarding the death sentences, and even so, he eyes them with suspicion and contempt, he now trusts only those in the army who remained loyal to him.

On my way back home I came across more young people wearing black ties. Betito is the one who explained to me, when we sat down to eat, that it's a form of protest by the university students, an expression of mourning for those executed and for Dr. Romero's capture. While she served us cannelloni, María Elena mentioned that she had just seen Chente on his way home for lunch from the university, and he was also wearing a black tie. Betito asked me if he could wear one of his father's ties; I answered that he isn't a university student, the tie of his school uniform is green, and black doesn't match, and anyway he doesn't like wearing ties, he is always complaining about it, and his father doesn't like other people wearing his clothes. But he insisted. In the afternoon he went out wearing Pericles's tie.

I had plans this afternoon to have coffee with Carmela and Chelón, but I got a very bad migraine. I slept for a while. I woke up with cramps, my spirits very low, and with an overwhelming desire to cry and stay in bed alone. The beginning of my period made me feel like I was being crushed by a huge log, so heavy was the load of nervous exhaustion I was carrying. I didn't leave my bedroom even for dinner; María Elena brought me tea and sweet rolls. Betito came in a while ago to ask me how I was and tell me that Chente said that six soldiers are guarding Dr. Romero at the San Miguel hospital, the delegation of medical students is already there to protect him, and they are looking for a way to help him escape once his health improves. I am not in as much pain now, but I don't know if I'll be in any shape tomorrow to attend the meeting at Doña Consuelo's house.

Wednesday April 19

Things have blown sky high: they've arrested Chente. There was a confrontation between the police and the students; several were arrested. The rector has decided to shut down the university. Raúl and Rosita are out of their minds with worry. It happened late this morning. I was lying on the sofa, a hot water bottle on my belly, when the radio reported the riots, the arrests, and the suspension of classes until further notice. I immediately had an intuition that Chente was among those arrested; afterward I became even more alarmed, imagining that Betito might have decided to skip school and join the university students. María Elena tried to reassure me: she said the radio newscasters hadn't mentioned anything about high school students or minors, and Betito was surely at school. But I was still worried; I even forgot about the discomfort of my period. I called his school to ask. Everything was fine, the principal told me. Then I called the Alvarados' house. I was right: Raúl had just called Rosita to tell her of Chente's arrest. The poor thing was crying her eyes out; and she was scolding him under her breath: she had warned him, but that boy is so stubborn, they're going to mistreat him, she can't understand why children don't pay attention to their mothers; she said what we often say as a defense against pain and fear. For a moment I thought she'd turn against me. But no; instead, she begged for help. She said that Raúl and the other professors were on their way to the Black Palace. I called Doña Chayito. She already knew, and she told me she had just spoken to the American ambassador to ask him to take a stand on this issue, and she said most of the students who'd been arrested were medical students, and the board of the Salvadoran Medical Association had made an urgent request for an audience with the general; she told me she'd have more news at the meeting that afternoon. I stayed to keep Rosita company until Raúl arrived; some neighbors came to visit, to offer their support; and two more plainclothes policemen have appeared on our street to watch us, as María Elena pointed out to me. At one moment, Rosita lost control: she let out some bloodcurdling screams, as if Chente were dead; she rued her bad luck, recalling the tragedy of her daughter Dolores, who was two years older than Chente and died of fulminating peritonitis, weeks before her *fiesta rosa*, her fifteenth birthday celebration, a girl we never had a chance to meet but whose photos I've seen on a kind of altar on a shelf in the Alvarados' living room. Thank God Raúl arrived when he did, because we couldn't find any way to comfort Rosita; the poor man looked quite shaken when he arrived but quickly pulled himself together, gave her some tranquilizers, and managed to convince her to lie down. Then he told us that the police had provoked the confrontation in order to arrest the students, taking advantage of the fact that the campus is only one block away from the Government Palace; he assured me that the board of the Salvadoran Medical Association remains in a state of emergency, and he said that final year students, who work as interns at the hospitals, are threatening to go on strike.

At lunchtime, Betito brought a leaflet from the university students that called for the overthrow of the general; though as yet there was no mention of the arrests of the morning, it ends with a sentence I will never be able to forget: "We must act like men, not dumb beasts: throw off the yoke of the tyrant." He offered to type up a copy I could take to our meeting in the afternoon. But there was no meeting: Doña Consuelo called, sounding very frightened, she told me the tea for Leonor had been canceled, she was very sorry, she would explain later, for now it would be better if we didn't pay her any visits. I assumed the general's spies had insolently positioned themselves in front of the house, intimidating her. Doña Chayito confirmed this when she came over this afternoon, having been alarmed by the number of policemen watching the committee members; she warned me that we must be extremely careful about what we say over the phone, it would be best to find ways of arranging our meetings when we are face-to-face or through messengers. For a brief moment while we were having coffee and *cemita* cakes in the living room, she looked overwhelmed, exhausted, as if she no longer knew where to go from here; I felt frightened because at that moment I understood that a large part of my own self-confidence to stand in the street and demand Pericles's freedom came from this woman, from her determination and drive, this woman who is not a friend of mine and doesn't even belong to my social circle. Fortunately, Doña Chayito quickly returned to her usual high spirits: she said we mustn't despair, these new arrests will rebound in our favor because our movement will grow, and we must be prepared for this to happen, for now I should focus on getting the Alvarados involved, and she would come visit me tomorrow, Friday, at noon, or would send Leonor, Doña Julita's daughter, with precise instructions.

I would have liked to go to my parents' house, but after Doña Chayito left, my period and its attendant discomforts obliged me to take to my bed again: I felt overwhelmed by sorrow and despair, morbid forebodings about Clemen, Pericles, and Chente, until I fell fast asleep. María Elena woke me up when she entered the room with a cup of tea; she told me it was time for dinner, said it wouldn't be good for me to spend the whole night with an empty stomach, and that Raúl had come a while ago to ask how I was. I asked if he had given her any news about Chente; he is still being held at the Black Palace, that is all she knew. It took a great deal of effort to get on my feet. Betito had stayed at my parents' house to eat, she said; then she insisted on forcing me to eat something even though I wasn't the least bit hungry. That's how María Elena is: based on her age, she could be my daughter, but sometimes she acts like my mother.

Two other doctors were at Raúl's house; when I arrived they were carrying on an animated conversation. Raúl introduced me; they were Dr. Salazar and Dr. Moreno, the fathers of two other students who had been arrested. All three men seemed anxious and were drinking whiskey; Rosita looked improved, though her gaze was unfocused, as if lost. Dr. Salazar told me he knew Pericles and Clemen, and he expressed his regrets, but he said it seemed the general had made a point of having at least one member of every family behind bars. I asked after the boys. Raúl told me they were being held at the Black Palace, but the director, Colonel Monterrosa, had given assurances to the board of the Salvadoran Medical Association that they would not be mistreated and that normal due process would be followed, though he warned that because they had violated the provisions of the state of siege, the students could remain detained for as long as the authorities deemed necessary. Dr. Moreno explained that the general hopes the Salvadoran Medical Association will lose heart and therefore cease to appeal for clemency for Dr. Romero, whom he plans to put in front of a firing squad as soon as his injuries heal. Raúl told me they have already organized a team of lawyers from the same university to defend the students, and they have received authorization to visit them tomorrow morning. Rosita cried out passionately that the only thing she wanted was to see her son, touch him, have absolute proof that they haven't done anything terrible to him. That is what we all wish for most, I told her. I then told the doctors about the difficulties we are having visiting our family members at the Central Prison, the ways we are working together to demand visiting rights, and the threatening and harsh responses we've gotten from the general, including all the ladies in the committee being under police surveillance. I wished them luck getting in to see their sons tomorrow and said it would be good in any case to support each other, combine our efforts, which—as they must surely already know—have the support of the American ambassador. Dr. Moreno said certainly, we could count on them, tonight they would speak to their wives and would have them get in touch with me and Rosita; Dr. Salazar agreed. Then, after discussing the reports of Dr. Romero's health, they threw back their whiskeys and left. "Who would ever have guessed we would find ourselves in such a situation," Raúl said as he saw me to the door; Rosita broke out in tears.

How strange this sensation of being an experienced veteran in the face of my neighbors' anguish and grief; I know it is sinful to feel superior, but I can't help it. Even stranger is this hint of pleasure at others' pain that puts us all in the same boat, a dreadful emotion I should never allow in my heart.

Thanks to my nap in the afternoon, the discomfort of my period has lessened and I can sit and write in this diary. I was missing Pericles so much a short while ago, I opened his wardrobe to make sure Betito had put his black tie back in its place: there it was, hung up perfectly. A few moments later I found myself touching and smelling his suits, his guayaberas, his underwear. My poor husband must be in a sorry state indeed.

(11:30 at night)

I haven't been able to sleep. I got into bed and soon found myself in the grips of great uneasiness, a horrible foreboding, as if something very terrible were happening to Clemen. I am riddled with fear so intense I had no choice but to get up and start writing. God willing, I am wrong, and my Clemen is not suffering; God willing this is merely a panic attack, the fruit of my imagination. I will find solace in praying for my son.

Thursday April 20

We human beings are bound together with invisible ropes. It was one in the afternoon when Mila phoned; I feared the worst, that my forebodings had come to pass and news of Clemen's demise would reach me from the mouth of this treacherous woman. But no, she called to tell me—again, excited and tipsy, according to what I deduced from her tone of voice—that she hasn't a penny to feed the children, they eat thanks to help from her parents, all because of Clemen's irresponsibility, she has no idea how she will pay the rent on the house at the beginning of next month, most likely she will move out and go to live with her parents, because the general will never pardon Clemen and if he's caught he's a dead man. She said all this with such malice, as if she really didn't care, or even that deep down this is what she is hoping for. I was outraged, but all I said was that she could bring my grandchildren to the house any time she wanted, that unfortunately I have no money to give her because I am in the same situation now that Pericles is in prison, I survive thanks to help from my parents, but these are the circumstances I have been called upon to live and it is no reason to dismantle my home. Then she exclaimed that my case was different, because Pericles might be set free at any moment, but in her case it was like waiting for a dead man, she was not willing to ruin her chances for the future for something so senseless and that's why she has decided to make a new life for herself, because even if Clemen manages to leave the country, she would never consider going to live abroad. "As if the general were eternal," I muttered without thinking, quietly, almost as if I were talking to myself. Mila got quiet for a few seconds. At that moment I felt like asking her what her Colonel Castillo had proposed to make her be in such a hurry to get out of her marriage to Clemen, but all I said was that I hoped her decisions were the result of reasoned reflection and not momentary upset, and I hung up. Chelón says the best method for calming the spirit is to try to put oneself in the place of the person who has upset us, attempt to mentally project oneself into the other person and understand his or her attitudes, but I must confess that this is impossible with my daughter-in-law—the more I think about her cowardice and treachery the more furious I become.

I recounted to María Elena my conversation with Mila, just to let off some steam, unburden myself of those injurious feelings. María Elena said that the best thing for me would be to accept that Clemen's marriage is over, perhaps then it would be easier for me to deal with my relationship with "Señora Mila," with ironic emphasis on the "señora," as she said it. I asked her if she knew something I didn't know, something she had recently heard from Ana. She answered that the love birds see each other every day at noon, the hour of day most convenient for Colonel Castillo, and that Mila returns full of sighs and with her eyes all glassy after each encounter. I asked her not to tell me more, because my blood was beginning to boil again; María Elena speaks about all this with a certain contained delight, as if her words concentrated the scorn of everybody who had always insisted that marrying Mila was my son's worst misstep. But now that I am alone and thinking about it, now that I see so clearly how irreparable that marriage is, I tell myself that María Elena is right, I must find a way to let Mila know I am aware of her relationship with Colonel Castillo, because what infuriates me is that she thinks I am some kind of idiot, and for the future of my grandchildren it is in my interest to force her to lay her cards on the table. The only thing I pray for is that Clemen not find out about this vile treachery until he is safe and sound outside the country, my son is already suffering enough trying to save his own life on the lam, he doesn't need to carry the additional burden of knowing that his wife is betraying him with the very man who is hunting him down so ferociously.

Exactly what I feared has happened to Chente: neither Raúl nor Rosita nor the appointed lawyers from the university were allowed to meet with him at the Black Palace. The same thing happened to the families of the other five students who were arrested. Raúl says Colonel Monterrosa informed them that orders came from the top to keep the young isolated for a certain period of time in order, that cynical man said, for them to reflect on their bad behavior, but he also guaranteed them that they were fine and would not be mistreated. Rosita is inconsolable. I stayed with her for a while this afternoon, to keep her company, share with her some of the difficulties I have faced every time my husband has been imprisoned; at a certain moment she said she now understands the burden I bear, she thinks it is admirable how I have been able to live through such situations. I answered her with a sentence Pericles often said: "Man is a creature of habit; woman is, too." And I realized I wasn't able to understand Rosita's suffering when she lost her daughter; although Clemen has been sentenced to be executed by firing squad and death is relentlessly pursuing him, my heart refuses to imagine the pain his loss would cause me.

Toward evening my mother and sister and I went to the Polyclinic; I accompanied them to visit Dr. Ávila's mother, and then they came with me to Don Jorge's room, where we stood outside for a long time chatting with Teresita. I sensed a different atmosphere in the hospital among the doctors and nurses; I don't know how to describe it: they seemed to move with a different level of intensity, a certain urgency and commitment. I suppose the capture of Dr. Romero, and the efforts to prevent his execution, as well as the general's attacks on the association, have endowed them with the strength of solidarity, and a new kind of zeal.

Fugitives (III)

1. THE AFTERNOON

Jimmy and Clemen, lying in hammocks side-by-side, are snoring through an after-lunch, after-whiskey, and after-conversation siesta. Suddenly, Sóter, the dog, jumps out of the lounge chair where he's been dozing and runs off barking.

"Someone's coming," Jimmy says, stretching.

Clemen is in a lethargic stupor.

The blades of the ceiling fan squeal overhead.

Jimmy stands up: he looks through the large picture window into the sea's shimmering glare; he can see some men jumping off a boat at the small dock.

"It's Mono Harris," Jimmy says. "He's come with somebody."

He goes out onto the terrace.

Clemen babbles something incomprehensible, his mouth full of saliva; he shifts around in his hammock.

With quick energetic steps, Mono Harris walks toward them along the gravel path through the sand under the almond trees. Sóter trots by his side, wagging his tail. The other man walks behind them, as if hiding under his straw hat.

"Get up, Clemen," Jimmy shouts to him from the terrace. "Something's going on."

Clemen opens his eyes; he tries to rouse himself.

"Hey there," Mono Harris says to Jimmy as he holds out his hand. "This is Adrián," he adds, pointing to the man with the hat then asking him to wait on the terrace.

They walk into the living room; Sóter leaps around between them and barks playfully.

Clemen places his feet on the floor, still dazed, still unable to shake off his drowsiness or find his way out of the hammock.

"What's going on?" he manages to articulate, his mouth all gummed up.

"You've got to leave, now," Mono Harris says. "National Guard soldiers are on their way here."

Clemen leaps out of the hammock.

"Shit!" he cries. "The Guard!"

Mono Harris asks them where the whiskey is; he needs a drink.

"What are we going to do?" Jimmy asks as he takes a bottle and a glass out of the cabinet.

"We'll get you to Punta Cosigüina, once and for all," says Mono Harris.

Jimmy looks at him, suddenly excited.

"Fantastic!" he cries. "It's about time."

"That guy outside, Adrián, is your guide. He says you can shove off this afternoon."

Clemen pounces on the table and grabs the pack of cigarettes.

"Where are the soldiers coming from?" he asks, dismayed.

Mono Harris tells him that starting this afternoon soldiers will begin to "comb" the island searching for fugitives, starting at the bay; he found this out from the commander of the National Guard post on the hacienda.

"There's nowhere else we can hide around here?" Clemen asks and lights another cigarette.

"Unless you want to hang out in one of the hidden channels in the mangrove swamps," says Mono Harris, as he tosses back a shot of whiskey. "We'd save the money we're going to pay the guide, but if they find you, neither Mincho nor I will know you guys from Adam."

"Don't pay any attention to this moron," says Jimmy. "When do we leave?"

"Right now. I'll take you in my boat to San Nicolás, the hamlet on the other side of the island, where you'll leave from."

Mono Harris takes an envelope with money out of his pants pockets.

"The agreement is that you'll pay him when you get to Punta Cosigüina," he says.

"Is he trustworthy?" Jimmy asks as he starts counting the banknotes.

Mono Harris shrugs his shoulders.

"Does he know we're fugitives?" Clemen asks.

"He assumes you can't leave the country legally and that's why we're hiring him, but he doesn't know who you are. It's better that way. Keep pretending you're livestock buyers; let him think you're rustlers."

Sóter runs to the front door; he lets out a couple of welcoming barks.

"Good afternoon, Señor."

It's Lázaro, the caretaker.

"Our friends are leaving us, Lázaro," Mono Harris announces.

The caretaker looks surprised, says he'll miss them, asks them if he can get them anything.

They say thank you; Jimmy promises he'll drop by soon to say goodbye to him, his wife Marina, and his girls. The family lives in a shack about thirty yards behind the house; she cooked for them and washed their clothes; he took them to look at the livestock and showed them all the nooks and crannies on the island.

"What do we need to bring?" Clemen asks after Lázaro has left.

"Nothing but your knapsacks with your few belongings," says Mono Harris. "There's a bag in the boat with canned food and other provisions."

"Did you bring more cigarettes?" Clemen asks, anxiously.

"There are a couple of packs in the bag," Mono Harris answers.

Jimmy goes quickly to the bedroom.

Mono Harris says in English that they can take Mincho's shotgun, he's given them permission, in case of emergency.

"How about the gun you gave me?" Jimmy asks.

Mono Harris says, of course, and urges them to hurry up.

"How should I dress?" Clemen asks, still confused, and lights another cigarette with the butt of the one before. "These shorts, or should I put on long pants?"

"This guy thinks he's going to a wedding . . . ," Jimmy says sarcastically.

Mono Harris reminds them they will still be Justo and Tino, in case they meet anybody on the way; then he goes out on the terrace to discuss things with the guide.

"You don't think it's a bit too sudden . . . ?" asks Clemen, while he's gathering up his toiletries.

"If you want to stay, stay . . . ," Jimmy says.

Sóter paces around the rooms, excited.

"All I want to say is that for the last ten days, every time Mono has come here he's said there's no way we can go by sea, nobody will dare take us," Clemen says; he picks the bottle of whiskey up from the table and places it in his knapsack. "And now he shows up here with a guide and tells us that some soldiers are on their way, and we have to take off right away . . ."

Jimmy throws his knapsack over his shoulder, sticks his gun under his belt, puts on his baseball cap, and picks the shotgun up in his right hand.

"Let's go . . . ," he says.

Clemen puts his straw hat on his head.

They go onto the terrace.

Lázaro and Marina, with the two girls, come to say goodbye.

"We'll be back in a month," Jimmy tells them, "to take the livestock we picked out. Thank you for everything."

Lázaro and Marina wish them luck on their trip; the girls—snotty, barefoot, wearing a few filthy rags—point to Sóter.

Lázaro sees Don Mincho's shotgun in Jimmy's hand; he says nothing.

Mono Harris and the guide have started walking toward the jetty. Sóter trots along behind them.

Clemen jumps into the boat; he sits down, apprehensively, facing Jimmy.

"It's been so nice here," he mumbles, but nobody hears him because Mono Harris has started the motor with one pull, and Sóter is barking from the jetty. He'd rather not leave, he's gotten used to the place, all the fear of their flight transformed into a peaceful vacation by the sea. And now, again, anxiety and fear.

"Are these the provisions?" Jimmy asks, shouting, as he rummages through a large paper bag.

The guide, curious, turns toward them from the bow; his tanned face, slanting eyes, and shaggy beard peek out from under his broad-rimmed hat.

"It's enough food for the trip," Mono Harris answers.

Clemen stares at the house, the silhouettes of the girls, and Sóter running on the beach as it all recedes; the bright light hurts his eyes.

"How long will it take to get there?" Jimmy asks the guide.

The boat suddenly lurches. Clemen grabs onto the side; his hat flies off his head, but Jimmy manages to catch it with a quick swipe.

"To Cosigüina?" the guide asks. "Depends on the current and the winds. If we leave before two thirty, we might catch the current."

Jimmy looks at his pocket watch: it's two o'clock.

"Will we get there before midnight?"

The guide shrugs his shoulders.

"Are we going in this boat?" Clemen asks, holding the hat Jimmy handed him between his knees.

"No," Mono Harris says, "in Adrián's canoe."

Clemen shoots Jimmy a sidelong glance.

"You wouldn't make it in this boat for long in the open sea," Mono Harris explains. "Anyway, it needs to look like one of Adrián's normal fishing trips..."

They are advancing parallel to the coast, not far beyond the breaking waves.

Clemen realizes the house is merely a spot in the distance, a blotch against the green of palm trees, almonds, and coconut groves; then he turns and looks forward, and the sea wind blows in his face.

"The canoe is strong. It hasn't failed me yet," the guide says from the bow.

A flock of seagulls fly over the waves in the opposite direction.

"You think he'll turn us in?" Clemen asks, looking at half a dozen abandoned-looking shacks lined up along the beach under the glaring sun; he's smoking frantically, compulsively, one puff after another.

They are standing on the small broken-down jetty where Mono Harris has left them. He gave them each a hug, wished them the very best of luck, and asked them to send word once they'd reached the American base in Punta Cosigüina; then he rushed off. The guide showed them the canoe tied to the jetty, and asked them to wait; he'd go get the two oarsmen and bring the rest of the equipment needed for the crossing.

"I don't think . . . ," Jimmy starts to say, carefully checking out the canoe: he wonders if it is strong enough for the high seas; he figures it's about fifteen feet long; inside, over a net spread out on the floor of the boat, the guide has placed the bag of food, and they have put down their knapsacks and the shotgun.

"There's something about him I don't like," Clemen says.

"What?"

"The guide . . ."

"I told you, if you don't want to go, you can stay here."

A couple of young women are walking down the beach, each with a basket on her head; they're following the line of foam the waves leave behind as they retreat, stamping their bare footprints into the wet sand.

"I don't trust this canoe," Clemen says, then turns to look at the women. It's been exactly twenty days since he's slept with someone;

the night before he counted while sitting in the sand, alone, facing the dark sea, wanting to scream like a madman or jerk off. He throws the cigarette butt into the water.

"What do you know about canoes?" Jimmy asks.

The women walk toward the jetty; a gust of wind blows their white dresses tight up against their bodies. They walk past.

"Where do you think they're going?" Clemen wonders out loud without taking his eyes off them.

"The things you think about . . . ," Jimmy says in a tone of reproach.

"What the hell do you want me to think about? Another week in that house and I would have ended up screwing Sóter . . ."

"Here comes Adrián and the oarsmen," Jimmy says. Then he takes out his pocket watch and mumbles, "We're still in time to catch the current."

They've appeared from between the shacks; they walk quickly toward the jetty. The guide is carrying a rolled-up sail; the two oarsmen are carrying a heavy barrel between them.

"What're they carrying in there?" Clemen asks.

"Drinking water," Jimmy says as he starts toward them.

Clemen turns, squinting, to the metallic blue horizon; then he looks at the clear sky. He rubs his face with both hands.

"I hope I don't get seasick," says Clemen, sitting on the starboard side facing the open sea, both hands clutching the side of the canoe; Jimmy is on the port side, his eyes glued on the coast, the shotgun held between his legs.

"You feel sick?" Jimmy asks him.

Clemen turns to look at the guide, who is back on the bow peeling an orange and throwing the peels into the sea.

"No," he says, "but I'm not used to being in a boat."

"What about when you went to Europe with your parents?"

The canoe is moving perpendicular to the coast, heading slowly out to sea, rocking as it goes.

"That was ten years ago," Clemen says, "and this isn't anything like an ocean liner."

The fat oarsman looks at Clemen and smiles. The other, an emaciated man with one eye, hasn't lifted his head; his eyes remain on the floor of the canoe.

"You think we'll catch the current?" Jimmy asks the guide.

He has just popped half the orange into his mouth and can't speak. He gestures with his head toward San Nicolás, the jetty they left about ten minutes before, which they can still see from this distance in spite of the glare.

Jimmy turns around and squints: a boat is approaching the jetty. The metallic shine is clear, unmistakable.

"I think we're in luck," the guide says then leans over the water to rinse off his hands.

Clemen turns to look. At first he's baffled, but a few second later he understands: he blinks anxiously, swallows hard, then turns to look out to sea.

The oarsmen, their backs to the jetty, haven't seen a thing.

"When will you raise the sail?" Jimmy asks the guide, as if nothing at all had happened.

The guide picks his teeth with his fingers, determined to get out the last pieces of orange.

"We've got a while yet," he says.

Clemen leans over to Jimmy, cupping his mouth with his hands, and whispers in his ear, "What if the soldiers saw us and decide to come after us?"

"We're too far away," Jimmy murmurs. "You can relax."

The one-eyed oarsman has a bout of coughing, but he doesn't stop rowing or look up.

Soon the boat and the jetty have become a blur, quivering through the mist and the shimmering glare.

"What did you think of Don Mincho's livestock?" the guide asks as he moves toward the center of the canoe and the barrel of drinking water. "That orange was too sweet," he says as he takes the drinking gourd filled with water out of the barrel.

Clemen again grabs hold of the sides of the canoe, which is rocking sharply from the guide's movements.

"Good stock," Jimmy says, "though we still haven't decided what to buy."

The guide gives him a sly look of complicity.

The coast has turned into a brown line. Jimmy shoots a parting glance at the jetty and San Nicolás, where only a few spots of color still sparkle.

"I want some water, too," Clemen says. "You guys want?" he asks the oarsmen.

"Too soon for them," the guide responds quickly.

The fat oarsman smiles again.

"Those shitfaces make me nervous," Clemen whispers in Jimmy's ear, looking at the oarsmen out of the corner of his eye. "They haven't opened their mouths since we left."

"Not everybody's a big mouth like you," Jimmy answers.

A breeze begins to blow; the canoe picks up speed.

The guide raises his hand and stretches out his palm; then he licks his palm and raises it again, swiveling it around to find the direction of the wind.

"Time to raise the sail," he says, moving toward the middle of the canoe. Clemen and Jimmy make room for him.

"Careful ...," Clemen cries, tense, again grabbing onto the side of the boat.

The guide and Jimmy lift the mast and unfurl the sail.

For the first time the one-eyed oarsman looks up; he smiles, toothless. The fat oarsman turns around, looks at the sail, and also flashes a smile. They say nothing, but they decrease the rhythm of their rowing.

The canoe moves forward faster, as if it were skimming over the water.

Jimmy lets out a shout of joy.

"Take it easy, pirate ...," Clemen cries, without letting go of the side, without even relaxing his grip.

The guide stays next to the mast, manipulating the sail; Clemen and Jimmy have moved to the bow.

"We got away from them ...," Jimmy says, a big smile on his face, raising and dropping his eyebrows several times in jest.

The breeze turns into a strong wind; the sail swells.

The guide repeats that they've got luck on their side; he looks off into the metallic blue sky, the immense and empty horizon, where there is no other boat anywhere in sight.

Jimmy glances at his pocket watch: it's five to three.

"At this rate we'll be there before eight," Jimmy guesses.

The canoe glides over the water with only the merest hint of swaying.

Clemen lets go of the boat with his right hand, takes a pack of cigarettes out of his shirt pocket, and with a practiced move pulls one out with his lips. Then he takes some matches out of his trouser pockets.

"You can let go," Jimmy tells him. "Don't be afraid. You're not going to be able to light it with one hand."

"I'm not afraid," Clemen says irritably. He lets go with the other hand.

But the wind is interfering with his efforts to light the cigarette. Jimmy leans over to help him shield the match with his cupped hands.

Clemen smokes, relaxed.

"Have you been to Cosigüina many times?" he asks Jimmy.

Jimmy says yes and assures him they will be warmly welcomed; two of his best friends, officers who graduated with him in Fort Riley, are stationed at that base.

"Now I feel like a whiskey," says Clemen, and he asks the guide to pass him his knapsack.

"Careful you don't get seasick," Jimmy warns him.

Clemen stares at him, annoyed.

"Too bad we don't have any ice," he says as he takes out the bottle.

At that moment, a gust of wind makes the canoe shudder and begin to lurch.

"It's getting choppy," the guide says.

Clemen puts the bottle back in his knapsack and again grabs hold of the side of the boat. Another gust, stronger than the previous one, carries Clemen's hat off into the waves.

"Shit, what was that!?"

The guide is trying to maneuver the sail, which is now being slammed with one gust after another.

"Strange wind, with clear skies and no storm in sight," Jimmy says as he gets up to help the guide.

The canoe rocks back and forth with each blast.

The sea has suddenly gotten very rough: the waves slam against the sides, sending walls of water into the boat.

The oarsmen are rowing with more effort.

"Is this a current?" Clemen asks, his face ashen, unable to hide his fear.

"It'll pass," says the guide, grabbing onto the mast with one hand and the barrel of water with the other, looking around as if for an explanation for this squall.

The fat oarsman has stopped smiling; his face clouds over with fear. The one-eyed oarsman, his head down, rows more vigorously.

Then several gusts of wind hit them from the front: the canoe founders.

"Pull down the sail," the guide shouts.

Jimmy tries to help him.

"Let's turn back!" Clemen cries.

The fat oarsman moves his head wildly up and down in agreement.

"It's no big deal," Jimmy says sternly, as if rebuking Clemen for his fear; they manage to fold up the sail.

The guide insists that very soon they'll pass through this gale.

"It's as if we're being attacked from all sides!" Clemen exclaims.

The canoe lurches forward; the waves are getting stronger and higher.

Clemen finds himself suspended in the air. When the boat slams down on the water, the boat shudders; the water barrel crashes down. Jimmy and the guide quickly set it right.

Another wave hits hard against the side of the canoe, drenching them with water.

"Turn around!" Clemen shouts.

The fat oarsman has stopped rowing and is holding onto the sides of the boat in terror.

"We can hold out a little longer!" Jimmy exclaims.

The wind whips around them.

The guide is bewildered: he looks at the oarsmen, then at Jimmy. And then, stunned, he sees the swell.

"Careful!" he shouts.

The canoe capsizes.

2. NIGHT

"Fuck! ... Jimmy! ... Jimmy! ..."

"Calm down."

"Where are we?"

"You fell asleep."

"I can't see anything."

"Stop squirming around so frantically, you're going to flip over the boat."

"I'm sitting down ..."

"I know, but first you'd better get used to the dark. You've been sleeping for about three hours."

"I can't see you, Jimmy. Where are you? Where's the lamp?"

"Here, next to me."

"Light it, so I can see where I am."

"You don't need it. Close your eyes then open them slowly. Soon you'll be able to see in the dark."

"Quit giving me advice and hand me the god damn lamp."

"We're not going to light it unless there's an emergency, a real danger. It's too risky ... You're sitting down now, there's nothing to see that you didn't see before it got dark."

"You never stop giving orders, do you, asshole? You can't get it through your head that I'm not your corporal ..."

"Sergeants have corporals. We captains have lieutenants. Ignoramus ..."

"It's horrible to wake up in the dark."

"It'd be more horrible to not wake up."

"What? What did you say?"

"Look at the sky. I'm always amazed at how many stars ..."

"Where are my smokes?"

"You missed an amazing sunset."

"Jimmy, did you see my cigarettes?"

"The sky turned lilac."

"Oh, yeah, the sky ... Cut out the sissy crap and light the lamp, I've got to have a smoke ..."

"Look in your pockets."

"Hand me the lamp, Jimmy, please, before I lose my patience."

"You're a moron, Clemen."

"And you're a pain in the ass. Give me the damn lamp ..."

"There're your cigarettes, look ..."

"Where?"

"From here I can see the reflection of the package next to the carboy of water.

"Oh, you're right ... Shit. I've only got half a pack left. Let me count ... Eleven cigs ... Let's hope Mono Harris comes tomorrow and bring us more supplies."

"Let's hope."

"He promised."

"He said he'd return tomorrow if the National Guard had quit snooping around the island."

"What if they stay? We've only got enough provisions for one day."

"We've got to be careful, Clemen. Use the least ..."

"What a drag to have to eat canned sardines and drink water after the fresh seafood and whiskey we had at Don Mincho's house. And you were thinking we'd be in Punta Cosigüina by now..."

"I don't think the soldiers will hang around for long. It's a private island. They'll finish their search tomorrow then leave."

"Unless the caretaker or his wife or daughters rat on us, or they go to the hamlet and the guide and oarsmen open their fat traps. Then they'll stay and look for us, Mono Harris won't be able to bring us provisions, and we'll go straight to Hell in a handbasket ..."

"Stop torturing yourself with what-ifs. If they rat on us, they rat on themselves. Nobody's going to say anything."

"The shipwreck this afternoon was a tragedy, Jimmy. I lost all my cigarettes and the bottle of whiskey."

"We lost the shotgun, the gun, our shoes, the money. We very nearly drowned. And all you think about is your whiskey? Be grateful we're still alive."

"A drink would do me so much good at this moment."

"Me, too."

"It's your own fault, and the guide's ... You think Mono Harris will pay him?"

"Of course ..."

"Why should he? He didn't get us to Punta Cosigüina, which was the deal, and he almost got us drowned. And it was his fault, when we capsized we lost the money we were going to pay him with when we got there."

"It wasn't his fault, it was the weather."

"The weather?! The shipwreck was your and the guide's fault, you were so determined to keep going when the waves were already dangerous. I warned you we should turn around. But since you're a stubborn ass ... Don't now start pretending to be all nice and understanding."

"We had to try to leave when we had the opportunity ... Don't be such an ingrate. You should thank the guide for going to get Mono Harris while we waited on the beach after the wreck ..."

"..."

"It was all so weird, Clemen: that squall, those swells, they appeared out of nowhere. There was no storm anywhere, the sky was completely clear. Doesn't that seem strange to you?"

"What, now you think the sea has to give you an explanation? Don't give me this shit, Jimmy. There weren't any clouds but that wind was very strong. There are none so blind as those who will not see, as my grandmother used to say."

"Pass me the water. I'm thirsty."

"Pass me the lamp, and I'll pass you the water."

"What do you want the lamp for?"

"What do you want the water for?"

"Look, Clemen, it's about time you started acting like a grown-up."

"You, too. Pass me the lamp. You know very well I don't like the dark."

"I don't understand what I'm doing with you. It's like some kind of a punishment."

"I tell myself the same thing."

"Pass me the god-damn water!"

"Don't shout at me, you turd!

"Don't call me a turd!"

"..."

"..."

"Jimmy, what was that?"

"What?"

"That splashing. Over here, on my left."

"I didn't hear anything."

"Shh ... You hear?"

"You're right."

"What the fuck is it, Jimmy?"

"A fish."

"Fish are in the water, not out of it. It's probably a snake."

"Here, Clemen, take the lamp. Turn it on and move it to that side ... careful."

"You got the gun ready?"

"Uh-huh."

"You see something?"

"Nothing."

"I think we're too close to the mangroves, Jimmy. A snake, or all kinds of other creatures, can jump down on us from the branches. We should move the boat more into the middle of the canal."

"We're about ten feet from the branches. And if we go more to the middle, we run the risk of being seen by a fisherman or the soldiers. Here we're more hidden: in an emergency, we can slip into the swamp and disappear."

"I'm afraid a snake or a monkey is going to jump on my neck."

"You and your dramas. Turn off the lamp and pass me the water."

"Let's leave it on for a while."

"We're using up the kerosene just for the hell of it."

"No, we aren't. The light scares off the creepy crawly things."

"On the contrary: look at the tons of mosquitoes. They're going to eat us alive. Turn it off, you'll be more afraid when we've got the soldiers on top of us."

"You think they're going to be poking around at night in these swamps?"

"Better not be overconfident."

"It's that asshole with the gold tooth who wanted to confess to you who's after us. Mono Harris himself said he was a motherfucker. By now he must have realized we took him for a ride ..."

"Too bad I didn't have a chance to confess him; it would have been a hoot."

"They must have wired our photos from the capital, and he recognized us."

"Mono Harris would have said something, but all he said was that the National Guard is inspecting the island, just like they inspect all properties; he didn't say they knew we were hiding there."

"We were doing so well at Don Mincho's, like a vacation ... The best ten days I've spent in a long time. The only thing missing were girls."

"Look: a shooting star ..."

"Where?"

"There, just above Mars."

"Let's make a wish."

"My only wish is to leave this country as soon as possible."

"We could also wish the soldiers don't catch us, and that they leave the island and don't come back, so we can get out of these swamps and return to Don Mincho's house."

"What then? We're going to spend the rest of our lives waiting till they just happen to drop in on us?"

"I'd rather that than drown. No way in hell I'm getting back in a canoe and back out onto the high seas. If you want to try it again, you can go to Punta Cosigüina alone ..."

"..."

"It's true, right, you learned your lesson, too?"

"It was a miracle, Clemen ..."

"Damn right it was a miracle. If it hadn't been for that sand bank, we would've drowned. And luckily the upside-down canoe was floating on the empty water barrel ... If the canoe had sunk, we wouldn't have lived to tell it."

"That's not what I was talking about."

"About how long were we floating around holding onto the canoe, adrift and about to drown, until we hit the sand bank?"

"I'm telling you it was a miracle because I prayed to the Virgin ..."

"At least a quarter of an hour, hovering between life and death. I still can't believe it."

"She heard my pleas ..."

"What the hell are you talking about, Jimmy?"

"The Virgin answered when I cried out, 'Virgin of Guadalupe, save us!'"

"The Virgin answered you?"

"That's right."

"You're crazy, Jimmy."

"It was just seconds after I prayed for her to save us, after I shouted out in despair, that we hit the sand bank."

"But, what ..."

"You don't believe me? You didn't hear me shouting?"

"We were all shouting, scared shitless, Jimmy, don't be an ass. The one who shouted loudest was that fat oarsman, the one next to me, who didn't know how to swim and was squealing like a pig ... He almost pulled me under, the motherfucker. He sure made up for his silence earlier ..."

"That good-for-nothing, he's why you didn't hear me shout."

"We all asked God to save us and now it turns out the Virgin answered you. I think it was really bad for you to dress up as a priest ..."

"I'm telling you, it was a miracle. You wouldn't understand."

"Okay, so the Virgin was right there, in the waves, waiting for you to pray to her. Really? She appeared to you, without the rest of us seeing her?"

"Stop making fun of me."

"So stop talking crap. We were lucky we capsized before we'd gotten too far from shore. That's what really happened."

"You don't believe in miracles?"

"Yeah, but the miracle wasn't for you, it was for all of us, and it wasn't because you shouted but because we all begged for help. You military guys think that even God is under your command ..."

"If we come out of this alive, I'm going to go to the Basilica of Guadalupe in Mexico to offer up thanks."

"Just pass me the water, I'm thirsty again."

"Here ... Careful! Don't fall!

"Calm down ..."

"..."

"Jimmy, about what time is it?"

"I lost my watch in the wreck."

"I know, but you're good at figuring out the time. You think it's about nine?"

"My father gave it to me, before he died."

"..."

"It was my best keepsake from him."

"I don't know why we had to get involved in this ..."

"What are you talking about, Clemen?"

"The coup. The whole thing. Look where we are: in a canal lost in the middle of a swamp in the bay, in this little boat, without the least idea what will become of us."

"We're alive, that's what matters most."

"You know what would be the worst, Jimmy? If after all this they caught us ..."

"Don't even think about it. I'm not going to let them get me. If you want to surrender, go ahead, but I've got this gun."

"That Mono Harris, what a guy, he even left you his gun."

"We owe him our lives. He got us this boat, he towed us into this canal that is difficult to find, and he came back to bring us provisions. He's like our guardian angel."

"My poor mother must be worried to death. And Mila and the kids ..."

"Truth is, Clemen, I don't understand why you got involved in the coup. You're not in the military and you're not even very interested in politics; you just like to be a radio announcer, work in the theater, drink, the ladies ... Why did you get involved?"

"Because we have to get rid of that son of a bitch ..."

"A lot of people think that but they don't take the risk and participate in a coup."

"And you, why did you get involved?"

"For me, it was simple: I'm in the military, and I swore to defend the constitution that scoundrel is violating. But you? ... Don't start getting nervous again."

"My father is in prison. Doesn't that count? There's no freedom anymore."

"You'll excuse me for saying so, Clemen, but you aren't anything like my uncle. He's a politician, a serious man who maintains a strong stand in opposition to the general ... But there's no way I can see you as a politician ... Did you think this was some kind of adventure that would turn you into a hero?"

"Man, dressing up as a priest really did mess you up ... Now you want to confess me ..."

"There's no way to have a serious conversation with you."

"The only thing I know is that I'll never get involved with anything to do with the military again. You guys are a fiasco."

"Don't let's start on this again."

"Defend the constitution ... ? Don't make me laugh, Jimmy. You think I'm going to believe you that a turd like Tito Calvo or that mama's boy General Marroquín got involved in the coup to defend the constitution? Who knows how much money Don Agustín offered them, not knowing they wouldn't have the balls to do it right ..."

"Stop defaming the dead."

"I hope that strike works, the one Mono Harris told us about."

"If we couldn't bring him down by force, there's no way it can be done with a strike."

"So then what? The motherfucker will be in power for the rest of his life?"

"That's why we should leave any way we can."

"What about the gringos? Why don't they get involved once and for all and finish off that Nazi?"

"I already told you what Captain Masey told me: 'You put him in, you take him out.'"

"How convenient for them, as if they didn't have anything to do with it . . . Look at those clouds, Jimmy: really weird . . ."

"You're right."

"A storm . . . That's all we need."

"No. It's fog, a fog bank's coming this way."

"Along the coast? That's strange. That only happens in the mountains."

"Well, here it is."

"Now there's a breeze. I really can't see anything, Jimmy. It's so dark . . ."

"Shhh . . . Quiet . . ."

"What's going on?"

"Listen . . ."

"What?"

"A noise . . ."

"It's the waves."

"No, listen."

". . ."

"I'm going to row us into the mangroves."

"Go on, then."

"Lower your voice . . ."

"I don't like this foggy air; it gives me goose bumps."

"We'll stay here behind the branches. Here we've got cover and we can see if anyone is coming up the canal."

"Jimmy, I can't see anything."

"Keep your voice down. Don't you understand?"

"This is like a nightmare. I've never been somewhere like this, it's so creepy . . ."

"It's just fog. Try to control your fear . . ."

"At any moment some vermin can attack us from these branches. They say the bats in the mangroves are savage."

"Something's approaching ..."

"Where?"

"Over there, at the entrance to the canal."

"Fuck!"

"Shhh ... Sounds like a canoe. You see the glow? They must have a lamp on the floor."

"Maybe it's the soldiers?"

"I told you, Clemen, we can't trust ... Let's hide."

"They might be fishermen ..."

"I don't think so. They're staying on the other side of the canal. If they were fishermen, they'd go down the middle."

"Don't shoot, Jimmy."

"Shh ... Here they come."

"I can't see anything."

"I can only see one silhouette. That's it."

"The soldier with the gold tooth?!"

"If it were him, there'd be two of them. A soldier never goes alone, they're always in pairs ..."

"I saw him, Jimmy!"

"Maybe the other one is hiding on the floor of the canoe. That's it: we can't see the other one, but he must have his rifle at the ready in the bow and we can only make out the one in the rear."

"It's not a soldier, it's a woman ..."

"How could it be?"

"Look at that hair."

"It's a helmet."

"No it's not, it's a woman's hair."

"You're hallucinating, Clemen."

"Did you hear?"

"I hope they leave ... I hope they leave."

"It was a laugh ..."

"Quiet ... They're going past us."

"The woman is laughing."

"Luckily, they're going toward the other end of the canal. If they come back this way, I'll take them by surprise."

"Didn't you hear the laughter, Jimmy?"

"What laughter? You're nuts."

"This makes my hair curl . . ."

"That's from the humidity. You're letting fear get the better of you . . . They're leaving."

"I swear I heard a laugh."

"I just hope they don't come back . . ."

Haydée's Diary

Friday April 21

Doña Chayito came over very early this morning, just as I was sitting down to breakfast. I wasn't expecting her. I asked her if there was an emergency. She said this was the best time of day to shake off the police who are tailing her, even the ones prowling around my house hadn't come on duty yet. I invited her to have breakfast with me; she said she'd already eaten, but she would love a cup of coffee. She explained that the time had come to show our opposition to the general's intransigence, that if we allow ourselves to be intimidated, who knows when we will see our imprisoned family members again, we must seize the opportunity, take advantage of this climate of deep unrest the students' arrests have generated throughout the society. She then said that we must call all our supporters to join the protest march from the El Calvario Church to the Central Prison on Sunday after ten o'clock Mass, but we must be sure to spread the word as discreetly as possible, keep it a secret, so we can take the general by surprise. She said it would be best if those who attend the earlier Mass or go to a different church not change their plans, to avoid raising suspicions, and they should arrive at El Calvario at precisely eleven o'clock, the time the march will begin. She explained the plan with excitement and great precision, as if she'd gone over and over it in her head. She said we should all wear black, and the men should wear black ties; we should all carry a piece of folded white cardboard in our handbags as well as a thick marker to write our slogans demanding freedom for our family members during the last few minutes of Mass without running the risk of being stopped by the authorities and caught red-handed on the way from our houses to church, and that after the march we can leave the signs in front of the Central Prison. I asked her whom we will ask to join us; she said everyone who supports our cause, but it is important we invite each person individually, not en masse, that way each person will take it upon him or herself to come and the secret will be kept, and we should never talk about it over the phone.

In spite of her doubts, Rosita has agreed to join the march. We went together to talk to Dr. Moreno's wife, Doña Juana, who not only seemed excited about it but also acted like a seasoned veteran and had very strong words against the general; then we went to see Dr. Salazar's wife, Doña Cleo, who was exactly the opposite and rekindled Rosita's doubts, afraid that her participation in the march would hamper her son's release. I had to remind them of my experience with Pericles, and especially that of Doña Chayito and the other mothers who have suffered with their sons, who are also students, being in jail for weeks now already; I tried to help them understand that the situation of our loved ones has gone from bad to worse, and the general has turned a deaf ear. I warned all three not to speak on the telephone about our plans or mention anything to anybody else, as there are spies and informers everywhere.

I had two surprises this afternoon. The first was a call from Angelita, Pericles's first cousin; we console each other over our lack of news about Clemen and Jimmy. It was a normal conversation, chatting about this and that, until she asked me if I knew anything about plans for a protest march in support of political prisoners. She caught me off guard, but I managed to react appropriately: I said no, I had heard nothing about it, and I asked her to tell me what she had heard. She told me that a rumor had reached her, and she thought that since I was in the group of families of political prisoners who had met with the ambassador, I would know about it, and she said if she heard anything more she would call to let me know. I told her that so many political rumors are circulating one no longer knows what to believe.

The other surprise came in the evening at Mother's house, where the Figueroas and my sister Cecilia were also visiting. They spoke excitedly about Luz María's wedding, which will be held in a month at the cathedral in Santa Ana, and about the party afterward at the Casino Santaneco. Carlota showed me a sketch of the gown her daughter will wear and compared it to the one she wore and those Cecilia and I had worn at our respective weddings, and she complained that because of the war in Europe it is well-nigh impossible to order an exclusive design from Paris. She told me there's been a disagreement in her family about the guest list, in the wake of the attempted coup and the executions, because Carlota's mother's family has always been involved in politics—her grandfather was once the president of the republic—and now several members of her family are repudiating the general and vow not to attend the wedding if old family friends who have remained loyal to the government are invited. I also found out that Nicolás Armando's sons will be groomsmen, about how excited Cecilia is to make her grandchildren's suits and attend the wedding rehearsals; I felt a stab in my heart to think what my poor grandchildren might suffer because of their foolish mother. Later, while I was in the kitchen making tea, Carlota came to tell me she is worried about Fabito, her eldest, who is studying medicine, and who has become deeply involved in organizing protests against the general, she fears he'll be arrested at any moment. I told her how surprised I was, I knew nothing about Fabito's political involvement, though I did not think it so odd considering the fact that the general has been attacking the medical society and medical students. But the conversation didn't end there: very secretively, so nobody else would hear, Carlota revealed that Fabito was a member of a delegation of students who traveled to the hospital in San Miguel to meet with Dr. Romero and prepare a plan for his escape, he could speak with him in French (Fabio senior took Carlota and her children with him when he went to Paris for a residency) and that way outwit the two soldiers stationed in his hospital room, but Dr. Romero convinced him that the escape plan wasn't viable, that it was, in fact, suicidal. I told her it was fortunate Fabito had escaped the sweep Chente and his fellow students had been caught up in. Then she told me that's precisely her fear: Fabito is organizing a march next Sunday to protest the arrests of the students, and she's afraid that this time he won't escape, and they will take him straight to jail. It was a pity that at that moment Mama and Cecilia came into the kitchen, along with other friends who had just arrived, and we couldn't continue talking.

I dined at Carmela and Chelón's house. I told them about the plan for Sunday, how desperate we are because the general is still keeping us away from our family members at the Central Prison, that this protest march is a last resort to pressure the government. I asked Carmela to accompany me to ten o'clock Mass, though I made it clear I was not asking her to join the march, because I know that she and Chelón abstain from any political activity, but my best friend's presence at church would bring me comfort and give me strength. She said she would, of course, she would be there. I said to Chelón teasingly that he was off the hook, for if Pericles found out that he had attended Mass, even to demand his release, he would never forgive the betrayal.

A while ago María Elena told me Betito has not been home since school let out. It seems he has something cooking with Henry and his other friends; I wouldn't be surprised if they too were planning for Sunday, together with the university students. I will speak with him tomorrow morning early. With so much commotion, Doña Chayito's appeal for prudence and secrecy will surely be to no avail.

Saturday April 22

An intense day, as if there had been electricity in the air. Seems like everybody and his brother knows about the march, though almost nobody speaks about it openly. Around mid-morning I ran into Mingo at the Americana drugstore. Irmita is doing very poorly; I promised to stop by to see her in the afternoon. Standing at the counter, while the pharmacist was filling our prescriptions, I was dying to ask Mingo if he had heard about the march, but I refrained. When we got outside, he beat me to it and told me under his breath that the university students were planning a protest against their classmates' arrest, that the situation is very tense; he then told me the good news that yesterday the government finally gave Serafín safe passage to leave the country for exile in Guatemala, apparently the Americans applied strong pressure on them to grant him authorization, and on Monday he will leave under the protection of the Guatemalan consul. We agreed we'd continue our conversation when I stopped by his house in the afternoon.

Then I went to my parents' house for a while. Father, Uncle Charlie, and Güicho Sol were drinking coffee on the patio; I joined them. I wanted to know if Father had heard about the march tomorrow. I didn't even have to ask: Uncle Charlie spoke about the need to organize other forms of protest to remove the Nazi warlock, he said the university students are preparing a strike, and it would be best to support them, their idea is that everybody will join the strike until the general understands that nobody in this whole country wants him; Güicho disagreed with him, he said the warlock understands only the language of force, and what's called for is another military uprising but this time led by officers who aren't as stupid and cowardly as those who let the general prevail, and if such officers don't appear the only choice will be for American troops to invade. My uncle insisted that the idea of a strike is not unreasonable, but Güicho replied that with a strike one runs not only the risk of it being infiltrated by communists but also of them taking over. Then Uncle Charlie asked what time it was. I told him it was ten to eleven. He asked me to please move my watch ahead ten minutes, he was desperate for a shot of whiskey, and he had made a solemn vow not to have his first drink until after eleven in the morning. That meant that I should stand up and go to the kitchen for the ice bucket, mineral water, and booze, because they were going to discuss men's subjects, which would be inappropriate for me.

Don Leo was loitering about the kitchen, so I asked him to drive me to the Figueroas' place. Mother asked if something was going on; I told her I just wanted to pick up the furniture catalogue Carlota still hadn't returned, it would only take me a minute. I asked Juani to bring the drinks to the men on the patio. On the way to the Figueroas', Don Leo brought me up-to-date on the war in Italy; he said the American troops are advancing relentlessly and soon they will liberate his village, he fears for his nephews who supported Mussolini and who will now take a beating, though he right away began to rant and rave against them, as he always does; he also predicted the Americans would occupy Rome within a few weeks. I noticed several policemen lurking around Carlota's house, then I remembered that several government ministers live along these few blocks of Arce Street, including Dr. Ávila. Carlota was very anxious when she greeted me. She confirmed that the university students' march to protest the arrests and executions will be held tomorrow morning, but she couldn't tell me if they would also leave from El Calvario Church, as I suspect they will, because Fabito comes home only to sleep, he spends all his time plotting against the general and doesn't tell Carlota anything, and that's why she scolds him every chance she gets for devoting all his time to politics instead of concentrating on his medical studies. I asked Carlota if she will join the march to demand that they spare Dr. Romero's life, for he is a good friend of the family; she answered that those are men's problems and she hates politics, it brings nothing but misfortune, and she cannot imagine running through the streets with the police chasing after her, she would die of fear. Then I recommended she be prepared because Fabito could be arrested at any moment, and she would have to come to terms with the situation, as my neighbors and so many others have had to. Carlota made a face of despair, then whimpered that hopefully God would spare her from undergoing such a trial.

I returned to my parents' house believing that the march tomorrow would be much larger than what I had thought and that of all of us, perhaps only Doña Chayito is aware of this. My belief turned into a certainty after I conversed with Mingo this afternoon: he told me all the journalists know about the protest march and if the journalists know, so do the general's secret police; he told me he wouldn't be surprised if by morning El Calvario Church and the entire downtown area is occupied by National Guard troops. Mingo was quite uneasy. And for good reason: Irmita is doing worse than I thought: she's having difficulty breathing, she has terrible back pain, and she's very pale. She does not have tuberculosis, the doctors already told her, though they still haven't been able to give her a diagnosis. God willing it isn't cancer.

I admitted to my parents that I intend to participate in the march. Mother is very worried, she tried to dissuade me, and she asked me to prohibit Betito from joining the protests; Father warned me to be careful, he told me about continued rumors of unrest within the army and about the Nazi warlock getting crazier than ever. I promised them I would do everything possible to convince Betito to stay home, but I also told them they must understand how difficult it is to reign in the enthusiasm of a fifteen-year-old boy whose father is in jail and whose older brother is a fugitive, fleeing from a death sentence. And that's exactly what happened at dinner when I told Betito that it would be best for him to remain at home, not to take any risks—he responded very decisively that he would not let me go alone, he would stay by my side; I did not feel I had the moral authority to order him to do anything else.

A little while ago, after cleaning the stove and turning off the kitchen lights, while we were listening to the radio theater, María Elena insisted she would also accompany me to church and on the march. I made it clear to her that it was not her duty, and that it might be dangerous, but she said she was doing it out of her own free will, because it simply isn't right that Pericles is in jail and that they want to execute Clemen.

***

A few minutes ago, just after I put away this notebook, Father called to tell me that this afternoon, under the cloak of secrecy, the war council has been reconvened and assigned the task of trying another group of coup participants; he couldn't give me names, but he said they were military officers captured since the previous war council. "There will most likely be a new round of executions tomorrow morning," Father said with rage and sorrow. I asked him, my heart in my throat, if Clemen might be among those captured. He told me he is certain he is not, because he was told they were all military officers, and Tonito Rodríguez would be their defense lawyer. I am appalled, my nerves are frayed. How can one sleep after hearing such news ...? And what will happen at the march if there are new executions?

Sunday April 23

What a day, dear God! I barely slept a wink all night. I turned on the radio at five o'clock in the morning, knowing there would be a news bulletin if there were executions even though it is Sunday. But at seven, there was still nothing. Then I received a call from Father telling me the war council had adjourned an hour earlier and would reconvene that night; Mingo, Doña Chayito, Angelita, and other friends also called because the news had spread like wildfire. Doña Chayito told me that Captain Gavidia, Merceditas's husband, is among the new officers on trial and will surely be sentenced to death. I just managed to cry out "God no!" then felt enormous pressure in my chest. I asked her if we would still hold the march under these conditions; she answered, of course we would.

Moments later I received my Sunday call from Pati; I tried to speak calmly, I didn't want her to notice how anxious I was, I avoided mentioning the war council or Chente's arrest, for she is very fond of him. My daughter knows me too well, she is too perceptive, and I didn't want to worry her because of her pregnancy. In spite of my best efforts, at one point she said I sounded strange, then insisted several times that I was hiding something important from her. I explained that I was suffering from exhaustion and worry precisely because nothing was happening, I couldn't see her father and had no news of Clemen. After hanging up, I crossed myself and asked God to forgive me for having lied.

During breakfast, Betito was ranting and raving against the general, in that same show-offy way Clemen has that so displeases Pericles. I asked him to tone it down, the walls have ears. At that moment we heard knocks on the door: it was Raúl and Rosita. They wanted to know if the march was happening in spite of the threats of new executions; I told them yes, it was. Rosita was very nervous. We agreed that each family group would go to church on its own so as not to arouse suspicions in the policemen watching our block.

Father sent Don Leo to drive us to church. I was dressed in strict mourning, even wearing a veil, and I had a marker and a piece of cardboard in my handbag, as Doña Chayito suggested; María Elena was also dressed in black, and Betito was wearing Pericles's tie of the same color. We didn't speak the whole way there; the streets were almost empty. But many groups of people were standing in front of the church, many more than usual. Don Leo told me he would park nearby and wait for us, for Father had given him orders to remain at my disposal the whole time and then to drive us home. Carmela, Chelón, and Mingo arrived at that moment. I saw Raúl, Rosita, and the other doctors standing near the door; Doña Consuelo, accompanied by her daughter, came to greet me. Mingo gestured to me, calling my attention to the secret policemen hanging around nearby. I looked for Doña Chayito among the various groups, but couldn't find her. We were all whispering angrily about the new trials. Soon the bells rang and we entered the church. I saw that a lot of people were already inside. Doña Chayito appeared by my side; while she was greeting me, she placed a small piece of paper in my hand. Betito went off with his friend; María Elena sat at a pew in the rear. I sat between Carmela and Mingo. The priest began saying Mass. The first time we kneeled I carefully unfolded the piece of paper and read it; Mingo was watching me out of the corner of his eye. A few moments later I stood up and went to the confessional; I wasn't burdened by any particular sin, but I felt anxious and thought it would calm me down to confess. While I was waiting my turn in line, the tension in the air was palpable: people were glancing at one another with looks of complicity, others were gesturing to each other, and many were whispering, not listening to what the priest was saying, as if everyone was simply waiting for Mass to be over and for the march to begin. I confessed that I had lied to my daughter to avoid worrying her, because of her condition: the priest sent me off quickly with one Apostles Creed as penitence. I returned to my place at the pew, but as I was settling in between Carmela and Mingo, I thought I espied, in the bright light pouring in through the church doors, Don Leo entering the church. I wondered, and worried: Don Leo doesn't like priests and never attends Mass. The priest was reading the part of the gospels with the parable of the good Samaritan; then he devoted his homily to the theme of forgiveness. Just as I was joining the line to receive communion, Don Leo approached and whispered in my ear that a squad of National Guard soldiers was stationed outside the church, and it would be best for us to leave as soon as Mass was over. My knees buckled with fear. I continued to the altar, contrite, praying to God that nothing would happen, then I looked up to see where Doña Chayito and Betito were, but didn't see them. I heard some noise behind me, near the entryway, but just at that moment the priest was holding out the host to me. Returning to my pew I could feel the agitation, the looks of fear and anger on everybody's faces, and the young people going to and from the front doors. I kneeled to pray for a few minutes. Mingo and Chelón said it seems the general has stationed a tank half a block away on the street the march would go down. "I told you," Mingo reminded me, when I came back to sit down, "the warlock is always the first to know." The priest concluded the Mass. Most people got up and began to move toward the door. I remained seated, took out the cardboard and the pen, and wrote "WE DEMAND A GENERAL AMNESTY!" exactly as Doña Chayito's little piece of paper had instructed. Carmela was watching me as I drew the large letters. Then I joined the others on the way out, the sign still folded in half. I saw Merceditas, walking with Doña Chayito, the poor girl looked completely distraught. A nervous crowd had gathered in the atrium. The soldiers were positioned on the sidewalk across the street, and I caught a glimpse of the tank about fifty yards away, in the middle of the street, its cannon pointed right at us. I was scared. The university students began to congregate in the street, to shout slogans demanding the release of the prisoners and against the dictatorship, and to shout insults at the soldiers. I saw Betito on one of the steps along with Henry, El Flaco, Chepito, and other classmates. Doña Chayito strode out into the street, her sign held high, defiant, face-to-face with the soldiers; several of us followed her. My legs were trembling as I walked down the stairs. At that very instant, the commanding officer ordered them to draw their guns, and they fired into the air several times; the soldiers then aimed their weapons at us, and a horrific blast was fired from the tank. There was a stampede in both directions. I dropped my placard and felt like I was going to faint, but then somebody took me by the arm. "Hurry!" Don Leo said as he led me quickly down a side street. "What about Betito?" I managed to ask, but Don Leo was almost carrying me because I was on the verge of shock. María Elena was running behind us. "Where's Betito?" I asked again, terrified, when we got into the car. "He took off with his friends in the other direction. He's okay," Don Leo said before driving off at full speed. The further we got from the area the more I worried about what might have happened to Doña Chayito, Merceditas, Carmela, Chelón, Mingo, and so many others. "Holy Jesus, God willing they haven't hurt or arrested anybody!" I cried out, reduced to a bundle of nerves. "The shots were fired in the air, to frighten and disperse the crowd," Don Leo said, then he asked me where I wanted him to take us. I asked him to go by the house to drop off María Elena, so she'd be there in case Betito showed up or called, and then he should take me straight to my parents so I could tell them what had happened. But they'd already heard and were waiting for us along with their neighbors out in the street: the news had reached them by telephone a few minutes after it happened, and Mother assured us she even heard the shots. The whole city was in an uproar. I fell onto the sofa in the living room, overcome by distress: Juanita asked me if I wanted some tea. Mother was anxious about what might have happened to Betito, though Don Leo had already told her what he had seen. The telephone was ringing off the hook; I asked them to keep their calls brief in case Betito tried to call. Father was giving instructions to Don Leo to drive around the area looking for his group when the call came. Thank God, they got away in Henry's car, Betito said; they were safe and sound at Flaco's house. I felt enormously relieved. I tried several times to call Doña Chayito, but her line was busy; finally, her husband answered, he said she was fine, but she wasn't home. I gave thanks to our Lord; I told myself that woman is made of steel, surely she was already organizing other forms of protest. Suddenly I had a terrible sensation, like an emptiness in my stomach and total exhaustion; I went to one of the bedrooms, curled up in a fetal position on the bed, and began to sob, quietly, so nobody in the living room would hear me, until I fell asleep.

Now, as I finish describing the events of the morning, I already feel better, thanks to Mother letting me sleep uninterrupted until late this afternoon. Don Leo then brought me home. We dined with Raúl and Rosita. We are all quite discouraged, fearful, anticipating news about the war council that reconvened at seven o'clock tonight. I don't think we'll hear anything until early tomorrow morning, but it seems quite certain that evil warlock will order the execution of more young officers. I must give thanks to our Lord that they haven't captured Clemen, and ask Him to keep protecting him.

Monday April 24

They executed them by firing squad at seven this morning in the General Cemetery: Captain Gavidia, Merceditas's husband, another captain named Piche, and Lieutenant Marín, the brother of Víctor Manuel, the young man from the Tax Collectors' Office whom they had so savagely tortured, the only civilian they've executed so far. I feel like there is a pendulum swinging back and forth in my chest, taking me from the bleakest desolation to outraged anger, back and forth, and back and forth. The university students have gone on strike to protest the executions. Raúl confirmed it: the university will remain closed; he also said that final-year medical and engineering students who volunteer at hospitals and government officers will soon go out on strike. Rosita is suffering from nervous depression, she is convinced the general will execute all political prisoners, including Chente.

Doña Chayito came by the house before lunchtime; as always, she was in a rush and didn't want to stay to eat, having only a glass of fruit drink. She had just come from Merceditas' house: the captain's body has been prepared and the wake will be held there, at the family home, so as to avoid trouble for any funeral parlor, she explained. I told her I would go there later in the afternoon and could remain all night to keep them company, if necessary. Doña Chayito also told me she had just spoken to some leaders of the university movement: they have decided that it is impossible to confront the beast on the streets, we just saw he wouldn't have any qualms about killing all of us; the idea now is to organize a general strike, shut down businesses, offices, hospitals, schools; halt all public transportation and trains; make sure everyone stays home and the country remains at a standstill until the warlock leaves. "Where will we get the courage to do nothing?" I muttered, as if to myself, faintly. Doña Chayito asked me what I meant. I told her people need to work, earn their daily bread, only single young people without families to support can go on strike like that. Doña Chayito kept looking at me, pensively: "That's exactly what I argued," she said. She then added that we must do something immediately to stop the warlock from executing Dr. Romero and force him to release our family members, or at least allow us to visit them, as is our right.

I went to the beauty salon this afternoon. I felt like something the cat dragged in, and I didn't want to show up at the wake looking like that; it's enough to have one's spirits so low they're sinking through the floor but one must, at least, keep up appearances. When I entered the salon, Angelita was lying in the chair; Silvia was finishing up combing her hair. Not realizing I had entered, she was talking contemptuously about the general digging his own grave, about the Americans being furious at him, how President Roosevelt will personally give orders to have him dragged out by the scruff of his neck, how in the world did he dare execute those young men, Captains Piche and Gavidia, Jimmy's classmates, Piche considered the best artilleryman in the army, the United States having invested a cartload of money in their training. When she saw me, she didn't flinch, but her anger seemed stronger than her prudence, and she asked me if I was going to go to the wake. I told her I was. Then Silvia asked if it was true that Dr. Romero is going to be the next one to face the firing squad. "God help us," I murmured.

I asked my parents to lend me Don Leo so he could take us to the wake, Betito came with me, and more importantly to pick us up at night, before the curfew. It was already evening by the time we got there. Don Leo raised his eyebrows to point out the secret policemen stationed around the house. I assumed that few people would attend the wake, out of fear, but I was wrong: many families of officers who'd been executed, both today and fifteen days ago, and also families of prisoners and the condemned, like us, were crowded into the house; groups of young people came and went. I had never met the Gavidia family, only Merceditas. Angelita was sitting with someone who looked to all appearances to be the mother. I offered my condolences. I thought she would be devastated, in a state of collapse, but I was surprised by the composure, anger, maybe even hatred, that I could see in her face. I can't and don't even want to imagine the pain of losing two sons in such an appalling way, but I would not be surprised if the desire for vengeance acted at such moments as some kind of salve for the spirit. Angelita explained to me that the families of all three men who were executed wanted to hold their wakes together, in one place, but the general forbade it; she also told me that Pepe, the other Gavidia brother who had been detained, was released this afternoon, as if the warlock had been satisfied with the blood revenge he had exacted from the other brothers in the military. I asked where Pepe was, as I wanted to know if he had seen Pericles at the Central Prison, but it seems Pepe and

Merceditas were both resting, they were devastated. I discovered Doña Chayito and Doña Consuelo conversing on the other side of the room. I went over to them. Doña Chayito announced that she would soon return to Lieutenant Marín's wake, where Doña Julita and some other neighbors were, and she asked if I wanted to accompany her. Doña Consuelo was feeling out of sorts, she had a migraine and would soon return home. I looked for Betito so I could tell him I was going to the Marín family wake, but I couldn't find him, he was neither in the house nor out on the patio. But I very nearly bumped into Fabito: he had just arrived with two other young people. He greeted me, very solemn and respectful, as always; he is identical to Fabio senior, even the same nasally voice. I asked him if he'd seen Betito; he said he hadn't. Then I asked after Dr. Romero's health, because Carlota had told me that her son is in constant contact with the doctors who are attending him in San Miguel. He explained that he is now out of danger, the machete wound on his face is healing, and the goal now is to not let him recover too quickly, to prevent the tyrant from ordering his execution. I noticed that Fabito and Doña Chayito greeted each other familiarly, like long-time accomplices. I asked him, if he ran into Betito, to please tell him I was going to the Marín family wake for a while and would soon return; I went to Angelita and asked her to do the same.

Doña Chayito was waiting for me out on the sidewalk. It was already getting dark. We had barely walked half a block when Don Leo pulled up alongside us in the car and stopped. This was unexpected, because we had agreed he would return to pick me up at nine at night, and I assumed he was at my parents' house. As if to excuse himself, he said that Father had instructed him to remain at my disposal. "Get in," Doña Chayito said quickly; two secret policemen were standing on the corner. I asked Don Leo if he had seen Betito leave. He said that Henry, Flaco, and Chepito had picked him up in Chepito's car. Halfway there, checking to make sure Don Leo didn't see her through the rearview mirror, Doña Chayito, without any fuss, put her hand down her belly, under her skirt and her underpants, and pulled out a small piece of paper, which she unfolded and gave to me; it was another communiqué from the university students, a different one than Raúl had brought over this morning, as I could see from the heading. It would have been very difficult for me to read it in that light. I folded it back up and hid it in my brassiere.

"Things are even worse here," Don Leo said, stopping the car. There was a National Guard checkpoint blocking the street the Marín's house is on. I got nervous. A soldier approached the car and asked for our documents; he asked Don Leo where we were going. "To the wake," I came out with, and I still don't know where I got the courage. The soldier went over to an officer standing nearby, looked over our documents for a few minutes that seemed to last forever, and wrote our names down in a book. "Two hours ago this checkpoint wasn't here," Doña Chayito muttered. The soldier returned and, as he handed back our documents, he leaned over and gave me a sinister glare. "Pass," he barked. I was in a cold sweat. "There might be one at the other wake by the time we get back there," Don Leo commented. But according to Doña Chayito, the warlock sending the soldiers here was yet another act of cruelty against the family, because they say he personally tortured Víctor Manuel, but failed to break his will, failed to get him to give anyone else away.

When we got out of the car, I feared my legs would buckle under me; I grabbed on to Doña Chayito's arm. Just a few family members were there; I had already met some of them outside the Central Prison and also at Sunday Mass. I gave my condolences and went to sit next to Doña Julita and her daughter, Leonor. The atmosphere was more infused with terror than mourning. I couldn't hold out any longer, and asked where the washroom was. While I was taking care of my business, I took out the communiqué I'd hidden in my brassiere; I tore it up into little pieces and flushed it down the toilet. I returned to the living room. Doña Chayito was complaining about the checkpoint, explaining that many people would refrain from coming to offer their condolences as a result of it. I accepted a coffee. I calmed down a little. I watched the Maríns' mother, the poor dear was weeping incessantly, and then would suddenly burst into sobs. I got chills wondering if they'd tortured Lieutenant Alfonso as they had his brother, Víctor Manuel. I told myself probably not, everybody says the general lashes out more violently against civilians. I felt like I was drowning, as if they had just notified me that Clemen had been captured. I took out my rosary beads and began to pray, trying to chase away those dreadful thoughts. But I was unable to lessen my agitation, the pounding in my heart and temples. I was determined to finish my rosary. Then I told Doña Chayito I wasn't feeling well and would soon leave; I asked her if she would be staying at the Maríns' or if she wished us to take her someplace else. She asked me to take her to Captain Piche's house. I felt somewhat guilty saying goodbye, so few people were in attendance, and the crushing density of the sorrow was felt acutely in that almost empty room. It was dark when we went out to look for Don Leo. I prayed to God we wouldn't have any trouble getting through the checkpoint. We passed without any difficulty, I didn't even see the soldier with the sinister eyes; I felt lighter, now that I wasn't carrying that communiqué, though I knew a migraine was hovering, about to attack and lay me low at any moment. Doña Chayito gave Don Leo directions. The city felt dismal, as if the wind were fear, blowing through the streets. There were no soldiers in the area, only secret policemen snooping around. I told Don Leo I would stop in only for a moment to offer my condolences, and we would leave in less than a quarter of an hour. There were the same amount of people here as at the Gavidias'. Angelita was near the door, greeting people; she told me she had just arrived, she had heard about the checkpoint in front of the Maríns' house, and she unfortunately wouldn't be able to make it there tonight. Then with some urgency she pulled me over to a corner and asked me if I had any news about Clemen. My heart skipped a beat. "No, why, my dear?" I managed to stutter. She told me she'd just been assured that Jimmy is fine, but they didn't give her any details, and she wanted to know if I had heard anything she hadn't. I told her the men in my family and Pericles's family share the opinion that life-and-death secrets should not be shared with women, so I was totally in the dark.

I returned home even more unsettled, and still now, after writing down all the events of the day, anxiety is gnawing away inside me, as if something important were happening right next to me without my being aware of it. Fortunately, the migraine has passed. Betito was dropped off a while ago; I scolded him for having disappeared without letting me know. He told me that when he returned to the Gavidias', I was already gone, and he and his friends had some other things to do. I saw in his eyes the fervor of someone who has embarked on an adventure; I warned him to be careful. Only now do I realize, with a heavy conscience, that I haven't thought about Pericles even once all day. My poor husband.

Tuesday April 25

A ray of sunshine after the storm! They released Chente and the other medical students who were arrested last Wednesday. The government lifted the curfew; they also authorized the opening of the Club and the Casino. And an assistant to Colonel Palma, the director of the Central Prison, called when I wasn't home and left a message with María Elena to tell me to appear early tomorrow morning because visits would now be allowed to political prisoners. We were all surprised, happy. I wouldn't have believed any of it if I hadn't been at my neighbors' house celebrating with Chente. God willing they will soon free Pericles, and tomorrow I can bring everything we have packed for him: clothes, food, personal grooming items. Betito will accompany me even if it means he'll get to school late. My mother-in-law called to tell me she regretted not being able to come, her arthritis has her bent over in pain, and would I please give Pericles her blessing. Doña Chayito and the other members of the group are hopeful that our family members will be released in the next few days; we'll meet in front of the Central Prison.

I dined at my parents' house; Uncle Charlie stopped by, but he only drank whiskey. According to him, the gringos are furious about the executions, and they have made it clear to the general that they are considering sending in the military police to protect American citizens in the event of a new uprising, and it is this threat that has forced him to back down. "He isn't cowered by a threat like that," Father commented. Then he said: "That warlock must have something up his sleeve: he's loosening things up to see who will lift their heads so he can lop them off." I put in my two cents: I told them that the why and the wherefore didn't matter, the important thing was that I would be able to visit Pericles and that the students had been released. Mother mentioned that Carlota is happy the clubs are open for there will be no problem now with Luz María's wedding.

I have checked and rechecked the provisions I am taking to Pericles several times; I don't want to forget anything. These twenty days without seeing my husband seem like an eternity. I am nervous, like a girl about to see her sweetheart after a long separation. All these bad experiences I've had in the last few weeks have turned a little red light on in my head, a warning light not to get shaken too badly if things go haywire again, if the Devil starts whispering again in the warlock's ear.

Wednesday April 26

Finally, I was able to spend an entire hour with Pericles! I have no words to describe what I felt. At first, while we were being searched, and the guards were rummaging through the suitcase and the basket, I couldn't contain my excitement, as if I were a little girl about to get the toy I had always wanted, but once I was face-to-face with Pericles, I controlled myself, though I was so happy I kept wanting to jump up and throw my arms around him. The first thing he did, after we greeted each other, was look through the basket to find the cigarettes and he immediately lit one up, then he asked me to pour him a cup of coffee from the thermos. He looked over the other things; he laughed at the after-shave lotion: he said he had made his peace with smelling bad, but the problem would be to keep it away from his fellow prisoners who would want to drink it. We talked about everything; he was very happy they let Betito in. I told him I had no news about Clemen, I told him about the fright we had upon leaving church on Sunday, about Chente's arrest and subsequent release, and all the political gossip. Betito excitedly told him about the prospect of a general strike led by university students. He told us to be very careful, to remember that one should never confront "the man" head on; he said most of the prison guards treat the political prisoners well, even with respect: among the prison authorities a lot of uncertainty reigns, many are convinced that sooner or later change will come and that "the man" will end up leaving. He asked me to call Pati as soon as we got home to reassure her that he is fine so she doesn't worry. I told him I would tell his mother the same thing, the poor dear wanted to come but her arthritis was acting up. As the time passed I started to notice the toll imprisonment was taking on him, a twitch in his right eye, his cough worse than ever, his pallor. I told him I would bring some cough syrup next time I came. He chain-smoked during the whole visit; it's the first time in jail that getting cigarettes has been the biggest challenge, he said. Then he asked after Mila and the grandchildren. I hoped to sound natural when I told him they were fine in spite of her complaints about her economic difficulties; but I've never known how to lie to my husband: he threw me an inquisitorial look, turned to Betito, then grew quiet. I told him that yesterday, when I heard about the lifting of the curfew, I called the lawyer, Mr. Pineda, who told me the conditions might now be more favorable for moving his case through the courts. Pericles told me not to build up any hope, that his release will have nothing to do with any courts—it will only come when "the man" orders it or because "the man" isn't in power anymore. It took all my strength to say goodbye, and hold back the tears. As I left I tried to find Sergeant Flores to ask him when we could visit next, but on the wall in the hallway there was a sign posted that stated that we could return on Saturday morning.

Chente came over in the afternoon; I thought his time in jail would have dampened his enthusiasm, but he has again plunged head first into organizing the strike. He said his fellow prisoners have also left jail even more resolved to struggle against the tyrant. Today, he informed me, final-year students who work as interns in the hospitals, legal assistants in the courts, employees of the Ministry of Public Works, and assistants in dental clinics will all go on strike. And he explained that he is part of the group responsible for raising funds to help students who work in public sector offices who have gone on strike and who have families to support. I offered to lend him a hand in whatever way I could. Later, I went to my parents' house; I explained the situation to Father. He told me he believes it will not be difficult to find honorable men who want to contribute to the strike fund to help defeat the warlock as long as their names, of course, are never revealed.

When I arrived home, María Elena was waiting for me with the news that Mila has let Ana go and begun to pack up the house, she will turn it over to the owners next Friday so they won't charge her for an additional month, and she will move into her parents' house. I felt wretched, as if the day had suddenly been spoiled. But there is nothing I can do: that woman is driven by the red-hot sin burning between her legs and nobody can stop her. What will become of Clemen when he finds out? I told myself I must focus on the tasks at hand and the memory of my meeting with my husband to avoid having bad thoughts. Fortunately Carmela and Chelón came by for coffee a while later, to find out in detail how Pericles is, what his living conditions are; they asked me if they could come with me for a brief visit once the visits become regular, just to say hello and have the pleasure of giving him a hug, without intruding for long on our privacy. I told them they could, of course, but that I hope Pericles will be freed before they allow regular visits. Then we spoke about the strike and I showed them the leaflet Chente had given me; they had a different one, also a typed carbon copy, more or less saying the same thing, calling on everybody to stop cooperating in any way with the government, nobody should go to the movie theaters the warlock owns, or buy lottery tickets, or pay local taxes. Both leaflets call for a boycott of the government newspapers and a large show of passive resistance, but the one Chente brought me asks everybody to always wear a token of mourning as a way of showing that they condemn the executions. Chelón commented that there doesn't seem to be any sign of the government re-authorizing the publication of opposition newspapers.

A short while ago, Betito told me he believes the high schools will soon call a strike, today there was an intense discussion on the subject at his school. I warned him not to use the excuse of a strike to miss classes if other students are attending, the struggle against the general is serious and there's no excuse for taking advantage of it in order to party with his friends; I know my sons all too well.

It has been an intense and gratifying day; to be with Pericles was like a gift from heaven for which I am deeply grateful.

Thursday April 27

Once again, intimidation and violence! The general is counterattacking rather than relenting. We were about to begin the novenas of mourning for Lieutenant Marín when the National Guard troops burst into the church. Doña Chayito had summoned me to attend: she said our presence was important to show our solidarity with the family. I didn't think twice about it. But when I arrived I realized there was a big crowd, even Chente and Fabito were milling around in the atrium, so I assumed this was an act of both solidarity and denunciation. What I never thought possible was that the warlock would dare to send his troops into the church with orders to evict us. He is sacrilegious, an apostate. Fortunately, the boys saw them coming and took off in time to avoid confrontations and arrests. I am still furious. This is the last straw. Lieutenant Marín's wife and his mother are both primary school teachers, and they have decided to go on strike with the support of many of their colleagues.

The day began with excellent good news. Mingo dropped by the house to find out how Pericles is doing, and he took the opportunity to tell me that the Americans have already firmly turned their backs on the general, yesterday the ambassador rejected the government's proposal for the United States to send officers to reorganize the air force, which was virtually dismantled after the attempted coup. "Such a rejection means they've lost all trust in the government," Mingo explained to me with great excitement. I went straight to Father with the news. He told me he'd speak with Uncle Charlie to confirm. By noon everybody had heard that "the man" is being left out in the cold.

Father dropped by in the evening to give me an envelope full of money for me to give to Chente, so that the strike committee can distribute it among those who need to support their families. I was amazed, surprised by the speed with which he had collected so much money. He explained that the warlock is digging his own grave, not when he executed the officers who had betrayed him but rather when he sentenced Don Agustín, Dr. Pérez, and Dr. Romero to death. He insisted I make it very clear to the students that they will never learn the names of the donors and that there should be no receipts or any other compromising paperwork. Minutes later I went to find Chente, but he wasn't there. I put the envelope away in my trunk and went to Mass.

As we were leaving church, under the strict surveillance of the soldiers, our fear subdued by our outrage, Doña Chayito told me that the government must know by now about the campaign to support the interns who have gone on strike in the hospitals and government offices, because this morning both government newspapers carried a furious tirade against them, and she said that perhaps he ordered the Mass cancelled for the same reason, just so we wouldn't get our hopes up that his resolve was weakening. What one hand gives the other takes away, as the saying goes.

A short while ago, just as I was about to go to my bedroom and María Elena had already gone to hers, Chente came over. We discussed the warlock's wickedness, his apostasy. He asked after Betito; I told him he was out with his friends but would return at any moment. I noticed he was nervous. I told him to wait for me in the living room; I went to get the envelope full of money out of the trunk, and I gave it to him. "What's this?" he asked as he opened it with amazement. "A contribution for the students who are on strike," I said. His face lit up; he was about to count the money, but I repeated the warning Father had given me. Before leaving, he gave me a carbon copy of a new leaflet, which I have here on my desk and looks like it was just written, which asks all to "pray together for our humble, saintly, and beloved archbishop, who has been repeatedly humiliated by the tyrant, a theosophist who does not believe in God and works in devious ways to persecute the Catholic Church." Betito came home later; he claims that enthusiasm for the strike is growing everywhere. I told him I would go visit his grandmother Licha in Cojutepeque tomorrow, and I would take María Elena with me, and if he doesn't want to eat lunch alone he should go to my mother's house. I repeated that he should be very careful.

Friday April 28

I was out of San Salvador for only ten hours, but when I returned I had the feeling that much more time had passed. Betito greeted me with the news that there were practically no classes at his school because most of the professors were absent, and next week will be worse, he says, because the entire teachers' union will be on strike. Then I found out, at Raúl's house, that Dr. Romero is recovering and, if nothing changes, in one week they'll release him from the hospital and the general plans to execute him immediately; Raúl said with absolute conviction that the Salvadoran Medical Association will do everything possible to prevent his execution. Events are hurtling forward: the students have formed committees to persuade diverse sectors to support the strike, and people seem to be slowly losing their fear, so much so that Mother told me that some of her friends are considering closing their shops starting next week and keeping them closed until the warlock is gone. The government is pulling out all the stops: Betito brought home a leaflet from a pretend committee that supports the government, saying the strike is being promoted by the wealthy who are outraged that the general has taken measures that benefit the poor. He is not only criminal but also shameless.

And there I was, as if coming from another world, because I love traveling by train; as soon as the engine whistles and the cars begin to clatter along the tracks, I get swept away into memories of my youth and adolescence, a sensation of idleness washes over me, as if the landscape rushing by were lifting me out of reality. I was also coming from a different world because my mother-in-law lives in her memories, talking to her is like climbing into an old attic, or rather, opening a chest full of stories; she always pulls out a couple of new anecdotes about Pericles, curious stories about his childhood and adolescence. I greatly enjoyed my visit to the market with María Elena and Petronila, my in-laws' old servant, to buy *chorizos, cuajada,* and *pepitoria*. The only thing I don't like is eating lunch with the colonel: the atmosphere is so silent, martial, like being in a mess hall with a commander who doesn't allow talking at mealtime; that's where Pericles gets all his manias. I noticed that in that city, merely one hour away from San Salvador by train, one doesn't feel any of the political agitation we experience here, as if the struggle to depose the general had nothing to do with them. Only when I spoke with Father Dionisio, the parish priest of Nuestra Señora del Carmen Church, who dropped by in the afternoon to have a cup of coffee with my mother-in-law, did I feel the excitement of the political situation. Father Dionisio asked about Clemen, whom he has known since he was a child; I told him I had no news. He crossed himself and muttered that he prays daily for the Lord to keep him safe and sound; he looked at me out of the corner of his eye. My mother-in-law gave me a basket of food for me to take to Pericles tomorrow. The poor dear was sitting down most of the time because of her arthritis; it was difficult for her to even take a few steps.

What really soured my mood upon my return, however, was to find two suitcases and a few boxes of Clemen's belongings, which Mila, taking advantage of my absence, had brought over in the afternoon, and which Betito had moved into what had been Pati's bedroom, which I now use as a sewing room. Tomorrow I will have to tell Pericles all about this, I wouldn't want him to be released one of these days soon and have his return spoiled by his sudden discovery of Mila's betrayal; better for him to know now, for he has said himself that in jail all other problems seem "like when you take off your glasses and everything shrinks." Ana spent the night in María Elena's room, for Mila has already moved out, and she wouldn't let her come stay at her parents', so she just threw her out in the street; they will both leave tomorrow early for their village. I have prepared some gifts for Belka.

Saturday April 29

They might release Pericles at any moment. God heard my prayers! Betito and I went this morning early to the Central Prison; there was a throng of visitors because it was also visiting day for common criminals. I don't know if it was just my impression, because I am very susceptible to suggestion, but there was something different in the air, as if people were feeling more optimistic, less afraid. Doña Chayito said we should talk afterward, many things are happening and she wanted to bring me up-to-date. Carmela and Chelón joined us in the line going in. Pericles was very happy to see them. Then Mingo arrived, and my brother-in-law, Toño, who came from Cojutepeque. It was the first visit like in the old days, when my husband used to be held in the Black Palace, in a room near the director. We drank coffee and ate sweet breads (everybody brought food for Pericles), we gossiped, we laughed at the latest jokes about the general and Doña Concha. My husband said that by the time he gets out of jail he'll have enough jokes and salacious stories to fill a book. Carmela and Chelón were the first to leave; then Toño and Mingo said they also had to go, but Pericles told the latter to stay with me for a few minutes because he wanted to discuss something. Betito said goodbye to his father and said he'd wait for me outside, using as an excuse that we were going to discuss issues he had no business hearing, as if I hadn't noticed his interest in Leonor, Doña Julita's daughter, while we were lining up to go in. Pericles revealed that Dr. Ávila had visited him yesterday afternoon, Friday, to make him a proposition: they will release him if he goes straight to Mexico and establishes contact between "the man" and Don Vicente Lombardo Toledano, the most influential workers' leader in the Mexican government, a man Pericles befriended during our years in exile. Dr. Ávila specified that this was just to test the waters, an initiative of his ministry, but now that the general is interested in promoting social programs to improve the lives of the poor, he may well be receptive to considering an initiative that would establish a closer relationship with the experience of the Mexican revolution, and Pericles would be the right person to do it. "What did you say?" Mingo asked him, looking quite surprised. "I said I have no desire to go from being a prisoner to being a messenger boy in exile, that if they wish to establish contact with Vicente, they have an ambassador, and that's what he gets paid for," he said. He then made it clear to Dr. Ávila that they should free him immediately, for there has been no crime and no trial, only an arbitrary arrest, and that once he returns to being an ordinary citizen, with rights and legal guarantees, he would be willing to listen, in the living room of his own home, to the government's social plans and any reasonable request they make of him. "What did he say?" I asked, because Don Ramón is quite sensible and I know he is fond of us. "What could he say, he doesn't make the decisions . . . ?" he answered in that typically derisive tone he uses when his meaner self overrides his intelligence. But I am hopeful that Dr. Ávila's gesture is a sign that my husband will soon return home. What leaves no room for doubt, Pericles added, "is that they're up to their eyes in you-know-what now that the gringos have thrown them overboard," and for the first time he has the impression that "the man" is going down a blind alley. Mingo was perplexed by the news; he muttered that not only was he being abandoned by the gringos, but he also had all the bankers and coffee growers against him, the students and teachers were on strike, and the medical society would be applying strong pressure starting next Tuesday for him to decree an amnesty to prevent the execution of Dr. Romero. Pericles asked after Don Jorge's health. Mingo said he was with him yesterday at the Polyclinic, Don Jorge is out of mortal danger, but nobody knows for certain how fully he will recover; then he looked at his watch, he said time was flying, there were only ten minutes left to visit, he would leave us alone and wait for me outside so he could accompany me home. I told him not to worry, I had already arranged to meet some friends on my way out. Then I mustered my courage and without any preambles I told Pericles, in a very low voice, that Mila had moved out of her house and intends to divorce Clemen and is the lover of Colonel Castillo, the prosecutor of the Military Court that sentenced my son to death. While I was tripping over my tongue trying to tell the story, I felt terribly anxious, as if I were to blame for what had happened, but once I'd finished, as Pericles screwed his face into a look of disgust, I suddenly felt lighter, as if a heavy burden had been lifted. I told him I thought it better that he knew now so as to avoid spoiling his return home. He asked after our grandchildren; he asked if Pati, the colonel, or Mama Licha knew. Then, chewing on his words as if he were going to spit them out, he simply said, "Every cloud has a silver lining." As we said goodbye I had this feeling I still carry with me, that we would soon be together again.

By the time I left, Betito had already hightailed it out of there, surely in hot pursuit of Leonor. I walked a couple of blocks with Doña Chayito; the sky was cloudy and for a moment there was a light breeze, which made me think we would soon get the first rain of the season, and we did, a few hours later. Doña Chayito told me that the struggle to free our family members had taken second place, and we must now put all our efforts into supporting the general strike called by the university students, we must convince our friends and acquaintances to join the strike, close shops and offices so that the country would cease to function as soon as possible and so the warlock will be forced to leave. I told her to count on me for anything I can do to help. She explained that it would be best for me to take advantage of my relationship with Chente, for the students are taking the lead and it is no longer an issue of protesting in the streets but rather turning the city into a ghost town, everyone should remain at home and then only policemen and soldiers will be left in the streets, wandering about like lost souls.

Lunch at my parents' was hectic. Uncle Charlie and some of Father's friends discussed the negotiations they were holding with the chambers of commerce and the business owners' associations to get them to keep paying their employees even though their places of business remain closed. Monday is May 1, anyway, a holiday, so the strike will begin on Tuesday, with the bankers taking the lead in the private sector. I confessed to Father that I feel quite lost in the maelstrom that has been unleashed. He told me not to worry, I can continue participating as I have been, passing funds to the student committee so they can distribute them to bus drivers, taxi drivers, government employees, train operators, and others, so they can buy food and survive day to day for as long as the strike lasts. As I was leaving my parents', I crossed paths with Juan White, together with Mono Harris and Winall Dalton, who were stopping by for a visit, rather tipsy for so early in the day. Winall is always quite flirtatious with me, though respectful, and he always seems like a gentleman to me, though Pericles says he is nothing but a "lecherous gringo" around whom I should never lower my guard.

This afternoon, after visiting Don Jorge and Teresita at the Polyclinic, I stopped by my neighbors, where they were celebrating Rosita's birthday, though the party was actually just a front for the doctors to meet to plan next week's strike. Raúl told me that I shouldn't worry, the warlock will fall before we know it, and we would have Pericles and Clemen with us again. Chente dropped by, as usual in a rush, and he whispered to me that pharmacists, justices of the peace, and even market vendors are poised to go on strike, and that they will need more cash support from the well-to-do. The excitement was so contagious that even I had a drink.

Now I am home alone. Betito went to a big party at the Club, the first since the government authorized it to open. I told myself this has to work, "the man" can't possibly face everybody down if nobody is standing in front of him; I also told myself that the coming days are going to be hectic, even though there won't be any protests in the street, and we'll have to keep our noses to the grindstone to achieve a total moratorium. My only regret is that this is the last page of my beautiful notebook from Brussels. On Tuesday I'll buy another one before the shops close for the strike.

Fugitives (IV)

1:08 p.m.

"It's hellfire out there, Clemen."

"What?"

"It's hellfire ... Look: nothing moves under this sun shining straight down like a lead weight. This is what Hell must be like. Luckily, we're in the shade of the mangroves ..."

"I'm thirsty."

"Again?"

"Uh-huh."

"Try to get a grip on your anxiety. You just drank some water. If you don't control yourself, you'll finish the little we have left."

"What'll we do when we run out of water, Jimmy? How are we going to get out of this swamp?"

"Calm down. Stop thinking about it."

"How can I stop thinking about it!? We're getting dehydrated! Look at how dry my lips are!"

"If you get all excited you'll use up more energy and get thirstier. Just relax."

"Something must have happened to Mono Harris! Why hasn't he come, Jimmy? He said he'd be in San Salvador for only three days and return yesterday, Saturday, bringing water and more provisions. Now it's Sunday noon, and we're running out of everything . . ."

"There was probably some emergency. But he won't abandon us. He'll be here any minute . . ."

"What if they captured him, huh? What if that soldier got suspicious, and they've got him locked up in a cell somewhere? What will become of us?"

"They wouldn't dare arrest Mono Harris. He's an American citizen. Anyway, he's done nothing, except help us."

"You think that's nothing!? . . . What if one of the oarsmen turned him in?"

"The soldiers would have already shown up here."

"We've got to get to dry land, Jimmy. We can't just wait here till we die of dehydration."

"Let's wait till tomorrow morning early. If Mono Harris hasn't shown up by then, we'll figure out how to get to land."

"I don't think our water will last till tomorrow."

"If you calm down and stop drinking every time you get anxious, it will."

"It's got nothing to do with anxiety. You yourself said it's like Hell out here. How am I supposed to not be thirsty!? . . ."

"You're too agitated. You're drinking almost twice as much water as me. Don't you realize that?"

"'You're too agitated! . . .' How the hell am I supposed to not be?! I'm going crazy in this boat! This is worse than the attic! At least there, at the priest's house, we could go down to the living room and the toilet twice a day . . . This is horrible, Jimmy! Ten days stuck in this boat eight feet long, surrounded by salt water, sleeping outside under the worst possible conditions, trying to protect ourselves from all the bugs, pissing and shitting outside, like animals! . . . It's worse than being in prison!"

"Nothing's worse than being in prison. Don't forget we wouldn't be in prison long, soon enough they'd take us out to face the firing squad … like they did my comrades, and Lieutenant Marín's civilian brother …"

"…"

"So, settle down."

"Poor man. You military men are savages, Jimmy. Mono Harris said that Marín was unrecognizable from the torture."

"The torturers are civilian, not military."

"Don't give me that shit. If they're civilians it's because you guys have taught them how to torture people …"

"I don't understand your obsession with the military. What about your grandfather, isn't he in the military? and your father, wasn't he in the military before he became a political journalist … ?"

"So what? My father now renounces you …"

"Who saved you, Clemen? Who pulled the chestnuts out of the fire for you when you got in over your head? Your grandfather, right? If it hadn't been for him, neither you nor I would be here, we'd probably already have been shot …"

"My grandfather helped me because he is my grandfather. Grandfathers help their grandchildren. It would be unthinkable for him to behave any other way … What do you think happened to Don Arturo?"

"The last thing Mono Harris told us is that he was wounded and in the hospital in San Miguel."

"I know that already. You don't have to repeat it to me. What I want to know is if your motherfucking general has shot him."

"God help us."

"It's fucked up to be incommunicado, have no way of finding out what's going on. At Don Mincho's house on the island we could listen to the radio. We've been rotting here in this swamp for ten days with no contact with the outside world except through Mono Harris. And now the sonofabitch has disappeared. I can't take it anymore!"

"Well, you don't have much choice. And stop crying, it doesn't do any good!"

"I'm not crying!"

"Sounds like it to me."

"Don't go acting all brave, Jimmy. It doesn't suit you."

"We need mental discipline to survive. Spending your time complaining only makes us weaker."

"We're already weak. If you could see yourself in the mirror you'd feel real sorry for yourself. You look like a scarecrow ..."

"And you, with your hysteria ..."

"*Hysteria*? Only you could think up such a degrading word, Jimmy ... Hysteria ... A cigarette is what I need. I haven't had a smoke in more than twelve hours. You think that's nothing? Last night, before I fell asleep, I smoked my last one. Twelve hours without a cigarette!"

"Because you're desperate, and anxious. I warned you to smoke less, I told you something unexpected could happen. Like now, again, I'm warning you not to drink so much water, because the water is for both of us, not just you. You could do what you wanted with your cigarettes, but you're going to have to be more disciplined with the water, you have to respect that it's both of ours."

"What if Mono Harris doesn't show up today or tomorrow morning? By noon we'll be without a drop, we'll be more desperate, more hungry and thirsty, we've only got two tins of sardines and those hard-boiled eggs. Why not leave right now?"

"Because Mono Harris will come, and then he won't find us, and we'll lose touch with him. How many times do I have to tell you ..."

"What if he never shows up? What'll we do then?"

"I told you: we'll try to get to San Nicolás. It won't be that difficult. But we run the risk of coming across a National Guard patrol."

"You sure you know how to get out of this labyrinth of swamps and canals? Mono Harris said this is one of the most remote canals, the most difficult to find among the mangroves, that's why he brought us here. Which direction is San Nicolás, Jimmy? Tell me!"

"Over there, where we came from ..."

"You don't know anything! You don't have the least fucking idea! We came from the other direction. I remember perfectly."

"I'm not going to argue with you, Clemen. Here, the one who has the training to survive and find his way is me. You're just a poor slob.

That's why, when we start for San Nicolás, you're going to follow my instructions ... Is that clear?"

"If you suck my dick ..."

5:13 p.m.

"Whoever understands you can have you for free, Jimmy. According to you we were supposed to conserve our energy so we don't die of hunger and thirst, so why in the world are you swimming?"

"I need to freshen up. I'm not swimming; I'm floating."

"Same thing."

"Not the same thing."

"It'll take a water snake or manta ray scaring you to set you straight ..."

"Don't be such a chickenshit, Clemen. I have the feeling you don't know how to swim, that's why you're so afraid of the water."

"I'm not afraid of the water; I'm afraid of creatures."

"I don't believe you ... Ever since we got on the canoe you've been shitting your pants ..."

"A while ago, while you were napping, you muttered the name Faustino Sosa several times ..."

"Really? The major?"

"Uh-huh."

"I must've been dreaming about him. But I don't remember ..."

"You've got a guilty conscience, don't you, you asshole?"

"Take a dip, Clemen, instead of talking nonsense."

"You sent him to his death and now you feel guilty."

"I didn't send him to his death. I already explained it to you several times."

"So why were you dreaming about him?"

"Nobody knows why we dream what we dream ..."

"You don't fool me."

"I've got no desire to fool you or justify myself to you ... The water is delicious. This is the best time of day to freshen up. But it's time for me to get out now."

"It's going to get dark soon and Mono Harris hasn't come ..."

"I know."

"And we're running out of drinking water …"

"Move over, Clemen, I want to get back in the boat."

"All we've got left is this one tin of sardines … Nothing for breakfast tomorrow."

"What about the hard-boiled eggs?"

"There was one left. I ate it while you were taking a nap. My guts were churning."

"You're a disgrace! So I get one sardine more than you."

"Don't mess with me, Jimmy. We'll go halves …"

"One extra sardine for me to make up for the egg."

"What we should do is get the hell out of this swamp and find a shack where we can get some food and water …"

"We agreed to wait till tomorrow morning."

"I won't be able to sleep thinking about waking up without food or water."

"Don't be a fool. You're better off sleeping. Your anxiety will only make you more thirsty and hungry."

"Let's get out of here now, Jimmy, before it gets dark! I'm really getting desperate … It's useless to wait if Mono Harris isn't coming. Tomorrow will only be worse: by then we'll be dying of hunger and thirst!"

"If we leave now, it'll get dark when we're halfway there, we'll have to light the lamp, and we'll be an easy target for the soldiers. I've explained it all to you. We'll leave at the first light of dawn."

"The soldiers aren't going to be riding around at night through these canals."

"Oh, yeah? What about the boat that passed right by us the first night we were here?"

"Those weren't soldiers …"

"We're not going to discuss this again, Clemen."

"Let's eat the sardines, then."

"We're going to wait a few hours."

"Why? I'm hungry now. It's already getting dark. It's dinner time. I'm going to open the tin …"

"No. We'll open it in a few hours so we won't be so hungry in the morning."

"Give me that tin, Jimmy!"

"I said no ... Don't be an ass."

"You're the ass! Give me that tin! There are four sardines, two each."

"I'm not giving you the tin and there aren't two each. There are three for me and one for you. Stop fucking ..."

"God damn sonofabitch!"

"It won't do you any good to insult me."

"Okay, so I'll take a sip of water. I've got this burning in the pit of my stomach. I need to drink something ..."

"You're not going to finish the water, either ..."

"Fuck you, Jimmy! Give me that water!"

"Calm down! We have to ration the water even more, otherwise we'll be so weak from thirst we won't be able to do anything."

"Give me the damn water, asshole!"

"Stop shouting like a madman! And calm down unless you want me to break your neck!"

"What, you think I've got my hands tied behind my back?! Give me the water and the sardines!"

"Calm down! You're going to capsize the boat!"

"Give them to me, you motherfucker!"

"Let go! If you so much as touch me I'll smash you one, Clemen!"

"Don't you push me, you piece of shit!"

"Let go of me!"

"Give 'em to me!"

"Oh no, we're capsizing!"

7:50 p.m.

"You see, there's enough moonlight for us to navigate. We can still leave, Jimmy ..."

"I told you not to talk to me. I don't want to know you're here."

"There's no reasoning with you."

"Shut up!"

"We still have one oar ..."

"Shut your damn trap ..."

"We can go near the hamlet and look for the guide's house, or one of the oarsmen. I'm sure they'll give us water and food ..."

"Do you not understand? Silence!"

"The more time passes, the more desperate we get ..."

"If you weren't my cousin, I would have already drowned you ..."

"You would be capable of killing me, Jimmy?"

"I'm never going to forgive you ... Because of you I lost my gun."

"It wasn't only my fault, we both ..."

"You are a total moron."

"It wasn't your gun, anyway, it was Mono Harris's ... And it's right there, in the water, nobody's going to get it. Mono Harris can come back with some fishermen and bring it up in a net."

"Don't start again, Clemen, this time I'm not going to be able to control myself, and you're going to end up getting very badly hurt ..."

"There you are, worried about the gun ... The worst thing is that we lost our drinking water and the sardines."

"It's your fault we have no way to defend ourselves and nothing to eat or drink. It's also your fault we lost the lamp and the other oar ... You've worn out my patience."

"If you don't want to row, I could start rowing with this."

"You're completely useless. You don't know how to row. You don't know how to do anything. You don't deserve to live. Any one of my comrades shot by the firing squad is worth a hundred of you ..."

"You're just cross ..."

"How could I not be?"

"It doesn't do any good to be angry."

"Shut your big fat mouth!"

"What are you doing, Jimmy?"

"I'm starting to row, can't you see?"

"We're going to San Nicolás then? How great, you finally decided! Bravo!"

"Don't get your hopes up ..."

"What are you doing? Why are you going deeper into the swamp? It's dangerous, Jimmy! It's totally dark!"

"Here's the mangrove I was looking for ..."

"What for? What are you doing?"

"Me, nothing ... You see that thick branch on your right?"

"Uh-huh ..."

"Climb onto it!"

"You're crazy!"

"Climb onto that branch right now, or I'll bash your head in with this oar!"

"You've gone mad, Jimmy! Calm down!"

"Climb onto the fucking branch, you bastard!

"You're hitting me, Jimmy!?"

"I'm going to smash you to pieces, you sonofabitch, climb onto it now!"

"Why do you want me to climb onto it?!"

"Now!"

"Stop hitting me, you crazy bastard!"

"That's it! Good! Up a tree, you bastard!

"You've gone crazy ..."

"You are going to stay right there ..."

"What are you saying?! Have you lost your mind?!"

"There, now you won't bother anybody."

"Come back, Jimmy! Don't leave me here!"

"I'll come back tomorrow with Mono Harris to get you ..."

"Jimmy! Don't be so mean! Come back! I beg you! Jimmy ... !"

6:15 a.m.

"All these canals look alike ..."

"Jimmy, are you sure we're going in the right direction?"

"I hope so. We've got to take advantage of this early morning light."

"We've been going around in circles for half an hour, and I don't see we've gotten anywhere. Just more mangroves ..."

"That's what I said, they all look alike."

"I remember when Mono Harris brought us here from near San Nicolás, it took about twenty minutes."

"Because the motorboat was towing the canoe."

"You're right..."

"That's why I think we'll get out of this bay soon."

"I hope, because the sun is rising... My mouth is dry."

"Mine is, too. And rowing is making me even thirstier."

"You want me to help row?"

"No. We'll be out of here in no time..."

"Listen to my guts churning from hunger."

"Must be here to the right..."

"Everything looks the same to me, Jimmy. How will Mono Harris find his way?"

"He said he knows it by heart, and if he didn't he'd get lost, he said even some fishermen prefer not go into these swamps because they're afraid of getting lost, they say they're haunted..."

"I thought he was just boasting to scare us."

"Now this way..."

"I don't see any way out, Jimmy. It all looks the same. Mangroves and more mangroves."

"I'm even starting to worry now."

"We should have made some exploratory outings a few days ago."

"Mono Harris warned us not to budge from that canal or we'd get hopelessly lost. That's why we didn't."

"Isn't this the canal we were in for ten days?"

"What are you talking about..."

"I'm sure it is, Jimmy!"

"You're kidding. It can't be..."

"Bring us around to this side!"

"It looks different to me."

"Because the tide has risen... Come up close... That's the tree you left me on!"

"How do you recognize it?"

"Because you left me there for more than an hour, you bastard... The worst hour of my life."

"But it was night, it was dark, how can you possibly recognize it now?"

"Here, underneath, look, level with the water ..."

"I think you're wrong."

"No. I pulled off those twigs and shoots so I could lean against the trunk!"

"I don't see anything ..."

"Right here: look carefully! That part's underwater now! This is the mangrove! We've gone in a circle, Jimmy! We're right back where we started!"

"It can't be!"

"But it is! What are we going to do now?"

"We're going to try again."

"We're lost! We're in a labyrinth!"

"It's okay, we'll get out of here ..."

"How?!"

"You row now ... Maybe that's why I got lost ... I was rowing so I wasn't paying enough attention."

"Let me sit there ... Give me the oar."

"Don't capsize us, Clemen, or we'll really be lost ..."

"Not a chance in the world."

"With you rowing, I'll be able to focus better, try to remember how we got here with Mono Harris ... Go this way ..."

"Okay. How do you change direction?"

"You move the oar that way ... That's right ..."

"It's hard."

"Come on."

"..."

"..."

"My hands are burning, Jimmy. I'm going to get blisters."

"You really are useless."

"I don't see that we're getting anywhere."

"Let me row ... My turn ..."

"Now what?"

"We keep trying. We've got no choice."

"I'm dying of thirst, Jimmy ..."

"Try not to think about it ..."

"How can I not think about being thirsty?! My throat is so dry. The sun is already up. If we don't get out of this labyrinth soon, we're going to die of sunstroke and dehydration!"

"Don't say that."

"But it's the truth!"

"I'm also extremely thirsty. Let's rest for a while in the shade. The worst thing is for us to get desperate."

"All these mangrove trees look alike."

"They look alike to us, but they aren't all alike."

"I hate being here! This is like a nightmare, Jimmy!"

"It is a nightmare."

"We have such bad luck!"

"I wish we could wake up ..."

"We've been wandering around now for about two hours in these canals and we haven't seen a trace of a fisherman. Nothing, zilch ..."

"We can't lose faith."

"There's not even a current, look ... The boat barely sways."

"Maybe the tide is changing, maybe it's peaked and soon it will start going down."

"We're worse off than we were before, Jimmy: even if we do manage to get out of the swamp, we won't be where Mono Harris will look for us when he gets back!"

"I know. You don't have to shout at me!"

"I'm not shouting!"

"You're letting despair get the better of you, Clemen ... Calm down."

"We managed to escape from that motherfucking general of yours just to come here and die like this! I can't believe it!"

"Calm down, already! If you get desperate and keep shouting, you're going to get even thirstier ... At least we're out of the sun here ..."

"We should try to go back to the canal where we were, Jimmy, where Mono Harris left us ..."

"Right now we need to conserve our energy. Not start rowing like crazy."

"You think Mono Harris will come?"

"He's got a motor on his boat. We'll hear him if he comes anywhere near."

"You're right."

"And if he doesn't find us in the canal, he'll look everywhere in the swamp for us."

"God willing."

9:12 a.m.

"Hey, Jimmy!"

"What? What happened?"

"We fell asleep."

"We did."

"How long has it been, you think?"

"Let's see . . ."

"The sun is pretty high."

"It's about ten."

"I think it's past eleven, Jimmy. I'm so hot."

"No, it's not that late."

"Damn, this thirst is unbearable!"

"Look where we are . . . The current has carried us, Clemen."

"That's why I woke up, the sun was blasting me in the face."

"Are we in the same canal?"

"I see the same mangroves everywhere . . ."

"I'll row into the shade . . ."

"I feel kind of dizzy, Jimmy."

"It's the sun. It was more on you than me. Good thing you woke up. Otherwise, you'd have gotten sunstroke."

"The water is twinkling."

"We're in the shade now. You'll feel better here."

"Where are we?"

"I have the feeling there's a way out of this swamp close by, just around the corner, but we've just had bad luck."

"I need some water, Jimmy. Really. I'm feeling terrible ..."

"I'm going to try once more ..."

"What?"

"To find a way out ..."

"You've still got energy to row? ... I can't."

"We've got to make the effort ... Anyway, we should take advantage of the current. It'll have to carry us out to sea ..."

"Let's stay under the trees, Jimmy, out of the sun."

"It's impossible. Look ... Some are too low, the branches touch the water ... We'll have to go down the middle of the canal."

"Shh ..."

"What?"

"You hear?"

"What?"

"Stop rowing and be quiet ..."

"..."

"It's a buzzing, Jimmy! It's a motorboat!"

"I don't hear anything ..."

"Yes! I hear it perfectly!"

"You're hallucinating, Clemen ..."

"No, I'm not hallucinating! ... Listen! ... It's a motor! ... It's Mono Harris! ..."

"Where?"

"Over there! It's getting closer!"

"You're right! I hear it now!"

"Row that way, Jimmy, so he doesn't miss us! ... It's Mono Harris! We're saved!"

"I hear it on the other side! ..."

"Don't be a fool! It's over there, Jimmy! Row over there!"

Haydée's Diary

Tuesday May 2

Two nights without writing and so much to tell. Yesterday, the government issued an arrest warrant for Chente and some other university students; fortunately, they were forewarned and there were no arrests. They are in hiding; according to Raúl, only the leaders of the Student Strike Committee know their whereabouts. He also explained that the general made the announcement in order to intimidate anybody who might want to commemorate the one-month anniversary of the armed uprising. Raúl is deeply committed to the medical society strike. This afternoon he attended a meeting of doctors called by the director of Rosales Hospital at which they drafted a resolution calling on the government to commute all death sentences and decree a general amnesty for political prisoners. Raúl says the doctors are united and determined, and if the general fails to respond they will halt medical services in San Salvador and will not allow the warlock to execute Dr. Romero. I asked him if this measure would also affect the Polyclinic, or only the public hospitals, and what would happen in cases such as Don Jorge's; he told me the strike would be general, but that patients in intensive care units would continue to receive medical attention. Poor Rosita is beside herself: again and again she asks herself what she did wrong that her son and her husband make her suffer so, as if it were their fault and not the warlock's. I've tried to reason with her, explain that each of them is acting in accordance with the dictates of his own conscience, that now is the moment for us all to take risks to force that cruel man to leave the country and let us live in peace.

A whole detachment of policemen is in front of our house keeping surveillance on us. I fear they will arrest Betito; I've asked him to be very careful. Mother has suggested he stay at their house until the situation returns to normal; Betito has said he doesn't want to leave me alone. Don Leo came by with the car this morning to drive him to school and brought him back in the afternoon, along with the news that as of tomorrow classes are cancelled until further notice. Betito said he and his classmates will spend all their time working to support the strike; there's nothing I can do to stop him. Last night I realized that Chente's disappearance has left me without a direct link to the university movement, and that it's imperative I find a way to safely funnel the funds Father collects to the strikers. Raúl told me he would communicate my concern to the students so they can designate someone. I called Doña Chayito but didn't find her. This morning I went to the Figueroas'; Fabito doesn't appear on the list of students on the arrest order, and I thought I might find him at home. No luck. Carlota promised me she would tell her son I was looking for him, though she warned me that sometimes Fabito doesn't even come home to sleep, he is always running around, working on organizing the strike. I was surprised that Carlota as well as Luz María are now quite receptive to the struggle against the general, the latter even admitting to me that she and her friends are forming a group to visit their friends and persuade them to close their shops when the strike is called. Carlota assured me her husband also supports the ultimatum the medical society gave the general, and he will do everything possible to stop the general from executing Dr. Romero, her gynecologist.

I told my parents about Dr. Ávila's offer to Pericles. Father said my husband did the right thing to refuse; Mother called Doña Tina yesterday to wheedle information out of her, but she didn't seem to know anything about it. I haven't wanted to get involved because Pericles would never forgive me, though I've been chomping at the bit to call Don Ramón. My visiting day at the Central Prison is supposed to be Saturday; I have tried and failed to get in touch with Colonel Palma to get him to authorize a visit before then, that way I can find out if any other member of the government had gotten in touch with my husband or if Dr. Ávila has returned. I would like to discuss with my in-laws the offer he made to Pericles, but I would have to go all the way to Cojutepeque—it's too dangerous to talk about it over the phone.

This afternoon I stopped by Hispania stationers to look for a beautiful notebook, one similar to my diary from Brussels, but I had no luck: there were several for schoolchildren, not convenient to write in. I asked Don Sebastián if by chance he had any notebooks in his storeroom; he said everything he had was on display. He asked after Pericles, his favorite client, as he calls him, because my husband is a fanatic about paper, pens, and ink; I told him about my visits to the Central Prison, about how arbitrary the authorities are acting, about my despair and my hope. Then I asked him what he thought about the strike as a way of forcing the general to step down, if he will support the effort and close his shop. He answered that he fears reprisals from the government, but if all the shops on the block close, he will also, and he'll join the strike. I bought this notebook, the one I'm writing in now, which is fairly ordinary, on the condition that in his next order he get me a diary as lovely as the one I bought in Brussels.

Don Sebastián's stationers is located on the same block as the Estradas' notions store. I took the opportunity to go and talk to Carolina. She told me the same thing as her neighbor: she would close her shop if the others did, because if everyone doesn't do it at the same time it will get them in trouble with the general and they'll lose money, all for nothing. She's right. I decided to tell her that the students have probably already decided on the date to start the strike, and that hopefully they will let us know soon. I took Don Sergio's taxi at the Plaza Morazán; I asked him his opinion about the strike, but that man is as silent as a tomb, the very soul of discretion.

I went to my parents' house after dinner. I asked Father about the strike date. He told me the students had wanted businesses to start shutting down yesterday, but business owners have asked for a little more time to prepare, so most likely the work stoppage will begin on Friday, though meetings are still being held with representatives of the associations and the guilds, especially with small businessmen, who are the most cautious, and among them, the Chinese and the Turks, who are afraid the general will throw them out of the country. The signal of the beginning of the strike will be the closing of the banks, Father said, and the biggest challenge will be to paralyze all public transportation, bring all trains, streetcars, buses, and taxis to a standstill. I told him that because of the warrant for Chente's arrest, I have been left with no contact in the student movement, so I have no way to collaborate or get them funds, should the need arise. Father told me not to worry, the shop owners and the students are well connected, and I needn't take risks, I should focus on convincing all my acquaintances to close their shops when the moment arrives; then he went to meet with his friends. I stayed a while longer talking with Mother, who told me how outraged she was yesterday, on the road to Santa Tecla, when she saw Mila riding in a car driven by a man she thought must be that Colonel Castillo. I frowned, but said nothing. I have no reason to allow my life to be embittered by that woman any longer. If the strike is successful, and the warlock and his minions are forced to leave, I will be satisfied—if and only if, of course, nothing happens to Clemens and Pericles.

As I write, a little before eleven at night, I wait for Betito, with fear and uneasiness, for although the curfew has been lifted, policemen and soldiers are swarming in the streets. I will scold him, for his own good, because under these circumstances, at his age and with his enthusiasm, if I give him an inch he will take a mile.

Wednesday May 3

Events are hurtling forward. A few minutes ago I got back from the Alvarados'. Raúl was in the living room with two other doctors; they were drinking whiskey and talking, fiercely indignant. I recognized Dr. Salazar. The other was Dr. Luis Macías, until a few hours ago the director of Rosales Hospital and the head of the delegation that met with the general this afternoon to give him the memorandum demanding he rescind the death sentences and declare a general amnesty. Poor Dr. Macías was quite upset: he was going from the fiercest indignation to terrible shame, from nervous laughter to horror, with astounding ease. He told me what happened at the Presidential Palace: the warlock made them wait for an hour, then he received them, coldly, in his office, told them to remain standing and silent; he took from his desk drawer the memorandum they had given a few minutes earlier to his private secretary and, without uttering a word, picked it up gingerly as if it were filthy, lit a match to it, and threw it on the ground in front of them. "Treason, gentlemen, does not go unpunished in this country," he said in a threatening voice. "Cowards cannot set conditions for my government, and if you fail to carry out your oaths as doctors, you will pay the price," he warned them before ordering them to leave and without letting them utter a single word. By the time they got outside, they were trembling, one was on the verge of passing out, and Dr. Macías decided to resign immediately his position as director of the hospital, because after the humiliation he had suffered at the hands of the warlock, he doesn't feel worthy of leading the doctors in the strike that will be declared any minute now. Raúl and Dr. Salazar insisted he shouldn't resign, but I understand his reasons, and his actions seem courageous to me, which is what I told him.

The whole day has been hectic, starting early this morning. While I was eating breakfast I suddenly remembered that tomorrow is Carmela's birthday; with all my running around I'd completely forgotten. Neither Carmela nor Chelón likes parties, they prefer to celebrate their birthdays privately, have a simple meal, but Pericles and I always arrive in the evening with a cake and a gift. I went to the

Bonets' patisserie to order a special chocolate cake with walnuts. Montse waited on me; she told me to come pick it up in the afternoon because she'd heard that the strike will start tomorrow or Friday, and they are not going to open the patisserie. Then I went quickly to La Dalia department store: I bought a lovely brocaded handkerchief for Carmela; Don Pedro told me he's heard rumors that the warlock plans to execute Dr. Romero on Friday at dawn, he said he will close his store starting tomorrow, it simply isn't possible to allow that evil man to continue to execute decent people whenever he feels like it. When I returned home, I quickly called the beauty salon; I don't want to look like a fright for Carmela's birthday or for my visit to Pericles. Silvia said she'll be open tomorrow, and she'll expect me in the morning.

Luz María left a message for me with María Elena: I should stop by her house at two for a cup of coffee so she could show me some sample wedding invitations. I guessed this was about Fabito, because the invitations are already finished. I was right: I talked to Fabito for five minutes because he was in a rush. He told me I should give any funds I collect for the strike to Luz María, she is the safest channel and will always know how to get in touch with him. I asked him about Chente; he told me he is fine, but he couldn't give me any details. And as to the date the strike would begin, he emphasized that the time had come, there was no reason to wait any longer, they (the students) have already been on strike for a week, and the goal is to create a snowball effect. Then he left. Luz María, who was never the sharpest knife in the drawer, asked what he meant by "a snowball effect"; then she told me—after warning me it was a secret I shouldn't repeat to anybody—that Fabito is the treasurer of the Student Strike Committee and, according to him, financial support is flowing in generously from all sides.

Doña Chayito came over before dinner with the news that the movie theater employees have already gone out on strike, and they will be closed as of today; she gave me a copy of the communiqué with this announcement and demands for the government to declare a general amnesty. Most of these theaters belong to the general and his family; it will undoubtedly be particularly hurtful that his own employees have been the first to go on strike. Doña Chayito was, as always, her energetic self and expressed confidence that the strike will force the warlock to step down and then our family members will be set free. She expressed regret, however, that the movie houses were closing because—she spoke in an undertone and gave me a wink—sensitive meetings were held in those dark theaters. According to her, the general strike will start tomorrow. And she invited me to a Mass that will be held on Friday at El Rosario Church for the peace of the souls executed by the general.

This is the second consecutive night I finish writing in this notebook and Betito still hasn't arrived. He didn't even come home for lunch: he called to say he was at Henry's and would have dinner at Flaco's. I don't like quarrelling with him over the phone. While we were eating breakfast I asked him to be very careful, to come home for meals and early at night, but my warnings went in one ear and out the other. I asked María Elena if she knew anything about his activities, for I spent a good part of the day out of the house; she said he hadn't returned since he left in the morning. Right now I have to think of the best way to confront him, try to figure out what Pericles would do in this situation.

María Elena regretted not being able to taste the cake; I also would have liked to have a piece to sweeten the wait for Betito. We both love chocolate, but María Elena collects recipes and asks me to buy ingredients for baking. A few months ago she told me she'd love to work as an apprentice a few hours a week at the Bonets', if I could ask Montse if that were possible, but with all this turmoil, I simply haven't had a chance. I admire her efforts to better herself. God willing, Belka, my lovely little girl, will inherit this and other virtues.

Thursday May 4

The first thing I did when I got out of bed this morning was call Carmela and wish her a happy birthday; every year since we became friends at school I've done the same thing: we each try to be the first person to wish the other one a happy birthday. Then, in this morning's newspaper—the official "yellow rag" as Pericles calls it—I learned that the government announced the release of civilians who had remained imprisoned for their participation in the failed coup. I immediately started calling everybody I could think of to make sure it was true, for although my husband didn't participate in the uprising, the fact that they were freeing the coup participants, who actually attacked the general, meant that they would also free Pericles. None of the other women in the committee knew anything; we were all quite excited, moving heaven and earth to find out what was happening. Until finally Doña Consuelo learned that it was one of the warlock's tricks: he released those who had been arrested by mistake, those who were still in jail but hadn't actually participated in the coup and had no record of political activity. I was so outraged I felt sick. How can he play with people's feelings in such a despicable way?! If I didn't despair it was thanks to the intense energy and excitement one feels in the streets, in every home, everywhere, a kind of magnetism in the air, and also thinks to the fact that María Elena brought me back to reality when she returned from the market and told me the vendors won't open their stands tomorrow, they all say the city will wake up at a standstill, without banks or stores or hospitals or pharmacies, and of course without a market, and many people were buying emergency provisions. Mother did so for us: she went in the car with Don Leo and Juani.

Silvia's salon was filled to overflowing, as if we were all afraid the strike would catch us with our pants down, so to speak. I waited half an hour, chatting with the other clients: rumor has it that several ministers think the general should resign, and if he doesn't in the next few days, they will. Mingo doesn't think they have enough guts. "They are afraid of what people will do to them if the general is toppled, so they send their wives out to spread rumors about them wanting to resign, but once they're face-to-face with the warlock, they start shaking in their boots," he said as we enjoyed the chocolate cake with walnuts on the front porch of Carmela and Chelón's house in the late afternoon. He also said, jokingly, that with the bankers spearheading the strike, all the shopkeepers will join, because there's not a single one who doesn't owe money or need a loan, "and if the people with all the money throw themselves off a cliff, we'll all follow because we'll figure there's more money down there." It's amazing how friends can end up resembling each other so much, because that comment could have come out of Pericles's mouth, as I told Irmita, who was looking much more hale when she came over with Mingo this afternoon. What I'm worried about is the possibility that if the strike starts tomorrow, the authorities may decide to suspend visits to the prison on Saturday; Chelón was the one who brought that up, with some concern. God willing, that won't happen.

Betito returned home early tonight; I thanked him for minding me and sparing me the worry. But he and his friends are going full steam ahead, according to what he tells me, they haven't stopped working on the strike for the last two days: they have groups visiting every shop, block by block, trying to persuade the owners to close their shops tomorrow; other groups are working to persuade the bus, streetcar, and taxi drivers to join the walkout; he says a secret committee of university students is coordinating all their efforts, and he and his friends are in constant touch with them. Betito's eyes shine as he talks, he is bursting with enthusiasm. It is obvious women my age are superfluous when there's so much energy and youth, to the point where even Father used him today as a messenger to distribute the funds, and he lent him Don Leo and the car to make a few visits, which Betito calls "operations." He showed me a few of the strike circulars they have distributed all over the city. I never tire of repeating to him that he should be careful.

I have prayed to Our Lady of Perpetual Succour from the bottom of my heart for the strike to be effective, for the warlock to step down without more bloodshed, for nothing to happen to Clemen, and for our family to soon be reunited. Tomorrow I will go to Mass at El Rosario Church with Doña Chayito and the other ladies. I am going to try to get some sleep because tomorrow will be a very nerve-racking day.

Friday May 5

What a day! My goodness! So many emotions, hopes, fears. The beginning of the strike has been a success! The city is paralyzed; the warlock gave a speech on the radio a while ago, at seven at night, to be precise, and denounced the strikers as "Nazi agitators" who are trying to wage "a war of nerves." Well, he has the nerve!? He must be in deep trouble; if he weren't, he wouldn't have spoken on air, with that horrible voice of his, but instead would have delegated it to Don Rodolfo or some other minister, so people would see that he couldn't care less about the strike. But that's not what happened. How I long for Pericles at these moments, how I miss his explanations of the general's secret thoughts and his state of mind based on the intonations of his voice over the radio . . .

At precisely nine o'clock this morning, María Elena, Betito, and I, all of us dressed in strict mourning, arrived at El Rosario Church. We walked there, even though a few streetcars and buses were still running, because the strategy is that nobody should use public transportation to make the drivers join the strike. The church was packed; there were groups of young people in the park and everywhere around. Expectation filled the air. We stayed near the entrance; I recognized several friends and my fellow committee members; I chatted with Angelita, Luz María, and Doña Chayito. But several minutes passed and Mass didn't begin. We soon learned that the priest was not going to come, he had not been authorized to celebrate the Eucharist. Everybody started talking about it, outraged. Then a student leader, speaking from the atrium of the church itself, announced between cheers and applauses that the general strike and walkout had begun. Groups of young people, including Betito and his friends, fanned out around the downtown area to persuade the owners of the few shops that had opened to close them immediately. On our way home, María Elena and I saw for ourselves that the banks and the large department stores along our way were shut, as were pharmacies, the Ministry of Health offices, and dentists' and lawyers' offices. But many people were in the streets, and everybody seemed excited and happy, as if it were a holiday, as if we all wanted to see for ourselves that the strike was real; hours later, however, the streets had emptied out; all the circulars stressed the importance of people remaining at home.

Before noon I went to eat lunch at my parents' house. It was a hotbed of activity: against Mother's will, Father and his friends had converted the house into a kind of "center of operations," as Uncle Charlie called it several times, where family acquaintances came and went with information about the strike and to report the latest rumors; whiskey was flowing and the telephone didn't stop ringing. When I entered the living room, Father was talking on the phone to Don Milo Butazzoni, the owner of the Milán grocery store, the most important one in the San José district, who was refusing to close his business; Don Milo is an old grouch, an admirer of Mussolini and the general, but he gets along well with Father, that's why Father took on the task of calling him, if not to support the strike, then at least to lower the metal grate in the afternoon. I spent some time in the kitchen helping Juanita prepare sandwiches for all the visitors. Mother was unable to contain her pessimism, and she kept saying that the strike will plunge the country into chaos and the warlock will remain on the throne. I learned that the bankers and the coffee growers were applying enormous pressure on the civilian members of the cabinet for them to resign this afternoon if the general did not tender his own resignation, but the general's response was the aggressive speech he gave on the radio, and as of tonight, as far as I know, there have been no resignations. Betito, Henry, Flaco, and Chepito showed up after dinner; they brought in their beer and were wearing their passion on their sleeves; they showed us the new circulars announcing that students and doctors in other cities, such as Santa Ana and San Miguel, had joined the strike and that many government offices, including the Customs Administration, are closed. Uncle Charlie said the greatest challenge is to bring the trains to a standstill, and the fact that the railroads are run by foreign companies means it will not be an easy task to do so; Betito and his friends talked about the difficulty they were having convincing the taxi drivers to support the strike, for most of them are police informers. At one moment, in the midst of all the enthusiasm and activity, I felt useless; I wondered how Doña Chayito and my other fellow committee members were contributing—what I could do, other than helping to prepare sandwiches and nervously biting my nails, because all my friends had already closed their shops and businesses, and I had nobody else to talk into joining the strike. After we ate, Uncle Charlie went to the embassy to find out firsthand, he said, the Americans' impression of the strike and to encourage them to offer their support. I decided to come home. Mother insisted on Don Leo driving me, because she didn't think the streets were safe. It was then, as we were crossing Arce Street, that the idea came to me as if a light bulb had gone on in my head: I told Don Leo to drive toward Plaza Morazán, I needed to run an errand in the vicinity. I felt like I had been hit by a lightning bolt, possessed by a burst of energy that was leading me along with a clear head and a precise purpose. When we got to the plaza, I asked Don Leo—without the slightest hesitation—to take me to the taxi stand, as I was eager to carry through with the task I had set for myself; I then instructed him to stop next to Don Sergio's taxi, told him to wait there, and said I trusted his discretion to say nothing to my parents. Don Leo understood immediately; all he said was: "Be careful, Señora." I got out of the car and entered the other one. Don Sergio greeted me, a bit surprised, but clearly pleased by my appearance, it seemed I was the first customer of the day. "What a miracle, Señora Haydée. Tell me, where can I take you?" he said. I told him to take me to Dr. Figueroa's house, located on the same block as Rosales Hospital, but I asked him to go very slowly, because I was early, and that way I could use the opportunity to talk to him. He turned to look at me in astonishment. "Talk to me? ..." Yes, Don Sergio, I told him, with inspiration from who knows where, and straight to the point, I launched into my speech: I said I didn't understand how they, the taxi drivers, can be so ungrateful, so insensitive to injustice, how they can refuse to support a strike the whole society is participating in, aren't they part of that society, don't they care about the future of their children, their families, their country, because if they are willing to go against the will of the entire people, who will stick their necks out for them when the general leaves? Who will help them? Where will they get the bank loans all respectable people need? Who will fix their cars? Who will renew their drivers' licenses? What doctor will attend to them? What professional will offer them their services? With what scorn will the average person view them? I told him it was shameful that even justices of the peace and many other public employees have joined the strike whereas they, the taxi drivers, carry on as if nothing were happening, as if the general were going to stay in power forever. Even I was taken aback by my vehemence, and I am even more so now as I review the sequence of events, Don Sergio driving, utterly stunned, speechless, surely imagining the very black future I had just painted for him. Furthermore, I told him, at any moment the ministers are going to start resigning, I had just learned—thanks to those in the know—that in a matter of hours or at most a few days the general will have to leave because nobody can govern a country without money, and they, the taxi drivers, will be left in the lurch. That was when Don Sergio mumbled something to the effect that that's the problem, they have families to support, and they don't have the luxury of walking away from their jobs, though, to tell the truth, this was his first ride of the day. I told him there was a solution to this problem, thanks to the fact that everybody supports the strike, honorable people are donating funds for those most in need, and he should tell me how much he earns a day on the average, and I will speak to the boys to get that money for the members of his association, but he will have to persuade his colleagues, explain to them what I had just said to him, and make them commit to a walkout, to going home. Again Don Sergio remained quiet; he was driving slowly, glancing at me from time to time in the rearview mirror. Finally, he muttered that I had convinced him, but I should please not mention it to anybody, it is an agreement between him and me; right away we spoke about amounts. We arrived at the Figueroas; I asked him to wait a few minutes in the car. God heard my prayers, because Luz María herself opened the front door. I quickly explained the situation: we had to find Fabito urgently. She told me it would be difficult because he was running from place to place. Since Luz María couldn't drive me to where her brother was nor did I want to scare Don Sergio, we agreed I'd go back to my parents' house where she or Fabito would bring me the money for the taxi drivers. Once back in the car I told Don Sergio that while I was collecting the money, he would return to the taxi stand and begin to talk to his colleagues, one by one, for it is always easier to persuade somebody one on one, and as soon as I had the agreed-upon sum, perhaps in a few hours, I would come find him, and if he got another customer in the meantime he should leave word as to when he would return; he warned me about the risk at the stand, he said it's being watched by spies and police detectives, and he suggested we arrange a specific time when he would come find me. My parents were surprised to see me back, so excited, and in a taxi; I couldn't hide the truth from them. Mother got upset, she said I was taking unnecessary risks. But Father was clearly quite impressed: we don't have to wait for Fabito, he said, I can collect that amount of money from my friends right away. And so he did: he made a few phone calls then left in his car with Uncle Charlie. While we were drinking tea and I was praying that Don Sergio would manage to persuade his colleagues, Mother proposed we let Luz María know that we no longer needed the money, so she wouldn't make the trip in vain; I said it was better to wait, just in case Father encountered some difficulty obtaining the funds due to the banks being closed. Mother insisted, frowning sternly, that she didn't think it prudent for honorable women, like Luz María and I, to get involved in the affairs of men and common folks. Father and Uncle Charlie soon returned. We shut ourselves up in his office: we counted out the money that he then gave me in a manila envelope along with some instructions. When the taxi arrived to pick me up, I was so anxious I was perspiring, especially because now that the rush of inspiration had passed, I was haunted by the thought of what could happen to Don Sergio if word got to the police; however, once in the car, and after he told me excitedly that he had persuaded four of his colleagues to join the strike, I again felt determined and full of energy. He also told me that the strike was beginning to take hold at other taxi stands. While he was driving me home, and we saw how deserted the streets were, I explained that in the envelope was the amount of money seven taxi drivers at his stand earn in three days, including him, of course, and this meant they should immediately go to their respective homes and wait, without going anywhere near

Plaza Morazán. He asked me if the three days included Saturday. I answered, with an edge of rebuke, that he shouldn't be such a skinflint, most people were making sacrifices, opposing injustice to follow their conscience and not for monetary gain, and if the strike continues past Wednesday he should come find me. I was thankful the policemen posted on our street had left that morning.

I entered the house for only a moment to ask María Elena if there was any news, then went straight to the Alvarados'. Raúl told me that Dr. Luis Velasco had taken on the directorship of Rosales Hospital this morning, and in order to avoid suffering any further humiliation at the hands of the warlock, all the doctors had decided to go out on strike. He was thrilled because he had been able to see Chente at noon; he says he is doing well in spite of the days he has spent in hiding. Rosita never stops complaining. I asked them if they had noticed that there was no surveillance on our street. Raúl said it seems the general has given orders for the policemen to return to their barracks, perhaps he fears another military uprising in support of the strike.

Then I came home to prepare the things I would take to Pericles tomorrow. I don't want to think about what God holds in store for us; it won't do any good to torture myself. I've spoken to Doña Chayito: she has assured me that all the ladies in the committee will show up at the Central Prison to demand our visiting hour; strike or no strike, it is our right. I'm not sure if I'll tell Pericles about my adventure this afternoon; it may only make him worry. I'll decide once we are together.

(10 at night)

I have just learned that an important meeting is being held tonight at the Alcaine compound: many people have gathered there to form a government to take over when the warlock falls, which will happen soon, in the next few hours, they say. God willing. Betito told me all about it, he came home a while ago, all in a flurry, rushing in then out. He saw Father there, and Uncle Charlie, and many of their friends, and Fabito and Chente, Dr. Velasco, Mingo, and even Doña

Chayito, among other people we know. I was quite moved: my son was upset that they didn't let him into the meeting; only one representative from the group of high school students was allowed in, and Chepito was chosen. I reminded him to be very careful.

Saturday May 6

I'm dead tired, exhausted, as if the fatigue of the entire week has suddenly crashed down on me. All I want to do is sleep. The strike is growing, but the warlock has counterattacked. Father says Monday will be the decisive day, the showdown.

I wasn't able to see Pericles. No visits were allowed; neither the director nor Sergeant Flores showed his face. The moment we arrived, early this morning, the guards warned us no visits would be allowed for the political prisoners, it would do us no good to wait or voice any complaints, they were only following orders. Doña Chayito and a group of students took the opportunity to pass out circulars and make speeches in favor of the strike to the dozens of families of prisoners who had gathered in front of the Central Prison. There were cheers, clamors, shouts of defiance. As if we had all shed our inhibitions.

At last night's meeting at the Alcaines', a Committee of National Reconstruction was formed, which will take charge of negotiating the warlock's departure; Dr. Alcaine himself is on the committee and is the bankers' representative, and Dr. Velasco represents the professional associations, according to what Father told me. The strike is going full-steam ahead: city employees, those in the Vice-Ministry of Public Works and in the Ministry of Foreign Affairs, have all decided to walk out on Monday, when it is hoped that other government offices will follow suit and join the strike. I mentioned that poor Dr. Ávila will have no choice but to resign, but Mother was not so certain after speaking with Doña Tina.

The whole day has been filled with rumors, meetings, to-ing and fro-ing. They say delegates from the Legislative Assembly and members of the cabinet itself have shown up at the presidential palace, trying to persuade the general to step down, but he will not budge, on the contrary, he has begun to apply pressure on business owners to reopen their shops, using circulars, telephone calls—an unknown group was even banging on the doors of La Dalia department store and issuing threats. The latest rumor is that hordes of peasants armed by the government are congregating at the army barracks, ready to enter San Salvador and force businesses to open. God willing, this is only a rumor.

I am going to bed; I can't keep my eyes open any longer. I've left a note for Betito on the dining room table, asking him not to forget to come give me a good-night kiss.

Sunday May 7

They killed Juan's son! The police fired into a group of boys as they were leaving his house and killed Chepito White. Betito was there, heaven forbid, with Henry, Flaco, and the rest of their friends. I thank God nothing happened to my son. Poor Chepito! He was only seventeen years old, what a terrible tragedy. That evil warlock! It's not enough for him to kill his own comrades-in-arms, now he orders the slaughter of innocent children ... Betito is very upset: he watched his friend bleed to death. My poor child. The things we are fated to see, Lord ... When we heard the news, we all poured into the streets in outrage. The Whites are Americans, one of the best families in El Salvador; they say Ambassador Thurston has gone to demand the resignation of that murderer. I have rushed home to change into mourning clothes so I can attend the wake.

(Midnight)

The warlock must fall soon, very soon, unless he decides to kill us all! Father and his friends say it is a matter of hours now that the entire cabinet has tendered its resignation. That's the least they could do. Not another soul could fit in the Whites' house; when I went outside to get some air I couldn't believe my eyes: thousand and thousands of people were filling several blocks in every direction, as if all the inhabitants of the city had come out to repudiate the general. Carlota and Luz María and I wandered around, taking it all in.

All our friends and acquaintances were there, entire families, even babies; many couldn't even make it into the Whites' house, though they tried. The university students set up security to keep the crowd organized and avoid disturbances; they even protected the houses of the ministers in the neighborhood, like that of Don Miguel Ángel and Don Rodolfo Morales himself, where they say the agent was standing when he shot Chepito. The police have remained in their barracks, warlock's orders. The burial will be tomorrow at ten in the morning; the whole country has come to a grinding halt. Uncle Charlie told us that Pan Am is cancelling all its flights. I spoke with my sister Cecilia from Carlota's house: she said that people in Santa Ana are also furious and have taken to the streets, city employees have gone on strike, and tomorrow the city will shut down. Luz María told me that late this afternoon she went with some friends to the house of the manager of the railroads, an old friend of the family's, to convince him that no trains should run to the interior of the country tomorrow; she said the man was dismayed by Chepito's murder, impressed that young society ladies were so dedicated to the cause, and he assured them he will make sure the engineers don't leave the station. When I got here, I met up with Chente; we hugged each other as if we were friends of the same age, as if he wasn't as old as my children; I was so happy to see him safe and sound. These young people are so resilient; Betito didn't want to come home, he said he was going to stay awake the whole night, with his friends, doing whatever there was to do. Don Leo brought me home. I must sleep a bit. María Elena told me Pati has been calling, very concerned. It's too late now. I will call her early tomorrow, before I leave for the funeral.

Monday May 8

The warlock resigned! He announced it over the radio, at seven tonight, while thousands and thousands of us stood in the plaza in front of the National Palace, where we had gone en masse after Chepito's funeral. I was with María Elena and Doña Chayito, next to the cathedral, when we heard the news. After embracing each other, surrounded by cries of joy and the cheering crowd, we left quickly for the Central Prison. There were droves of us gathering in front of the gates to demand the release of our family members. The prison guards were terrified; they took cover and said their chiefs weren't there and they could not make any decisions. We didn't cease with our demands, with slogans and chants, which were answered by the prisoners inside. There was a festive atmosphere; even the security guards were joking around and celebrating. Then Sergeant Flores appeared, he said he had just spoken on the phone with Colonel Palma, who said the prisoners would not be released until tomorrow, just as soon as the order signed by the new minister had arrived. Not one of us wanted to budge until our family members were released, but then I realized that the best thing would be to find Father so his friends would put pressure on the new minister. We went back to the plaza. We found Carmela, Chelón, and many other friends, all happy and celebrating. I ran into Chente, Fabito, and Raúl, who explained to me that negotiations to form a new cabinet will take all night, the strike will continue until the warlock leaves the country. I came home to call Pati and tell her what was going on, the poor thing was quite worried there in Costa Rica. I was about to pick up the handset when I got a call from Mila. My God, the woman was completely drunk! I hung up immediately because I have no desire for this joyous moment to be spoiled in any way. I told Pati that her father will come home tomorrow and her brother can now come out of hiding, wherever he may be, as soon as they declare the amnesty. God has answered my prayers!

Part 2
The Lunch (1973)

SARPEDON: Nobody ever kills himself. Death is destiny.
—*Dialogues with Leuco*, Cesare Pavese

Old Man Pericles called at ten thirty in the morning. Carmela answered the phone: surprised to hear his voice, she invited him over to eat, telling him she was making a casserole he would love. A bit apprehensive, I took the handset: he told me he needed to talk to me; he wanted to know if it was a good time for me. I asked him where he was calling from. He said he was in the public phone booth in front of the hospital. I told him Carmela had already invited him, and he should come without delay. I wanted to believe his voice sounded as it always did: a stranger to dismay. When I hung up, Carmela questioned me by raising her eyebrows; I must have given her a look of resignation.

I returned to the terrace and my rocking chair, where I spend my mornings, but I couldn't take up my reading again. Old Man Pericles was barely two years old than me, and his time was coming. I felt uneasiness waft over me like a light breeze from the patio. I got up and stretched. Then I went to my studio, to my writing desk, and reread the notes I'd written at dawn. I was thinking that what I needed was a scarecrow to scare off the crows in my mind.

A short while later, I thought I heard Carmela in the living room dialing the phone. I assumed she was calling María Elena, the Aragóns' maid, the only person who now lived in the house with Old

Man Pericles. Carmela whispered so I wouldn't hear; I disapprove of her meddling in other people's lives, fretting over the old man as if he were a defenseless child and not a seventy-five-year-old adult.

It would take Old Man Pericles approximately forty-five minutes to get to the house. We live at the top of the mountain, across the street from the last bus stop, in front of the entrance to Balboa Park, which is bustling every Sunday with people who come up from the city. The house is small, but more than enough for two old folks like Carmela and I; the patio abuts the most heavily forested section of the park. The air is clean and the night sky is awe-inspiring. We've been living here almost fifteen years. It is true, the area is getting more and more crowded. There's more noise: during the day, youngsters play on the street, and buses arrive and depart every twenty minutes. But at night, silence takes hold, broken only by the chirping of the crickets.

Old Man Pericles would take a bus from Rosales Hospital to downtown, then get on the number 12 bus, which would bring him here. Once a month, at least, he came for lunch, whenever he was in the country—and not in jail or in exile, which fortunately he hadn't been for the last year and a half. The last time was when he was stopped by customs at Ilopango Airport, interrogated, then immediately deported by plane to Costa Rica. The press said the authorities had prevented a well-known communist from entering the country and bringing money from Moscow to finance subversive activities. I told myself that some perverse fear must be eating away at people who can treat an old man this way.

Once in a while, at dawn, I still write a few lines in my diary, I jot down a verse, an aphorism; in the mornings, as the sun is rising, I draw, make sketches, sometimes just a few lines; toward evening, I like to pick up my brushes, stand in front of the picture window overlooking the park, and contemplate the swath of green that joins the deep blue. For more than fifty years such idleness has been my vocation. Old Man Pericles always said that no art makes sense; I never argued with him, though on one or another occasion a crack would show up in his hard shell, and he'd admit to having "sinned," that is, written a few verses. Never, of course, would he have read them to me: he would say that this business of lifting up one's tail feathers to display one's rear end is only for peacocks, not leathery old birds. "Bitter ones," I would answer, and he would just smile, because I'd reminded him that at the beginning he too had illusions, the muse of poetry had also tempted him, but he had succumbed to a different temptation, the one he called "the perfidious wench"—wretched politics.

Carmela entered the studio, walked up to the desk where I was sitting and digressing; she placed her hand on my shoulder and offered me a glass of fresh watermelon drink. She also had not stopped thinking about Old Man Pericles. Fifteen days before he'd confided in us that he had just been diagnosed with lung cancer. We were sitting in the rocking chairs on the terrace, drinking coffee after lunch. And he said, without any preamble and without any particular emphasis, while smoking, that they had told him that morning at the hospital, the exam results in hand. "No return," he said with a grin, words I remember precisely because they were the same two words he would use whenever he wanted to mock the possibility of the eternal return, an idea I sometimes liked to entertain.

But the doctor had told him they could treat him to prevent the spread and that he should return in fifteen days for his first session. That's why, as the sun was getting hotter and hotter, we waited to find out what was going on.

"What could have happened, why did he leave the hospital so soon?" Carmela muttered behind me.

I asked her if she had spoken to María Elena. She had been working for them forever, Haydée even brought her with them once when they went into exile in Costa Rica.

"She told me she thought he was at the hospital. He left the house early this morning, carrying a bag with his pajamas and a few toiletries, ready to check in for his treatment. She was surprised when I told her he had called us and was on his way here."

"Maybe there was some delay," I said.

María Elena also told her that in the last few days Old Man Pericles had been even more withdrawn than usual, he ate little, and he barely left the house, spending all his time in his office with the door closed; his cough had gotten worse.

It now feels as if I've always known him, because memory is deceptive and attaches itself capriciously to things. But it must have been around 1920, shortly before I married Carmela. Old Man Pericles was already married to Haydée, and Clemente was about three years old. Carmela and Haydée were classmates, neighbors, friends in the same club.

As for Pericles, all I remember from those days was his military haircut, his upright bearing, his stern gaze, and his wrinkled brow, as if he were already old. He was a second lieutenant in the cavalry, a graduate of the military academy. He was following in the footsteps of his father, who was then a lieutenant colonel. He would, however, suddenly abandon his military career and enroll in the university to study law. As he would say, this was his first insubordination: the eldest son's break from paternal authority. An insubordination against the military world of his father, which as the years passed, would become the central theme of his life. "They'd already passed me the baton when I saw the folly of continuing in that world," he once told me. "That's my story."

The moment I met Haydée, on the other hand, stands out perfectly clear in my memory. It was an afternoon at Carmela's family's house during our courtship: a slender redhead with milky-white skin, freckles, and green eyes, Haydée was sitting on the sofa holding a cup on her lap. Dazzled, I reminded myself she was Carmela's best friend, the one I had heard so much about, the wife of Second Lieutenant Aragón, the mother of the baby my future mother-in-law was holding. A thought slipped past me: Haydée could have been the girl for me.

Not even half an hour had passed since Pericles had called when there was a knock on the door. I told myself it was impossible for him to have gotten here so quickly, unless somebody had driven him. But it was Don Tobías, the postman. Twice a week he came to deliver mail to these last houses along the highway beyond which is the enormous park and, further on, the uninhabited highlands. He was a thin, short man with a narrow, Cantinflas-style mustache, and was perspiring; he had been delivering the mail in this area for five years. Carmela invited him in, as always, to have some fresh watermelon drink. The letter was from Maggi, our only daughter; Carmela opened it eagerly while Don Tobías was enjoying his refreshment, then she began to read it, some parts out loud. Maggi wrote about some late cold spells and the miraculous arrival of spring, about her companions at the convent in Maryland, the pastoral work she so much enjoys, and her recent trip to Baltimore.

Don Tobías asked us if we'd heard the latest news: the authorities had learned that the big blue house at mile nine had been inhabited by a guerrilla group for several months. He said he couldn't believe his ears when he heard it on the radio news that morning. He had not delivered any mail to that address that whole time; he delivered the utility, water, or telephone bills to a post office box; there was nothing unusual about that, many people in the neighborhood preferred to receive their personal mail in a box in the city, given how remote this area is. I told him we had also heard the news on the radio, and fortunately the house had already been vacated by the time the authorities burst in, and there were no victims to mourn.

"Hard to believe the things that are starting to happen," Don Tobías said as he handed the glass back to Carmela; he wiped off his mustache, thanked us, and said goodbye.

Carmela read the letter again, then she handed it to me. I went back out to the terrace to sit down in the rocking chair. The temperature was rising; the dry season was in its final gasps, the earth was parched and the vegetation withered, and we still had at least a week to go before the first rains. At the end of the letter, under her signature, Maggi drew the same drawing she has been drawing ever since she was a little girl: the sun with a bird in the middle. She was about to turn fifty. I put the letter aside; I offered my gratitude to the invisible ones that my daughter was still alive. Clemente had been murdered a year before, and Old Man Pericles had taken it badly, very badly, even though he tried to convince himself of the contrary. Clemente, the eldest son, had died unreconciled with his father.

One night, as he was leaving an Alcoholics Anonymous meeting in the Centroamérica district of San Salvador, he was shot in the back. At first we thought it was a political assassination because the country was in the turmoil of the elections. Old Man Pericles was still in exile in Costa Rica; the authorities gave him permission to return. They never caught the culprit, and I assume the case has been shelved. According to hearsay, it was most likely a powerful military officer's act of revenge for a cuckolding. From the time he was a young man, Clemente had had a knack for getting into trouble over women.

A few days after the funeral, Old Man Pericles came over and confessed to being plagued by contradictory feelings: on one hand, his grief at Clemente's death; and on the other, his blind rage, at him, the world, life. That's when I told him that by some strange law that seems to follow a swinging, pendulum-like movement, children always position themselves at the opposite extreme of where their parents want them to be, and the more foolishly we try to determine their futures, the further they go from where we wish them to be. I'm the perfect example: I'm an agnostic, awash in esoteric ideas, always having disdained the emptiness of Catholic rituals and rejected the corruption of the Church, and I've had to accept that my only daughter became a nun, out of her own free will and vocation.

"The best proof, Old Man, that life makes decisions to spite us," I told him.

But Old Man Pericles was a hard nut to crack.

"The difference, Chelón, is that you believe there's something beyond this, an afterlife, that's why you can forgive. I don't," he said.

"You don't believe in the afterlife or you can't forgive?"

"Neither . . . ," he said, as if to settle the matter.

"You still can't forgive Clemente for not being like you?" I insisted. "Perhaps he simply broke from your concept of the world in the same way you broke from the colonel's."

Old Man Pericles wrinkled his brow.

I was tempted to tell him that sometimes what we most hate and never forgive in those around us is some hidden part of ourselves we neither recognize nor accept, but the old man just would have looked at me scornfully and asked where I had left my cassock.

Old Man Pericles used to call Clemente "that blundering fool," a way of mitigating his disappointment in his firstborn, for whom he'd had such high expectations. Clemente participated in the attempted coup against the dictator in April 1944. At the time, he was condemned to death by firing squad but miraculously managed to escape. So great must have been his terror that, from then on, he foreswore politics and for the rest of his life supported military governments.

"Nobody should judge another's fear," I told the old man that day after Clemente's funeral. Who knows what that young man felt, sentenced to death, the shock and disorientation at the prospect of facing a firing squad, something he could never quite get over, and despite his father's example of struggle, he was grateful to his conservative grandfather, who had saved his life.

"One thing is fear, another is shamelessness. He could have simply abstained from politics without turning into the priestly confidant of alcoholic military officers and the shoulder for their sluts to cry on," he said, without mitigating his scorn and bitterness one iota.

I didn't insist, though for me Clemente's portrait had to be drawn with heavy brushstrokes: from the terror of death he sank into alcoholism, and to emerge from both he needed faith, which he found in AA, where he became a fierce activist. He ended up organizing groups of recovering alcoholics among the top brass of the military, and that's the world he moved in.

Clemente's private life also provoked Old Man Pericles's wrath: first he married a floozy who left him; then he married a Honduran girl from a good family who represented everything Old Man Pericles hated most, but whom, after Clemente's murder, he'd begun to visit and had grown quite fond of. And there was, moreover, the family secret, his trampling on a reputation when he was a young man, an episode that was never so much as mentioned.

That morning, sitting in the rocking chair, wandering through my memories and waiting for Old Man Pericles to arrive, I reminded myself yet again that the history of the Aragón family was not material for a short story but rather a tragedy, one I would never dare write—out of modesty, loyalty, incomprehension, lack of skill, and because life had already passed me by, and if I went back and lived it again, I would perhaps opt for silence, as Old Man Pericles did, but without his bitterness. And then I told myself that we humans are hopeless, there I was gloating over Old Man Pericles's misfortune, wondering about the best way to write it, as if I didn't have my own cross to bear, as if the rage that devoured me during Maggi's tragedy wasn't still with me, forever and unutterable. And now, while writing down these recollections of the old man, I can assert that we men are incorrigible, inconstant, we almost always end up doing what we have set our minds to avoid, and vice versa.

The telephone rang again; it startled us. I feared the old man may have had some mishap, but no, it was Ricardito, Carmela told me, the young man who was selling my paintings. I took the handset: he asked me if he could stop by in the afternoon. I told him I already had plans, we should put it off till the following day. He was curious, kind, and meddlesome; he told me he wanted to be my agent, manage my entire oeuvre, as if that's what I needed. I explained that between the galleries, he, and Carmela, it was enough, I wasn't that prolific. He loved to get me wound up so I'd talk to him about esotericism, Eastern thought, maybe hoping I would give him a greater percentage of sales if I could make him my disciple. I gave him free reign to ask questions and offer his opinions as much as he wished, and once in a while I'd get fired up and run off at the mouth. Carmela warned me there was something about him she didn't like, she could smell the bird of prey in him. I told her that when vultures start circling it is because they are attracted to something that's putrefying, so it is best to keep them distracted and thus defer the moment they start pecking at our flesh.

But what really bothered Carmela was that sometimes Ricardito arrived in the company of gorgeous young women who called me "maestro," praised my work to the heavens, and asked me why I didn't teach, how much they would love to take classes from me. She was made particularly uneasy by a rather bold, skinny, curly-haired blonde; her name was Andrea, and she frequently and fervently exclaimed how much she wanted to be my model.

It was 1927 when I had my first show—some oil paintings I was quite proud of at the time—and Old Man Pericles had quit law school and plunged headlong into journalism and politics. I visited him at the newspaper office where he worked; he'd written an article in which he spoke quite generously about my show. One year later, when I had the nerve to send some verses I'd been working on for publication, I again visited him at the newspaper; Old Man Pericles leafed through the chapbook and, totally serious, asked me if I really thought I could be a painter and a poet at the same time. I said yes.

"Is your wound that large?" he asked.

I didn't understand.

"I mean, painting should be enough for you," he said with that sarcastic frown I would always recognize from then on.

Then he told me he couldn't understand how the muse of poetry, so insolent and depraved, could pick a guy like me—sober, a devoted husband, not given to excesses of any kind—that there must have been a mistake somewhere because no lasting art can come from politeness and a good heart.

I didn't know what to say.

The following week he published a short article in which he welcomed a new poet who was already a painter, but he didn't say a word about the quality of my verses. The clarity of my recollection is proof of the slight I felt to my self-esteem.

Then came that fateful coup d'état in December 1931: suddenly

Old Man Pericles became—probably through the intrigues of his ex-comrades-in-arms and his father, Colonel Aragón—the private secretary to the new president, a general with a warlock complex who would rule over us for twelve years. I stopped seeing him during this period; the exercise of power always isolates men, and Old Man Pericles was no exception. But I heard about his adventures through Carmela, who continued to see Haydée as frequently as ever.

Barely a month after the coup, the peasant insurrection began, led by the communists. There was total chaos. We felt uneasy in San Salvador, but the situation in the western sector of the country was much more dire. When the indigenous hordes armed themselves with guns and machetes, my in-laws were at their finca in Apaneca; they managed to escape by the skin of their teeth and arrived, terrified, in San Salvador. The government's response was strong. There was a massacre, and the leaders were executed.

I've never known the passion for power, but I have read about it and thus am not surprised that Old Man Pericles lived those weeks of the insurrection with great intensity, awash in adrenaline and with enough vehemence to crush his enemies. I imagined him whispering in the general's ear, drawing up plans, displaying his brilliance. He had been educated at a military academy, but he'd also attended law school, where he had shared classrooms and perhaps even adventures with some of the communist leaders, whom he was now fighting, and whom he would soon defeat.

The insurrection was a disaster; its chief military leader—Negro Martí, a former law-school classmate of Old Man Pericles—was captured almost at the outset. He was court-martialed and sentenced to be executed by firing squad. The night before his execution, the old man went to the prison with a box of cigars, shut himself up with Negro Martí and his two deputies—who were also sentenced to death—and they remained there talking and smoking until the dawn. At five in the morning he accompanied Martí to the wall of the General Cemetery. It was the first of February 1932. That's when his life changed.

Old Man Pericles wasn't one to make confessions and give detailed accounts, and I never met Martí, but I can picture the scene as if I had been right there, several yards away from the site of the execution, sitting on the grave of a stranger, my sketchbook resting on my lap, trying to capture every last detail under the blue-gray light of dawn, when there appears a rather small, thin man with dark skin, a mustache, a receding hairline, the little hair he has left curly and tangled, his hands in manacles, flanked by a priest and the commanding officer of the firing squad, surrounded by guards, his step firm and determined, with a proud bearing, conscious that he had the central role in this scene and was, thus, the one who set the tone and the rhythm. Old Man Pericles is walking to the side, silently; the priest holds forth, invoking God and gesticulating affectedly. With a disdainful look on his face, the condemned man says no, no he is not going to confess, would the priest please leave. The priest insists, stubbornly, obsequiously. The commanding officer and Old Man Pericles exchange looks. It's time, the officer says gravely, and he removes the manacles. The old man approaches the condemned man and embraces him tightly, his nerves and muscles clenched; they exchange no word, only a glint in the eyes. The commanding officer takes out a handkerchief to blindfold the prisoner, who says he doesn't need a blindfold, they should proceed without. The priest relents and, still muttering his mumbo-jumbo, he embraces the condemned man, who responds coldly. The old man starts to walk away, eager to gain some distance; when he gets alongside the firing squad he hears the voice of the condemned man shouting: "Pericles!" The old man turns around. "Come here, give me a hug," he says. "But I already did," the old man answers, discomfited. "Come, give me another one, I don't want the last hug in this life to be from a scheming priest," the condemned man says. The sky lightens. Pericles retraces his steps. They embrace again; the condemned man uses the opportunity to whisper in his ear: "You are going to be one of us." The old man walks away, bewildered, his head down, his back to the scene; he pauses briefly to light a cigarette. The condemned man stands and faces the firing squad, his chest out, defiant. The officer shouts: "Ready!" He orders them to prepare their weapons. Then, the condemned man's voice rings out forcefully: "Aim!" The officer suffers a moment of confusion but right away lifts his whip and energetically nods to the squad to carry out the condemned man's order. At which point the condemned man shouts: "Fire!" The officer swings the whip through the air and the shots ring out. The condemned man has slumped over. All present hold still and silent amid the curls of smoke. Breathing heavily and clearly agitated, the officer approaches the body, still in its death spasms; he draws his forty-five, brings it to the condemned man's temple, and shoots. A car's engine has started nearby.

I repeat: Old Man Pericles wasn't one for details—he never told anybody what he talked to Martí about during the more than five hours they spent in that prison cell awaiting the execution, smoking cigars, anticipating the moment he would lead Martí to the wall. And I could imagine that scene, innocent and heroic, thanks to the many times I'd read and heard about similar ones, but I could never paint it as I wished because I was somehow permanently incapacitated, and I could never do anything more than draw half a dozen sketches, nothing presentable, especially not to the old man, who would have turned to look at me without a stitch of compassion, raised his eyebrows, and asked me since when I thought of myself as Señor Goya of the Candelaria district.

Carmela called out from the kitchen to tell me that Old Man Pericles would arrive any minute now, and I should get out the ice cubes in case he wanted a whiskey. I told her not to be so pushy, I would take care of it. I stood up; pain shot through my spine. I walked over to the cupboard—very carefully, afraid of exacerbating the pain—to make sure there was enough whiskey left in the bottle; then I placed an ashtray on the dining room table and another on the coffee table out on the terrace. I told Carmela there was no point in taking out the ice until we heard the bus arrive, otherwise it would melt. Carmela asked me to help her set the table. At that moment we heard the clatter of the bus on the street below.

I opened the door. I took the cutlery out of the drawer of the china cabinet and was about to set it out when the old man appeared.

"Just look at you, making yourself useful as always," he said, putting his bag down on the sofa. He was dressed as he almost always was: a white short-sleeved guayabera, dark gray slacks, black loafers, and tortoiseshell glasses; his face was impeccably shaved.

He held out his hand to me, gave a kiss to Carmela, who had just appeared at the kitchen door, then asked to be excused, he had to use the washroom.

Old Man Pericles always claimed that his rebelliousness came from way back, that he had inherited his bitterness from his mother. He came to this conclusion with the passing of time, and the older he got, the more his certainty grew. His grandfather was a famous general, commander of a troop of indigenous soldiers and a liberal leader, who was executed by the conservatives around 1890 after leading a revolt. Old Man Pericles's mother, Doña Licha, then a young lady of fifteen and the general's eldest daughter, was taken to the main plaza to watch her father face the firing squad; the rebel general's head was then placed on top of a stake at the entrance to the town to dissuade the natives from offering any further resistance. "That's the only way I can explain the rage I feel against those bastards," Old Man Pericles told me one night he allowed himself to confess. What he didn't say was how disappointed he was that neither of his sons had inherited his rebellious spirit, his resentment of the powerful, which he considered to be one of his own dearest virtues.

"I didn't go in," Old Man Pericles said, sitting in the rocking chair, a glass of whiskey on his lap.

"Why not? What happened?" Carmela asked from the kitchen, raising her voice.

"The older that woman gets, the keener is her hearing," I noted, because Old Man Pericles was with me out on the terrace, and he was speaking so only I would hear him.

Soon Carmela was there, standing behind us, drying her hands on her apron, worry etched all over her face.

"They postponed your treatment? Till when?" she asked.

"I said, I didn't go in," Old Man Pericles repeated, looking at me out of the corner of his eye, appealing to my good offices, because Haydée had died twelve years before, and he had probably lost the habit of explaining himself, of being questioned by a woman. "I was in the waiting room and I decided not to go in, so I didn't. I came here instead," he said and took a long sip of whiskey; then he turned to look at Carmela, for just a few seconds, but enough for her to understand.

"Then what? . . ." she asked, dismayed.

"Then nothing," I intervened. "Can't you see that he's here now?" I said somewhat emphatically.

Carmela returned to the kitchen. I knew she was on the verge of tears because she had understood that Old Man Pericles had decided to let himself die, and she, Haydée's best friend, had promised her, at her bedside when she was dying so suddenly of breast cancer, that she would take care of the old man as if he were her brother.

"I don't need to go through any more ordeals. The doctor warned me the treatment would be painful and, with luck, it could only hold the cancer at bay but never reverse it," Old Man Pericles said as he lit a cigarette.

Noon had come with its steamy breath, its glaring light: not a touch of a breeze; the leaves on the trees, unmoving.

"But you don't stop smoking," Carmela said, carrying a plate of toast with beans and avocado; she said it angrily, as if the harm he was causing was to her.

"What for, said the parrot, the hawk's already caught me . . . ," the old man mumbled, repeating an old folk saying.

"I remember when you used to smoke a pipe," Carmela said, now in a different tone, as she offered us the plate of hors d'oeuvres. "That did you less harm, smelled better, and you looked more elegant."

Old Man Pericles was extremely circumspect, a stranger to speechifying; his style was the caustic or sarcastic phrase, the query, or the doubt. Two years after that insurrection, he left for Brussels with Haydée and the three children, as an ambassador; he would return after becoming an opponent of the general, who jailed him more than a few times during his twelve-year dictatorship. I never knew how he became a communist, where he had been recruited, nor by whom. Once I asked him; he answered that so many many years had passed, and his memory was in such poor shape, that it wasn't even worth trying to recall; this was his elegant way to avoid digging through the garbage of the past. But one afternoon, with the snippets I'd heard over the years and my shameless imagination, while lying idly in the hammock on the terrace, I elaborated a story that begins at a cocktail party at a Latin American embassy in Brussels around 1935, perhaps the following year, after the Civil War in Spain had broken out, a cocktail party where Old Man Pericles is wandering around alone carrying a glass of whiskey, looking for his Central American colleagues, when he is suddenly approached by a man he has never seen before.

"Are you Ambassador Aragón?" the man asks in perfect Castilian Spanish. He is blond, with pale skin and blue eyes.

"At your service," the old man says.

"Allow me to introduce myself," the man says, with a touch of an accent the old man can't quite place. "My name is Nikolai Ogniev. I am a journalist, a correspondent for the Soviet newspaper, *Pravda*."

The man holds out his hand.

"My pleasure," the old man says, politely but already on his guard. "How can I help you, Mr. Ogniev?"

"I understand you were once a journalist, before you devoted yourself to politics and diplomacy."

The old man takes a sip of his whiskey, then places the glass on a shelf and pulls a silver cigarette case out of his pocket.

"Would you like one?" the old man asks; the other man says no.

The old man lights a cigarette just as a fat jolly man with a stentorian voice approaches them. He is the host.

"If I may, I would like to borrow the ambassador for a moment," the fat man says to Nikolai, as he takes the old man by the arm and leads him away. He quickly whispers something to him than goes to join another group.

"Forgive me. You were telling me that you are a journalist," the old man says when he returns, picking his glass of whiskey off the shelf.

A waiter offers them a tray of sandwiches.

"Precisely. And my specialty is Spanish-speaking countries..."

"You are quite far away from your specialty," the old man comments.

"Please allow me to explain," Nikolai says. "I am stationed here in this city, at a bit of a remove from the whirlwind in Europe precisely so I can use my spare time to write a book about the current situation in Hispanic America."

At the far end of the hallway, past a swarm of other guests, the old man catches a glimpse of his colleagues from Guatemala and Nicaragua. He longs to join those clowns in their banter.

"I have no doubt," Nikolai continues, "that you are deeply knowledgeable about the reality in your country, as a participant and as a witness, and I feel quite fortunate to have met you at this precise time and place. I would like to request an interview, have the opportunity to ask you a few questions about Central American history. Nothing formal. We could meet for dinner any day that's convenient for you."

From the other end of the hallway, the eagle-eyed oaf from Guatemala gestures to the old man with a barely perceptible nod of his head—a question and an invitation.

"In particular, you might be able to help me understand the events that took place in your country three years ago at the time of that bloody insurrection," Nikolai says and makes a grimace, fleeting, slightly malicious, or perhaps it is just a nervous tick, the old man isn't sure.

Old Man Pericles blows out the smoke and stares into Nikolai's blue eyes; he wonders how old this Russian is: forty? forty-five?

"Were you in your country during the October Revolution?" the old man asks, off the cuff, before finishing his whiskey.

Nikolai smiles, then nods and winks.

They agree to dine one day that week in a restaurant in that city I never saw and never will, but it wasn't difficult for me to imagine the afternoon in question, while lying in my hammock with the story of

Pericles in Brussels playing in my head like an old movie, which took place in a restaurant of Nikolai's choosing, with private rooms suitable for intrigue, in one of which the old man would sit after giving his coat to the waiter, with that astonishing lighthearted sensation that accompanies a man who has decided to take on his own destiny.

It is not difficult for me to imagine the freedom Old Man Pericles felt when he made the decision to resign from his diplomatic post and become the opponent he would be from then on, the "Soviet agent," as the authorities would call him each time they jailed him or sent him into exile; that sensation of freedom and adventure of knowing that he was returning to his country as somebody else, his own opposite, without anybody at first suspecting; the lightheartedness that comes from having finally divested himself of the contradiction of belonging to and representing a camp he found utterly repugnant. It was in the last few months of 1937, if I remember correctly. Old Man Pericles returned all grown up, saturated with the events taking place in Europe; he told stories, amazing at the time, about Nazis and fascists, and he could talk for hours about events in Spain, about the Republicans and the Franco uprising.

Haydée experienced the old man's resignation differently, as she admitted to us when she returned: hers were the concerns of a mother (Clemente and Pati were teenagers and Alberto was still a boy), the concerns of a woman from a conservative family who doesn't fully understand her husband's decisions, but who is also enormously happy to be returning to her own land and her own people.

Before serving lunch, Carmela said she would bring a glass of watermelon drink to the poor Viking, who was waiting outside, sitting in the shadow cast by a silk cotton tree, he himself a shadow of Old Man Pericles for years already. Carmela always took pity on him, brought him a cold drink, and told him he mustn't worry, he could have lunch in the dining room where the park employees ate, Old Man Pericles would be at the house until late in the afternoon, as if he were a friend and not the police spy assigned to tailing our friend. The Viking wasn't as old as we were, but I had the feeling he was aging more quickly, as if he were suffering from a secret malady.

When I first met Haydée, as I've said, she was a tall, slender young woman with red hair; beautiful, brimming with life, and so expressive that next to her, Old Man Pericles—who at that time wasn't old but was already scowling and reserved—seemed mute. For decades, and every time she wanted to irritate him, Haydée would tell the story of how her heart was pierced by that handsome, dashing young second lieutenant of the cavalry, who paraded around proudly on his sorrel, leading his sweaty troops through the central plaza in Santa Ana. The eldest and favorite daughter of Don Nico Baldoni, a fellow coffee-grower and friend of Carmela's father, Haydée had the wisdom to take what life offered her with a good dose of wonderment. I never heard her once complain about the tribulations she was forced to undergo at her husband's side: sometimes she spoke enthusiastically about one or another of their periods of exile and the juggling acts she had to perform to survive when her husband spent time in jail. But I am also certain her family never left her to fend for herself. Don Nico respected Old Man Pericles, and he must have supported him at least until 1944, when the dictator fell, because at that time we were all in the opposition; later, after the Second World War and once the old man had already been branded a communist, things may have changed. But Haydée was loyal to him for better and for worse. Until she was stricken with breast cancer, sudden and devastating, which finished her off before we could even get used to the idea of her being gone.

Carmela had made a casserole of ground beef, vegetables, and green plantains; she served the beans separately in soup bowls topped with cream and grated cheese, just as Old Man Pericles liked.

"Have you heard anything from Estela and Alberto?" Carmela asked, as if wanting to liven up the repast, perhaps seeing that the old man was even more withdrawn than usual, whereas I perceived him as he always was: laconic, and averse to small talk.

"They're fine," Old Man Pericles mumbled, "and Albertico is, too; he's happy at the university."

Carmela said they had done well to make lives for themselves there, in San José, Costa Rica, where they'd gone into exile a year earlier, after the failed coup that Alberto's close friends had participated in, and maybe he had himself, though he denied it; his daughter Pati had also been living in that city for more than three decades.

"We got a letter from Maggi today," Carmela said, as if she was determined to intrude on every silence; later I understood she wasn't doing this out of compassion for Old Man Pericles but rather for herself, for both of us, for it was frightening to think that we were eating with death sitting in the chair next to us.

"Without the treatment, the pain is going to knock you out," I told him, taking the bull by the horns.

"The pain will knock me out with or without the treatment," Old Man Pericles said as he took another bite.

At the previous appointment, the doctor had told him that if he didn't undergo the treatment he'd have only a few months left, it would become increasingly hard to breathe, and he would suffer unbearable pain.

I felt as if Haydée had entered the dining room, a strange, fleeting presence; Carmela turned to look at me. Old Man Pericles finished eating the meat casserole, then pulled the bowl of bean toward him with relish, breaking into a smile and saying:

"Horrifying, don't you think?"

The rumble of the bus broke the heavy midday silence.

"You should make another appointment. If you don't get the treatment, you'll regret it," Carmela said, clearly upset. Then right away, before getting up, she asked, "Are you going to want more juice?"

Old Man Pericles asked her also for more tortillas, toasted rather than fresh, the way he liked them.

"Did you ever find out who was living at that house at mile nine?" I asked.

The old man wiped the plate of beans with a piece of tortilla. He nodded, without looking up.

"Nothing good is in store for us . . . ," I commented.

"Things here are always worse than we imagine," he said before bringing the dripping piece of tortilla to his mouth; he left the bowl clean, pure, without a trace of beans and cream. "Fortunately, I won't be around to see it," he added with no self-pity, as if he really did foresee what was coming.

Now I understand how grateful Old Man Pericles was that Albertico had left the country: some of his companions at the university, his age, were already appearing in the newspapers as supposed members of the burgeoning guerrilla cells that were confronting the military government. Surely the old man was staring at the specter of the insurrection of 1932, at the butchery armed struggle can lead to.

Albertico was the grandchild with whom the old man most identified; this was evident when he told us that the young man had started studying sociology at the University of Costa Rica, and that he took on politics with a dedication and lucidity that neither his father nor his Uncle Clemente had ever had; he called Clemente's children "futile flesh," and Pati's "meek Costa Rican lambs."

Carmela insisted that the best thing for Old Man Pericles to do after the treatment was to go to San Jose, where his two children were living, so he could spend his last few months with has family. I was certain he would never take that comfortable and predictable route; nothing would have horrified him more than to watch his privacy suddenly intruded upon by his children and grandchildren and their concerns: he didn't have the temperament of a patient, much less of a dying man.

Of his two remaining children, Pati was most like Old Man Pericles: she was a tall, graceful, haughty brunette; she had a fiery temperament and no time for trivialities. Married to a powerful Costa Rican communist, she had a couple of children and had made her home in that city, where Haydée had spent long stretches, especially toward the end, when the cancer was ravaging her. Old Man Pericles always called his daughter's house "the Costa Rican rearguard," because that's where he went into exile each time the baboon currently in charge gave the order. I met Pati when she was little: she always was a livewire; then I heard about her marriage and didn't see her again until her mother's funeral.

"What are you painting, Chelón?" he asked me while Carmela was making coffee in the kitchen.

"I'm still on the fallen angels," I answered.

"You've spent more than two years on them," he said. "Have you found your gold mine?"

"The buyers like them, and they still aren't boring me," I explained, which was absolutely honest; every week I painted one oil and one watercolor of an angel with a different occupation, and they came to me on their own, without much effort. "As far as it being a gold mine, not..."

"He's now painting one where a poor ice-cream vendor, with his wings and dripping with sweat under the burning sun, is pushing his little cart," Carmela said from the kitchen. "He modeled it after the ice-cream vendor's cart that parks here at the entrance to the park on Sundays."

"Not only the cart," I said, "the hat as well."

"It's a source of solace," Old Man Pericles said as he lit his cigarette.

"What do you mean?" Carmela asked, walking toward us with the coffee pot.

But I understood right away.

"People like to buy solace, the rich most of all," he answered.

"There you go with your notions," I said. "The poor are the ones who need solace."

"But they don't have the means to buy it..."

"The Italian ambassador already reserved the ice-cream angel," Carmela said, pleased, while she poured out the coffee.

He was one of those boors who begin to fancy themselves renaissance men after being posted to a backward country like ours. When I described to him what I was painting, he said he loved ice cream and asked me to put it aside for him, and he even had the nerve to offer me some suggestions. He'd been at the house the previous Saturday, insisting we come to a reception at the embassy; he appeared incapable of comprehending that his world was so alien to me that his offer to send his chauffeur would do nothing to induce us to attend his party—we had already had our share of protocol for our lifetimes.

"He brought me some first-rate cigars," I said, remembering the Italian's good side. "Would you like one?"

"Of course. I hope such high quality doesn't irritate my taste buds . . ." Old Man Pericles said, ironically, for he smoked the cheapest cigarettes around.

"What they'll irritate are your lungs," Carmela cut in, glaring at me reproachfully for what she considered to be my imprudence, as if she still didn't want to accept that there was no return, our friend had already crossed the line, his refusal to submit to the treatment was not a mere whim, not a reaction to fear, but rather the result of a final, resounding decision—and Old Man Pericles had always been a decisive man.

I went to the studio to get the box of cigars off the bookshelf.

We rarely spoke about politics, only when there was pandemonium in the streets due to strikes, elections, or a coup d'état. Old Man Pericles always had the latest bits of gossip, but he doled them out slowly as if they were old jokes everybody had already heard. Already before Haydée's death his tone had become sardonic, even when he talked about his own comrades' adventures, as if he no longer believed what he preached and belonged to that gang because one has to have something to cling to in this life. He despised the military even though he, his father, and his grandfather had been in the military; more than anything, though, he despised the rich: the fourteen packs of hyenas, he called the so-called fourteen families who own this parcel of land. It was his loathing of the arrogance of the powerful that made him remain a communist to the very end rather than any illusion about the supposed goodness of that other world. "There's deep shit everywhere, Chelón. This is mine. What is to be done?" he said one day after returning from a long trip to Moscow and Peking, when those two cities were still on friendly terms.

At some point in the afternoon he'd always enter my studio: he would cast an eye over the canvas I was painting, rummage through my books with the hope that I had bought something that might interest him, then look pensively out the picture window. He never offered an opinion about my paintings, always claiming to be incapable of evaluating the visual arts; he was contemptuous of non-figurative art and was grateful I had never wasted my paint on such things. Whenever I showed him any of my poems, published or not, he'd make a measured comment, but would always end by saying: "You're right to prefer painting." That was another of his characteristics: he seemed to go through life forgiving the world. I reminded him of it that afternoon when I noticed him looking attentively at the ice-cream vendor as a fallen angel:

"What is His Lordship's judgment?" I asked in a sarcastic tone, much like his own, as I handed him a cigar.

"You should give the ice-cream vendor the Italian ambassador's mug," he said.

Then he stood looking out the window in intent contemplation, as if he didn't want to miss a single detail. He asked me for the binoculars. I told him I'd lent them to Ricardito, and he still hadn't returned them. He looked at me as one looks at a man who has been swindled despite the warnings.

"And that girl, Andrea, has she returned?" he asked me in the conspiratorial tone of an accomplice, because I had told him about the visits of the young lady who wanted to sit for me, of Carmela's chagrin, of the fantasies and fears that even old age fails to temper.

I said no without parting my lips, only waving my index finger back and forth.

Carmela appeared in the doorway.

Now, while reminiscing, I realize that ours was, more than anything else, a friendship of old age. We had, of course, met in the twenties, and the friendship between Carmela and Haydée had been indissoluble since they were children, but for the following thirty years we'd seen each other only sporadically while his and Haydée's lives were swept up in the old man's political adventures—their periods in exile and the displacements—and Carmela and I went to live in the United States, where we remained for ten years, at first thanks to an arts scholarship and then as the embassy's cultural attaché. The same baboon who put Old Man Pericles behind bars on more than once occasion was the one I had to thank for my appointment, which allowed me to live for several memorable years in Washington and New York. In 1958, when we returned home to stay, our friendship solidified, despite the constant turmoil of his political life, and Haydée's cancer, which finished her off a few years later.

"I don't understand why your returned," Old Man Pericles would say to me, shaking his head as if I had disappointed him. "You should have stayed in New York, or moved to Paris, where artists are worshiped."

Ten years earlier, when I had told him about my scholarship from the American Embassy to attend a fine art academy in New York, fearful that he would be devastatingly critical of me because of his anti-Yankeeism, and doubtful myself if it was worthwhile to go live in a city where we had no family and knew not a soul, Old Man Pericles spared no arguments to convince me to accept the scholarship.

"Everything has its time, Old Man," I told him, "and my time up north is over."

We returned to the rocking chairs on the terrace; Old Man Pericles seemed content with his cigar in his mouth.

"They're the same ones Fidel smokes, according to Signore Ambassador Strasato," I noted.

The old man shot me a withering look; I knew my friend had spent one year on Castro's island after the triumph of the revolution, something of an ambassador for our native communists. It was a few months after Haydée's death. The change must have helped him deal with his grief. After his surreptitious return, I invited him over, hoping to satisfy my own curiosity about his Caribbean experience. "The Cubans get high on noise," he declared sententiously. A few weeks later he was arrested and again sent into exile.

Carmela was cleaning up in the kitchen. She asked if we wanted her to make us another coffee before she took her nap.

Old Man Pericles said he'd rather have another whiskey, unusual as he always drank only before lunch.

I went to get it for him; fortunately, there was some ice left.

"Recently I've felt like death has always been here, lurking, waiting," Old Man Pericles said, touching both hands to his chest, where his lungs were.

A breeze from the park swept over the terrace, spreading its shards of mist.

"It's not poetry or cheap metaphysics. Don't get me wrong, Chelón," he said, taking another drag off his cigar; he always referred to "cheap metaphysics" whenever we talked about the afterlife, the invisible, or other possible worlds. "It wasn't some revelation or a sudden urge to discover new worlds, just a sensation, as if my body were telling me ... Very strange."

"I thought you didn't believe in anything," I said, without reproach, just to needle him.

"You know well enough that it has nothing to do with belief," he mumbled, the cigar held firmly between his lips. And I knew that he knew that I knew, I thought playfully, with a small burst of ingenuity, and to avoid remembering the spot where my death was lurking, waiting.

He gulped down his whiskey.

"Difficult to get used to the idea that one is finished," he said, rocking back and forth in his chair.

I assumed that if that cancer had always been lurking in his lungs, it must have flexed its muscles and decided to spread only about a year ago, in February, when Clemente was murdered. I could be wrong: maybe there'd never been any hope for the old man, and his body's hour had simply come, as mine will, very soon now.

I never quite understood how Old Man Pericles subsisted during that last period, how he scraped together the little money he needed to survive. After his return from Europe, he began to work for the newspapers that opposed the dictatorship; the general was ruling in all his splendor, but soon the Second World War would come and with it his decline. Then there was a long stretch during which I associate him with the radio; that was when he struck up his friendship with the Pole, a Jew with whom he founded a radio station and who, as the years went by, became the most important radio impresario in the country. While the old man was getting poorer and poorer because of his communist activities and having to live from hand to mouth between jail and exile, the Pole was swimming in money and founding new businesses right and left. They stopped seeing each other, but the friendship persisted, and especially the Pole's respect for Old Man Pericles. I know of this first hand, because one of the Pole's daughters bought a couple of my paintings; she said her father always spoke about Old Man Pericles with great admiration, for he had been like a big brother to him and had taught him about integrity, even though he didn't share his political ideas.

After Haydée's death, he told me he was earning a small salary as a clandestine correspondent for a Soviet news agency. I've always assumed Haydée must have left him something from what she inherited from Don Nico.

"These last few days I've been waking up afraid. I know I've been dreaming something horrible, but I forget it the moment I open my eyes. I don't want to remember," Old Man Pericles said, placing the half-smoked cigar in the ashtray, as if he'd smoked enough.

"Maybe it's death," I suggested.

"That's what I think," he said.

"Did you used to remember your dreams?" I asked him.

"There you go ..."

The neighbor's cat walked across the patio; he gave us a passing glance out of the corner of his eye, but didn't stop. When Layca was alive, that cat didn't dare come near here: our boxer bitch never even had to chase him, she'd paralyze him with a single look.

"Is it true you can do anything you want in your dreams, as if you were awake?" he asked, shifting his position in his chair.

I told him about that once; at the time, he was intensely curious, but he never fully believed me.

"It's just that sometimes I'm awake while I'm dreaming, so I can move around fairly easily, but there's a big difference between that and being able to do anything I want," I said.

"So you can fly or go anywhere you want in a split second? What's it like?" he insisted.

"So-so. It's simple: while you are dreaming, you know you are dreaming. That's the only extraordinary part of it."

"Hard to believe."

"As you say, Old Man, it's not a matter of belief; it's a gift," I explained.

"If that's true, there must be something after."

"I'm telling you there is, but it has nothing to do with all that church nonsense about Heaven and Earth that you hate so much. Anyway, death is a personal matter and each of us experiences it differently," I said, feeling somewhat ill at ease and fearing I was simply repeating clichés. "Are you afraid?" I asked him.

He took off his eyeglasses and rubbed his eyes, as if the glare were burning them.

"Of pain, that's all," he murmured. "And it's right here, devouring me," he said, touching his chest.

"Almost all suffering is futile," I said.

"Indeed, Mr. Schopenhauer," he said with his old grimace. Then he said, "I wonder what would happen if you decided you didn't want to return ..."

"What?" I shot back, confused.

"If, when you are conscious that you are dreaming you suddenly decide you don't want to return, you are doing quite well there and badly here, and you want to remain in the dream. What would happen then?"

"One can't decide when to return," I said. "Your body brings you back."

I asked him if he was going to smoke the rest of his cigar, Carmela didn't like the stale smell of burned tobacco. He told me I could toss it. I picked up the ashtray and went to the washroom to dump it.

"A while ago I read that there's an exercise for people who want to wake up inside their dreams," I told him when I got back; I placed the clean ashtray on the coffee table. "You've got to get into the habit of taking a little hop every five minutes, no matter what you're doing, and while you are taking the little hop you ask yourself, 'Am I awake or am I dreaming?' It's a method so that the little hop, together with the question, get etched into your unconscious ..."

"A little hop ..." he noted with a frown and a lifting of his eyebrows.

"That's right. And if you come back down to earth the way you normally do, that means you're awake, and if you don't, if instead you keep floating, it means you're dreaming, because there is no law of gravity in dreams.

"Have you tried it?"

I told him I hadn't. And I laughed.

"I can just see me on my way home, taking little jumps every five minutes. Worse than Vroom ..."

Vroom was the madman of La Rábida, the district where Old Man Pericles lived. He ran around the streets barefoot pretending to be a car, he'd stop at the traffic lights, imitate the sound of a car engine, honk, hold up traffic and even sometimes overtake an absentminded driver, while other drivers either waved or insulted him.

I suggested we take a walk in the park through the dense forest, so the stifling heat wouldn't do us in.

Old Man Pericles had an aversion to the occult. I could understand why: the general who fancied himself a warlock read books about the occult sciences and professed ludicrous notions to justify his brutal acts, as when he would say that it is worse to kill an ant than a man because the man will be reincarnated whereas the ant will not. On several occasions I tried to explain to the old man that the occult had nothing whatsoever to do with the sick mind of a criminal, any ignoramus can convert knowledge into grotesque superstition, that the depth of the mystery is inaccessible to a man corrupted by power. But Old Man Pericles had been marked by that experience, and his mistrust of any metaphysics was equal only to his sarcasm whenever—in private—he mentioned Marxist dogma.

I clearly remember Haydée's wake, during those early morning hours when the visitors had all left and the only ones left were a few family members and the closest friends, Old Man Pericles asked me what I thought about the idea of the eternal return. I told him I preferred to call it recurrence, and said I didn't forswear the possibility that things could happen again in precisely that way—that time was circular and the moment of our death coincided with that of our birth, and we would have to live the same life over and over again. Old Man Pericles remained pensive for a while then said that such a possibility seemed macabre to him, that if such a recurrence was an invention of a "superior intelligence"—as I liked to call the will from the invisible—it was not, in fact, a superior intelligence but rather a perverse, sadistic one. And he gave the example of a man who'd suffered the worst possible torture and death, who would be born over and over again only to die in the same brutal fashion.

"It hasn't got heads or tails, not heads or tails," the old man repeated, aggrieved, because at that moment his atheism was weakening, and he could find nothing to replace it.

I didn't tell him that I was wont to pray to my invisible ones, asking them to leave me forever in the void.

The Viking was sitting in the shade of a pink poui tree, leaning against the trunk, dozing off. He was the sleuth assigned to keep watch over the old man; apparently he was supposed to never lose sight of him and to keep a record of all his movements. He was a bitter old cop, but he had a certain way with people; in his youth he had been a professional wrestler—hence his nickname, "The Viking," for at the time his hair, now gray, was blond. At first, Old Man Pericles treated him with disdain: he ignored him and at the slightest opportunity gave him the slip; then he took pity on him, and if he found him hanging around the house when he went out in the morning, he'd tell him not to waste his time, they were both too old for this game of cat and mouse, then he'd tell him his plans for the day so he wouldn't have to follow him and could still present his report to his bosses. The Viking did his part, too: the last time they were expediting the order to expel him from the country, he let the old man know, which gave him several hours to get ready before they arrested him and drove him to the airport. And whenever they exchanged even a few words, The Viking always, and with great respect, called him "Don Pericles."

I would have liked to paint The Viking as a fallen angel, the old worn-out bloodhound assigned a quarry who is even older and more infirm than he. But I never found the path that revealed him to me: an old man sitting in the shade of a tree doesn't say anything; putting him in a policeman's uniform would have been forced and unnatural. Maybe I should have painted him precisely like that: a bloodhound with weary wings.

Old Man Pericles and I had both married women who were one tier above us, socially and economically speaking. Needless to say, things were different at the beginning of the century: the prejudices and alienation arose later with the advent of the middle class and the nouveau riche. Back then, there were the wealthy few on the one hand and the people—the masses—on the other. None of us had any pretentions or ambitions; ours was simply the preordained encounter of persons of the same class and social standing. That's why Old Man Pericles made so much fun of his son Alberto, and was so disparaging of his longing to cut a figure in society, a desire that ruled his life ever since he was young; he always wanted to be a dandy, parade around the clubs, dress in the latest fashion, drive fancy cars to impress the girls. "That one was born in the wrong place: a pearl among swine," the old man would say. And that's what he'd call him, "The Pearl," when he wanted to scoff at his adventures. I always thought Alberto exhibited behavior typical of the youngest son, the spoiled one, the one who believes the world is made for him; but Old Man Pericles explained to me that he spent too much time with his maternal grandmother when he was little, hence his mother-in-law was to blame for his son's frivolousness. "Even when he dabbles in politics he acts like a playboy on a safari," the old man said, laughing, derisive; at moments Old Man Pericles even accepted Alberto's frivolity, but he never forgave what he once in a broadside called Clemente's "betrayal." At the time I sensed that he was not referring to Clemente's friendships with the same military commanders who ordered the old man's arrests and expulsions but rather a specific, crushing, painful, and unmentionable act they would both carry with them to their graves, as I would in the case of Maggi.

"What would you do, Chelón?" he asked me.

We were walking down the road toward the path that led into the grove of Guanacaste trees, where those tall broad-leaved evergreens shade out the sun and the air is cool, damp, and comforting. I was wearing my cap and carrying my cane.

"I don't know," I answered.

Although the rains had not yet begun, and the mountain was dry, the color of straw, inside the forest the greens of the vines and the bushes emerged seductively.

"Well, you should know, because your turn will come," he said with touch of a grimace.

"Maybe it's better when it arrives all at once, no warning," I noted.

I had an intuition, a fleeting idea, but I shooed it away, like one shoos away a fly.

"What I would do, Old Man, is settle any outstanding accounts; let go of any resentments, hatreds, lay my burdens down, for where we're going it's all just excess baggage anyway," I said.

"And if we're not going anywhere ..."

"Still, the lighter, the better."

"I have a fever," the old man said, suddenly stopping.

"You want to return?"

"No, let's do our usual route."

He seemed exhausted, and he had always been the one to set the steady, almost martial, pace, never showing the least consideration for my fear of falling.

"If you don't do the treatment, you'll soon not have enough air to go out of the house," I said.

"I feel badly for María Elena," he said.

Since Haydée's death, María Elena spent half the week at the house with Old Man Pericles and the other half with her family in her village.

"We're going to avoid all that," he said.

That was when I understood the raven's reasoning.

We walked across the small hanging bridge over the spring; he stood for a while holding onto the lateral ropes, his gaze lost in the thin tongue of water.

"This morning, after talking to you, I called The Pole," he said. "He'll take care of the wake and the burial."

With my cane, I pushed aside an orange peel that was littering the path.

"He's very fond of you," I said.

"It's no skin off his back: he'll write off the cost of the funeral home and the cemetery as publicity for his radio stations," he said, smiling.

"Don't be such an ingrate," I rebuked him.

But Old Man Pericles was like that: he never missed an opportunity to get in a jab.

We emerged from the forest into an open field; from there we could reach the highway circling the park that would take us home.

"Pati and Albertico will come to take care of everything," he said. "Truth is, the only objects of any value in the house are Haydée's."

We walked along the sidewalk that ran parallel to the highway.

I would have liked to tell him to take it easy, not to let himself get carried away by his obsessions, even in the worst-case scenario he still had a few months, but he was laying all his cards on the table.

"Can't let the pain have its way with me," he mumbled as he took a deep breath, just to make sure I understood.

I've often asked myself what we had in common, what united us, apart from the friendship between our wives. He didn't admire my paintings, or my poems ("metaphysical poetry," he'd say, despite my enthusiasm), or my way of understanding the world ("too much Eastern marijuana, Chelón," he'd insist in his mocking tone).

I couldn't care less about his passion for politics, his militancy alongside people he himself disdained, his loyalty to the interests of communists in faraway land. But we never argued, not in the sense of ideas clashing head-on. It seems we met over an ineffable, inviolable terrain, someplace far beyond any generational empathy. Or as if deep down I was doing what he would have liked to do and he was living an adventure I would have liked to live. It's not worth delving into too much. Some friendships are destiny.

Carmela was waiting for us with two glasses of fresh fruit drink. Then she made coffee and cut a lemon tart she had baked earlier in the day. Until that moment I hadn't realized how much Pericles had declined in the last two weeks: he was ashen and was having difficulty breathing, as if he would never recover from what had been our traditional evening stroll for the past decade.

"If my lungs were in better shape, I would have liked to go to the Devil's Doorway," Old Man Pericles said as he drank this last coffee and smoked a cigarette.

The Devil's Doorway was a huge cliff about three-quarters of a mile into the park, where the mountain abruptly ended. The view there was spectacular: one could see the sea and a good chunk of the coast; at night it was crowded with cars full of furtive lovers.

"It wouldn't have been good for you in this heat," Carmela said.

Before I had so many ailments, I used to walk to the Devil's Doorway more often; I went many times with the old man. Watching the sunset from those heights is a revelation.

But the name was derived from its more sinister side: Milena, a feather-brained ballerina and a friend of ours from childhood, knocked off balance by the ravages of old age, was the last to throw herself off the cliff into the void, six months before. The list was long.

The old man lit another cigarette.

"It's time for me to go," he said.

Carmela gave him a piece of pie for María Elena; he put it in his bag.

We walked him to the bus.

"Don't be stubborn, old man. Get the treatment," Carmela said to him, with the voice of a scolding mother as he kissed her on the cheek. I know how she must have struggled over whether to say those words, but now she was on the verge of tears.

We hugged each other, as if it were just another parting, wordless.

The Viking had scampered onto the bus through the back door.

Old Man Pericles sat two rows behind the driver; he barely waved.

A few times, later that afternoon, amid waves of melancholy, we would reminisce about Haydée. Above all, her enthusiasm during the general strike, when she got involved in a way we never would have expected, with courage and audacity, relentlessly demanding the old man's release and amnesty for Clemen; clearly etched in my memory is that night we found her in the crowd next to the National Palace when we heard that the dictator had stepped down. Haydée was jubilant, shouting and dancing with joy. And the following morning, when we accompanied her to the Central Prison, in the midst of those throngs of people waiting anxiously for the release of their families and friends, she was radiant, shouting slogans, cheering, until finally Old Man Pericles and all the other prisoners emerged, Pericles with that roguish expression on his face. That same afternoon we learned that Clemen was alive and hiding on the island of Espíritu Santo, along with his cousin, Jimmy Ríos. I never again saw her so happy, so unreserved, so fulfilled.

Then we remembered the period toward the end of the fifties, when we had just returned from New York and they from their exile in Costa Rica. Haydée and Carmela suggested using their savings to start a patisserie. All four of us were excited by the idea. Old Man Pericles joked around, saying I would dream up exotic pastry designs and he would be in charge of the texts for promotion and publicity. I warned him not to get his hopes up, that considering our wives' characters, the most we could aspire to would be to paint the walls of the place they rent. But when the old man was suddenly arrested by the new colonel and again expelled from the country, all our plans were dashed.

"You remember how she used to love to play dominoes?" Carmela asked, her eyes tearing up, on that late afternoon of gray clouds that were not going to burst, an afternoon of lethargy and nostalgia. And it was true: Haydée played dominoes with the ferocity of a card shark, making bets, challenging her opponents, and making fun of them; she was proud to show off the skills she had acquired during one of her periods of exile in Mexico.

"Haydée died believing the old man would live to be eighty," Carmela recalled as we were preparing dinner.

"We thought the same thing about ourselves," I said, just to irritate her, to break through the grim atmosphere.

That's when I remembered the sketches I had made while in the waiting room at the hospital when we visited Haydée every day in the late afternoon; sketches of others, waiting just like we were, to go in and see their sick, or of some irritable nurse; sketches of the waiting room or any other notion my pen came up with. Once, Haydée asked me to show them to her, then warned me that under no circumstances should I draw her now, ravaged as she was by the cancer, and if I ever did she would never forgive me and would come to me in the middle of the night and pull off my covers. I promised her I never would; but that same night, after I came home from the hospital and Carmela had already gone to bed, I shut myself up in my studio and sketched her just as I had seen her that day in the hospital: all that withered beauty between the sheets. Before going to bed, I went out on the patio and burned the sketches.

The call came at seven thirty at night. I answered it. It was María Elena; she was crying so hard she could barely talk. The moment I heard her voice I knew that Pericles had gone on ahead; he always asserted that as far as making decisions went, the sooner the better.

María Elena told me she had been in her room, at the back of the house, watching her telenovela, the door closed because the sound of the television disturbed the old man, when she heard a loud noise, as if a can had fallen off the shelf in the cupboard. She went to check in the kitchen but found nothing out of place. Then she had a premonition. She knocked on the door of Old Man Pericles's office, where he always went to read after dinner. There was no answer. She opened it and immediately smelled the gunpowder: his body was lying draped over the desk.

Carmela was watching me from the kitchen doorway. Without thinking, almost automatically, I pointed my index finger into my temple; she began to cry, inconsolably, heartrending sobs. I clung to my memory of the old man's embrace.

Then I called Ricardito, the first person I thought of who could come immediately in his car to take us to the old man's house.

It was going to be a long night.

I've just finished the painting of Old Man Pericles as a fallen angel. He is sitting in the rocking chair on the terrace, as he did that last afternoon, holding his glass of whiskey on his lap in both hands, the cigar in the ashtray on the coffee table; most conspicuous are his tortoiseshell glasses and his wings that fall over the shirttails of his white guayabera. There is a thin line of blood coming out of a small hole in his right temple. His eyes came out too sad, moist, but it's too late to correct it. I've painted it for myself, my last effort; it's called THE FALLEN ANGEL WITH NO OCCUPATION. When Carmela saw it, she cried out, "Haydée would have loved it."

Author's Note

I began this book in Frankfurt am Main, Germany, in March 2005, and finished it in Pittsburgh, Pennsylvania, at the end of 2007. I am grateful to Henry Reese and Diane Samuels, directors of the City of Asylum program in Pittsburgh, for their generous support, without which I would not have been able to complete this work.

This book is a work of fiction. The principal characters are fictional. However, the historical setting of the first part ("Haydée and the Fugitives"), as well as many of the situations and characters alluded to therein are based on historical events in El Salvador in 1944. Let me be clear: in this book, history has been placed at the service of the novel, that is, I have taken liberties with it according to the needs of the fictional narrative. Do not, then, look for "historical truth."

Herewith are the titles of several books that aided my understanding of that period and were of great use to me: *Relámpagos de libertad* [Flashes of Freedom], by Mariano Castro Morán (Editorial Lis, San Salvador, 2000); *Insurreccion no violenta en El Salvador* [Nonviolent Insurrection in El Salvador], by Patricia Parkman (Dirección de Publicaciones e Impresos, San Salvador, 2003); *April y mayo de 1944* [April and May 1944], by Francisco Morán (Editorial Universitaria, San Salvador, 1979); and *El Salvador, 1930–1960* [El Salvador,

1930–1960], by Juan Mario Castellanos (Dirección de Publicaciones e Impresos, San Salvador, 2002). I wish to thank Beatriz Cortez, in Los Angeles, and Miguel Huerzo Mixco, in San Salvador, for sending me these texts. Jimmy and Clemen's escape was inspired by the testimony of Captain Guillermo Fuentes Castellanos, recounted in the book by Colonel Castro Morán, mentioned above, though Jimmy is not Captain Fuentes nor is Clemen Lieutenant Belisario Peña. The Gavidia brothers were executed by firing squad in real life, but Merceditas is a fictional character.